A Life
Worth
Living

OTHER TITLES BY LOUISE GUY:

Everyday Lies

Rival Sisters

A Life Worth Living

LOUISE GUY

LAKE UNION
PUBLISHING

Text copyright © 2018, 2020 by Louise Guy
All rights reserved.

Previously self-published in Australia in 2017.

Published by Lake Union Publishing, Seattle

www.apub.com

Amazon, the Amazon logo, and Lake Union Publishing are trademarks of Amazon.com, Inc., or its affiliates.

ISBN-13: 9781542015981
ISBN-10: 1542015987

Cover design by Sarah Whittaker

Printed in the United States of America

For Ray, JJ and Jamie,
who make my life worth living.

Chapter One

Leah took a deep breath, let the front door snap shut and checked her watch.

Five minutes.

That was all it had taken Grant to end their six-year relationship. No explanation. No, *It's not you, it's me*. Just, *It's over*.

She brushed a stray tear aside, moved down the narrow hallway of the art deco apartment, and into the kitchen. The candlelit table she'd set earlier was wasted. She plonked down on one of the retro bar stools at the counter and poured herself a glass of Cab Sav, which she'd bought specially to mark their sixth anniversary, and stared across the open plan layout to the couch where Lewis's purrs and soft snores confirmed he was oblivious to all that was going on.

Oblivion: much more appealing than admitting it was over.

While she'd been thinking of their future – their wedding, their children – he'd been looking for an exit. She gulped her wine. She really was an idiot; she had thought they were happy. They had well-paid jobs, a great circle of friends, loving families, good sex, a future mapped out. What wasn't working for him?

Her phone beeped and she drew it across the counter.

Sorry. I know this is a shock. Didn't want to live a lie any longer. Will come over Tuesday night and collect my things. If you aren't home, I'll leave my key. G.

Live a lie? What the hell did *that* mean? That he was never into the relationship? Was he seeing someone else? Was he gay?

She switched the phone off and refilled her glass.

Leah groaned as her mother's familiar ringtone roused her from a deep sleep. Light seeped in through the curtains.

She'd forgotten to set her alarm. She reached across the still-sleeping, fluffy white body of Lewis to the bedside table and picked up her phone. 'Hi, Mum.'

She stroked her cat, almost managing a smile at the motor-like sound of his purr as she waited for her mother's predictable question.

'Leah, darling. How are you? How was the anniversary dinner? Any news?'

Tears welled. Her parents were expecting news of a ring, not the end of the relationship. Leah took a deep breath and did her best to sound normal. The last thing she needed right now was to listen to her mother's disappointment. 'No. Nothing to report.'

Silence greeted her.

Eventually her mother spoke. 'I hope you still had a nice night, love.'

Leah swallowed the lump in her throat. How could she explain her relationship was over when she didn't even know why? 'Mum, I have to feed Lewis and get ready for work. I'll call you later, okay?'

'Of course. Dad and I are still away for a couple more days, so if my mobile's out of range I'll call you back. Have a good day, and show that boss of yours how valuable you are. Love you.'

Leah smiled and set the phone on the bedside table. It was unlikely her arrogant, chauvinistic boss would ever acknowledge her value, but it was nice to know she had her mother's support.

She gathered Lewis in her arms and rocked him like a baby. The distinctive sound of trams clunking along St Kilda Road eight floors below her apartment reminded her to hurry. But she always had enough time for her cat. This was their morning ritual, except on the mornings Grant had slept over. Lewis was banned from the bedroom then. Grant had merely tolerated him.

'That should've been a red flag in itself, shouldn't it, Pud?' She rubbed her face against the cat's as he nuzzled into her. 'How could anyone not love you?'

Leah glanced at the clock; it was nearly seven thirty. She needed to get moving if she was going to make the nine o'clock staff meeting.

She threw back the bedcovers, and with Lewis still cradled in her arms, hauled herself out of bed.

Leah pulled her coat tight as the sharp Melbourne winds drove into her body. She followed the line of commuters off the tram, past the Arts Centre and into the heart of Southbank.

She'd been doing this short commute for eight years now, since landing her dream job at *The Melbournian*, the city's leading newspaper. After six years of going from one local paper to the next, the move had been symbolic; she was finally on her way.

Leah's disappointment had been palpable when, after only two weeks in her role as a reporter for the business section, she was moved into Property to replace a reporter who'd been let go. Her job was to write about residential real estate for the weekly *Property Push* magazine. It was a step above reporting for the local papers, but no longer fitted the description of her *dream job*.

To make matters worse, she'd been praised for her work, even awarded a Quill for Excellence in Journalism at the industry awards. It had firmly cemented her position at *Property Push* and made it virtually impossible to move within the paper. Not that she hadn't tried.

Barry Fitzgerald, or Fitzy, as her pit bull-resembling boss was called, had rolled his eyes when Leah applied for an internal transfer to Finance only a month ago. He rolled his eyes every time; even months earlier when she'd applied for a position back in Business, and before that in Arts.

'Leah,' he'd said. 'Face facts: you're good at property so you aren't moving. You'll have to leave if you want to try something new.'

She was often tempted.

The morning dragged. The staff meeting had taken up the first two hours as Fitzy had droned on. Once back at her desk, Leah's thoughts kept shifting back to Grant. Only a week ago, he'd surprised her with flowers at work and whisked her off to No35 for dinner before checking in to Crown Towers for an overnight stay. They'd had to pull themselves away from the bed and each other in order to make the check-out time the following morning. Why would he go to all that trouble then end it? It made no sense.

She sighed. She had two properties to view that afternoon in order to write up features for Saturday's magazine. Leah checked their listings and reviewed their photos. The reality was, she could write a feature from that information alone, but she was expected to slap on a smile and meet with the realtor to acquire any additional information.

One of the realtors was North to South Realty – the company her sister worked for. There'd be no need to fawn over this property, or even view it. The hour would be much better spent having a coffee with Eve.

Chapter Two

Eve scrolled through her emails, smiling at the familiar name of Ben Styles. She quickly scanned the message then glanced towards her open office door. She could just see her assistant's head tilted towards her computer. She picked up her desk phone and dialled Penny's extension. 'Would you mind getting me a coffee?' Eve asked.

'Sure,' her assistant said. 'Was there something wrong with the one I got you earlier?'

She noted the half-filled takeaway coffee sitting on her otherwise clear desk. It was still hot. She swallowed. 'I think it has sugar in it. Get yourself one too. Put them on my account.'

Eve waited until Penny had collected her bag and walked down the corridor towards the elevator before closing her office door. She was being overly cautious making Penny go out – her assistant probably couldn't hear through the closed door – but she wasn't willing to risk it.

She slipped out the mobile phone tucked at the back of her desk drawer, and switched it on. It contained just one number. Eve pressed the call button and waited only a moment.

Ben's deep voice came on to the line. 'Hey, gorgeous.'

Her stomach fluttered. 'Hey, yourself.'

'Usual spot?'

'Definitely. Three o'clock?'

'No appointments this afternoon?'

She looked at her schedule. Penny had scheduled an appointment at the O'Reilly residence with the property reporter from *The Melbournian*. As much as she'd enjoy seeing her sister, an hour with Ben was much more appealing. 'Nothing I can't postpone.'

'Okay, gotta run. See you at three.'

Eve smiled, switched the phone off and slipped it into her bag. She was being dramatic having a phone exclusively for calling Ben – there was no reason Sean would ever check her calls; after all she worked in real estate, she was always on the phone, but she also didn't want to take the chance.

She scrolled through her other emails, sending quick answers to those that needed immediate action. She was just double-checking her schedule for the day as Penny pushed open the office door, her expression anxious. She made her way to Eve's desk, a steaming cup of coffee in hand.

'Everything okay?' she asked.

Her assistant flashed a small smile. 'Oh, just a bit of a run-in with the coffee guy. Assured me he didn't put sugar in your coffee before. Nothing major.'

A pang of guilt stabbed at Eve but she quickly dismissed it. 'It's only the coffee guy. Don't give it another thought.' She stood. 'I'd better get going. I've got a ten o'clock in Richmond. Need to convince John Miller his three-million-dollar terrace should be listed with us.' She slung her winter jacket over one arm and picked up her briefcase. 'I'll be back by twelve. Could you confirm my one thirty while I'm out?' She'd postpone her three o'clock meeting herself.

Penny nodded and held out the coffee.

Eve indicated her full hands. 'Sorry, no room. You enjoy it.' She turned, doing her best to ignore her assistant's look of irritation, and left the office.

'Hey, Nic.' Eve took the call from her best friend and indicated right to exit the underground parking on to Chapel Street. 'I've only got a few minutes. I'm on my way to an appointment in Richmond.'

'I'm checking if you're still on for Friday?'

'As if I'd miss your fortieth, you old bag.'

Nicola laughed. 'You'll be joining me in a few years, so I wouldn't get too cocky.'

'And you'll be turning forty-five by then,' she retorted. 'Sorry, but age is one thing you're always going to be ahead of me in.'

'One thing? I can think of plenty of others,' her friend joked. 'You know it's costume, don't you?'

Eve sighed. 'Nic, I helped plan the party. I sent out the invites. I'll be there with bells on. Well, perhaps not bells, but certainly an incredibly sexy costume.'

'Are you coming alone?'

She hesitated. 'Do you mean, am I bringing Sean?'

'No, I meant Ben.'

Her pulse quickened and she glanced out of the window. Did she really think someone was listening? She was getting paranoid. 'Of course I'm not bringing Ben.'

Nicola laughed. 'Thought I'd check. I've got you down for two, so you can bring Sean if you want to.'

'I'm coming alone. He'll need to look after the kids.'

'You could always get a sitter.'

'No, he won't want to come,' Eve said. 'No offence, but other than you he won't know anyone and small talk's not really his thing. I'm not sure I'd want him there anyway. He's been very moody lately.' Her husband actually hadn't come near her in a month. Or was it two?

That was unusual. She frowned. He annoyed her at times but they had a good marriage. He was probably working too hard; his firm demanded a crazy commitment from its lawyers.

'If you change your mind, he's welcome.'

'Thanks, lovely.' Eve stopped in front of the Richmond terrace. 'Now I'd better go – client to woo and all that.'

'Male or female?'

'Male. Why?'

The smile in Nicola's voice was obvious. 'Just checking. Don't do anything I wouldn't do.'

'He's a client, nothing more.'

'So was Ben, if I remember rightly.'

She smiled. 'Okay, you win. I'll see you Friday night. Love you.'

Eve shivered as a biting wind whipped up the narrow street and into her bones. She was grateful she'd brought her jacket.

With briefcase in hand, she pushed open the iron gate and strode towards the front door.

It was close to one by the time Eve returned to the office. John Miller had expected her to work hard for the listing. She'd turned on the charm and enjoyed a coffee and a long chat with him before exclaiming her great interest in the features of the house.

The property was quite deceptive. The single-block terraced front was only one of Miller's houses. He also owned the block directly behind the house and the ones on either side. He'd built an enormous home spanning the four blocks. The indoor pool added a whole other dimension.

'How did it go?' Penny asked as Eve exited the elevator and passed her assistant's desk.

'Good.' She tapped her briefcase. 'Contract's signed and sealed. Peter should be pleased.'

'Actually, he stopped by your office about an hour ago. Asked you to pop in and see him when you got back.'

Eve checked her watch. 'Okay, I'll go down now and then I'd better dash again. I've got the one thirty and the three p.m. with *The Melbournian*.' Her cheeks flushed speaking of the later appointment.

She deposited her coat and briefcase on her desk and made her way to Peter's office.

Joel, Peter's assistant, waved her in as she approached his desk. 'He's expecting you.'

Peter looked up from his desk, a smile lighting up his rounded face. 'Grab a seat. This won't take long. How did things go with Miller?'

'Signed,' Eve said.

'Great job. I've had a phone call from Ben Styles. You remember him? You sold his penthouse about twelve months ago.'

Her heart raced trying to retain a neutral look.

'You know, the penthouse in Albert Park?'

'Yes, I remember him,' she replied. 'What did he want?'

'He's got a development in South Melbourne he's wanting some advice on. Could be twelve townhouses on our books if he goes ahead with his plans.'

'Sounds good,' Eve said. 'What does he need? An appraisal?'

'Sort of. He wants *your* advice before he renovates. What you think he needs to do to get top dollar. He'd like you to be involved in overseeing the renovations to ensure they meet your vision.'

Eve shifted uneasily in her seat.

'Look, it's a bit unorthodox, but he's willing to pay for your time on a consulting basis. He thinks he'll need you for a day next week and a few hours on different days once the project commences.'

'He wants *me?*'

Peter nodded. 'Was adamant. No one else would do.'

She swallowed. She'd kill Ben if this was an excuse to spend more time with her. They might have met through work but he needed to keep well away from her professional life. 'Okay, I'll give him a call – tee something up.'

Her boss stood. 'Good. Let me know what he ends up needing, as far as your time's concerned. And Eve, great job this morning with Miller, keep it up.'

She forced a smile and retreated from Peter's office, checking her watch. It was already one fifteen. She wouldn't have time to ring Ben before her next meeting. She'd leave her questions until she saw him at three.

Eve made a hasty departure from her one thirty. Luckily it'd been a straightforward contract signing and scheduling for open homes. The house, a small terrace in Port Melbourne, would sell easily. The land value alone would reach the price the client was hoping for.

She was due to meet Ben in twenty minutes, which gave her just enough time to drive from Port Melbourne to Collins Street and quickly freshen up. As she hurried towards her car, the second phone in her bag beeped.

Eve checked Ben's message to discover a change of venue, to an address in South Melbourne. She frowned and messaged, *Okay.*

He wasn't having her meet him at the new development, was he? She wasn't planning to work this afternoon. She shook herself. No, the longing in his voice when they'd spoken earlier had assured her they were both looking forward to this.

She slid into the front seat of her Audi, excitement building within her. She hadn't seen him for over a week. It felt like a month. She did a quick make-up check in the car's mirror, fishing in her bag for her lipstick and reapplying it.

She'd taught herself to dismiss all feelings of guilt when she saw Ben. Technically she was cheating on Sean but it made her a happier person, more tolerant with the kids, more loving to her husband. Ben made her feel wanted and sexy, and her time with him gave her the chance to be the real Eve. Not Eve the mother, Eve the wife, or Eve the real estate agent.

The relationship had its rules. Ben was married too, happily he'd said, but he needed more. Like Eve, he wanted adoration, escapism. So they'd agreed that if they were discreet, no one need know, and no one would get hurt. They'd put their families first, and snatch whatever time they could for themselves.

Her phone rang as she pulled out into the traffic on Beaconsfield Parade. Irritation replaced her excitement. The number showing on the Audi's navigation screen was St Roberta's Primary. The girls were both booked in for after-school care that afternoon and she was tempted to not answer but then they'd ring Sean, who was in court and couldn't be interrupted.

She pressed the receive button on her steering wheel reluctantly. 'Hello.'

'Mrs West?'

'Yes.'

'Mrs West, it's Mary Steed from St Roberta's. I'm afraid Ava isn't feeling very well. We need you to come and collect her.'

'But she's booked in to after-school care.'

'We're aware of that, but since she feels ill and has a temperature of thirty-nine, we're required to ask you to collect her.'

Eve wanted to pummel the steering wheel. This was not happening. She was only a few minutes from South Melbourne, a few minutes from Ben.

She did her best to compose herself. 'And if I can't?'

Mary cleared her throat. 'I'm sorry, Mrs West,' she said crisply, 'that's not really an option. If you are unavailable, could your husband or another family member or friend collect Ava? We did call your nanny, Kate Spencer, but her phone went straight to voicemail. We can call your emergency contacts if you aren't able to.'

She sighed. If only Kate wasn't still on holiday. 'Fine, leave it with me. I'll see if I can get someone to come and pick her up. If I can't, I'll be there within half an hour.'

Eve hung up. Of all days for Ava to be sick. Her parents always offered to do jobs like this but they were away for a few days. Leah?

God, she'd never rung her sister to postpone their three p.m. appointment. Would she dare ask her to pick up Ava? An image of Ben, bare-chested, filtered into her thoughts and she shivered.

Yes, she *would* dare to ask Leah.

Chapter Three

Leah pulled up to the O'Reilly residence in the company car at two forty-five p.m., fifteen minutes before her scheduled meeting time. She'd needed to get out of the office, clear her head a little before catching up with her sister. She'd tried to distract herself with an audiobook during the thirty-five-minute drive to Hampton but switched it off because her thoughts kept flitting back to Grant.

Leah sank back in her seat and closed her eyes just as her phone rang. Eve's number was on the caller display. Instinct shouted her sister would cancel.

'Thanks for the notice,' Leah said, not bothering with a greeting. 'I'm sitting out the front of this place in Hampton. I thought we'd get a coffee.'

'I'm so sorry, Lee. I meant to call you hours ago. An opportunity has come up that Peter wants me to chase immediately. I've had to cancel my entire afternoon.'

She sighed. 'Fine, I'll go for a walk down the beach instead. I'm assuming I don't actually need to see this property?'

'No, I'll send you enough info for your write-up.' There was a brief pause. 'If you aren't already mad at me, you might be in a minute. I need to ask you a favour.'

'What do you need?'

'The school's called and Ava's sick. The twins were both booked in to after-school care, but she's got a fever so they won't let her go. Is there any possibility you could pick her up? If you're in Hampton, you're less than ten minutes away.'

'What? Now?' Leah had planned to go back to the office after she'd met with Eve. If her niece was sick, she could hardly take her back to the paper.

'Yes, sorry.'

She didn't respond. Leah had been looking forward to seeing Eve and talking to her about Grant. She needed to talk to *someone*. Jackie, her best friend, would know all the right things to say, but she couldn't bring herself to ring her. Not yet. Not until she knew why he'd ended it.

'You there, Lee?'

Leah pushed all thoughts of Grant from her mind and made a quick decision to call the office and say she'd be keeping the car overnight and would work from home for the rest of the afternoon. 'Of course I'll pick her up. Do you want me to take her to your place or mine?'

'To mine if that's okay? That way you can put her to bed. You might as well collect Harriet while you're there too. No point us doing a separate trip to the school later. You've still got your key, haven't you?'

'Yes. What do I need to do? Does she need a doctor or medicine or anything?'

'I've got no idea.'

'You're her mother. Surely you know what to do when she's sick.'

'Just take her home and put her to bed. Ask the school nurse, she'll tell you what to do. Gotta run, thanks again.'

Leah stared at the phone. Eve had already hung up. Surely her sister should know what to do? The twins must have had fevers and illnesses before?

She drove back out on to the road in the direction of Brighton and the girls' school.

Leah pulled into a park and noticed a long line of traffic was queued at the exit. She walked past the sports fields to the heart of the school and found the main administration office. She was quickly directed to the sick bay and after-school care facilities.

She opted to collect Harriet first. If Ava felt rotten, it would be best to get her straight into the car and home.

Leah pushed open the door to the after-school care room and was greeted by the noisy chatter of children as they painted, completed puzzles and read books. She scanned the room. An ache tugged at her heart as she spied her blonde-haired niece deep in conversation with a girl around the same age. Only two days ago, she'd contemplated having her own baby, a baby with Grant.

In a split second that dream was now out of reach. She managed a smile when Harriet threw her hands in the air and burst out laughing at something her friend said.

It was only because Ava was in the sick bay that she could easily identify Harriet. When they were in their school uniforms, until Leah spoke to them, it was very difficult to tell them apart. It was easier in their casual clothes. Ava loved purples and pinks and Harriet loved blue and yellow.

No doubt her own parents had had the same difficulties with her and Eve when they were younger, although Leah had opted to wear her own long blonde hair up in a ponytail or bun from an early age, whereas Eve liked hers loose around her shoulders.

Harriet looked up, her face breaking into a huge grin. She jumped to her feet, rushed over and flung her arms around Leah, giving her a tight squeeze. 'Aunty Leah, what're you doing here?'

Leah laughed, returning the hug with equal force. 'How is it I can't tell you and Ava apart, yet you can easily tell the difference between me and your mum?'

'Lipstick,' Harriet said. 'Mummy always wears tons and you never wear any. You have nice shiny lips. I wish Mummy had lips like yours, and eyes too; I hate all those colours she puts on hers.'

'One day, you might decide you want to wear lipstick and eyeshadow too. Mummy wears it to look nice for her job.'

The child shook her head. 'Your job is much more important than Mummy's. She only sells houses. You work at a paper and you look nice. And your hair is beautiful; having it up makes you look smart. What're you doing here?'

'I've come to kidnap you.' Leah smiled again, as Harriet's eyes grew wide.

'Really? Wow, that'd be so cool. Will I come and live at your house or will we sneak off to another country?'

Leah drew her niece in for another hug. 'I'm kidding, silly. Ava's sick and your mum asked me to come and pick her up and take her home. So it made sense that I pick you up too.'

Harriet grinned. 'And you came and got me first, because I'm your favourite.'

'Come on, let's go find your sister. You can show me where the sick bay is.'

Ava was sitting in a comfortable chair, flicking through a book when they arrived. She gave Leah a weak smile, confusion registering in her eyes.

Harriet bounced over to her before Leah had a chance to explain.

'Avie! Aunt Leah's kidnapping us and taking us to a kingdom far away where there are unicorns and chocolate rivers. Get your stuff, we need to go.'

'Mrs West?'

Leah glanced at a thin, dark-haired woman with a friendly face and smiling eyes. Her badge confirmed she was the school nurse. 'No, I'm the girls' aunt. I'm Leah.'

'Sorry, I've seen you at the school before. I assumed you were the girls' mother.'

Harriet shrieked with laughter. 'You did see our mother. They look exactly the same.'

'Oh, I see! Twins run in the family?'

Leah nodded. 'Is there anything I need to know or do for Ava?' She glanced across at her niece, whose face was very pale.

'Put her straight to bed,' the nurse said. 'A cold drink and some food if she'll eat anything. She was complaining of a headache, so you might want to give her some paracetamol. It will help bring her temperature down. See how she is once you get home.'

'Okay, thanks.' She smiled at Ava. 'Do you think you can walk up to the car, sweetheart?'

'Your car?'

She put her arms around her niece. 'Yes, of course. I'm taking you home and looking after you until your mum finishes work.'

'Will she be very late?'

Leah couldn't help but notice the look of hope on Ava's face.

'I'm not sure, she didn't actually say. But regardless, I'll stay until you've gone to sleep.'

'Both of us?' Harriet asked. 'You can read me stories and put me to bed too.'

'Sounds like the perfect way to end the day.'

As Leah helped Ava out of the car and across the path to the front door, she glanced around at the perfectly manicured garden – the hedges were cut to the same height, the winter roses all neatly standing to attention and blooming. On one hand it was very pretty, on the other, it seemed rigid and formal. She preferred a garden that grew a little wilder.

She checked on Harriet, who'd insisted on carrying both school bags. 'You okay, Harry?' she called.

The little girl's face was red from struggling under the strain of the bags, but she nodded. 'Ava must have rocks in her bag,' she announced. 'It's crazy heavy.'

'Library books,' Ava said. 'Big fat ones. But no rocks.'

Leah unlocked the front door, pushed it open and led Ava inside. Harriet followed, dropping the school bags on to the floor the moment she crossed into the house. 'Now what?' she asked.

'What do you normally do when you get home?'

Her niece gave her a sly look. 'Mummy usually lets us make a chocolate cake or muffins. Or she gives us some chocolate.'

Leah hid a smile as she heard a sharp intake of breath from Ava.

'You liar,' her other niece said. 'Mummy's never home, but when she is she never lets us have anything like that. She makes us eat fruit or carrot sticks.' She lowered her voice. 'She doesn't want fat kids.'

A lump rose in Leah's throat. Fat kids? They were seven, and there was nothing of them. If anything, they could both do to put on a few kilos.

'How about I help Ava up to bed, then you and I look at what we could make for afternoon tea,' she suggested.

Harriet's eyes glistened. 'A chocolate cake?'

She shook her head. 'Probably not today. Ava's not well and chocolate is the last thing we should be feeding her.'

Harriet's little face clouded over with disappointment.

'Don't worry, we'll make something yummy. Now, you go and put the school bags in the kitchen so I can unpack them. Wash your hands and I'll be down in a few minutes.' Leah put an arm around Ava. 'Come on, let's get you into bed.' They walked slowly up the stairs.

The girls shared a huge bedroom that led off their own play and television room; a rope lay on the floor at the halfway point, creating a clear division. One side of the room was full of pinks and purples, with stuffed toys strewn about and a doll's house sitting in the corner. A shelf above a small desk proudly housed around twenty miniature fairy figurines.

The other side of the room was blues and aquas. A skateboard was propped up in one corner, and a basket full of Nerf guns stood in pride of place in the middle of the floor.

Leah helped Ava over to her pink princess bed, sat her down, untied her shoes and pulled off her socks. 'How about we put your pyjamas on? That way you'll be nice and snug and comfy.'

Her niece reached under her pillow, pulling out a pretty pair of floral flannel pyjamas.

She helped her change and tucked her in, bringing a soft blanket snug around her. 'How're you feeling?'

Tears welled in Ava's eyes. 'Horrible.' Her voice was a whisper. 'My head and throat hurt.'

She gave her a cuddle. 'Oh, you poor little thing. How about I go downstairs and get you a nice cold drink? I'll see if I can find some medicine for your head too.'

Ava nodded, laying her head back against the pillow. Leah snuggled the blanket around her once again and tucked her soft toy squirrel in with her. She leant down and kissed her niece's forehead, noting that it was very hot. 'I'll be back in a few minutes,' she promised.

She made her way back down the stairs. She could hear clanking and banging coming from the kitchen. What on earth could Harriet be up to? She'd probably be covered from head to foot with flour and cocoa, having decided to make a chocolate cake anyway.

Leah stopped at the kitchen door, tears pricking her eyes, as she saw what Harriet was doing.

The little girl was hunched over the kitchen table, her tongue poking out of the side of her mouth as she concentrated on spreading a piece of bread with butter. Next to her was a tray, with a small vase which had one pink rose sticking out of it, and a glass of something clear and fizzy with ice cubes in it.

Leah got herself together and joined Harriet. 'What you doing, chipmunk?'

Her niece looked up. 'I thought I'd make Avie some afternoon tea. I'm making her a sprinkle sandwich.' Her eyes widened. 'That's okay, isn't it? I know Mummy wouldn't normally let us have that, but it is Avie's favourite. And I don't think she'll notice I cut the rose from the garden.'

Leah put an arm around her. 'Of course it's okay. It's lovely, in fact.' She felt Harriet relax against her. 'What's the drink?'

'Mineral water. I wanted to give her lemonade but we don't have any. I've squeezed some lemon in it to make it a bit nicer.'

She was surprised Harriet had even found sprinkles if Eve was that strict about what the girls ate. 'It looks great. I'm sure she'll love it. Now, you finish, and we'll take it up. I'll see if I can rustle up some medicine for her headache and fever.'

Harriet concentrated on applying the sprinkles to the bread while Leah opened the pantry and went in search of the medicine. She let out a breath, relieved to see a large box on the top shelf marked 'First Aid'. She took it down and opened it, taking out the paracetamol and the ear thermometer. She checked the dosage to give Ava and rummaged back through the box for a medicine cup.

'I'm finished,' her niece announced.

Leah crossed to the kitchen table and admired Harriet's work. The sandwich had been cut into little bite-sized pieces.

'It's a sandwich poppa,' Harriet explained. 'When you're sick, you don't want to be taking big bites.'

'Poppa?'

Harriet nodded. 'Poppa it in your mouth.' She grinned. 'I made that up, do you like it?'

'I *love* it, and so will Ava. Let's take it upstairs. Shall I carry the tray until we get to the top of the stairs, and then you can take it so she knows you made it?'

The little girl beamed with delight. 'Really? I can walk into the room with it?'

'Of course,' Leah said. She placed the medicine and thermometer on the side of the tray and followed Harriet up the stairs, stopping outside the girls' room to hand it back to her niece.

Harriet smiled proudly and walked into the room. She stopped as she neared the bed, her face clouding with disappointment.

Ava was asleep.

'Set it down there and come with me.' Leah pointed to the bedside table.

Harriet followed her back into the playroom.

'Have you got paper and coloured pencils?' she asked.

Her niece nodded.

'Great, let's make a lovely card to sit on the tray. When Ava wakes up, she'll know you made her the food.'

'That's a fantastic idea.' The little girl made her way across the room to a chest of drawers. She took out a sheet of paper and reached into the second drawer for a big packet of coloured pens. 'Can you help me fold the paper so it's like a real card?'

'Of course.' Once it was folded, Leah put the paper on a table. 'You work on this while I clean up the kitchen and pack your lunchboxes away. Would you like me to make you a special afternoon tea too?'

The little girl didn't look up from the card she was adding something purple to. 'Yes, please.'

Leah smiled as she headed back down the stairs. Her niece had such a good heart and Eve was lucky to have the family she had. Her smile slipped and a lump formed in her throat. She was supposed to have had that with Grant. What she'd lost was enormous. Not only the man she loved, but she'd wasted six years. The likelihood of finding a new relationship and having children in her thirties was slowly moving out of reach. It was quite possible she might need to settle for being an aunt.

Chapter Four

Eve pulled up in front of a run-down townhouse at the address Ben had sent her in South Melbourne. She opened the car door and stepped out on to the cracked footpath.

There was no sign of Ben's Mercedes. She peered at the house in front of her; number thirteen, according to the broken letterbox propped up with rocks against a small concrete pillar.

Roof tiles were missing, the paint was peeling, and the small garden was completely overgrown. The two properties to the right looked the same. Either side of the three run-down blocks stood new terraced houses. If this was the development Peter had mentioned, where were the other nine properties?

Eve shivered. It really was freezing. She turned to wait in the warmth of her car when a sleek silver vehicle parked behind her. A lightness spread within her and her breath quickened as Ben stepped out.

He stopped, their eyes meeting, his grin causing dimples to bloom on his cheeks. His jet-black hair had been cut short, and his aquamarine shirt brought out the brilliant blue of his eyes. His black Armani suit and gleaming black shoes completed his trademark look.

Ben's eyes swept up and down the street as he approached her. He didn't embrace her, or even touch her. 'Hey, beautiful lady.'

'Hey, yourself.' Eve forced her eyes away from his to the run-down house. 'What's with the dump? It's hardly the Sofitel.'

'Don't judge a book by its cover.' He pushed open the old iron gate, which was half hanging off its hinges. 'Come in. I want to show you something.'

She followed along the uneven path to the front entrance. The three steps leading to the door were broken in parts, and the door itself was scraped and cracked. 'Nice,' she said.

Ben laughed. 'Glad you can see past its rustic charm.' He pushed a key into the lock and turned it.

The hallway was dark but at least it didn't smell. Eve had expected the dank, mouldy smell she was often met with in old places, but was pleasantly surprised. They moved down the hallway into a bright kitchen. The room was old but spotless. The outside of the property had been let go, but it appeared the inside had been looked after. 'How long has this been empty?'

'A month or two,' Ben replied. 'The owner died a few weeks before the lease was due to be renewed. The family chose to evict the tenant, and eleven others, so they could look at selling it.'

'Eleven others? So this is the project you contacted Peter about?'

Ben nodded. He stepped closer and took her in his arms. 'God, I've missed you.' His lips met hers with urgency.

Eve found herself responding but her mind wasn't allowing her to surrender. She still didn't understand why he'd brought her here today. Today was about them, not about work.

He drew back. 'What's wrong?'

Heat rushed to her face. 'Sorry, I'm trying to work out why we're here and not at the Sofitel. This is hardly comfortable.'

Ben grinned and took her hand. 'You haven't seen it all yet.' He led her to another small hallway off the kitchen. He pushed open the first door to reveal a large, empty room.

'Gorgeous fireplace.'

'It's at least a hundred years old,' he said. 'A bit of work to restore it, and it'll be an amazing selling point for the house.' He continued down the hall and pushed open a second door.

They were faced with a similar room. This one, however, housed several old chairs and a broken bed frame. Frustration was growing in Eve. The afternoon of escapism she'd been longing for seemed to be slipping through her fingers. Appraising a run-down house had not been her plan.

Ben must've sensed her irritation. 'Be patient,' he murmured and kissed her again. This time his tongue lingered in her mouth and he ran his hands down her sides and cupped her bottom. She could feel his hardness through his suit pants.

He pulled away and led her to a third door. 'Last one.' His voice was deep and husky as he stood back and signalled for her to open the door.

She pushed it open and stopped. 'Wow.' The word was out before she had time to think.

The room was beautiful. The floorboards had been polished and the walls had been stripped of wallpaper and painted cream. The fireplace had been restored and some kindling was piled in the grate along with some scrunched up newspapers ready to light. But the main feature was the bed in the middle of the room.

Ben's arms circled her waist from behind while his mouth nuzzled at her neck. 'What do you think?'

Eve swallowed. The bed in front of her was nothing short of glamorous. It was round, with a rolled fabric finish and at least a dozen plump cushions strewn around it. She faced Ben, no longer needing to question why he'd brought her here today. 'Did you do this all for me?'

He nodded. 'For us. I'll tell you more about the South Melbourne project later. For different reasons, we'll be renovating this house last. For the next six to nine months this room is ours and, while we're working on the project together, it makes sense that you'll need to meet me here on a regular basis.'

She grinned. 'You've really thought this through, haven't you?'

'I organised for this room to be done last week. I wanted to surprise you. Don't worry. The contractors I used aren't the ones working on the development. No one except *us* will be aware that this room even exists.'

'You've thought of everything.'

Ben kissed her again. This time he removed her coat and started on the buttons of her shirt. 'Hold on, I forgot something.' He moved across the room to the fireplace and lit the newspaper. Very quickly the sticks began to burn and he leaned down to blow on them, then stopped.

Eve stood before him completely naked.

Ben rolled on to his back, sweat beading his brow. 'Wow!'

Eve smiled, curling her spent body around his. 'That was amazing.'

He dragged the soft duvet over them. The room was warm with the fire crackling in the hearth.

He stroked her thigh. 'You're the one that's amazing. How lucky are we?'

They *were* lucky, extremely lucky to have found each other. If they'd met before they'd both been married would their life together seem so exciting?

'Don't think,' Ben said, allowing his fingers to travel over her body. 'You do too much of that.'

Eve sighed. 'Guilty.'

'We're perfect as we are, Eve, you know that.'

He appeared to be able to read her mind.

'It's part of the excitement. It gives us a break from everyday life. Reminds us we're desired. Full-time wouldn't be the same.'

She didn't respond. She agreed, but there were times, particularly after amazing sex, that part of her wanted this life, not her regular one. She snuggled closer, closing her eyes as the combination of his body heat and the warmth of the fire enveloped her.

The ringing of her phone instantly killed her post-sex glow.

Ben tugged her back when she pushed off the covers. 'Leave it. It'll only be work.'

Eve hesitated then fell back against him. 'Good idea.' Her mind briefly flickered to the girls. They were with Leah. She didn't need to worry about them.

Her lover pinned her under him as the phone stopped ringing. 'You have other things to worry about right now.' He moved beneath the covers, his tongue trailing down her body.

She tensed in anticipation. But as he continued his explorations, her phone rang again.

'Shit!' Eve sat up. 'I'd better at least check who it is.'

Ben sighed and rolled off her and she slid from the bed and reached for her bag and phone. The caller ID showed Sean's name. 'Shit,' she repeated. She hesitated. She'd never spoken to her husband while she was with Ben.

Guilt stabbed at her.

She looked across to Ben, mouthed 'Sorry', then pressed the receive button and put the phone to her ear.

'Just checking if you want me to pick the girls up from after-school care?' Sean asked.

'You're on your way home already?' Eve checked the time; it wasn't even five.

'Court was cancelled. I thought I should check in with you guys. I've been working late so many nights I'm worried I might not recognise the twins.' He gave a soft laugh. 'Luckily, I only have to remember what one of them looks like.'

'Leah picked them up earlier.' Eve cringed. She hated that this discussion was in front of Ben. Keeping her two lives separate was what made them work. 'The school called. Ava was unwell. I thought you were in court, and I couldn't get away.'

'What's wrong with Ava?'

'A temperature, not feeling great. Nothing serious.'

'And you really couldn't cancel your day to collect her?'

'No,' she said. 'And Leah was in Hampton at a property, so it wasn't inconvenient.'

'Finishing work during school hours might have been,' Sean said. 'You should've cancelled your afternoon and gone to her. She's sick; she needs one of us.'

Eve sighed. 'Don't be so dramatic. Leah's with her. She adores Leah. She's probably loving every minute of it.'

'What time will you be finished up?'

Ben was propped on one elbow watching her.

Her heart skipped a beat. 'I'm not sure. I've been brought in on a major development project in South Melbourne, and they want me involved in the planning stages.'

'Fine,' Sean said. 'I'll go home now and look after her.'

'You don't need to,' she said. 'Leah will manage fine.'

'That's not the point. I don't want our daughter at home feeling miserable and not having one of us there. I feel guilty, and it amazes me *you* don't. So you can relax and enjoy whatever it is you're doing and not worry at all.'

'That's not fair,' Eve said. Although looking around, he couldn't have been more accurate if he'd tried. She crossed her fingers. 'I've got a huge opportunity here, and I can't afford for it to go to another agency. If you're happy to play Father of the Year and race home then I'll stay until the meetings are done. I'm not sure if they'll be finishing with a dinner or drinks but if they are, I'll text you.'

'Don't bother.'

She glanced at her phone. Sean had hung up.

'Trouble?' Ben asked.

'Nothing we need to discuss.' She slipped the phone back into her bag.

'You look so sexy on the phone naked,' he said. 'Maybe you should consider that your new office look.'

She rolled her eyes. 'That sounds appropriate.'

Ben pushed himself up and got out of bed and Eve took in the beauty of his full nakedness and swallowed.

He held out a hand and took her left hand in his, lifting it to his lips and kissing her ring finger. 'You don't have to take off your wedding ring when we get together. I know you're married.'

'I don't. I said no to an engagement ring and the same to a wedding ring.'

Ben raised an eyebrow. 'Really?'

Eve nodded. 'Men don't wear engagement rings. They give them to brand a woman, declare *she's mine* so no other guys hit on her. It's archaic. I guess there's a bit of a feminist lurking in me.' She held up her right hand, which was also bare, and grinned. 'I'm not a ring person, unless they're earrings of course. Earrings are always very welcome, diamond preferable.'

Ben laughed. 'I'll keep that in mind. Now, back to bed with you. You told your husband you're working on a major development and we've got some planning to do.'

She raised an eyebrow as Ben hardened in front of her. 'I take it that's the major development?'

He nodded. 'It's definitely in need of your expert handling.'

Eve took his hand and moved back on to the bed with him. She wouldn't wish illness on either of her girls, but today it'd turned into a bonus.

Leah was rummaging through the fridge to see what she could put together for dinner when Harriet came into the kitchen.

'I put the card on the tray,' she said. 'Avie was still asleep.'

'Good girl. Now' – she pointed to the table – 'I've made you a little plate of afternoon tea. Why don't you have that while I work out something for dinner.'

Her niece's eyes widened as she moved to the kitchen table. 'Chocolate biscuits? Where did you get them?'

She laughed. She'd found an open packet of Tim Tams pushed to the back of the pantry. Leah remembered how much her sister loved them and assumed she'd uncovered a secret stash. 'I magicked them here. The deal is, you must eat the fruit on your plate and the cheese and then you can have the treat.'

Harriet looked around the kitchen. 'What if Mummy comes? She won't let me eat them.'

'This one time she will. Don't you worry, you enjoy them.'

Her niece reached for the fruit, but her eyes were glued to the chocolate biscuits.

Leah continued her search for ingredients for a meal. She'd found mince and plenty of garlic, basil and tomatoes. She'd found pasta and the other items in the pantry she'd need to make her Bolognese. The girls loved spaghetti, so it was an easy choice. She could also make a salad. As she started preparing the ingredients, the sounds of the garage door caught her attention.

'Oh no,' Harriet said. 'Mummy's home.' She pushed the plate of afternoon tea away from her. 'I didn't eat the biscuits, so it's okay.'

Leah's heart contracted. Her niece was scared about eating chocolate biscuits? She mentally kicked herself. She should never have given them to her.

They both turned as they heard the internal garage door open and shut, and footsteps approached the kitchen. Expecting to see Eve, Leah was surprised when her brother-in-law's broad figure filled the doorway.

'Daddy!' Harriet leapt from the kitchen chair and rushed over to Sean, flinging herself at him.

He dropped his briefcase and scooped her up, swinging her around. 'Hello, my beautiful poppet, how was your day?'

'Great, but Ava's sick. I made her afternoon tea and a card.' Her face clouded over. 'But she's fast asleep, so she doesn't even know yet. Aunty Leah has been looking after me.'

Gratitude filled Sean's warm chestnut eyes. 'Thanks so much. I only just heard from Eve that Ava was sick. If I'd known earlier, I could've picked the girls up myself. Court was cancelled.'

She smiled as Sean put Harriet down and loosened his tie. 'No need to worry. Ava needs to rest, and Harriet and I are having a great time. Actually, I was getting some dinner organised. I'd be happy to stay longer if you'd like me to.'

'You have to,' her niece said. 'You promised to run my bath and read my stories. Remember?'

'Of course I did. But Daddy might have other plans?'

'None at all,' he said. 'We'd love you to stay. Unless Grant's expecting you?'

At the mention of her now ex's name, a lump immediately formed in Leah's throat. She took a deep breath, and hoped her face didn't give away how rattled she was. Sean wasn't the right person to confide in. 'No, nothing planned for tonight.' She leaned closer and lowered her voice. 'Well, I did have one plan but I might need your help.'

'Sure. Doing what?'

She winked at Harriet. 'I magicked up a packet of chocolate biscuits, you see, and for being such a good helper I added two to Harriet's afternoon tea. She's eaten her fruit and her cheese, but she was worried she might get in trouble if she ate the biscuits. I need you to help convince her she's earned a lovely treat.'

His eyes widened as he looked at Harriet. 'A treat? A chocolate biscuit treat?'

The little girl nodded.

'And you said no?'

Harriet nodded again.

Sean held her out from him and started to examine her. 'You have toes that look like mine. Legs that look like mine.' He turned her around. 'Even your hair looks like mine. But saying no to chocolate biscuits? That confirms it, you can't belong to me. It isn't possible.'

Harriet giggled. 'Yes I do, Daddy.'

'Then we'd better examine these biscuits, because if you don't like them, then you definitely don't belong to me. I can see from here they're one of my favourites.' He took his daughter across to the table, sat her down and pushed the plate with the two biscuits in front of her. 'Take your time and enjoy them, sweetheart.'

Harriet reached for a biscuit, her face crinkling in delight. She took a tiny bite. 'Mmm. Yum.'

He laughed. 'Phew, turns out you do belong to me, after all. Now, I'd better have a chat with your aunt and help her get some dinner ready.' Sean moved back to the kitchen counter.

Leah opened the fridge and held a bottle out to him. 'Beer?'

He grinned and sat down at the counter. 'Thanks. We could get used to this. Chocolate biscuits and beers on a Monday. Whatever would Eve say?'

She raised an eyebrow. 'Really? She won't let you have a beer?'

He twisted the top off his drink and took a swig. 'She'd prefer I didn't. That doesn't mean I don't. I just have to put up with her tutting the whole time.'

'And the kids aren't allowed any treats?'

'Not on her watch. She's crazy strict about it. Convinced they'll end up overweight, pimply teens.'

'They're seven,' Leah said. 'That's not exactly healthy for their body image or self-esteem.'

'I agree,' Sean said. 'I take them for secret treats. Don't I, Harry?'

The little girl's mouth was coated in chocolate. 'And we don't tell Mummy.'

She smiled. 'I'd better get on with this sauce. Hopefully Eve won't object to pasta and salad.'

'Grab yourself a beer too,' her brother-in-law said. 'Or a glass of wine? I'll make the salad.' He moved from the stool, washed his hands and started to prepare the ingredients.

Leah took a frosty bottle of light beer for herself and enjoyed the first sip as the cool liquid trickled down her throat.

They worked in comfortable silence for a few minutes. She fried the garlic and onion before browning the mince for the sauce. She hadn't seen Sean since the girls' birthday party three months ago, and she certainly hadn't spent time alone with him in years.

Not that they were alone; Harriet was still licking chocolate off the second biscuit. Did her brother-in-law ever think back to the months before he and Eve had got together? The months where he'd flirted with Leah. Where her heart had soared every time she'd seen him.

They'd been at university; he was studying law, she journalism. Finally, he'd asked her out. They'd been to dinner and then on to a party at one of his law student friend's houses.

After arriving at the party and being introduced to Sean's friends, Leah had excused herself to go to the bathroom. There was a line and with only one toilet in the house, she'd been gone close to ten minutes.

Ten minutes she'd used to reflect on their laughter and flirting over dinner and the amazing night they'd had so far. She'd hugged herself; she'd never felt like this before.

When she returned she'd frozen in the doorway of the living room. Sean was sitting on the couch laughing, his arm draped around Eve. His laughter had been replaced with confusion the moment he saw her. He'd pulled his arm back and glanced from sister to sister.

Eve had jumped up and rushed over, flinging her arms around her. 'Lee, come and meet this gorgeous guy. I've only known him for five minutes, and I'm going to marry him.'

Her heart had sunk. She'd forced a smile as she'd explained that Eve was her identical twin sister. He'd appeared mortified at first, but Leah couldn't help but notice that his eyes kept travelling to Eve.

'Didn't you notice we were dressed differently?' her sister had asked, laughing, one arm on Sean's.

'I'm so sorry, I was concentrating on what you were saying, I really didn't notice to be honest. Your tops are different colours but you're dressed similarly.'

Leah had dressed in black trousers, boots and a blue sequined top, and other than her top being a different shade of blue, Eve had been dressed almost identically. Even though they appeared identical, and were dressed similarly, Sean's attention was captivated by Eve. He'd seemed mesmerised by her.

Her sister had taken her aside when he went to get them drinks. 'How much do you like this guy?'

A lot. But he didn't look at her in the same way he was looking at her twin.

To Eve, she'd forced a laugh. 'It's our first date, I'm just getting to know him.'

'How would you feel if I stole him off you?' Eve's eyes twinkled.

Leah hesitated. Eve usually got what she wanted but it didn't mean she wouldn't put up a fight for something that was important to her. But then she thought of the way Sean had looked at Eve. She couldn't force him to like her better than her sister. 'I'd wish you both all the best,' she'd answered.

'Hold on, don't be silly,' Sean said, returning with their drinks. 'This is *our* date. It's lovely to have met Eve, but I'm here with you.'

Her twin had laughed. 'Leah, you don't have to leave. Sean and I have only spent five minutes together. If he wants to get to know me better, and you really don't mind, we can go out another time.' She looked across at Sean. 'Right?'

'I guess so.'

Leah had laughed at the indecision on his face. It was obvious that the two of them wanted to get to know each other right now. 'Honestly, don't worry, it's not a big deal.' She'd put her glass down on a nearby table, hugged Eve and grabbed her coat. 'Thanks for dinner,' she'd said to Sean.

She hadn't waited for further discussion. He'd appeared confused and slightly embarrassed so it was easier to leave the two of them to it.

Leah saw Sean at uni occasionally after that, but it was at a distance and she'd generally chosen to look the other way and get on with things.

He and her sister had started dating, and it was over a month later when she'd seen him in a social setting when Eve had brought him home for dinner to meet their parents.

Sean had seemed uncomfortable around Leah and she'd been friendly but distant. She'd liked him, a lot, but deep down instinct told her if it was Eve he was into, there was no point fighting for him. He'd resent her down the track and her sister would be furious.

And anyway, her relationship with her twin would always be her first priority. To be fair to Eve, she'd checked numerous times that she was okay with her having interrupted their date. Leah had assured Eve that having seen Sean's reaction when he'd met Eve, there was no denying who he was attracted to. There was no point trying to fight chemistry.

Eve and Sean had been together for fifteen years now. Happily married with two gorgeous children. It'd been the right choice.

'How's work?' Sean's deep voice shattered her memories.

They chatted companionably while they continued with the dinner preparations. Harriet went up to check on Ava every fifteen minutes, reporting back each time that her sister was still asleep.

The pasta had boiled, the sauce and salad were ready and Harriet had made a fantastic attempt at laying the table. Leah looked at the clock on the kitchen wall. 'Should we feed Harriet first and wait for Eve?' she asked Sean.

Her brother-in-law placed his second beer down on the counter. 'Nope. Who knows when she'll be home. She'll probably use the fact we're both here for an excuse to stay out even later.'

She was about to laugh but his face was deadly serious. 'Surely she'll hurry back after her meeting? She knows Ava's sick.'

He rolled his eyes. 'Don't count on it. I'd say her *meeting*, if there even was one, probably finished hours ago.' Sean seemed to force a smile. 'Now come on, let's eat. That sauce smells amazing.'

Leah stared after him as he made his way to the table. Eve hadn't mentioned any marital problems, but Sean's tone certainly implied something was going on. She hoped it wasn't serious.

Her niece patted the chair next to hers. 'I've saved you a seat.'

A satisfied smile played on Eve's lips while she waited for the tram to pass before pulling out into Clarendon Street. She was relieved Ben had also ensured the bathroom was functional, and she'd been able to shower, fix her messed-up hair and redo her make-up before leaving.

They'd ordered Thai and lain in bed eating and chatting. It'd felt incredibly luxurious to have spent so many hours together. Usually they were only able to snatch two hours here or there.

Twenty minutes later, she took a deep breath and turned into her own driveway, her headlights lighting up the house. As far as Sean was concerned, she'd been working. Eve had nothing to feel guilty or apologise for. What she didn't understand was why Leah's work car was parked out the front. She'd assumed her sister would've left when Sean arrived home. That would've been hours ago.

She checked her reflection in the rear-view mirror; her cheeks were flushed, but that could be attributed to the chill in the air. She pushed the remote to open the garage door and drove forward to park her car.

Eve frowned when she heard Leah's gentle laugh as she pushed open the internal access door. She scanned the kitchen, taking in the two empty beer bottles on the counter and the additional two being consumed at the table by her husband and sister.

Leah was the first to notice her. She jumped to her feet. 'Eve, you're back.'

She deposited her bag and computer case on the kitchen bench. 'I didn't think you'd still be here.'

'Eve!' Sean's eyes flashed with anger. 'That's incredibly rude.'

'What?' she asked. 'I thought once you got home, there would be no need for Leah to stay. I'm not saying she shouldn't have, only that I'm surprised.'

'I'd already promised Harry I'd put her to bed,' her twin said. 'And I wanted to check that Ava was feeling better when she woke up. She fell asleep the moment we got her home.'

'How is she?'

'She woke at about seven. Her temperature was back to normal, and she was able to eat the meal that Harry made her.'

Eve raised an eyebrow. 'That Harriet made? God, what did that consist of?'

Leah smiled. 'She made her a beautiful sandwich, and a mineral water to drink. Put it on a tray with a flower and everything. She's an amazing kid.' Her sister moved into the kitchen and stirred a pot on the stove. 'There's plenty of dinner left, if you're hungry? I've kept it warm in case.'

Eve shook her head. 'No, thanks, I've already eaten.'

'Where were you?' Sean asked. Her husband's face was hard. He was obviously still annoyed at her.

'Working. Like I told you.'

'Until eight?'

She sighed. 'That's hardly unusual, Sean. Coming from you, it's a bit of a joke, really. We're lucky to see you before ten any night of the week.'

'Which is why you work a job that allows you to be home for the girls.' He took another swig of his beer.

Eve felt Leah's eyes on them.

'Perhaps I should go,' her sister said.

Her husband stood. 'No, you stay, and thanks so much for all your help today.' He picked up his beer. 'I've got some work to do.' Sean went towards the front of the house, pulling his office door shut with a firm bang.

'Everything okay with you guys?' Leah asked.

Eve sighed again. 'Yeah, he's annoyed I asked you to get Ava and didn't get her myself. Thanks, by the way.' Eve poured herself a glass of water. 'Sorry, I should've said that when I first came in. I really appreciate you picking the girls up. I know you would've had to cancel your afternoon.'

'No worries. Actually, they perked me up a bit.'

'Everything okay? Is work getting you down again?'

Leah's dreams of being a hard-hitting journalist were not being met in the property section of *The Melbournian*.

'Yes. Well, no,' her sister said. 'It's not only work. It's Grant too.'

Eve sat on one of the kitchen stools and motioned for her twin to do the same. 'What's going on with Grant? Mum's sure he's going to propose soon. I think she has the engagement party planned already.' She glanced at her sister's left hand. 'Still no ring?'

Leah shook her head and her eyes misted over. 'He ended it.'

She gasped. 'What? Really? Why?'

'He didn't give me a proper reason. Just said it wasn't working for him.'

Eve closed her mouth, aware that it was hanging open. Like her parents, she'd expected Leah to announce her engagement any day. She'd even seen a beautiful necklace she'd planned to buy for a special engagement present. Grant was like one of the family. It had to be a misunderstanding.

She wrapped her arms around Leah. 'I'm so sorry.'

Her sister sank into her embrace and her short sharp breaths told her she was crying. She rubbed her back.

Eve was going to kill Grant when she saw him.

After a few minutes, Leah pulled away and reached across the kitchen bench for a tissue. 'Sorry,' she said. 'You're the first person I've told, and it makes it real.'

'It doesn't make sense. Six years and that's it? No explanation?'

'Appears so.'

'Are you sure it's definitely over? You didn't get your wires crossed?'

Her sister sighed. 'Nope, it's over. He's coming to get his stuff tomorrow night.'

Eve touched her twin's arm. 'I really am sorry, Lee. What a prick. But then, I'm beginning to think most of them are.'

A flicker of surprise flashed across Leah's cobalt-blue eyes. 'Who? Sean?'

'Yes, he's so bloody moody. You'd think he had his period the way he acts most of the time. I can't seem to do anything right. I work too much and parent too little, according to him.'

'Sounds tricky.'

'You're hardly disagreeing with him,' Eve said. 'What, do you think I work too much too?'

'It's not my life, Eve, so what you do is your own concern.'

'But?'

Leah hesitated. 'But you've got two amazing girls, and I think they'd love to spend more time with you.'

Eve threw back her head and laughed. 'Really? You really think they want to spend more time with *me*? I'm not the fun one, Sean is. They tiptoe around me.'

'Why do you think that is?' Leah asked.

'I'm sure you have your own opinion on that,' Eve said tightly. 'I hardly need to answer for you.'

'If you tried to lighten up a bit on them, I think you'd see a huge difference. Let them be kids, enjoy treats, get messy, have fun. We did all that when we were little.'

'I try sometimes,' Eve said. 'But to be honest, motherhood doesn't suit me. I know it is an awful thing to say, but I should never have had kids. I'm not cut out for it. From the day they were born, I wanted to hand them off to someone else, someone who'd do it better. Give them what they needed. I thought it would be different, easier. On top of that, they're wrecking my relationship with Sean. He's critical of my parenting, then we fight and that's about it for our communication. We hardly ever get any time for the two of us.'

Leah's face hardened. 'Two little girls rely on you to be their mother. Whether you think you're cut out for it or not you need to make more time for them and more of an effort. If you need help you only need to ask. But, Eve, you need to be more involved. It's the only way you'll ever build proper relationships with them. Imagine if Mum hadn't spent time with us. We'd hate her now.'

Although she hated hearing Leah's words, deep down Eve knew she was right. She did need to make an effort, only it felt so hard at times.

Leah's face softened. 'You need to make some time for the girls, that's all. And regarding Sean, I'd be happy to babysit so you can go out. I'd love to.'

She fiddled with her water glass. 'Maybe. Although, I'm not sure I want to be around him at the moment. In fact, I don't even want to talk about him. It's *you* we should be talking about. I can't believe Grant's walked out. Do you want me to speak to him? Find out what the hell he thinks he's doing?'

'No, but I appreciate the offer. I'll see him when he picks up his stuff. He's not walking out without a proper explanation.'

'If you want me to come over and be there when he arrives, I'd be happy to.'

'Thanks, but this is something I need to do on my own.' Her sister took a deep breath. 'Now, I really don't want to talk about him anymore. Tell me about something different. How's work going? What's this big development?'

Eve dived in about the development Ben was proposing.

'Ben Styles?' Leah asked.

She nodded.

'Be wary of him.'

Eve arched an eyebrow. 'Why? He seems like a nice guy. Do you know him?'

'I've never met him, but he comes with quite a reputation. I heard the guys at work laughing about him. I think a few were jealous. Apparently he likes to work with female suppliers. Has a very high hit rate with getting them into bed. Seems to prefer the married ones. I assume it's because he can be assured if they're cheating too, then they're probably not going to let on to *his* wife what's going on.'

Eve's chest ached with each breath. Her relationship with Ben was special. At least she'd *thought* it was. Was she the first woman he'd brought to the plush round bed in South Melbourne?

'You okay?' her sister asked. 'You look really pale. You might be getting whatever Ava has.'

Eve didn't respond. She'd assumed she was the only woman – other than his wife – in Ben's life. Had she been stupid to believe that?

'You're right,' she finally managed. 'I'd better go and check on the girls and I might go to bed too. I'm beginning to feel a little hot.'

Leah felt Eve's forehead. 'You are a bit warm. Let me tidy up a bit, and I'll get out of your hair.'

She helped her twin clear the beer bottles from the table and poured the pasta sauce into a container ready for the fridge.

Warm? She was downright boiling. If Ben was sleeping around, where did that leave her?

The sounds of the girls playing filtered into Eve's sleep. She groaned, opened one eye, and peeked at the alarm clock. It was only five thirty. She turned over, ready to poke Sean and tell him to go and shut them up, but the other side of the bed was empty. If he was up already, why didn't he quieten them?

She lay back, her annoyance now ensuring she was fully awake. Sean had still been working when she'd gone to bed the previous night. She assumed he'd come to bed, although the neat pillows on his side suggested he hadn't. He'd probably slept in the guest room. Again.

A scream of laughter jolted her upright. Eve threw off the covers and stormed out on to the landing. She opened her mouth about to tell the girls to quieten down but froze.

Sean was lying on his back, arms and legs in the air with one of the twins balanced on them. He was pressing his arms up and down as if doing reverse push-ups.

Their other daughter stood next to them, squealing with delight. 'My turn, my turn,' she shrieked. Both girls were having a great time which was at least one positive in being woken so thoughtlessly. Whichever one was Ava was obviously feeling better.

Eve shook her head. She couldn't even tell the girls apart this morning. They were wearing the same pyjamas, which was unusual; usually Harriet insisted on dressing differently.

Her husband laughed, lowering the child to the floor. 'Next victim,' he called. He glanced across to where Eve was standing. His face immediately hardened. 'Oh, you're awake.'

Morning to you too. Of course she was awake. No one could sleep through this.

'Mummy,' squealed the twins, rushing over to her. They looked like they were about to fling themselves on her but suddenly stopped. The girls knew better. They stared up at her, their faces full of love.

Eve swallowed. She really wanted to tell them to quieten down so she could get another hour's sleep. She'd tossed and turned, obsessing about Ben the night before and was going to be a zombie today if she didn't.

However, the girls were excited to see her and Sean's expression told her to tread carefully. She leant down and gave them both a quick hug, noticing Ava's stuffed squirrel poking out from one armpit. That at least confirmed who was who. She ruffled Ava's hair. 'Feeling better this morning?'

The little girl nodded. 'I slept forever. Daddy says I should stay home from school today but I think I'm okay to go.'

Eve shot her husband a look. 'Are you working from home today?'

Sean pulled himself up off the floor. 'No, of course not. I'm in court at eleven.'

'Why suggest Ava stay home then? I can't take today off either.'

He rolled his eyes. 'Why not? What's happening in the world of real estate that's so important?'

Eve glared. 'Don't undermine my work, Sean. What you do is no more important.'

'But Daddy helps people, Mummy,' Ava said. 'People who wouldn't have anyone to reper . . . reper . . . present them. His job is very important.'

She looked at her daughter. When had he fed her *that* speech? 'I think you mean *represent*, honey. And yes, Daddy does represent people, but they usually have quite a lot of money to pay for that representation.'

The little girl's face clouded with confusion. 'But I thought they had no money, and that's why Daddy had to fight for them.' She turned to look at Sean. 'That's right, isn't it, Daddy?'

'Sure is, pumpkin. I do a lot of pro bono work. It's not something Mummy knows much about. Now, how about we head downstairs? We'll make some pancakes for breakfast and let Mummy go back to bed. She looks like she needs a bit of extra beauty sleep.'

The girls giggled and followed her husband.

Eve retreated to the bedroom. Pro bono work? Since when was he doing that? And why had he told their seven-year-old and not her?

She was now wide awake, so she might as well forgo the extra sleep. Eve pulled on her running gear instead. It was still dark out but the early chill of the winter morning would do her good.

Eve slipped out of the front door without seeing Sean or the girls. They'd assume she was still in bed, which was fine by her. She shivered in the fresh morning air. The streetlights were on but the sky was beginning to lighten. She put on her thermal running gloves and set off down the driveway.

She'd started running at university. Initially it'd been to get the attention of a boy she'd liked but quickly she'd enjoyed the time to herself. The rhythmic thump of her feet pounding the pavement brought her to a state of relaxation she rarely experienced elsewhere. Yoga certainly hadn't done it for her. All that breathing and calm talking.

Eve turned left and ran out past the letterbox. She'd head along Bay Street to The Esplanade and continue a short way along the beach track – not that she'd be able to see much this early in the morning. That would have her in the shower before seven, and out of the door by quarter to eight.

Ben.

What they had felt so real. Like him, she wasn't expecting it to turn into anything more, but she couldn't imagine him sharing the same intimacy with anyone else, not even his wife. But then Eve still had sex with Sean. Was she kidding herself to think Ben wouldn't be doing the same?

Sean had been so moody lately. Ever since Kate had taken holidays, in fact. Her running slowed. Sean and Kate? That couldn't be why he was moody, could it? A lump rose in her throat. Screwing the nanny? It was textbook, but not her husband. Surely not? Kate was hardly his type, and she was only twenty-three. Although that could be in her favour; a younger woman.

Eve shook her head. No, she was too solid, too frumpy and too forthright. Anyway, wasn't she a lesbian?

Sean had joked when she'd started working for them that her unshaved armpits suggested that might be the case. Eve had whacked him when he'd said it. She had three lesbian friends – acquaintances really – and they were all groomed beautifully.

No, Kate wasn't the reason Sean was moody. Sexual frustration, perhaps? She tried to recall the last time they'd had sex. It'd been ages.

She eventually reached The Esplanade and joined the throng of other early-morning runners. Eve increased her speed, enjoying the sensation of her lungs burning, pushing herself to go faster. She reached Highett Street and turned around to start the run home. She could see her breath as she puffed out the cold morning air.

Eve needed to talk to Sean. They were drifting further apart, and deep down she didn't want that. Her husband's mood was generally a reflection of his work, and no wonder if he'd slumped to doing pro bono work, but she'd better make an effort.

Although her heart was often with Ben, her reality was with Sean. He earned good money, was a great dad, and until she'd met Ben, they'd always had a good time together.

Until she'd met Ben.

That looped in her mind as she turned into Bay Street and headed home. If she were honest with herself, her interest in Sean had slipped when she'd met Ben. She had withdrawn, her mind often preoccupied. It was out of respect for Sean: she couldn't be laughing and joking with him one minute and wishing she was being seduced by someone else the next.

She sighed and slowed to a brisk walk at their driveway. Bloody men, they always complicated things. She pushed open the front door to the smell of pancakes and sound of laughter.

Sean's voice floated through the house. 'I'm sure Mummy has something special in mind for your lunchboxes today, so let's leave it for her, shall we?'

Eve stopped. Was he kidding? He'd been up with them for hours and he expected her to make their lunches? Whether he was screwing her or not, she really couldn't wait for Kate to return. Only three more days.

She couldn't imagine how anyone managed to parent and work full-time. Lunches, homework, after-school activities, play dates with other kids. It wasn't conceivable that one person could manage all that and have any life of their own.

Eve glanced at the clock at the bottom of the stairs. It was almost seven, there was no way she'd have time to make lunches. She contemplated Leah's words about being nicer, giving the girls a treat now and then.

Her sister was right; she did need to relax more with the girls. Stop telling herself that she was a bad parent. If she tried harder, maybe she'd even enjoy it.

Regardless, for today, a treat was in order. Eve would give the girls ten dollars each for the tuck-shop with specific instructions to buy whatever they liked. She smiled, imagining the shock on their little faces. They'd probably think she'd gone mad.

Eve raced up the stairs, her mind already having moved back to Ben. She needed to work out how she was going to approach him, and the possibility he was seeing other women.

Chapter Five

Leah heard the key turn in the lock at exactly seven o'clock. He hadn't knocked.

She lifted the sleeping Lewis from her lap, put the book she'd been trying to distract herself with down, and stood.

Surprise registered on Grant's face. 'Sorry, I assumed you'd be out.'

She folded her arms across her chest. 'What, and make it easy for you to skulk off after six years?'

He had the decency to blush. 'How are you?'

She shook her head. 'I don't think that's any of your business right now.'

Her ex nodded. 'Fine. I'll get my things and go.'

Leah moved and stood in front of the two boxes she'd packed for him. 'No, I want a proper explanation first. None of this, *it just isn't working*. We've been together for six years. Only a couple of months ago, you were the one talking about where we should go for our honeymoon. It doesn't make any sense.'

Grant struggled to meet her eyes. 'Not everything has to make sense. I woke up one morning and decided I didn't want to do this anymore.'

'Sorry, that's bullshit.'

He ran a hand through his hair. 'It's not bullshit, it's how it is.'

She stared at the man she'd loved so deeply for the past six years. He'd sparked in her the same feelings Sean had many years before. She'd never had the opportunity to explore those feelings with Sean, but with Grant it'd been wonderful and real. How could he switch those feelings off so quickly? A pain developed in her chest thinking about it.

'What did you tell your parents?' Grant's mum and dad had accepted her into the family like a daughter from day one. The thought of never seeing them again caused her stomach to twist.

His mouth turned to a frown.

She sucked in a breath. 'Really? You haven't told them? Your mum was expecting a wedding, not a breakup. So was I.'

Grant finally met her eyes. 'Mum will probably get one.'

Leah stared at him. 'What does that mean?'

'Oh, Jesus.' His eyes filled with tears. 'I really didn't want to have to tell you this.'

Her legs began to tremble. She had a strong feeling she didn't want to hear what he was about to say. 'What?' her voice was a squeak.

'I'm sorry, Lee, so sorry.'

A lump formed in her throat and her gut cramped. Her voice was barely a whisper. 'For what?'

Grant cleared his throat. 'I did something terrible while we were together. It was stupid, really. Remember that weekend trip I took for work a couple of months ago?'

'What about it?'

He and six of his colleagues had gone to Sydney for a team-building retreat.

'We had a few drinks, and I sort of ended up in bed with Katrina.'

'Katrina Dixon? Who you complain about constantly and can't stand?'

Grant nodded. His expression spoke of his misery and guilt.

'Why didn't you tell me when it happened? Break up with me then?'

His eyes were fixed firmly on his feet. 'Because I didn't know she was pregnant then.'

Leah's legs crumpled and she barely made it to the couch.

'Oh, Jesus,' Grant said. 'I really wish I hadn't done this, but it wasn't only once. I've been with Katrina a few times in the last two months. It just happened. Turned out, we didn't hate each other after all.'

'Obviously not.' She couldn't believe what she was hearing. His behaviour towards her hadn't changed at all the past two months. If anything he'd been more loving.

'When she found out she was pregnant, I knew I had to tell you.' Guilt tinged his tone.

'But you didn't tell me. You were just going to leave.'

'I'm sorry, Lee. Really, I am. I didn't know how to tell you. I love you. That hasn't changed. I wish . . .' He pushed his hand through his hair. 'I wish I could turn back time. This isn't how I want things to be, either.'

'But you made the decision to leave without any discussion,' Leah said. 'You hardly know Katrina.'

'We need to give it a chance. If our relationship doesn't work, we're still going to be connected by the baby.'

Leah stared. 'I don't get why you're doing this. You don't seem all that happy about it.'

Grant sighed. 'Whether I'm happy or not is irrelevant. I have responsibilities. It's my baby too, which Katrina's father keeps pointing out.'

She might vomit. This was really happening. Their future, their plans were all destroyed. She pointed at the boxes near the door. 'It's all there.'

'I'm sorry, Leah. I really am. I never meant for this to happen.'

Anger flooded her senses. She pulled herself up from the couch and faced her ex. 'Never meant to accidentally screw someone else multiple times while we were together? You're a cheating bastard.' She pointed to the door. 'Get out.'

He opened his mouth then appeared to think better of it. He placed a set of keys on a small table by the front door and stacked the two boxes on top of each other. He looked back at Leah. 'I really—'

'I said *get out.*'

Grant opened the door, allowing it to snap shut behind him.

She sat back on the couch next to Lewis, her anger turning to tears. How could he? He'd acted like a complete stranger.

Her phone vibrated as she stroked Lewis. Caller ID said it was Jackie. Jackie, who was expecting news of an engagement.

Leah picked up the phone, willing the tears to stop. 'Hey, Jacks.' It was all she could manage before bursting into tears again.

The sickness in the pit of Leah's stomach carried over to the next morning. She'd spent over an hour on the phone with Jackie. Her friend was as shocked as she was. They'd finally hung up with Jackie promising to ring again that night to check up on her.

She dragged herself out of bed, considered calling in sick, but then dismissed the idea. Leah needed something to take her mind off Grant, not wallow in self-pity.

Vomit rose in her throat; her thoughts consumed with Grant. She made her way to the bathroom and turned on the shower.

Would he even have told her if Katrina wasn't pregnant or would he have kept on seeing both of them? Had Katrina known about Leah?

She shook her head. The man she thought she knew better than anyone on the planet, she obviously didn't know at all.

Showered and with a strong coffee in hand, Leah reached the offices of *The Melbournian* feeling marginally better. She waited for the elevator to reach the sixth level, then stepped out into the empty reception area. It wasn't yet eight, so the offices would be quiet for the next half hour or so.

Fitzy passed her on her way to her cubicle. 'Hey, hot stuff,' he said, then stopped, his eyes searching her face. 'Although not looking so hot this morning.' He took a step backward. 'Not sick are you?'

She shook her head. 'Didn't sleep well.' While he made her cringe with his inappropriate greetings and horrible manner, she needed him on her side if she had any hope of moving to a different part of the paper.

Fitzy laughed. 'Good, glad that's all. Now, no sleeping on the job okay? There's plenty of hard-hitting stories out there waiting for you to grab.'

Leah rolled her eyes. 'Not sure Property really brings out the hard-hitting stories.' Fitzy needed to give her a chance. 'Can I ask you something?'

'Anything for you, doll.'

'As you know, I work hard and do a good job with Property.'

'Can't disagree with that. Clients love you. Can't get enough of you, in fact. Best damn reporter I've ever had in Property.'

She forced a smile. 'That's great, but don't you think my skills should be tested elsewhere? Business, Finance, general reporting? I'd really like the opportunity to show you what I can do.'

Her boss patted her arm. 'Don't be silly. You don't need to prove anything to me or anyone else. I already know you're good. Moving to another department and wasting the talent and insight you have for real estate isn't going to prove a thing.'

'That's not really the point. I need a change. I'm sick of Property. You said when I accepted the position there would be opportunities to move within the paper.'

Fitzy's smile no longer reached his eyes. 'The only opportunities to move right now would be to move straight out the door and get yourself a job somewhere else. Don't push it, Donaldson. I like you but you're dispensable.'

Anger rose in Leah. She studied her boss. He'd told her she was the best reporter he'd ever had in Property and now she was suddenly dispensable?

'Let me get this straight,' she said. 'You're quite happy to lose me?'

'That a threat?'

'Of course it's not a threat. I'm wanting to make sure I've got the picture clear.'

He moved his hands to his hips. 'Like I said, in Property you're fantastic, but not indispensable. There are a lot of amazing writers out there, Leah, ones that would kill for your job. They come with fantastic references and a lot of experience.'

'So would I if I was going somewhere else.'

Fitzy's grin was sly. 'Experience maybe. Don't count on the fantastic reference.'

She stared as he continued through the office towards reception. He was a pig. A sexist, nasty little pig. He shouldn't be able to get away with the way he spoke to staff, particularly females, in this day and age; although somehow he did. She should probably lodge a complaint but she'd likely be the one who'd end up worse off.

Leah sighed as she reached her own workspace. She dumped her bag and coffee cup on her desk and switched on her computer, glancing around the office while her system booted. She'd looked at these same walls and same faces for eight years now, all the time expecting she'd move sideways to another department at some point and that was when she'd get her big break and work on the sort of stories that interested her, rather than writing up descriptions of over-the-top, ridiculously priced, elitist homes. But that wasn't going to happen. She opened her internet browser and typed in 'SEEK' to bring up the job search site. It was time to find out what her options were.

Leah was exhausted by the time she arrived home from work that evening.

Lewis greeted her enthusiastically, and she was glad of the distraction he provided. He rubbed around her, helping take her mind off the fact that it was Wednesday night, the night she and Grant usually went to Victoria Street for Vietnamese.

She'd just changed into her sweat pants and flicked the television on when there was a knock on the door. She wasn't expecting anyone; it had better not be Grant.

Leah opened her front door and immediately burst into tears.

Jackie stood in front of her, a bottle of red wine in each hand. Her best friend's smile was instantly replaced with concern. 'Hey, I'm here to cheer you up. Not make you cry.'

She smiled through her tears. 'They're happy tears.'

Jackie stepped into the apartment, placed the bottles of wine down, and drew her into a tight hug.

Leah sank into her friend. 'It's so good to see you.'

'You too, Lee. I had to visit after what he's done.' She gently pulled herself back from the hug and picked up the wine bottles. 'Now, this wine has a specific purpose; to get you drunk. So, let's get started.'

She laughed and led Jackie through the living room into the kitchen. She took two glasses from the cupboard and allowed her friend to pour them a glass each.

Jackie raised her glass to her. 'To my very best friend. May you see how beautiful and special you are and move forward without looking back. He's not worth it, but *you* are.'

They clinked glasses.

'You're right, he's not. Now, let's not even talk about him. Tell me everything. How's Richard and how are Poppy and Dustin?'

Jackie launched into updates about her husband and kids.

They sat up until well past midnight chatting and laughing about mutual friends and things from their past. The conversation, of course, kept turning back to Grant and what a bastard he was.

'I assume you told Richard you were staying tonight?' Leah asked when the second bottle of red wine was nearly empty.

Jackie nodded. 'I told him I'll be home sometime tomorrow morning. He'll get the kids to school, so if you don't have any early meetings we can grab some breakfast and then I'll head off.'

'Thanks, Jacks. Tonight means heaps to me. With Grant and work, things have been feeling miserable. Thank Richard for me too. I know leaving the kids overnight probably isn't ideal.'

Her friend tut-tutted. 'You've done me a favour too. He needs to get used to me having some time away. It's long overdue.' Her eyes twinkled. 'In fact, if you aren't feeling better in a week or two, and I think you won't be, perhaps we should organise a spa weekend away. Just the two of us. Imagine that?'

Leah laughed. 'I'm happy to do that anytime. Let me know when you can escape your madhouse.'

'Okay, let's do it. I'll tell Richard what a mess you are when I get home and that it is an emergency.'

She laughed again. 'Do you think he'll buy it?'

Her bestie grinned. 'He'll have to. We'll use it to aid your recovery.'

Leah dragged herself up from the couch. 'Sounds good. But for now, bedtime.' She wobbled on her feet. 'Nearly two bottles between us! We're going to need a weekend to recover from the wine, let alone anything else.'

Chapter Six

The week was dragging for Eve. Her early morning run on Tuesday had reinvigorated her and given her the energy and confidence to face the day, and Ben. That'd quickly evaporated when she'd called him to discover he was about to board a plane to Sydney and wouldn't be back until late the following night.

She'd wanted to see him, no matter how late, but he'd insisted they leave it until Thursday morning. He needed her to meet him and the team employed for the new development in South Melbourne and promised they could *talk* after that. He'd sounded slightly irritated when she'd told him she *had* to see him.

'It's not like you to be so needy, Eve. We'll chat on Thursday.'

Eve had somehow managed to get through the day, but her thoughts were consumed with Ben, and she found that exceptionally annoying. The thought of losing him made her feel physically ill. If he was seeing other people, she'd have to end it. Wouldn't she?

She left work early and picked up the girls from school. Expecting them to be delighted to see her, she was annoyed when it became obvious they would rather she hadn't.

'Why are you asking so many questions? I thought I'd pick you up and take you for a treat.'

The girls had exchanged looks.

'Like ice cream?' Harriet asked.

Eve smiled. 'No, like sushi. Or fruit salad. A yummy but healthy snack.'

The girls' smiles faded.

'Oh.'

Her annoyance rose as the girls stood before her. 'Come on then, get your bags and let's get out of here.'

'You'll have to sign us out of after-school care,' Ava said.

'They might not let us leave,' Harriet added. 'They're making biscuits this afternoon and they were expecting our help to ice them.'

She ignored her daughter's hopeful look. For God's sake, the kid would rather stay at school to make biscuits than go home early and have a treat?

She marched over to the after-school desk and signed the twins out.

'Let's go.'

The girls had already packed their bags and were waiting for her.

She'd taken a deep breath and tried to inject some enthusiasm into her voice as she asked about their days.

Over their sushi snack, the discussion revolved around Kate's return and when Aunty Leah would next visit. By the time they'd arrived home, Eve was in a foul mood. She'd ended up sending the girls upstairs while she made dinner.

Ava had managed to spill her water all over the table during the meal, which gave her the perfect excuse to cancel her bedtime stories and send her to bed early.

Harriet had piped up to defend her sister so Eve cancelled her stories too. Guilt stabbed at her while the girls showered, brushed their teeth and put themselves to bed. The afternoon had hardly turned out as she had hoped. Turning over a new parenting leaf wasn't going to be easy. However, with the twins out of her hair, Eve was left alone with her thoughts of Ben.

Now, Thursday morning finally having arrived, she found her heart beating a little faster than it should as she stopped in front of the South Melbourne development.

Ben arrived a few seconds after she did. She jumped straight out of her car hoping to speak to him, but three other members of the team arrived before they'd barely had a chance to say hello.

The development team consisted of Ben, a foreman and nine contractors. Eve listened to their plans and provided some input in areas where she could see opportunities to add value. It was the excuse Ben had used to include her in the project, and she was glad to be contributing, even though she was completely distracted.

By the time they finally said goodbye to the rest of the team, she was itching for her opportunity to talk to him.

The last car pulled out from the kerb, and Ben turned to her, eyes shining. 'Got time for a quick look over number thirteen?'

Eve flushed as desire flooded through her. 'Yes, but I need to ask you something first.'

He raised an eyebrow.

'Not here,' she said. 'Let's go inside.' She led him across the footpath, pushed open the old gate, and walked down the paved path. Her heart raced.

'So?' He drew her to him once the front door closed behind them.

She found it hard to make eye contact. 'I've heard a few things and I need you to confirm whether they're true.' She glanced up at Ben's face.

'Go on.'

'I have it on pretty good authority that you choose to work with female contractors and suppliers, preferably married ones, so you can get them into bed.'

Surprised flickered over his face then he let out a loud laugh. 'Where did you hear that?'

Eve shook her head. 'It doesn't really matter, but someone close to me warned me about you. Are you sleeping with anyone else other than me?'

He locked eyes with her. 'Yes.'

The air drained from her lungs. Breathing became nearly impossible. How stupid had she been? A million thoughts raced through her mind. What about diseases? She was an idiot. She was on the pill but that was the only protection they'd used.

She pulled back from his embrace.

Ben took her arm and guided her down the hallway. 'Come with me. You've turned white and you need to listen.' He pushed open the door of the renovated bedroom. 'Come and sit down.'

Eve allowed herself to be guided to the bed. Tears welled in the corners of her eyes.

'There's more to my answer.' He took her hands. 'Look at me, Eve.'

She shook her head, tears threatening.

He gently lifted her chin, so she was forced to look at him.

'I'm sure if I asked you the same question, the answer would be yes.'

Eve shook her head.

'Really? So you and Sean never sleep together?'

'Oh,' she replied. 'I wasn't counting Sean. Mind you, we haven't had sex in ages.'

Concern flickered in Ben's eyes. 'Really? Is everything okay between the two of you?'

She shrugged.

'The answer to your question is yes, but only with my wife. I made that very clear when we started our relationship. Lauren and I are happily married. I love her and don't intend to leave her. What you and I have is special, and I'd be devastated if it ended, but it has to take second place to my marriage.'

Eve nodded. Even though she hated hearing about his happy marriage, these were the terms she'd agreed to before starting the affair.

'I'm not sleeping with anyone else, Eve. Yes, I used to get around, but it was because no one satisfied me emotionally or intellectually. It was only sex. We both know what we have is different.'

A lightness spread through her. He was so sincere; he was telling the truth. They had an amazing connection. There was only room for their spouses, no one else.

Ben cupped her face in his hands and brought it slowly to his. He kissed her, lightly at first before spreading her lips with his tongue and delving deeper into her mouth.

Eve returned the kiss, passion building within her.

'How long have you got?' he murmured.

''Til twelve,' she whispered.

'Then let's make the most of the next ninety minutes.' Ben pushed her back on to the bed and covered her body with his.

When she arrived back at the office at lunchtime, Eve was surprised to receive a message from her mother inviting her and the girls to dinner. Leah must have told her about Grant as her mother's message was clear that the dinner was to be supportive of her sister.

Kate didn't start back until tomorrow, which meant if they weren't going out for dinner, Eve would need to collect the girls this afternoon from after-school care then cook a meal for them and put them to bed, so her mother's invitation was a welcome relief. The girls loved going to their grandparents' house, and by the time they left to go home were usually bathed and ready for bed.

She sent a quick text to accept the invitation.

The afternoon disappeared in a cloud of euphoria. Her body was still tingling from the morning's encounter with Ben. They were so compatible in bed. The sex was hot – a completely different level to sex with Sean, which, on the rare occasions they had it, had become routine and predictable.

At four thirty, Eve called it a day. Before leaving the office she told Penny to forward any calls.

The girls had their school bags ready and were waiting to go when she arrived at the after-school care classroom.

She smiled. 'We've got a treat tonight.'

Harriet rolled her eyes. 'More sushi?'

Eve managed to keep smiling, deciding to ignore this dig. 'No, dinner at Gram and Gramps's house.'

Her daughter's face lit up. She grabbed her bag and marched towards the door. 'Come on,' she called back over her shoulder. 'We should hurry, they'll be waiting.'

Eve looked at Ava and shrugged. Her other daughter grinned, picked up her bag and hurried after her sister.

Twenty minutes later, Eve's black Audi drove into the driveway of her parents' Queen Anne style home. The white picket fence had recently been given a new coat of paint. This was not the house Eve and Leah had grown up in; it was the house her mother had always dreamed of owning. As young children, she remembered her mother pointing out the houses with steeply pitched terra-cotta-tiled roofs. She particularly loved the decorative embellishments – the dragons, gargoyles and finials.

When Eve had first started working in real estate, she'd saved up the details of any houses she visited in the Queen Anne style to tell her mother about. When she'd seen this house, which had been recently renovated and featured the most beautiful leaded light coloured-glass windows, she'd invited her mother to come and have a look. She hadn't for one minute expected her parents would buy it. She'd thought her mother would enjoy the chance to see both the outside and inside of such a gorgeous home.

Her father had come too, and after two hours of her mother wanting to take one more look at one of the ornate fireplaces or study the detail of the wallpaper in one of the spacious bedrooms, he'd approached Eve and asked her how they could set about buying the house.

Eve and Leah had both been stunned at this decision, but sixty days later, they'd helped move their parents in.

The car doors burst open when she came to a stop and the girls dashed to the front door, shrieking and laughing. Eve watched the front door open and her father reach down and scoop the twins to him in a warm bear hug.

Sean always did this with the girls too. They loved it. A fleeting thought crossed her mind. Her hugs with the girls were few and far between. She wasn't touchy-feely.

As her father and the twins disappeared inside, she made a mental note to ensure she hugged each girl at least once a day.

As she stepped out of the car, Leah drove up and parked behind her.

'Jesus,' she said as her twin approached. The large, dark glasses did nothing to hide her pale, drawn face. 'Are you okay?'

Leah shook her head. 'Not really.'

'Grant?'

She nodded. 'And Jackie came over to cheer me up last night, which was lovely, but we drank my sorrows away and my head's wishing we'd stopped after the first bottle.'

'You've told Mum?'

'She knows the whole story.'

'Whole story? So you found out why he wanted to end things?'

Leah nodded again. 'Let's go inside. Even with the hangover from hell, I need a drink. Anything to numb me. Work was rubbish today too.' She forced a smile. 'I'm wallowing in self-pity so you can help me drown my sorrows.'

Screams of delight from the back garden could be heard as they let themselves in through the front door, expecting to find their mother in the kitchen. Eve's stomach rumbled at the succulent aromas of a roast that were filtering through the house. She hadn't eaten since breakfast. Her post-sex glow and a black coffee had carried her through the afternoon.

Their mother looked up from chopping vegetables when they entered the kitchen. She dropped her knife, rubbed her hands on her apron, and opened her arms to Leah.

Eve watched her sister sink into her mother's embrace.

'I'm so sorry, love,' her mother said. 'It's a despicable thing he's done. Something you can never think was your fault.'

She raised an eyebrow. *Despicable?*

Her mother looked across to her. 'There's a bottle of white in the fridge, honey. Why don't you get us some glasses and pour it? I'm sure Leah needs one, and after hearing about Grant, I could use a drink myself.'

Eve moved to the fridge. *He must have cheated.* That was the only explanation that would evoke that kind of reaction in her mother.

'He did,' Leah said.

She stared. Ever since they were little, they'd had a connection that, at times, made it feel like they were reading each other's minds. It was more a case that they knew each other so well, each could guess what the other was thinking.

Her twin forced a small laugh. 'It's not too hard to imagine what conclusion you'd draw.' She accepted the drink Eve held out and went on to tell the full story of his cheating and the pregnancy.

Eve refilled their drinks. 'What an arsehole.'

'That's an understatement,' her mother said. 'He'd better hope your father never runs into him – he'll skin him alive. He's furious, and so am I. To think he could sit around our dining table only two weeks ago and play happy families is a disgrace.'

Leah got up and reached for a vegetable peeler. 'Let me give you a hand, Mum. The last thing I really want to do is talk about him.'

She was shooed away. 'No, I'm nearly done and if you want to be distracted, go and find the girls and your father. They'd all love to see you.'

She nodded and left the room.

'What about you?' her mother asked Eve. 'Are you going to join them?'

She shook her head. 'No, I need a break from them.'

Her mum raised an eyebrow. 'The half-hour between school and here was too much for you?'

Eve ignored her mother's dig. She didn't understand how hard it was to juggle full-time work and kids. She hadn't worked when Eve and Leah were little, so how could she?

'Kate's back tomorrow, thank God.'

Her mother put down the tea towel she was holding and sat down across from her. 'This situation with Leah and Grant, it's very upsetting.'

'Very,' Eve agreed.

'Doesn't it make you think about what you're doing? How devastating the consequences could be?'

She shifted in her chair. A few months back she'd rung her mother and asked her to pick the girls up after school. When she'd arrived home just after seven, her mother had taken one look at her and practically launched an attack.

'You'd better tell me that *meeting* you've come from was with Sean,' she'd said. 'I only have to look at your glowing cheeks and messed up hair to know exactly what you've been up to.'

The garage door had opened part way through the diatribe and she'd immediately coloured and started apologising. 'I'm so sorry, love. I'm just so relieved you were with Sean. You worried me there for a minute.'

Eve hadn't responded. She'd mentally kicked herself that she hadn't taken the time to run a brush through her hair or fix her make-up. She'd been momentarily relieved when her mother had assumed Sean arriving home so close to her was because they'd been together.

However, when she'd started asking Sean about his day it'd been very clear he hadn't seen or spoken to Eve or the girls since that morning.

As her mum was about to leave, she'd turned to Eve. 'You're playing with fire, my girl, and I can guarantee you'll get burnt. You need to stop it right now. Respect those vows you made the day you agreed to be Sean's wife.'

She'd said goodnight and nothing more. It was none of her mother's business.

Sitting across from the table now, her sentiments were the same.

Her mum would never understand. She was nothing like Eve; she had no idea how it felt to be trapped in a marriage with demanding children. She had loved everything about being a mother. In fact, her mother had used up all the maternal genes in the family and there'd been nothing to pass down. It certainly would explain why she found the whole thing so hard.

'It's none of your business, Mum.'

'It will be if Sean finds out.'

'How do you figure that?' Eve asked.

'Because I imagine he'd leave you and you'd be trying to dump the girls on your father and me every weekend they were in your custody.'

She stared. "'*Dump* the girls'? That's lovely. Sorry, I thought you enjoyed spending time with your grandchildren.'

Her mother gave a snort and got up to check on the meat in the oven. 'Don't twist what I'm saying. You know exactly what I mean.'

Eve stood, not wanting to continue the conversation. 'I'll go out and see if Dad and Leah need a hand.'

Leah had had to wipe her tears again when her father, Bill, had embraced her. He hadn't had to say anything, the look in his eyes told her everything, and she loved him for it. She'd always been very close to her father.

When she and Eve were little, she'd often come and spend time with him in the garden. They'd work side by side planting new garden beds, mulching, weeding, and whatever else needed doing. He'd tell her stories about when he was a boy and always ask about her day, about what she was doing and what was important to her.

When she was ten, her father had taught her how to play chess. They'd spent hours over the years sitting across from each other, sometimes chatting, often enjoying a comfortable silence as they played. It was a far cry from the whirlwind of Eve and the many dramas that seemed to follow her right through school and beyond.

He'd brought out a ball, and the girls were trying to get it through the hoop he'd hung for them on the side of the garden shed. They squealed and laughed taking turns.

Her dad squeezed Leah's arm. 'If you need me to do anything, let me know. I'm happy to go and have a chat to that young man if you'd like.'

Leah could just imagine her father *chatting* with Grant. He kept himself in shape, and even in his late sixties could easily flatten an opponent.

'Thanks, Dad, but I want to move on now; forget all about him. There's not much point talking to him, or anything else,' she added. 'We can't change what he's done.'

Forget all about him. How Leah wished she could. She'd done nothing but obsess about Grant and how she'd missed all the signs that something was wrong in their relationship. He was having an affair and at the same time she'd thought he was about to propose. How stupid was she?

Her dad shook his head and sighed. 'No, we can't. There are plenty of good men around, love. It turns out he wasn't one of them. Don't give up on men altogether because of him.'

'I won't,' she promised. 'Although meeting someone else is definitely not a high priority at the moment.'

He caught the ball as it rebounded off the hoop and bounced towards him. He looked from the twins to Leah. 'Time for a game,' he said. 'Me and Harry against Ava and Aunty Leah. First to five goals is the winner.'

Her dad was always good for offering a distraction.

Leah snatched the ball from his hands and passed it to Ava. 'Come on, Aves,' she cried. 'Let's beat them.'

Leah smiled while she washed the roasting pans. Splashes and giggles were coming from the bathroom. She doubted one could even see the twins in the huge bathtub with the amount of bubble bath they'd used.

She frowned hearing Eve's voice speaking sternly, causing silence to fall immediately in the bathroom. She wished her sister would lighten up on the girls. So they'd made a mess. A few towels and it would all be wiped up, no big deal. Eve needed to let them enjoy themselves.

Throughout their own childhood, she remembered a lot of laughter and her father's famous bear hugs. Leah had known she was loved every day. Did Eve's girls feel like that?

She glanced up as her mother led Eve into the kitchen. 'Leave it to me,' her mum was saying. 'It's my fault, anyway. I put the bubble mixture in. Have a cup of tea. There's some of that horrible green stuff you like in the cupboard. You're here to relax and cheer up Leah. The girls are my responsibility tonight.' Their mother headed back to the bathroom.

'Made a mess have they?' Leah asked.

Eve shook her head, switched on the kettle and opened the cupboard in search of the tea. 'Mess is an understatement. Mum's having a go at me because I told them off. What she doesn't realise is that the mess they make here, they then make at home. Cleaning up after them the whole time is a pain.' She sighed. 'I know, I know. Don't say anything. I need to lighten up. I'm trying, Lee, I promise I am. It's going to take a bit of time.'

She was surprised to hear her twin admit she needed to relax. Perhaps their chat the other night had had an impact?

'Anyway, what are we going to do about Grant? Surely we don't let him get away with what he's done to you?'

'Revenge?' Leah asked. 'I hadn't really been thinking of revenge.'

'We should at least make sure the new girlfriend knows he was cheating on you,' her sister said. 'It's despicable what he's done.'

'I think I should probably stay right out of it. Don't forget there's a baby involved. Not that he seemed overly happy about that, but if I deliberately try to ruin their relationship I'd feel guilty towards the baby.'

'Are we even related?' Eve sat waiting for the kettle to boil. 'We might be identical in looks, but that's about it. You got all the nice genes, and I got none.'

Leah pulled off the rubber gloves, dried her hands and came and sat next to her twin. 'You got more than you like to admit. You just seem to like to hide them sometimes. As for Grant, I need to try to move forward. Yes, he did something despicable to me, but what am I going to achieve if I try to get revenge? I need him out of my life. There's nothing he could ever do now that would have me take him back, so it's a finished chapter.'

'In that case we need to start you a new chapter.'

'I tried that myself today,' she said. 'Started looking for another job.'

'Really? I thought you'd hoped to move into another section with *The Melbournian*?'

Leah shook her head. 'Not going to happen. Fitzy made that very clear. Even threatened that I'd get no reference if I tried to move to another paper.'

Eve shook her head. 'Unbelievable. What is wrong with these men? Did you want me to have a chat to Nicola? She's friends with Tom Barnaby. He might have some openings at *The Age*.'

'That'd be great. Hopefully he's not a friend of Fitzy's.'

'I'll call her.' She took out her phone.

'You don't have to do it right now,' Leah said.

Her sister looked up, 'I'll text and check she's still in touch with him. If she is, it will give you something to focus on, other than your prick of a boss and bigger prick of an ex.' She sent off a text, her phone pinging back only seconds later. She grinned. 'Knows him and he's coming to her fortieth, which means you are too. It's tomorrow night.'

Leah immediately shook her head. 'I can't crash her party uninvited.'

Eve passed her phone over. 'Read her message.'

Know him? He's a BFF and will be at my party. Bring Leah, would love to see her and will introduce. He's a great guy, won't stuff her around. xx

She handed the phone back to her sister. 'I don't know, I'm not really in a party mood.'

'Don't be silly,' Eve said. 'You don't have to be. Think of the party as a business opportunity. You won't get a meeting or interview with someone like Tom Barnaby very easily on your own.'

Leah sighed. 'Yeah, you're right. Okay, I'll come.'

'Excellent. It's costume, but don't worry, I'll organise your outfit. I have an idea you'll love.'

She raised an eyebrow. 'Really? In the thirty seconds since Nicola invited me you have a costume sorted? What is it?'

There was a glint in her twin's eye. 'You'll have to wait and see.'

Chapter Seven

Eve manoeuvred the Audi out of the underground car park and into the long line of traffic on the main road. She'd taken the afternoon off work under the guise of attending an event at the girls' school. The girls and their schooling couldn't have been further from her thoughts.

Kate had arrived bright and early for work that morning, her face fresh and tanned, reflecting her holiday. She would be picking the twins up that afternoon, allowing Eve to enjoy the feeling of being free.

She'd stowed the outfits for herself and Leah in the boot of the car. It was going to be some night. She grinned, then braked when the car ahead pulled to a stop in front of a red traffic light. She pressed the talk button on her steering wheel and instructed the car to call her sister, willing Leah to pick up.

It was close to a minute before her familiar voice came down the line.

'Eve?'

'Yep. What're you doing?' The light turned to green and she accelerated, keeping up with the cars in front of her. The phone was silent. 'Leah?'

'I'm here.'

'Just letting you know I'll pick you up at seven,' she said. 'I have your outfit with me, so you can change and then we'll go.'

'I don't think I'm up for it.'

'Yes you are. You promised you'd come and it could be a great job opportunity. Don't you dare pull out now. Nicola's gone to the effort of talking to Tom Barnaby this morning on your behalf. It would be incredibly rude to not turn up.'

More silence at the other end of the phone.

Eve shook her head. She glanced in the rear-view and changed lanes in order to do a U-turn.

'Maybe she could organise a meeting at his offices,' her twin said. 'A party isn't really my thing right now.'

Eve gave an exaggerated sigh. 'Fine. If that's how you feel, I'll speak to Tom Barnaby myself tonight and see what we can sort out.' She ended the call, hearing the relief in Leah's voice and grinned.

Leah stared at her phone. It was unlike her sister to back off so quickly. Perhaps Eve was actually prepared to give her some space.

She moved into the bedroom and took one last look around to make sure all traces of Grant were gone. A lone photo stood on her dressing table of the two of them in Fiji. They were holding hands, walking through the shallow water with the sun setting behind them. It was a magical photo taken on the first day of what had been a magical holiday. They'd snorkelled, jet-skied, done day trips to local villages and islands. They'd made love and talked about their future. A future together.

Leah picked up the photo. How could she have got it so wrong? This photo was taken six months ago. It wasn't like it was four years earlier, and things had changed.

She carefully slipped the photo out of the frame. Tears welled in her eyes as she looked at their happy faces. She blinked them away. Eve was right. She was wasting far too much energy on him. He was probably in bed with Katrina right now. Rubbing her belly and speaking to his baby.

Leah tore the photo straight through the middle. A sense of satisfaction overtook her. She tore it again and again until she held a handful of pieces.

She glanced at the clock. It was only four. A bit early for a glass of wine. She'd made a last-minute decision to call in sick today. It wasn't something she'd done very often but she couldn't face Fitzy or anyone else. She needed some time to herself. She'd go for a walk. Perhaps come back via the local Thai and order a red curry for dinner.

She grabbed her keys and bag and went in search of her sports shoes. She was pulling them on when the doorbell rang. She quickly tied her shoe and hurried to the door.

Her heart sank when she opened it and was greeted with Eve's grinning face. Of course her sister wouldn't take no for an answer. She should've known better.

Leah turned her back on her twin, scooped up Lewis, who was rubbing around her legs, and plonked herself on the couch. 'I'm not going.'

Eve, carting a huge shopping bag, followed her. 'Yes, you are. Grant's an arsehole, and he's gone. It's time to move on. But more importantly, this party is an amazing opportunity to discuss a new job. If you don't go, I don't ever want to hear another word of complaint from you about *The Melbournian* or your prick of a boss. And' – she held the shopping bag out to her – '*this* is another reason you have to come. Have a look.' She passed the bag over.

Leah moved her cat on to the couch beside her, opened the bag and removed a purple costume. 'Wonder Twins? Really?'

Her sister laughed. 'Come on, it's to cheer you up. Remember how long you bugged me to wear that costume in high school.'

A small smile played on Leah's lips. 'And you refused.'

'Now you get your chance to wear it. I've got one too. No one will know who's who. Come on, Lee, it'll be fun; like old times.'

She pushed the costume back in the bag and shook her head. 'I'm not ready to answer questions about Grant.'

'Focus on Tom Barnaby and imagine that this is a job interview. If any of Nicola's friends ask, say you're single. I doubt any of them know Grant anyway.' Eve put her hand back in the bag and pulled out the costume. 'How about this for a deal?' she asked. 'We'll be dressed identically, so no one is actually going to know who's who. If you find yourself having to answer any questions you don't want to then we'll switch. You can be me.'

Leah raised her eyes. 'Really? But then you'd miss out on being Eve. The centre of attention. Life of the party.'

She shrugged. 'Tonight is more about getting you out.' She held the Wonder Twin outfit in front of her and twirled. 'Now come on, say you'll go.'

While they spent less time together as adults, her twin was still always there for her when she needed her. She struggled to show it with her kids, but deep down Eve was kind and generous. She'd do anything for Leah.

She took the outfit. 'Okay. I'll come.'

Her sister squealed and threw her arms around her. 'Fantastic. We're going to have a great night.' She released her and rummaged in her handbag. Extracting a sheet of paper, she unfolded it and handed it over.

Leah stared. It was a photo of Eve dressed in the Wonder Twin suit, her long blonde hair straightened to cascade over her shoulders and down her back. Her make-up was minimal.

Leah looked closer. Other than Eve's eyes, which appeared huge with the mascara she'd used, a bit of blush and silver lips were all that were required. She opened her mouth ready to speak, then shut it again.

Eve held out a silver lipstick. 'Figure you've got the rest?'

She nodded.

'Great, now I'd better go. I want to see the kids before I head out again tonight.' She smiled. 'I'm turning over a new leaf. Being engaged, giving them hugs and occasional treats.' Her mouth melted into a frown. 'Although, I don't think they've noticed yet.'

'They will.' Leah followed her to the front door. 'Keep it up and give it time.'

Her sister gave her a quick hug. 'Will do. I'll see you at seven. We're going to have a great night.'

Leah swallowed, shutting the door behind her. That she doubted.

Eve pulled into the driveway, hearing a Justin Bieber song blaring from the upstairs window. She frowned and waited for the garage door to open.

Sean's car was inside. It wasn't even five thirty. It was unheard of him for him to be home so early on a Friday night. Even though it was Kate's first day back, she'd already organised for the nanny to stay late tonight to allow her to get ready for the party and be gone well before her husband came home.

She parked beside the Mercedes and pushed open her door. As she entered through the internal access, the music had been switched off and replaced with screams of delight coming from the girls. Sean's booming voice caused them to shriek louder.

Eve paused at the bottom of the stairs.

'Mummy!' Harriet's delight forced a smile to her face.

She took a deep breath. She wanted to spend a few minutes with her daughters but she also needed to get ready. She hoped Sean hadn't let Kate leave early.

Eve opened her arms to Harriet who bounded down the stairs and flung herself at her.

Ava followed, more conservatively, as she put her arms around Harriet and pulled her to her. 'How were your days?' she asked.

Harriet started babbling a million miles an hour while Ava waited patiently for her turn. As Harriet continued to talk, Eve disentangled herself and started to ascend the stairs. The girls followed.

Sean moved out of the girls' room and on to the landing as she reached the top.

'You're home early,' Eve said.

'I'm sick of getting home at ten or eleven on a Friday night.' He drew Ava and Harriet to him and tickled them. 'I miss my girls and want to take you all out somewhere nice.'

'Daddy's taking us to TGI Fridays,' Harriet shouted. 'And I'm going to have a caramel sundae.'

She forced a smile and shot him a look. 'Tonight?'

Her husband's jaw clenched. 'Yes. It's been too long since we last did something as a family. It'll be good for us all to spend a night together.'

Shit. Eve should've mentioned Nicola's party earlier.

Ava squeezed her hand. 'It will be fun, Mummy. I won't order a sundae, I'll have fruit salad. I just want to be a family.'

A lump formed in her throat. Did Ava really think they weren't a family? She squeezed the little girl's hand back. 'I'm sorry but I can't come tonight.'

Sean's eyes flashed. 'Why not? I've come home early specially to do this tonight.'

Eve's anger rose. He should've discussed this with her earlier rather than making her look like the bad guy now. 'You should've told me, not assumed I'd be available.'

'You're out all the time lately,' he retorted. 'Who are you going out with?'

She shook her head. 'I'm not out *all* the time. It's work.'

'So tonight is work?' Her husband threw his hands up. 'Let me guess, you're holding an auction at nine p.m. on a Friday night, because it's such a great time to sell a house.'

Eve stared. God, he could be a sarcastic prick. Footsteps on the stairs snagged her attention.

Kate's voice rang out. 'Ava, Harriet. Come with me and we'll have a bath and get dressed for dinner.'

Harriet looked from her parents to Kate and burst into tears. 'We can't go,' she said. 'No caramel sundaes tonight.'

'No family night,' Ava added, her voice low, her eyes downcast.

The nanny took the girls' hands and led them towards the bathroom and Eve overhead her telling them she'd make them a special dinner instead.

Sean's eyes softened as he turned to face her. 'Eve, we need to spend time together. You and me and the girls. It's been ages.'

She swallowed. It *had* been ages. Months in fact. He was usually so busy with work it was easy to avoid spending too much time with him or the girls. 'I know and I want to,' she said. 'Let's do it tomorrow night. Tonight's important. It's Nicola's fortieth. I can't miss it.'

'Nicola's fortieth?'

She nodded.

'How come I wasn't invited?'

'You were. Sorry, I thought you wouldn't want to go. You've never really liked her, and the last time we went to one of her events you said her friends were superficial.'

'They are,' Sean said.

'That's why I didn't mention it. I thought you'd prefer to either work or spend time with the girls.'

He stared. 'Really? That's why I didn't get an invite?'

She nodded again.

'Not because you're taking another guy with you?'

'Like who?'

'I don't know,' her husband said. 'The guy you're having an affair with, perhaps?'

She tried to calm her breathing. Adrenaline pumped through her. He couldn't know about Ben. There was no way. She'd been so careful.

Eve willed herself to act normally. She managed a small laugh. 'Which guy is that?'

Sean crossed his arms. 'You tell me. You're the one out late at night for hours at a time on most weekends. I don't know his name but I'm going to find out and when I do, we're over, Eve. Completely over.'

She forced another smile. 'Babe, I have no idea what makes you think I'm having an affair, but I can tell you right now, you've got your wires crossed. There's no guy. No affair.'

He continued to stare. 'The late nights at work? The sudden need to pop out for two hours on a Sunday afternoon? That's not because of a guy?'

She shook her head. 'You work late most nights of the week. You spend many weekends at the office too. Not once have I ever accused you of having an affair. You've got plenty of opportunity too.'

'I'm not having an affair,' Sean said.

'And I never suggested you were. And I really resent that you have accused me of having one.'

'So, the fact that you're so distant with me, a bitch to the girls, that's got nothing to do with you having an affair?'

Heat flushed her cheeks. A *bitch to the girls*? 'Nice, Sean, really nice.'

'Come off it. Why did you even want to have kids? From the day they were born, you've spent every minute possible trying to escape or palming them off on to other people. Nannies, babysitters, your parents, friends. Anyone. As long as it means you aren't expected to spend time with them.'

'Did it ever cross your mind that perhaps I was struggling?' she asked. 'Perhaps I had no idea what I was doing and couldn't handle it?'

He shook his head. 'They're seven. I think you could've worked it out by now if you bothered to make an effort. When was the last time you baked a cake with them or took them to the park?'

'When was the last time you did either of those things?' Eve retorted.

'Last weekend. Although it was biscuits, not a cake. You would've known except you had to rush out for that property inspection on Sunday afternoon, remember? The client who supposedly couldn't see you at any other time. The client who you got dressed up so nicely for and spent three hours with.' Sean slammed his fist against the railing at the top of the stairs. 'It's bullshit, Eve, we both know it. You've totally disengaged from this family.'

A twinge of guilt stabbed at her. Sunday afternoon she'd spent in bed with Ben. Still, her husband couldn't prove it, and that didn't give him the right to tell her she was useless. 'So, I'm a shit mother and I'm having an affair?'

'And a shit sister and a shit daughter too,' he said. 'Ask anyone in your family. How much time do you have for any of us?'

Eve's gut clenched. There was no way Leah or her parents would've said anything like that to Sean. 'You have no idea how often I speak to them when you're not around. You have no right at all to say that.'

Uncertainty crept into Sean's face. 'Okay, fine, but that's my observation of you when I do see you with them. It's all about you, what's happening in your life. You show no interest in them at all. I'm surprised they even bother with you.'

'With everything you've said to me tonight, I'm surprised *you* bother,' Eve said.

'I have no idea why I do. We're a big fucking mistake, that's what we are.'

She swallowed. She had no response to that.

'You go to your stupid party on your own, and I'll take the girls out for dinner. There's no reason they should miss out on a good night because their mother is a selfish bitch.'

Eve stood shell-shocked as her husband turned his back on her and stalked off in the direction of the girls' bathroom. She heard their screams of delight a few moments later. He must've told them that caramel sundaes were back on the menu.

Sean had never spoken to her like that before. They'd argued. Said a few hurtful comments, but nothing like *this*. Nausea churned in Eve's stomach. He suspected she was having an affair. She reflected on the amount of time she'd spent with Ben and realised if anyone was noticing her absences, which it appeared

Sean was, it would be obvious. She thought back to Leah's earlier words. *You need to be more involved. It's the only way you'll ever build proper relationships.* Sean's outburst was certainly reinforcing the need to spend more time with her family. But his anger was beyond anything she'd experienced from him. Would she be able to convince him she loved him? That she'd make an effort to do better? A lump rose in her throat. Was this even what she wanted?

She glanced at her watch. It was almost six already. She only had thirty minutes before she needed to leave to get Leah. For now she would have to do her best to push all thoughts of Sean's outburst from her mind. She couldn't allow it to ruin Nicola's party. She hurried down the hall towards their bedroom. She'd deal with this later. Right now she needed to get a move on.

Following a quick shower and transformation, Eve reappeared in the kitchen. Her purple Wonder Twin suit clung to her fit, curved body. She'd straightened her hair as she'd instructed Leah to do, and her lips sparkled with silver lipstick. The girls were sitting at the kitchen table letting Sean help put their shoes on.

'Wow,' Harriet said. 'You look beautiful, Mummy.'

Sean looked up from tying Ava's shoelace when their daughter spoke. His scowl sharpened, taking in her costume. 'Bit young, isn't it?'

'Young?'

'I mean you're a bit old for that get-up. Would have been a knock-out when you were a teenager.'

She opened the fridge, grabbed a bottle of wine and poured herself a small glass, doing her best to ignore her husband's comments.

Ben. How she wished she was with him right now. He'd appreciate the tight fit of the costume. He didn't play games. There were never any snarky comments or hidden agendas.

Sean raised an eyebrow. 'Wine? Aren't you driving? You never drink when you're driving.'

'One won't hurt, and after the last hour I need it.' She did.

His words kept replaying in her head. The criticism of her as a mother had hurt, which he'd no doubt intended. She sipped her wine, enjoying the relaxing sensation it provided.

Her husband was a good-looking man. He maintained himself. His sandy-blonde hair was slightly darker than when they'd first met, but it was thick and styled. Physically, he was a catch, but the anger flashing in his eyes towards her right now made him anything but attractive.

Eve drained her wine glass and moved over to the twins. 'Now, you two be good for Daddy, okay?'

Harriet and Ava nodded.

'And remember, I love you both very much.' She winked. 'And enjoy those caramel sundaes. I want to hear all about them tomorrow.'

Ava gasped. 'Really?'

The look of surprise and delight on her daughters' faces helped lift her spirits. 'Definitely.' She gave them both a quick peck on the forehead and grabbed her bag, ignoring Sean as she headed out through the laundry to the garage. Calling her a *shit mother*, she'd never forgive him for that.

Eve slid into the driver's seat of her Audi and started the engine. Her head spun slightly. One glass of wine shouldn't have her feeling like that. She shook herself. She'd be fine. It hadn't been a very big glass.

She pushed the button to open the garage door and carefully backed out and into the street.

Leah paced up and down inside her living room waiting for her sister. She'd poured herself a drink but was too nervous to drink it.

She'd dressed exactly to Eve's specifications, and they would create quite a buzz, but she also felt self-conscious. The outfits would've looked great when they were seventeen, but eighteen years later they seemed silly, especially when the party had the potential to be a job interview too.

She jumped as her phone ringing jolted her.

'I'm out front,' Eve said. 'Did you need me to come up or are you ready?'

'I'm ready,' Leah said. 'I'll be down in a minute.' She slipped her phone into the vintage black and gold purse Eve had given her the previous Christmas.

Her twin had the identical bag and had sent her a text an hour earlier with strict instructions about what bag to bring and what jewellery to wear. Leah rubbed her wrist. It felt naked without her watch, but Eve didn't want her wearing anything that could differentiate them.

After giving Lewis a quick stroke on the head, she opted to take the stairs and dashed down eight flights. She was bursting with pent-up anxiety and any attempt to get rid of some was welcome.

Her sister's Audi was parked directly in front of the apartment block. She opened the door and smiled when her identical self stared back.

'Perfect,' Eve said. 'You look amazing. You should wear your hair loose like that more often. Stop always putting it up. You really look stunning.'

Leah laughed. 'I look exactly like you. You wear your hair like this most days.'

Her sister grinned. 'I know. Like I said, absolutely stunning.'

Leah relaxed, the muscles in her neck loosening. Having her twin by her side always made things easier.

Eve switched on the internal car light and moved her face closer. 'Make-up looks identical,' she said. 'Earrings?'

Her hands shot up to her ears. 'Oh, sorry, must've forgotten to take them out.' She unclasped each earring and slipped them into her bag. 'I think we're all good now.'

Her sister started the car but then hesitated.

'Everything okay?' Leah asked.

'Not exactly. Sean and I had a huge fight before I left. He was being a real prick.'

'That's men for you,' she said. Although, she was surprised. Eve rarely spoke of any problems she might be having; she tended to keep things to herself. 'Do you want to talk about it?'

Her sister shook her head. 'Not particularly. The thing is, I skulled a glass of wine, which I never do, and I can really feel it. I'm not sure I should drive.'

Leah smiled. 'Is that all? Jump out and we'll swap places. I haven't had a drink tonight.'

'The party's at Nicola's holiday cottage,' Eve said, buckling the passenger-side seatbelt. 'It's tucked away in the Dandenongs, so it'll take us at least an hour to get there. How was your day?'

She shrugged. 'So-so.'

'Did you hear from Grant?'

'No, nothing. I don't expect to hear from him again. I keep hoping I won't bump into him.'

'And work? Your boss?'

'Don't know. Called in sick. No doubt he would've been his usual arrogant self. He keeps coming by my desk and laughing. Asking when I plan to move to the next big paper. The way he says it is creepy – like he thinks he can control it.'

'Well, he can't,' Eve said. 'Who knows what'll come out of your discussion with Tom Barnaby tonight. You might be walking in on Monday with your resignation.'

Leah nodded. 'That'd be nice.'

They quickly connected with the Monash Freeway, since it would be the fastest route out to the Dandenongs.

'Were the girls happy to have Kate back today?' she asked.

'Happy is an understatement,' her sister said. 'You should've seen them this morning. Their lunches were perfect, they didn't have to go to after-school care, and they baked muffins with her this afternoon. While I was getting ready, they were having a wonderful splash in the bath and she retold them one of the many stories she can recite from her childhood. She's like some bloody nanny magician. I don't know how we ever coped without her. Sean's taking them out for dinner tonight, so they were extra excited.'

Eve's phone beeped with a text message while they continued out of the city lights into the darker suburbs.

'Damn.'

Leah glanced at her sister, who was frowning at her phone. 'What's the matter?'

Her twin appeared to take a deep breath. 'Bad news. I'll read it to you. "Sorry, you might want to pre-warn Leah that Tom Barnaby is a good friend of her boss. Her boss has contacted him, and he believes most of the other editors of the leading papers, to ensure they don't employ her. Tom said he's sorry but he needs to tread carefully. He's happy to have a chat but there are no opportunities at *The Age*. Sorry, hon. CU soon." 'That's bullshit,' Eve said. 'He can't do that.'

Misery cascaded over Leah, making her shoulders droop. 'Yes, he can. It's a tight-knit industry. They all scratch each other's backs.'

Her sister fell silent for a moment, and when she spoke, it was in her practical, no-nonsense voice. 'No, that's bullshit. I'll speak with Tom Barnaby myself. I'm happy to pretend that I'm you, if you like. He'll employ you, I guarantee it.'

She laughed. 'No, he won't. It's a party. Let's not make it awkward. To be honest, I'd rather go home.'

Eve shook her head. 'We're halfway there, and we *are* going to speak to him. It'll work out fine, trust me.'

For all her sister's faults, deep down, when it came to Leah, her loyalty was unwavering. She'd seen it first hand when they were four and Leah was being teased by an older, nasty boy at kindergarten.

Eve had walked over with a long piece of wood she was supposed to be hammering bottle tops to and threatened to bring it down on the boy's head if he ever went near her again. Her sister had looked upset being told off by the kindergarten teachers and was banned from the woodwork area for the rest of the term, but the moment they turned away from her she'd grinned and gave Leah a thumbs up. Leah had felt terrible that Eve had been banned from her favourite area but her sister had shrugged and said the boy had deserved it, and she'd make mud pies instead.

Eve reached across and turned up the volume on the Friday night top forty countdown. 'Don't give it another thought. Enjoy the music and get in the mood. Leave Barnaby to me. It'll work out.'

Leah concentrated on the road ahead. She loved Eve for her enthusiasm and certainty that she could talk Tom Barnaby into employing her, but it was too much of a men's club. She knew it deep down. He might smile and say the right things tonight but it was unlikely to go anywhere.

Nothing was going right for her at the moment. First Grant, and now work. Although she could control the work issue. Resigning was her choice, but being unemployed was not something she could handle right now.

Leah sighed. She wished she hadn't agreed to come to the party. It was the *last* thing she felt like doing right now.

Chapter Eight

Leah manoeuvred the Audi on to a small bridge that crossed Big Sky Creek and, following Eve's instructions, turned through a gate on to a narrow, winding side road.

'Where on earth are we?'

'Shortcut,' her sister said. 'It's actually someone's property but Nicola said they don't mind if locals use it. It takes us up over the hill rather than having to go around the long way. Knocks at least ten minutes off the trip. It's hardly used, other than the people who own the farms around here. The scenery is stunning during the day. Rolling hills, magnificent gum trees.' She laughed. 'You'll have to take my word for it tonight. The moon's giving a bit of light but not enough to see much.'

The Audi gripped the corners as it glided up the hill. Leah noticed the headlights of another car in her rear-view mirror. Were they guests of Nicola too? She contemplated pulling over and letting the car pass, but it dropped back to a comfortable distance as the road became windier and soon they were twisting down the other side of the hill.

'Not feeling sick, are you?' Eve asked.

Leah was, but it had nothing to do with the winding road. Her life was in such a difficult place and she couldn't see a way out. Sure, in time she'd get over Grant and what he'd done, but her career was a huge thing for her. She couldn't believe Fitzy would go to the extent of calling their competitors – it made her blood boil.

'Leah?'

She glanced across at Eve, who was now staring at her.

'You okay?' her sister asked.

There was no chance to respond. Her eyes refocused on the road, but it was too late.

'Shit! Watch out!' Eve grabbed the steering wheel and the car swerved, skidding sideways as a kangaroo flashed in front of them.

Leah's heart was in her throat. The car was moving completely out of her control.

If they'd been on a flat piece of road, they would've stopped on the embankment, but they weren't. They were on a corner, a corner with an already broken barrier.

The Audi spun until it faced backward and smashed through the guard rail, rolling over in seconds.

Leah was stunned. Something hit against her side and a powder filled her lungs and the surrounding air. She heard screaming. She closed her mouth and the screaming stopped.

Her hands remained gripped to the steering wheel. Her seat belt had her pinned in the seat, as did the side airbag when it had hit her. Metal crunched as the car continued to roll. It wasn't slowing.

'We need to get out.' Eve's voice was verging on hysteria. 'There's a huge lake at the bottom.'

Her twin had released her seat belt before Leah could even consider whether it was a good idea. She heard a sickening crunch as her sister immediately slammed into the roof and the windscreen when the car rolled again.

What the hell was she thinking? She tried to reach her but Eve was being thrown about the car like a puppet.

Another sickening crunch, and the car came to an abrupt stop, leaving Leah feeling like she'd been punched in the face. She sat speechless; at least they weren't upside down. The front airbags had deployed when they'd hit the tree, explaining the punch to her face and head.

Leaves and sticks were poking through the shattered windscreen. She coughed, her chest burning. The air was thick with powder.

Eve was crushed into Leah's left side pinning her left arm.

'Eve?' The word came out a croak.

Her sister groaned.

She closed her eyes with relief. Somehow, she couldn't even begin to imagine how, they were both alive. She opened her eyes. She needed to do something.

They needed to get out of the car and get help. Thank God for the car behind them. Surely they would stop or call for help?

Her eyes had begun adjusting to the dark. The moon filtered through the trees, providing a little light. If they could get out of the car they'd be able to use the torch on their phones.

Leah pushed her sister gently back into the passenger seat. The roof was so crushed that, even hunched over, Eve barely fit. She prayed she'd be able to get the door open and help her sister out.

'Eve, are you okay?' she asked.

Her twin managed another noise. It was a strange sound, like she was trying to get air but couldn't breathe properly.

Leah's heart thudded as the light filtering through the windscreen revealed Eve's face. One eye was swollen shut, the other only half open. There was so much blood. It covered her chest and her arms.

They needed help, and quickly.

With a shaking hand, she managed to unbuckle her seat belt. 'Don't worry, Eve, we'll be fine. I'll get you out and then we'll get help.'

She pushed at her door. It took five attempts. Agony rippled through her body and she had to use all her weight against it to push.

It finally opened.

Leah stepped out on to the uneven ground and stumbled. The front of the vehicle was locked firmly with the tree they'd hit.

She heard a male's voice calling from the road above. A mild feeling of relief washed over her. She could barely make out his words. He'd called the emergency services.

Help was coming.

She steadied herself before edging around the back of the car to the passenger side. Her sister's door was smashed in, as hers had been, and was nearly impossible to open. Her left arm was no help. It throbbed, and she was unable to put weight on it.

Using her right arm, she pried the door open a few centimetres. She tugged again only moving it a few more. She leaned against the side of the car and wedged her foot in through the gap of the slightly open door, pushing it from the inside again and again until finally it swung open.

Eve was hunched over the centre console when she got to her. Indecision regarding moving her or not rushed over Leah, but there was a lot of blood and she needed to stop that if nothing else.

She found the lever for the passenger seat and reclined it before gently pulling her twin back into the seat. Her foot, now inside the car, bumped against something. She could make out the shape of her bag. Retrieving it from the floor she opened it, hands still trembling, and took out her phone. She quickly turned it on and switched on the torch function. Light filled the vehicle.

She gasped at the amount of blood that covered the once beige seats. They were saturated. She turned the torch on Eve. The seats weren't the only thing covered. She gently pushed her sister's hair away from her face.

Eve was barely recognisable. Blood was oozing from a slash on her forehead and a piece of mirror was wedged in the side of her neck. Blood streamed from each side.

She needed to stop the bleeding immediately. Sirens sounded from a distance. Thank God. She'd been worried it would take ages for anyone to respond since they were so far from civilisation.

'We're going to be okay, Eve,' Leah said. 'I can hear an ambulance. They'll be here any minute. In the meantime, I'm going to find something to stop the bleeding.'

'Lee?' Her nickname was barely a whisper. Her sister's eyes remained closed. Her body unmoving.

She took her hand, her own shaking uncontrollably. 'It's okay, I'm here. We need to get you fixed up. You're not looking your best.' She tried to smile. Tried to make Eve think everything would be okay.

'Lee.'

Leah had to move her head up to Eve's mouth to hear her speak.

'Tell Sean I love him and the girls.' A tear mixed with the blood rolled down her sister's cheek. 'Please look after the girls for me. Become like a mum to them. They love you more than anything.'

She squeezed her hand. 'Of course I'll look after them, but only while you get better. You're going to be fine. I can hear the ambulance even closer now.'

'Promise me, Lee. Promise you'll be a mum to them.'

'Of course, I promise. I'd do anything for those girls.'

Eve's hand relaxed in her grip.

'We need to concentrate on you now. You need to stay with me, okay?'

Her sister didn't respond. Her chest rose and fell with small breaths.

Leah let go of her hand and hunted for something to stop the bleeding. She found tissues and managed to bunch them on either side of the piece of mirror protruding from Eve's neck.

They were soaked within seconds. She took more and applied pressure to the spot. She was too scared to remove the mirror; it appeared to be lodged deep.

She willed help to hurry. The sirens were now on the hill somewhere above them.

'It's okay, Eve. They're almost to us. You need to hang on.'

'Love you, Lee-Lee,' Eve managed. Her words were slow, slurred.

'I love you too,' Leah said, fear evident to her own ears. 'Just hold on. Don't you even think of leaving us.'

'Sorry.' Her sister whispered the last word before her head tilted to one side.

Leah looked down at Eve's chest, willing the rhythmic rise and fall to be there.

It wasn't.

She shook her sister. 'Eve? Come on, wake up.' Blood gushed from the cut the moment she moved her fingers from it. She pushed the tissues back around it, her own heart pounding while she tried to figure out what to do.

She needed to do CPR but how did she do that and stem the blood at the same time?

Leah had to act, it was Eve's only chance. Her breathing was a priority now. She willed her not to bleed to death while she tried.

She pushed her twin back in the chair. Her arm was likely broken, and the confines of the crunched Audi would be a challenge, but she had to try.

Leah checked Eve's mouth to ensure it was clear. She bit her bottom lip and placed both hands on her sister's chest, then started compressions.

White-hot pain exploded through her arm. She counted to thirty, and leaned forward to breathe two breaths into Eve's mouth. Then she resumed the compressions.

Blood continued to pour down Eve's neck as Leah continued CPR. She was sweating. The pain in both her arm and heart was almost unbearable.

She knelt in a pool of her sister's blood trying to bring her back to life. Tears poured down Leah's face as she continued. Where was help?

The sirens had quietened.

She continued, her concentration only broken when she heard the crashing of bushes and trees and voices.

A strong light hit the car. The paramedics were here.

Eve had a chance.

'Over here,' a deep male voice called.

Leah continued the compressions, but was aware of the commotion and footsteps around her. She leant across to give Eve another breath.

Someone was now standing at the door.

'I'll take over,' the man said. 'You've done an amazing job.'

He helped her out of the car and resumed CPR, yelling instructions to the other paramedics around him.

A strong arm went around Leah and moved her behind the car. 'It's all right, help's here now. How many of you were travelling in the car?' The man spoke gently.

Leah managed a whisper. 'Two. Me and my sister.' Tears spilled down her cheeks.

The paramedic put down his medical bag and opened it. 'Your sister is in good hands. We need to look after you. The others will help her.'

She nodded. There'd been so much blood. Whether the CPR had an effect or not, she wasn't sure. The blood loss, surely that was too much? She was unable to speak.

'I'm Gary.' The paramedic pulled on plastic gloves. 'What's your name?'

Leah hardly heard him. Her eyes were locked on the car. Maybe there was hope. Maybe they could do something for Eve. 'Eve, oh Eve.' She buried her head in her hands.

Gary rubbed her shoulder. 'Eve, I need to help you. I know this is terrifying but we need to treat your injuries.'

She didn't bother to correct him. She didn't have the energy to say anything more. She sat on a foil blanket he'd produced while he examined her. She could hear other voices talking about Eve, moving her from the car.

'We'll need to get you to the hospital,' Gary said. 'You've got a nasty cut and bump on your head and your left arm's definitely broken. How on earth you were able to perform CPR with that is a miracle. It must've been agony.'

Tears ran down Leah's face. It had been. In more ways than one. If only it saved Eve. She would've done it with two broken arms if necessary.

'We're going to carry you out of here. The boys will prepare a stretcher and we'll get you up to the ambulance.' Gary was still talking.

She started to nod, then stopped. Her head throbbed. It was better not to move it. She could hear the others talking, their voices low. She closed her eyes as she made out some of their comments.

'No pupil response.'

'No pulse.'

The cold night air rushed at her. Bile rose in her throat.

Eve was going to die.

They hadn't said it outright, but she'd known it in her own heart the moment her sister had told her to look after her girls, to be a mum to them.

She leant over to one side and emptied the contents of her stomach.

Gary was immediately by her side.

'It's okay, Eve,' he said. 'We're nearly ready to lift you out of here.' He was holding her head, shining a small torch in her eyes. 'Can you hear me?'

'Yes.' Her voice was a whisper. 'My sister. Is she—'

Compassion filled Gary's eyes. 'We're doing everything for her. The boys have her out of the car and are preparing to carry her out as well. She has extensive injuries, but she has a chance.'

A chance.

Leah didn't feel any hope at those words. Eve had left her already. She could feel it. Part of her was empty.

Harriet and Ava.

She bent over. Tears streamed down her face as giant sobs shook her body. Those poor, poor little girls. Her heart tore, recalling their innocent young faces.

Leah would have to be the one to tell them. She needed to hold them, comfort them. Pain throbbed in her head.

Eve's death. Her parents would be devastated. So would Sean. It was all wrong; it should've been the other way around. Eve's life was too full, too busy to leave it so early.

It should've been her who died, not her sister.

What did Leah have going for her? Nothing. No husband, no children, no future in her career. Eve had so much to live for and so many people relying on her.

A stretcher had been placed on the ground beside her.

'We're going to lift you on to this now,' Gary was saying. 'Eve, do you understand?'

Leah couldn't muster any more strength to communicate. She wanted to lie down and sleep. Pray this was all a nightmare she would wake from. She let her eyes close.

A hand touched her face. 'Try to keep your eyes open.' The paramedic's gentle tone made her jolt. 'We need you to stay awake.'

She shook herself as Gary and another of the paramedics helped her on to the stretcher. She couldn't afford to sleep now. She had a huge lump on her head. She might have concussion or something worse.

Leah tried to focus her attention on something else but all that filled her mind was Eve's bruised and bloody face followed by Ava and Harriet. She couldn't move past these images and the knowledge there was absolutely nothing she could do to make this better for them.

If it hadn't been for her throbbing head and arm, Leah might've remained completely unaware while the paramedics prepared her for the stretcher and lifted her and began the trek back up to the road. Her neck was in a brace, her arm in an inflatable splint, her body covered with a blanket and strapped in numerous places to the stretcher.

Gary told her she needed to respond to his questions with a basic yes or no, so they could gauge how she was doing. She did her best to spit the word out when necessary.

They continued to call her Eve. She'd need to correct them when she could muster up the strength to mutter more than one word.

A fire engine pulled up just as they reached the road. Leah shuddered. Fire. Thank goodness the car hadn't caught fire. She closed her eyes as the bright lights of the ambulance infiltrated them.

A female paramedic was inside the ambulance. Her voice was friendly and soothing. 'Eve, we're going to transport you now to the emergency department at Dandenong Hospital. They'll look after you and contact your family.'

Tears streamed down her face. She opened her eyes and stared into the woman's kind eyes. She managed to spit out the word, 'sister.'

Compassion filled the woman's eyes. She took Leah's hand and squeezed it. 'Your sister is the passenger in the car?'

'Yes.'

'The boys are doing everything possible for her, Eve. There'll be more news once we reach the hospital.'

Leah closed her eyes as the doors of the ambulance were shut and the vehicle began to move. She wished they'd given her something to knock her out. Remove her from this nightmare.

Eve was already gone. It was hardly a comfort knowing that once she reached the hospital her family would be contacted. The grief they were about to encounter would be unbearable.

Bright lights and noise greeted Leah as she was wheeled from the ambulance into the emergency department of Dandenong Hospital.

They bypassed the waiting area and went straight into a consulting room where they were met by a doctor.

'Eve, I'm Dr Logan.'

The middle-aged man smiling at her reminded Leah of Sean. He had the same caring eyes and dimples that made him look a lot younger than he probably was.

'We'll run a few tests and make sure everything is okay, then we'll have a chat. Your family will also be contacted. Okay?'

'Thank you,' she whispered.

He squeezed her right hand and gave instructions to two nurses.

The next hour and a half saw Leah undergo a CT scan, a number of other tests, and her arm was set in plaster. Her costume was cut off, and the nurses bathed her and put her in a hospital gown.

Her body was sore, particularly across her chest and the side of her head. One of the nurses had explained that the seat belt had caused the chest pain, and the side airbag the pain to her side and head.

Once Leah had been cleaned up, the doctor returned. His eyes were soft, full of compassion. 'In addition to your arm, which is broken in two places, you've got a nasty concussion, but the CT scan showed no other brain trauma. We've stitched the cut on your forehead and there will be some discomfort from bruising that you'll have to contend with. Your nose is bruised but not broken. The front airbag most likely caused that. You may find your memory a little hazy but that should return to normal over the next few weeks. If you do experience any ongoing issues, we'll book a full MRI scan. At this stage I don't think that's necessary.' He cleared his throat. 'I am very sorry to inform you that we were unable to save the passenger in the vehicle. Her injuries were too extensive.'

Tears escaped Leah's eyes. She already knew Eve was gone, but hearing the doctor confirm it made it real.

He gave her a moment to try to compose herself before continuing. 'Due to the serious nature of the accident, the police would like to talk to you. They're waiting outside. Do you think you're up for it?'

Leah managed a brief nod.

The doctor gave her a sad smile and patted her arm before leaving the room.

Moments later two female police officers entered.

'Eve, I'm Detective Sergeant Jenkins and this is Detective Sergeant Cosh. We need to ask you a few questions.'

Eve? They still thought she was her sister. She opened her mouth but the lump in her throat prevented her from speaking. Instead she gave a small nod.

'Firstly, we are very sorry for your loss. I believe the passenger was your sister?'

Leah nodded again.

'The paramedics retrieved your bags from the vehicle. This is rather an unusual case for us and makes identifying your sister a little tricky. Your licenses show that you are twins. Is this the case?'

'Yes, identical.'

'And you were dressed the same. Where were you going?'

'To a friend's fortieth birthday party. We were taking a shortcut through that property to her house.'

'Can you tell us what happened? The forensic team will have more information later, but we hoped you could tell us.'

'Kangaroo,' Leah said. 'It came out of nowhere.' She squeezed her eyes shut while the scene replayed before her. 'I swerved to miss it and the car spun and went through the barrier. I think I hit the kangaroo, but I'm not sure. We went through the barrier backwards and then the car rolled.'

'And your sister wasn't wearing a seat belt?'

'She was. She took it off on the way down. Said she was getting out.' She recalled the crunch when Eve slammed hard into the roof of the rolling vehicle. A lump formed in her throat. 'But she couldn't.'

Jenkins' eyes filled with sympathy. 'Thank you, Eve. There will be further investigations of course but those details make our job a lot easier.'

Leah stared at the police officer. They still thought she was Eve. She almost smiled through her tears. Eve would like that even in death, she'd been able to fool people.

When they were in primary school it had always been Eve suggesting they switch for the day. She'd loved sports class and Leah art, so her twin had organised that they traded places for those classes.

Eve would get to do sport twice, and Leah art twice a week. When they chose to dress identically, no one could tell them apart. Their personalities were very different, but when they needed to act at being their twin, it was easy. Leah had enjoyed it. It'd given her the chance to act more confidently, say things she normally wouldn't. It must've been hard for Eve, having to be quiet and good for an entire lesson.

The police officer was still talking, but she'd tuned them out.

They thought she was Eve. They thought Leah had died in the accident.

If only that had been the case. Her family would grieve, but it wouldn't leave the same gap in the lives of the girls that Eve's death would.

They were referring to her as Eve again. Was there any way they could tell that she wasn't Eve?

Leah stared at the ceiling, her heart rate suddenly quickening. She could be Eve. The girls wouldn't lose their mother. Sean wouldn't lose his wife. She could use the memory loss to her advantage, play on that anytime something didn't add up. But what about her life?

Her parents would be upset, and her nieces, but other than a handful of friends, who would miss her? It would serve bloody Fitzy right too. He wouldn't be able to control her career if she was dead.

'We'll need to contact your family, Eve,' Jenkins said. 'We've accessed the emergency contacts in your phone and see that you have Sean West and Leah Donaldson listed.' Her face was full of kindness. 'Leah also had you listed as one of her emergency contacts. We will of course call Sean immediately. Is he your husband?'

This was Leah's chance to correct her. She hesitated. Was there any way the doctors or police could tell them apart? Fingerprints maybe? Neither she nor Eve had ever been arrested, so there wouldn't be a record of them.

She'd be living a lie, but she'd do anything for Eve, and she'd do anything for her nieces. Not only could she prevent them from losing their mother, she'd become the best mother possible. She could keep the promise she'd made to her sister in her dying seconds.

Leah looked Jenkins in the eye, tears rolling down her own cheeks. Her answer would seal her fate. She cleared her throat. 'Yes . . . Sean's my husband. Please call him.'

Chapter Nine

Sean couldn't concentrate on the game. He'd hardly touched his beer. The cruelty of what he'd said to Eve that evening replayed in his mind. While there'd been truth to some of it, it'd been unfair.

They hadn't communicated properly in months, and to spew all those things out was not only out of character for him, but horrible. The fact she'd reached for a glass of wine showed how much the conversation had affected her. Eve hardly ever drank and never – not even a glass – before driving.

They needed to sit down properly and discuss where they were at. They were both busy, neither of them saw enough of the girls, and while Kate was fantastic to have around, the girls needed more of their parents.

They also needed to be doing things as a family. Weekends were usually spent tag teaming. Eve would go for a run or to the gym, or he would, or one of them would be at work. The four of them rarely spent any quality time together. He couldn't remember the last time they'd taken the girls out to the park or to the zoo, or even the movies.

Sean picked up his warm beer and walked through to the kitchen. He poured the contents down the sink and added the bottle to the recycling. He needed to apologise to Eve.

The look on her face when he'd suggested she was having an affair had been complete shock. While they'd drifted apart recently, her reaction made him think he was wrong. She felt strongly about cheating, but her behaviour seemed to fit the pattern.

Sean probably needed to have a look at his own behaviour. She was right. Through the week, he was rarely home before ten. Weekends, he was out as much as she was, putting his own needs ahead of the family. In many ways his behaviour was no better than hers. He was a lot better with the girls, but they loved her. The disappointment they'd both displayed when she'd said she couldn't go out for dinner was obvious.

It wasn't only them spending time as a family, though. He and Eve might sleep side by side some nights but of late, that was all. They needed to go out on a date – go for dinner or a movie or even bowling. Something fun that they used to do. Something that made them laugh. Enjoy being together.

He smiled, switched off the kitchen light, and made his way up the stairs. For every nasty thought he'd had about Eve, this relationship and this family was not only up to his wife to make work. Sean could – and needed to – play a big role in fixing it too. First step would be an apology. If Eve had spoken to him like he'd spoken to her today, he would've been as shocked and hurt as she was.

He'd make that up to her and organise some time for the two of them to be together. He might even call his parents in the morning and see if they'd look after the girls so he could take Eve down to the beach. A walk along the foreshore would give them a chance to chat. Take small steps towards reconnecting.

Sean stripped down to his boxers and climbed into bed. He felt like a weight had lifted from him making those decisions. It was already past twelve.

He didn't expect Eve to come home tonight. She'd probably have a few wines and stay at Nicola's. That would give him and the girls a chance to go out in the morning and get some flowers. To do something nice.

Sean was drifting off to sleep when his phone rang. He grabbed for it, expecting it would be Eve at this late hour, probably drunk, letting him know she was staying the night or needed a lift home. 'Eve?'

The voice that greeted him belonged to a male, definitely not his wife.

'Good evening, am I speaking with Sean West?'

'Yes, that's me.'

'Mr West, my name is Dr Philip Logan. I'm sorry to tell you but your wife has been involved in a car accident.'

A lump rose in his throat. He tried to speak through it. 'Is she all right?'

'She's received cuts and bruising, a broken arm and a severe knock to the head, but yes, she's all right.'

He released a breath, his voice now a whisper. 'Thank God.'

'She's been admitted to Dandenong General Hospital. Are you able to come to the hospital?'

What about the girls? Kate. He'd ring her first then his parents if she wasn't available. 'Of course. I'll organise someone to look after our girls and then I'll come straight there.'

'There's no hurry, Mr West. Eve will quite likely be sleeping by the time you arrive. I suggest you bring a bag of her clothes, toiletries and any personal items you think she might need. She will be kept in for at least a night or two for observation. Now, take your time and please drive carefully.'

Sean stared at his phone as the call disconnected. Eve had been in an accident? Was it his fault? The nasty things he'd said had driven her to have a glass of wine, something she never did before driving. Was she so upset by what he'd said that she'd lost concentration?

Guilt flooded through him. He pulled his clothes back on and rang Kate's number. It clicked straight to voicemail. He didn't bother to leave a message and instead dialled his parents.

Sean explained to his mother what'd happened, then hung up. He needed to organise an overnight bag. He stood in the walk-in wardrobe and stared at her clothes. Work suits, dresses and designer labels stared back at him. Eve had class, he'd give her that, but these clothes were hardly comfortable for a hospital stay.

He dismissed them and instead opted for the few comfortable pairs of sweat pants, an aqua hoodie he'd always loved and two other sweatshirts. He could always bring her some fancier clothes if she felt she needed them but these were the clothes he liked her in. More casual, less uptight.

Sean added underwear and runners to the bag before moving into the bathroom. Her toiletry bag was missing. She must've taken it, expecting she might stay at Nicola's. She probably had spare clothes with her. She'd hardly redress in her Wonder Twin outfit. Did she have those items with her now? In case she didn't he put together a selection of toiletries and make-up from what was left in the bathroom.

He ducked his head into the girls' room, his breath catching as he watched them sleep. Their beautiful blonde hair spilled on to their pillows. Their faces were so innocent. How could he have thought for one minute that he and Eve splitting up would be good for them?

The sound of a car on the driveway caught his attention. He closed the bedroom door and made his way down the stairs to the front door to greet his parents.

Forty-five minutes after falling into his mother's tight embrace, Sean parked his car in a multi-storey car park adjoining the hospital and hurried through to the emergency area. He'd contemplated calling Eve's parents on the way, but decided to leave it until the morning. It was already late, and if Eve was sleeping, it would do nothing but worry them unnecessarily. He'd call them and Leah first thing.

The automatic doors opened as he walked into the emergency area and made his way to the front desk. Eve had been moved from Emergency and was now on a ward in a private room.

A nurse stopped him as he reached the ward. 'Mr West?'

Sean nodded.

The nurse's smile was warm and friendly. 'Your wife's sleeping. We've given her some medication to help her get off to sleep. She was very upset and in shock. I'm afraid she might not wake for a few hours.'

'But she's okay.'

'Physically, yes. Emotionally, it may take some time.'

'Do you know what happened?'

'No,' the nurse said. 'The police have spoken in detail with Dr Logan. He's in surgery at the moment, but will come and talk to you once he finishes up. For now, why don't you go in and sit with your wife? The chair next to the bed is quite comfortable. Hopefully you'll get some sleep too.'

Sean hesitated in the doorway of Eve's room before pushing open the door. His stomach contracted looking at his wife. The

109

blonde hair visible from beneath the bandages was spread across the pillow, exactly as the twins' hair had been. However her face did not reflect childhood innocence.

The parts that weren't deathly white were bruised and swollen. Her head was bandaged and her nose was bruised black. Her left arm was in a sling.

He moved to the chair next to Eve's bed and took her right hand in his. 'I'm here, sweetheart.'

Eve's steady breathing continued.

He tried to block out the jumble of thoughts and what ifs that kept playing through his mind. He hadn't even thought to ask the nurse if anyone else had been hurt in the accident. Eve was going to be all right but what if she'd hurt, or even killed, someone in the other vehicle?

He shuddered.

It was close to two o'clock when the door opened and a doctor entered. He beckoned and Sean followed him into the corridor.

'Dr Logan,' the man said, holding out his hand.

Sean shook it.

'Your wife was lucky based on what happened. Her injuries are fairly minor. A CT scan showed no brain trauma, however clinically she has a concussion. For now we must monitor how she progresses.'

'Do you know what happened?' he asked.

Dr Logan's eyes narrowed. 'I'm sorry, I was under the impression the police were returning to discuss the accident with you. It is possible they're escorting Ms Donaldson's parents to the hospital.'

'Ms Donaldson's? That's my wife's maiden name, not her married name. It's Mrs West. I'd planned to ring her parents in the morning. Is there really any need to wake them in the middle of the night? I'm her next of kin, not them.'

'Mr West, I'm afraid Eve wasn't alone when the accident occurred. Her sister, Ms Leah Donaldson, was in the vehicle with her.' The doctor lowered his eyes. 'I'm afraid her injuries were incompatible with life. She died before reaching the hospital.'

The air was sucked out of him. He stumbled and Dr Logan grabbed his arm to stop him from falling. He led Sean over to a row of chairs lined up against the wall of the corridor.

Leah was dead.

He put his head in his hands. How would Eve live with herself? How would *he* live with himself?

Dr Logan was still sitting with him.

Sean looked up at the doctor. 'It's a huge shock. Leah is, was, a big part of our lives. Eve will be devastated as will her parents and my girls. So many people.'

'I'm very sorry.'

'Was anyone else involved?' Sean asked. 'Another car?'

The doctor shook his head. 'No. I'm sure Eve or the police will provide you with more detail but it appears the car swerved to miss a kangaroo and skidded through a barrier and off the side of the road. Unfortunately, they were on a steep hill and the car rolled. It was a very unfortunate incident. No alcohol was involved, and whilst there will of course be further investigation, at this stage the police aren't treating the accident as suspicious.'

No alcohol? How did they work that out? He'd seen Eve drink the wine with his own eyes.

The doctor rose. 'I'll be back in the morning to check on Eve, and determine when she can be released. I'd suggest at this stage she'll be in for at least another thirty-six hours for observation, but will confirm that in the morning.'

'Thank you.'

Once the doctor left, Sean sat, head in hands.

Leah. Beautiful, gentle Leah. Grief built inside him.

He wanted to scream but instead dug his fingers into his temple until the pain was almost too much. He deserved to hurt. Deserved to be punished. He'd pushed and pushed at Eve. Said despicable things to her. Accused her of horrible acts. Told her what a bad mother she was. The shock from his words had been written all over her face. The gulping of the wine to block them out.

A hand touched him gently on the shoulder. 'Mr West, Eve is awake.'

Sean met the nurse's eyes. They were full of compassion. She knew about Leah. They all knew about Leah.

What they didn't know was he didn't deserve compassion. He hauled himself to his feet and stopped momentarily outside Eve's door before pushing it open to face his wife.

Leah's heart pounded when the door to her room opened and Sean hesitated in the doorway. His eyes were red-rimmed, his face pale. She still had time to back out, to admit she was Leah. Declare herself to be muddled and confused.

His eyes met hers, the depth of his pain revealed. She sucked in a breath. She hadn't imagined Sean to be so upset on hearing the news of her death.

He moved to her bedside and sat next to her on the bed. He put one arm around her and without saying anything, drew her gently to him, unlocking a tidal wave of tears within her.

She'd been so busy working out how to protect the girls, debating whether she could really take on Eve's identity, that she'd managed to push the thought that her sister was dead out of her mind.

Not now. Sean's warmth, his comforting embrace, brought it all out.

Giant tears caused Leah's body to shudder as she clung to Sean. Eventually, he pulled away, wiped her tears with his finger and forced a weak smile to his face.

'Oh, babe, I'm so sorry. I can't believe this happened.'

She could only nod. The lump in her throat was preventing words.

'How are you feeling?' Her sister's husband's eyes searched hers. 'Are you in a lot of pain?'

Leah shook her head, finally managing a few words. 'Not too much. My arm throbs a bit and I've got a cracking headache, but other than that, if I don't move too much, I feel fine.'

Fresh tears welled in Sean's eyes. 'Thank God. I don't know what I would do . . .' His voice cracked. 'Or how the girls would cope, if it had been you. We couldn't survive without you, Eve. I'm so, so sorry.'

She took another deep breath. His words helped confirm she'd made the right decision. The grief of losing their mother would change the girls forever. Her act was not for self-gain. It was for them. She only hoped she could pull it off. 'Who's looking after them?' she asked.

'My parents.'

Leah nodded. His parents. She'd only met June and Abe a few times. Nervous energy coursed through her – how well did Eve know them?

She'd be expected to know things about the family that she didn't know. Thank goodness for the knock to her head, she had a feeling she'd need to play on that.

'The doctor said they wanted to keep you in for at least one more night. Would you like me to bring the girls in to see you?'

'Yes, please. I think I should tell them about Leah. Tell them what happened and how much she loved them.'

'I can do that,' Sean said.

She gave him a small smile. 'Let's do it together. I think they're going to need both of us.'

Surprise flickered in Sean's eyes. He didn't say anything, but it was definitely there. Was he surprised she wanted to tell the girls, or that she thought they should do it as a team?

'Do you know if my parents have been told yet?' she asked.

He squeezed her good hand. 'I think the police told them. The doctor suggested the police would be bringing them in to the hospital. I'm not sure if they need to identify her.'

Leah closed her eyes. Her poor, poor parents. 'They can't see her.' Her voice cracked and more tears rolled down her face. 'She was a mess, Sean. Blood everywhere. She . . . she took off her seatbelt. Wanted to jump out. She thought there was a lake at the bottom.' She opened her eyes. 'Why would she do that? We were rolling down the hill so fast.'

'It was her survival instinct, I guess,' Sean said, his voice gentle. 'Perhaps she thought it was her only chance.'

'And it killed her. She might still be alive if she hadn't done that.'

He hugged her to him once more and she closed her eyes again, the warmth of his embrace bringing her a sense of safety.

Sean leaned back, his tear-filled eyes meeting hers. 'Eve, I'm so sorry about what I said last night. So very sorry. I was angry, I didn't really mean all of those things.'

Eve had said Sean was being a prick. She swallowed. Another reason Eve couldn't be dead. It would be awful for Sean to have to live with that as his final memory. His final conversation – or shouting match – with his wife.

With her good hand she squeezed his. 'It's okay. It's not important now.'

'But—'

His words were interrupted as the door opened and her parents stepped in. Her mother was wiping her eyes with a tissue, her father pale-faced, his eyes swollen. They both looked like they'd aged ten years since she'd seen them on Thursday.

Sean stood and wordlessly embraced Peggy first, then Bill.

More tears ran down Leah's face as she watched them. Her mother was the first to move to her bedside. She took her hand and sat in the chair next to her bed.

'Oh, Mum,' was all she could manage.

Her mum tried her best to give a smile, but instead her face contorted with grief. She closed her eyes for a brief second then reopened them.

'Thank goodness you're alive, Eve. I couldn't bear it if it had been both of you.'

The pain in her mother's face was beyond anything she would've imagined.

'And the girls.' Her mother shuddered at the mention of Eve's daughters. 'It's going to be devastating enough to tell them that Leah's gone, but if it had been you too, I can't even begin to imagine.'

'Neither can I,' her father said, moving over to them. 'The accident has taken our beloved Leah, but God spared you. He knew you were still needed here.'

Leah nodded. Her father's faith would ensure he made sense of the accident and got through it. Her mother wasn't as devout. On this occasion she was glad her father had that higher belief. Their words helped reinforce she was doing the right thing.

Sean remained at a distance during this exchange, but now he moved back and sat on the edge of the bed.

'Babe, while your parents are with you, I might go home and check on the girls. I need to let my parents know what's happening and see if they can stay until you come home. Are you sure you want me to bring the girls in?'

A lump rose in her throat. Telling the girls was going to be the hardest thing she'd ever done and on top of that, would they see through her act?

Oh God, what a nightmare.

Sean squeezed her hand. 'It's going to be rough but we don't have to do it today. Have a day of rest first.'

'No, I'll be okay. Why don't you go home and try to get some sleep?' She gave him a small smile. 'You look exhausted. Come back with the girls this afternoon. We'll tell them together then.'

'There are a lot of other people to get in touch with,' her father said. 'Family, friends, Leah's work.' His voice broke and he wiped at his eyes. 'How on earth are we supposed to do all that?'

A lump lodged in her throat as her sister's husband left her bedside and went and put an arm around her father.

'Leave it to me, Bill. There's no hurry. We can't change anything now. How about, after I bring the girls this afternoon, I drop them back with my parents and come over to see you and Peggy? If you prepare a list, I'll make the calls.'

'Really? You'd do that?'

'Of course,' Sean said. 'Not knowing a lot of the people will make it easier for me than it would be for you.'

Her father pulled Sean to him. 'Thank you, son, you're a good man.'

He was right. Sean was a good man. Eve had been lucky. Her time on earth might've been far too short, but at least she had the best while she was here.

Her sister's husband gave her a quick peck on the cheek, said his goodbyes to her parents, and promised to be back around three with the girls.

Leah watched as *her* husband walked out of the hospital room, his head drooping down the moment he thought he was out of sight.

'You're very lucky, Eve,' her father said. 'He's a good man.'

Peggy nodded, her eyes searching Eve's. 'Very good. I think you need to remember that sometimes.'

'I know he is.' Her eyes filled with tears looking from her mother to her father.

Eve was dead, never coming back. In an instant their family had changed forever.

Sean opened the door of the Mercedes and slipped into the warmth of the cream leather interior. He sat, unable to move for a few minutes. Eve had said to forget about what he said. That it didn't matter now, but how could he forget?

He'd never spoken to her like that before. Never been so venomous with his words. She'd had a terrible accident, quite likely the result of her anger at him and the glass of wine she'd thrown back like it was a shot. Her reaction time would definitely have been less. If he'd said nothing, would she have seen the kangaroo earlier? Been able to stop? Saved her sister's life?

The magnitude of what he'd done to Leah, to her family and to all those who loved her, including himself, was almost too much to bear.

The car purred to life while he clicked his seat belt in. He was going to have to pull himself together. He made his way down the winding exit ramps and out on to the main road. The next step would be telling his parents, then the girls later that day, before helping Bill and Peggy make the phone calls.

Sean took a deep breath. He owed it to all of them to be strong. To help them through this.

Mid-morning, Leah suggested her parents go home and try to rest. They'd both been woken in the early hours and that, combined with their shock and grief, had left them exhausted.

Her own guilt rose within her over the accident, and looking at her parents' distraught faces made her feel worse. She'd been the one driving. She'd glanced across at Eve for a brief second before the kangaroo had jumped out in front of them. If she'd had her eyes on the road, she might've seen it in time to brake or swerve in a more controlled manner.

Eve had asked her to drive to keep them safe. The request played on a loop in her head; it wouldn't leave her alone.

After Sean had left, she'd had nurses and doctors come in to see her. Been poked and prodded. It was a minor distraction each time from her parents' grief, but also exhausting. She needed rest. She needed to gather her energy and thoughts before Sean returned with the girls.

Tears flowed again as her parents said their goodbyes. Her mother hugged her, not wanting to let go. Eventually her father separated them and guided her out of the room.

Leah closed her eyes when she was alone again. Images of the accident, the screaming, the blood, Eve's lifeless body, ran through her mind. She tried unsuccessfully to clear them away. It appeared sleep was going to be too difficult. Instead she tried to focus on the girls and what she was going to say to them. For once, she was glad of her father's faith. She'd draw on that and hopefully get the girls to believe their aunt had gone somewhere beautiful and would always be watching over them.

Eventually, her fatigue got the better of her and she fell into a fitful, dream-filled sleep.

Sean fell into his mother's comforting embrace as he let himself in through the front door.

His father's footsteps hurried down the passageway.

'How is she, love?' she asked.

Guilt and tears overcame Sean and he buried his face in his mother's shoulder. He felt her tense while she rubbed his back. He hadn't rung from the hospital, so at this stage they had no idea what'd happened. He sniffed and tried to pull himself together.

He leaned back. 'Sorry, it's all been a bit of a shock.' Sean looked up the stairs, half-expecting Harriet or Ava to appear at any second.

'We dropped the girls at school a couple of hours ago,' his father said. 'Harriet reminded us they had their drama workshop this weekend. We told them you'd gone into work early, which was why we were here.' He checked his watch. 'I have to pick them up at two. Why don't you come and sit down and tell us how Eve is?'

He followed his parents into the living room. 'She's going to be fine. A broken arm is the worst of the injuries. She'll be able to come home tomorrow. They want to keep her in overnight again to keep an eye on her concussion.'

His mother smiled. 'Oh, what a relief. We've been so worried.'

Sean couldn't return her smile.

'What's wrong, son?'

He was drawn into his father's trusting eyes. The older man would be horrified if he knew how Sean had spoken to Eve the night before. How his words might've caused the accident. Sean cleared his throat. 'Leah was in the car with her. She—' His voice broke. 'She died.'

His mother's gasp brought more tears to his eyes.

'Oh, son.' His father ran his hand through his thinning hair. 'How is Eve taking this?'

'She's in shock. The accident was horrific. Eve tried her best to keep Leah alive. They said she'd done CPR for around ten minutes with the agony of her broken arm. She's had a pretty rough time.'

'The poor girl,' his mother mumbled. 'And her poor parents. The poor, poor things.'

Sean stood. 'I think I might go and have a quick shower and a lie-down if that's okay. If you want to go home, I'll be fine. I'll pick the girls up from drama and take them to see Eve.'

'Won't you need us here for the girls tonight?' his mother asked. 'You might want to go back to the hospital to see Eve on your own later?'

He remembered his promise to Bill and Peggy that he would help them with the phone calls. 'That would be great, thank you.'

His mother drew him to her and hugged him tight. 'Eve's okay, Sean. She's alive. The girls still have their mother. Dealing with Leah's death is going to be difficult for all of you, but you'll get through this.'

Sean nodded. Tears rolled down his cheeks at his mother's touch and words. He pulled away. While he appreciated it, he didn't deserve to be comforted.

Leah kept glancing at the clock above the door of the hospital room. It was already three. Sean and the girls would be here any minute. She'd rehearsed what she planned to say at least a hundred times.

She kept reminding herself what she was doing was for the good of the girls. They'd be upset, but their lives wouldn't be destroyed as they would've been if they knew their mother had died.

Oh, Eve. Tears welled and spilled. She'd been so consumed with working out how she'd fool everyone into believing she was Eve, for a moment she'd distracted herself from her own loss.

At ten past three, the door opened and Leah's breath caught.

Harriet and Ava looked tiny as they hesitantly came inside. Their eyes were wide. She could only imagine what they were seeing. She'd had a shock looking in the mirror earlier. Her face was a swollen and bruised mess.

Sean placed a hand on each of their shoulders and guided them towards her bed.

A tear ran down Leah's cheek. They were so beautiful. So innocent. They didn't deserve any of what was happening.

'Don't cry, Mummy,' Harriet said.

Luckily one twin was dressed in pink, so Leah knew immediately that was Ava. Harriet wouldn't be caught dead in anything pink. The little girl presented a flower from behind her back. 'We've brought you presents.'

A lump formed in Leah's throat. It was going to take some getting used to, hearing her nieces call her 'Mummy'. She patted the bed. 'Come and sit up here, I need a hug. I need you on this side so I can use my good arm.'

Sean helped the girls up on to the bed and she wrapped her arm around them both. More tears ran down her face.

'Why are you crying, Mummy?' Ava asked. 'Are you sore? Does your arm hurt?'

'A bit. But it's my heart that's sore right now.' She glanced across at Sean, who nodded his encouragement.

He moved closer to the girls, putting his hands on their shoulders again.

'Did you hit your heart on something?' Harriet asked, her little face crunched in confusion. 'I didn't know that was possible. We learnt at school that your ribs protect your heart. Did you break them?' Her eyes widened. 'Oh, no! Are they poking into your heart?'

Leah shook her head and took a deep breath. 'No, darling, it isn't that. Something very sad happened. That's why my heart is hurting.' She stopped. For all her rehearsing, the words caught in her throat. She looked to Sean for help.

He made the girls face him; hands still on their shoulders. 'Your Aunty Leah was in the car with Mummy when they had the accident.'

'Did she break her arm too?' Ava asked.

Sean shook his head. 'No, honey, but she was hurt. She was hurt so badly the doctors couldn't fix her.' His voice quivered, and he squeezed his eyes shut momentarily. He cleared his throat and opened his eyes. 'Very sadly, she died.'

Leah's gut contracted watching the two girls stiffen.

Their dad pulled them to him, his tear-filled eyes meeting hers over their heads.

Muffled sobs could be heard coming from his chest where the two little girls had their heads buried. They'd never dealt with death before, so Leah wasn't confident they'd understand what it meant.

Harriet shrugged him off and turned to Leah. 'Are you sure? Did you see her? It might be a mistake?'

She held her good arm out for Harriet who untangled herself from Sean's embrace and cuddled into her. 'Yes, we are sure. She died straightaway so she wouldn't have felt anything at all.' She tried to smile again.

The lie was necessary for the girls. They didn't need to know any of the details of Eve's final words, of her struggle to breathe and Leah's unsuccessful attempts at CPR.

'I expect she's looking down at us right now, wishing she was here and sharing our hugs.'

'I wish she was too.' Harriet dissolved into a fresh round of tears.

The girls cuddled into her and Sean and cried on and off for over an hour before he suggested they should go home and let Mummy have some rest.

Ava became hysterical. 'What if Mummy dies too? We can't leave her.'

Leah pulled the little girl to her. 'I'm not going to die, I promise. The doctors have checked me all over and I'm fine. A bump and a cut on my head, a bruised nose, and a broken arm. An arm that's going to need some fancy artwork from the two of you.' She held up the cast. 'How about when I come home tomorrow, you get out your best markers and pretty this up. The white is very boring. I need flowers, rainbows and maybe a few animals drawn on it.'

'Really?' Ava asked.

Even Sean looked surprised. Of course, Eve wouldn't have asked them to do this. She probably would've requested some kind of designer cast to begin with. Too late now, she'd need to go with it.

'Of course. When you get home, why don't you try planning on some paper a great scene that you can draw on the cast tomorrow?'

'I think we should draw butterflies,' Harriet said to Ava.

Ava nodded. 'And zebras. Aunty Leah loves zebras.'

Leah smiled; she did love zebras.

'I don't think we'll have time to cook dinner tonight either,' Sean said. 'How about you two give Mummy a hug and we'll stop off somewhere and pick up something yummy to take home. Gran and Pops will be at our house and will probably be hungry.'

'Chinese?' Ava asked, her face hopeful.

He ruffled her hair. 'Whatever you'd like tonight, princess.'

'Chips?' Harriet added hopefully.

'We'll get both,' Sean said.

Harriet gave a small cheer, then stopped, her face clouding over. 'Sorry,' she whispered.

Leah drew Harriet to her. 'Don't be sorry. When she was seven, Aunty Leah would've been cheering too, if she was allowed to have hot chips. She'd want us all to be happy and have fun. It's okay to be sad, but it's okay to be happy too. She'd want you to be.'

The girls hugged her.

'Get better, Mummy,' Ava said. 'And remember your promise.' She lowered her voice to a whisper. 'You promised you wouldn't die, remember?'

Leah did her best to block out all thoughts of Eve so she wouldn't start crying. 'I promise. And you two make sure you have all the supplies ready and designs worked out for my cast, okay? That can be the first thing we do when I get home.'

The twins nodded.

'I'll come back after dinner,' Sean said. 'Unless you are expecting anyone else?' His eyes searched hers. There was something in them, something questioning that she didn't understand.

'I told Mum and Dad not to come back in today. They need time to process what's happened and I haven't called anyone else yet. Don't forget you told them you'd help with the phone calls.'

'It's not something I'm likely to forget. I'll drop the girls and the food off with my parents and drive straight over there.'

The girls hugged her one last time, then, hand in hand with Sean, led him out of the room.

He looked back at Leah and gave her a sad smile. 'See you in a bit.'

She lay back against her pillows, giving in to the exhaustion suddenly overcoming her. She heard Harriet's voice as they walked away from the room.

'Mummy seemed really different.'

'She's had a huge shock, poppet. We'll need to give her extra care and love when she comes home,' Sean replied.

'Do you really think she'll let us decorate her cast?' Ava asked. 'Or was she trying to be nice to us because of Aunty Leah?'

Leah couldn't hear Sean's reply; they had moved out of hearing.

Guilty tears ran down her cheeks. She'd done what Eve had asked her. The girls hadn't lost their mother, but was lying fair to any of them?

She took a deep breath. Whether it was right or wrong didn't really matter now.

It was too late to back out.

She closed her eyes. Sleep eventually came as images of the accident, mixed with images of the girls' faces, enveloped her.

The hospital's windows were shrouded in darkness a few hours later when Leah woke. She had no idea what time it was, but she was conscious of someone sitting in the chair next to her bed.

Her head throbbed when she turned, and surprise washed over her.

Eve's friend, Nicola, was watching her. Her eyes were red, her face tear-stained. 'Hey you.' Nicola forced a smile. 'Pretty extreme measures to get out of coming to my party.'

The party. Leah had completely forgotten why they'd been in the car in the first place. It hadn't even crossed her mind to contact Nicola. She hardly knew Eve's best friend.

She'd met her a handful of times, but Nicola was the type of woman that Leah found hard to like. Superficial, self-indulgent and judgmental. Eve had said there was more to Nicola. She'd explained the way Nicola came across was a defence mechanism for anxiety.

She'd claimed once one got to know her, there was a whole different side to Nicola.

Whether that was true or not, she was going to have to be careful. If anyone would see through her act it'd be her sister's best friend.

'Sorry,' Leah said. 'Your present. It was probably wrecked.' She thought of the prettily wrapped box Eve had sitting on the back seat.

'I don't care about a present,' Nicola said. 'I care about you. Oh, honey, I'm so, so sorry about Leah. Sean rang me. I can't believe it.'

'Me either.'

'Are you okay?'

'I will be. I need to get out of here. Get home and look after the girls. Everyone's devastated.'

Nicola glanced towards the door. 'What about Ben? Have you been able to contact him? He'll be beside himself when he hears what has happened.'

Ben?

'You look confused,' her sister's best friend said. 'Is everything all right?'

'I'm having trouble remembering things. Did I work with Ben?'

Nicola's mouth dropped open. 'You don't remember?'

Leah shook her head.

'You worked with Ben Styles. You mentioned a large development in South Melbourne you would be *working* on.'

Working on?

Nicola's tone implied something other than working.

Leah remembered her discussion with Eve about Ben Styles. She'd warned her to be careful of him; he had a terrible reputation. Her sister hadn't given her any reason to believe there was anything going on between them. There was no way Eve would cheat on Sean. Leah was certain.

Nicola squeezed her good hand. 'You look really pale. Are you okay?'

'Mainly just a headache.' She touched her bandaged head. 'Whacked it pretty hard, apparently. It's making me confused.'

Her sister's friend raised an eyebrow. 'Yes, I'd say it is. If you need me to call Ben for you, let me know. He'll want to see you.'

Leah nodded. 'Thanks, but I'm fine. I'll contact him later. Sean's coming back soon, so I'll get him to check whether they've released my belongings. I haven't got my phone back yet.' She needed to go through the contacts on Eve's phone and see if she recognised any of them. She imagined numerous awkward conversations moving forward.

Nicola stood. 'I won't stay long now I've seen you. I was so worried when Sean called.'

'Thanks.'

Her brow creased in obvious confusion. 'Are you sure you're okay? You seem kind of weird.'

Leah shrugged. 'The accident. Shock. No sleep. It's caught up with me.'

'That, and a face covered in bruises rather than make-up. That's probably what it is. Did you want me to drop back with some for you? I'm sure you'll have a lot of visitors, and I know how much you hate not wearing it.'

She touched her face. Make-up? Her sister was dead, and Nicola was offering make-up. But . . . she *was* Eve, and even in these circumstances she'd consider her appearance high priority. So instead of declining Nicola's offer, she smiled. 'Thanks, but I'll be going home tomorrow. I'll worry about my face then.'

Her sister's best friend rummaged through her handbag and produced a black Chanel make-up purse. 'Take this for now. It's got all the basics.'

'You know me better than I know myself. Thanks.'

It was past eight by the time Sean returned. His face was pale, and he looked like he was ready to drop from exhaustion. He gave a small smile and took his place in the chair next to her bed. 'I made the calls,' he said.

'How did it go?'

He pushed a hand through his sandy-blonde hair, his eyes filling with tears. 'Honestly? It was the hardest thing I've ever done.'

Her own eyes filled.

'How do you break that kind of news to anyone? It was mainly your relatives we called tonight. Your parents didn't have the numbers for any of Leah's friends, or her boss. We'll need to go through her phone for that.'

'I'll do it.' Her voice was low. 'I think she would've wanted me to. I know some of her friends and work colleagues.'

Jackie. Leah closed her eyes. She'd be devastated. Absolutely devastated. They'd been friends since the first day of kindergarten, when they were four. She couldn't imagine how she'd cope if she received a phone call saying something had happened to Jackie.

A squeeze of her hand brought her back to the present. She opened her eyes to find Sean staring. 'I can help if you like?'

Warmth spread through her body at his touch. 'Thank you.' Tears filled her eyes again. 'You're being amazing with all of this. I know Mum and Dad would be really grateful.'

Sean opened his mouth, as if to say something then closed it again. He moved out of the chair and sat on the edge of Leah's bed. Careful not to hurt her broken arm, he took her in his arms.

She melted against his strong chest and closed her eyes, conscious of the tears dripping. The rhythmic circles his hands were rubbing on her back cleared her mind and helped her to only focus on this moment.

Eventually he stopped rubbing and leaned back. 'You'll be okay, Eve,' he said. 'You always are.'

'It won't be the same,' she said, her words the truth. 'Ever. I feel like part of me died in the accident.'

'It did. You two had a connection not everyone is lucky enough to have. Leah loved you.' He smiled. 'Even though you drove her nuts and bullied her into doing lots of things she didn't want to do, she loved you.'

'She loved all of us,' Leah said. 'She envied us too. Married, kids, a happy life. It's what she wanted.'

Sean stared again. 'Is that how you see our life? Happy?'

She swallowed. She was a stranger within their relationship. She needed to slow down, learn about Sean, and what he and Eve had had together.

Eve certainly had suggested things weren't perfect, and that he was constantly grumpy. She'd witnessed the hostility between the two of them the day she'd brought Ava home sick from school. Then there were her sister's comments that he was acting like a prick the night of the accident.

'That's how I'd like it to be. We have amazing kids and a great life. We should be happy. We owe it to ourselves and my sister.'

Sean gave a slight shake of his head and managed a weak smile. He stood and kissed her forehead. 'I'd better get back and relieve Mum and Dad. The girls should've been asleep ages ago but I want to be there overnight in case they wake or have bad dreams.'

'Good idea.'

Doubt crept into Leah's mind as Sean walked out of the door and turned into the corridor without looking back. It was one thing to step in and save the girls from going through the pain of losing their mother, but another altogether to pretend to be Sean's *wife*.

A nurse with a broad smile entered the room after he left. She placed a plastic bag on the tray table at the end of Leah's bed. 'The police dropped this in for you,' she said.

Leah stared at the bag. The once-carefully wrapped present for Nicola was visible, now ripped and smeared with dirt, in addition to one of the black and gold clutch bags Eve had insisted they both bring.

She already had her phone. She'd made the call from the scene of the accident and had kept it with her since.

She waited for the nurse to leave the room then opened the plastic bag and took out the clutch. Inside were a silver lipstick, a phone, a small make-up case and Eve's purse. What had happened to her own bag?

Leah switched on her sister's phone and was immediately confronted with the password screen. When they were younger Eve had used their birthdate for every pin number. She smiled, a tear rolling down her cheek, remembering her sister's complete incompetence for numbers. Their birthdate and year were supposedly the only four numbers she could remember. Leah punched in 1184 and the phone automatically opened to the home screen.

She shook her head. At least she'd have no problem accessing anything of Eve's that was password protected.

She opened the contact section and carefully read through the names. Leah recognised some of them as friends, others were work colleagues and of course, under Donaldson, there were plenty of family.

There were at least two hundred contacts but Ben Styles wasn't one of them. Nicola had certainly implied something was going on between Eve and Ben. An affair? There was no way her sister would do that. Eve had always referred to it as a deal-breaker. She'd been disgusted by Grant's behaviour.

Eve's contacts wouldn't be given the chance to grieve. They wouldn't even know she was gone. Leah squeezed her eyes shut. She was doing this *for* Eve.

She reached to the cupboard beside the bed and took her own phone from it. She looked through her contacts. It wasn't going to be easy to make these calls. The hardest of course would be to Jackie.

She switched her phone off and tossed it back on the cabinet. She couldn't do it now. She was exhausted. She promised herself she'd do it first thing in the morning. She didn't want people finding out from anybody else.

She closed her eyes. It was unimaginable, what she was going to do. Ring people, her own friends, and tell them she was dead. They'd believe her. They'd mourn her. It was a huge lie.

Would she be able to live with it? She'd have to live with it.

Two little girls were counting on her.

Chapter Ten

Sean smiled at his mother, grateful for the warmth of her hug. Both she and his dad had been wonderful. They'd ended up staying overnight and offered to help him this morning.

He'd have Kate's help that afternoon. She'd returned his call from the following night and, sounding shocked and upset, had insisted she come in and help with the girls. He'd gratefully suggested she come in around lunchtime, once Eve was home.

Sean had woken to find his mother already in the kitchen, the girls' lunches packed neatly into their lunchboxes, and a stack of pancakes warming in the oven. She'd even poured him a coffee.

'I couldn't sleep, so thought I'd make myself useful.'

He studied her carefully as he took a seat at the counter and gratefully accepted the coffee. She had dark rings under her eyes and was uncharacteristically pale.

'Thinking of Leah?' he asked.

His mother nodded. 'And Peggy and Bill. I don't know them very well, but I can only imagine what they're going through. On one hand, they'll be relieved that Eve is all right but on the other . . .' She busied herself pouring juice into cups for the girls, unable to meet his eyes.

He sipped his coffee, the lump that'd stuck in his throat since the moment he'd been told about Leah's death making it difficult to swallow. He closed his eyes. If only he hadn't spoken to Eve that way. She must've been distracted, angry, as she drove. Why her blood test had showed up without alcohol in it, he still couldn't fathom. That glass of wine would've affected her.

'You okay, son?' His father crossed through from the living room into the kitchen. He sat on a stool next to Sean and put an arm across his shoulders. 'Anything I can do?'

Sean shook his head. 'No, you guys have been great. Thank you.' He glanced at the clock on the kitchen wall. 'I'd better make a couple of quick calls and get the girls moving. I wasn't sure whether to send them to the drama workshop today or not, but I think it'd be a good way to keep their minds off things.'

'They're already dressed and moving,' his dad said. 'They're finishing off the last touches on a Welcome Home banner they've made for Eve. They'll be down any minute.'

As he finished speaking, the girls' voices floated down the stairs. They were speaking softly, not full of their usual raucous early-morning excitement.

They entered the kitchen, stopping when Sean and his parents looked them over simultaneously.

'Where's Kate?' Harriet asked. 'I thought she'd be making breakfast today.'

'Gran's made you breakfast,' Sean said. He crouched in front of them and drew them into a hug. 'Kate will be here when you get home from drama. I asked her to come at lunchtime to help Mummy once she's home.'

'We could help her,' Harriet said. 'We don't need to go to drama. It's all pretend stuff, anyway.'

'No, it does matter. You've both been looking forward to it for weeks. Gran and Pops need to go home to their own house, and I need to go and get Mummy. You'll be helping all of us if you go.'

The twins nodded.

'Now sit yourselves down,' his mum said, placing the girls' drinks on the table. 'I'll bring your pancakes.'

'Pancakes?' Harriet said. 'Whose birthday is it?'

'No one's,' June said. 'I thought it would be nice to start the day with a treat.'

Ava shook her head. 'Mummy would say no. I think we should do what she says today. Don't you?' She glanced at Sean.

'I think you'll find Gran's made healthy pancakes,' he said. He winked at his mother. 'Haven't you, Mum?'

'Sure have. I've used whole wheat flour and if you like I can cut up fresh fruit and we can have yogurt to go on top, rather than maple syrup. Would that make Mummy happy?'

Harriet's face clouded over. She glared at her sister.

Sean stepped in. 'How about we have both? Gran will put some fruit and yogurt in a bowl and you can eat it separately or put it on your pancake. Okay?'

Harriet's pancake dripped with maple syrup, her fruit and yogurt untouched, while Ava left her pancakes and concentrated on the healthier option. Once they finished, Sean excused himself to make the calls before getting the girls to drama. The twins went upstairs to brush their teeth.

They were hurtling past him as he walked towards his office and his phone rang. The caller ID showed it was Leah's phone. His heart caught in his throat. Leah's phone? Who could be ringing from Leah's phone? For a split second, he prayed it was all a mistake, a horrible dream. Was Leah still alive?

Please God, let her be alive.
He answered. 'Hello?'

Leah pushed the tray of food away. She had no appetite. She'd slept during the night, thanks to a sleeping tablet the nurses had given her. She'd woken, unsure of where she was until the dull throb of her head and arm reminded her.

Tears immediately filled her eyes at the memory of the accident. Would she wake every day with the vision of her sister coated in blood? The recollection of trying to revive her? She shuddered, her stomach churning.

She took a deep breath and reached for her phone. It was seven thirty. Sean was probably giving the girls their breakfast. She'd ring them first to say hello and wish them a great day before moving on to the calls she was dreading.

Sean answered his cell on the third ring. 'Hello?' His voice was quiet, tentative.

'It's me Sean. Eve.'

'Oh, of course, I saw Leah's number and got a shock.'

'Sorry, I didn't even think.' Leah had automatically used her own phone. She was going to have to get up to speed quickly with being the right person. 'I used her phone at the accident and I guess the paramedics assumed it was mine.'

'Everything okay?' His voice was full of concern.

'I needed to speak to the girls. Reassure them I'm okay.'

There was a silence at the end of the phone.

'Sean?'

He cleared his throat. 'Um, sorry. I'll put Harry on first. Ava must still be brushing her teeth.'

'Hello, Mummy.' Harriet's voice sounded so young.

'Hello, darling. I wanted to tell you I can't wait to see you today. I hope you and Ava will have your markers ready to decorate my cast.'

'You still want us to do that?' Harriet asked. 'Daddy thought you might change your mind.'

That was because Daddy thought she was Eve.

'No, I haven't changed my mind. I can't wait to see what your butterfly is going to look like.'

'I might draw a flamingo too. The same colour as your favourite lipstick.'

Leah smiled. 'I'd love that. Now you have a great day.'

'I'll try. Ava's here, Mummy, I'll put her on.'

'Love you, Harry,' she said but the little girl had already passed the phone to her sister.

'Mummy?' Ava's voice was shaky.

'Are you okay, love?'

The little girl started to cry. 'I want Aunty Lee-Lee.'

'Oh, honey.' Tears welled in her eyes. 'We all do. She loved us all so much, you know. She'd be sad seeing you upset. You know that, don't you?'

'I can't help it, Mummy.' Ava sniffed. 'I'm sorry, I'll try to be better.'

Leah blinked, trying to hold back her tears. 'Don't be sorry, and it's not that you aren't being good. Aunty Leah would want you to try to think of all the happy things you and she did together. Of all the things you loved about her. I'm sure she's still here with us in spirit. She'll be watching over you, surrounding you with all her love.'

'I hope so,' Ava said. The tears stopped, and she sounded a little more cheerful.

'Now, I was telling Harry I'll be home this afternoon when you get back from drama and the cast on my arm needs decorating.

I wondered if you had any of the glittery stickers you could put on it?'

'The ones you told me to take off my door?' Ava asked. 'The ones I got in trouble for and had to go to bed early?'

Leah grimaced. She had better get used to tripping up. 'Yes, they're the ones. I really love them, although perhaps not on your door. I think they'd look great on my arm.' She held her breath. She'd managed to inject a tiny bit of Eve into the conversation but she hoped not enough to upset Ava.

'Okay, Mummy. I'll go and find them before I go to drama. We'll get our pens ready too, so we can start the minute we get home.'

'Great. Ava, I love you very much. You know that, don't you?'

'I think so.'

Think so? Leah cleared her throat. 'I need you to do something for me.'

'What?' Ava asked.

'I need you to go and find Daddy and give him a huge hug. Squeeze him so tight he squeals and tell him that it's from Mummy. Then tell him he has to give you one and Harry one. I'm sending all my love to the three of you this morning.'

She closed her eyes at the sound of Ava's giggle, a tear rolling down her cheek.

'You sound funny, Mummy. Are you sure you're okay?'

'I'm better than okay. I can't wait to see you all later. Now I should go. A doctor has come in to chat with me. Love you, Aves.'

'Love you too, Mummy.'

Leah pressed end on the call and turned her attention to Dr Logan.

'How are you feeling today?' he asked.

She managed a smile. 'Sore, but alive.' The word *alive* brought tears to her eyes. She wiped them. 'Sorry. Physically, a lot better but

137

it's going to take some time. Every time I think of the accident or my sister . . . well, you know.'

Dr Logan nodded. 'It's going to be a hard road for a while. I'm here to talk about your physical injuries, but I will give you some information before you leave, as I highly recommend you seek counselling. I have a couple of great recommendations for psychologists. Other members of your family might benefit from some counselling too.'

Her parents. She doubted her dad would agree, he was too old school, but her mum might.

'I'd like you to go and see your GP in three days, to check that all is okay. While things are still a bit hazy, we'll need to keep an eye on you, particularly the trauma to your head. Make a note if you find you're struggling with your memory. Record the date, time and what you've forgotten. We'll review that in a few weeks,' the doctor continued.

'Is there anything you can do if I'm unable to remember things?' Leah asked. She'd struggle with Eve's memory. Not due to the bump on her head, of course.

The doctor shook his head. 'Not a lot, other than monitor you further. Make sure there's no swelling. We didn't detect any in the initial examination. Now, I'd better get on with your paperwork so you can be discharged.'

She thanked him and waited until he had left before reaching for her phone. She had a couple of hours before Sean would be there to pick her up. She took a deep breath.

The first call was the one she dreaded most.

Sean stood watching the girls chase each other around the school playground. They were a few minutes early for their drama work-shop and had begged him to let them have a quick play.

He couldn't shake the guilt that'd stayed with him since he'd learned of the accident. If only he'd spoken to Eve when he was calmer, not as she was about to leave the house for the night. She'd had that drink, and she'd been angry. On this occasion, it'd proved to be a lethal combination.

The police had said alcohol wasn't a factor. Her body must've been able to metabolise it more quickly than he imagined. But . . . he knew her well enough to know even a few mouthfuls would've been enough to fuel the hurt and anger his words had created.

He blinked away the threatening tears and waved at Harriet, who was now hanging upside down from one of the climbing frames.

There was nothing he could do to change what'd happened. Leah's death was something he was going to have to work out how to live with. They all were.

Fear, guilt and panic overcame Leah as she stared at Jackie's number. How could she do this to her best friend? She half contemplated telling Jackie the truth.

What would her friend say? But there was no way she'd let Leah give up her own life and take over Eve's. Jackie would point out all the reasons it wasn't a good idea. How Leah could still be like a mother to the girls. It wouldn't work, though. She had to be there with them. In their house. She couldn't do that if she was still Aunty Lee-Lee.

Jackie would consider it a betrayal if she ever found out, and that was exactly why she couldn't confide in her. There was nothing malicious in what she was doing. It wasn't something she would've even considered doing until Eve had asked her. She loved her sister, and she loved those two little girls more than anything in the world. She'd do anything for them.

Leah took a deep breath. Part of her wished she'd asked Sean to make this call, but she owed her friend this – at least. She pressed the call button before she could back out.

'Lee-Lee,' Jackie's smiling voice filled her ear. 'How are you, hon? I was going to ring you later today. Check what date suits you for our spa weekend. More bastard cleansing and all that.'

She closed her eyes. Her friend would be looking forward to that weekend. She cleared her throat. 'Jackie, it's Eve. Not Leah.'

'Oh. Sorry, I saw Leah's name on the caller ID and assumed.' She paused. 'Is everything okay?'

Leah swallowed. She could picture her friend in her kitchen sipping her morning coffee and reading the paper. She'd probably packed Richard and the kids off to one of their weekend sports, and was going to spend the next couple of precious kid-free hours relaxing.

'No, Jackie, it's not. There's been an accident.'

She heard a sharp intake of breath on the other end of the line.

Leah continued, scared if she stopped she wouldn't be able to get the words out. 'Leah and I were going to a party and a kangaroo jumped out in front of us. I swerved to miss it, but the car skidded off the road and rolled down a pretty steep embankment.'

'Oh my god.'

'Leah didn't make it, Jackie. I'm so sorry.' Tears rolled down her cheeks as she listened for her friend's response.

When she finally spoke, Jackie's voice was so choked she could hardly understand her. 'So sorry,' was all she could make out through the tears.

'Me too, Jackie. She loved you so much, you know,' Leah found herself saying through her own tears. 'She would've done anything for you.'

Except continue to live. Except tell you the truth right now.

'Are you okay, Eve?' Jackie managed.

Of course her beautiful friend would be concerned about Eve too. 'Just a few cuts and bruises.'

'Oh, Eve. I don't know what to say. I think I need to go.' Her best friend choked back a sob. 'I can't believe she's gone.'

'Me either.'

'I'll call you tomorrow,' Jackie said. 'When I can think properly. Should I call this number or your number? I don't have that.'

'This one's fine,' Leah said. 'I'll speak to you tomorrow. We haven't made any arrangements yet, but of course I'll let you know when we have. I'm still in the hospital, but will be discharged soon.'

'Eve.' Her friend's voice dissolved into tears again. 'I'm so sorry.'

Leah ended the call and stared at her phone, imagining what her friend was going through. The reality of what she was doing was beginning to sink in. She took a deep breath. Was she going to be able to do this? Watch her friends and family grieve for her?

Her head pounded as she lay back, tears spilling down her cheeks and on to the pillow. It would get easier, with time. Leah had to believe that. She had to believe she was doing the right thing.

Sean gave the girls another five minutes before walking them into the large school auditorium. He sought the drama teacher while they put their lunches in the fridge and got themselves organised.

He explained what'd happened and ensured she had his number in case either twin became upset and needed to be picked up early. He hugged them goodbye and spent a few minutes reassuring Ava he'd drive safely, before leaving and driving to the hospital.

The fear in his daughter's eyes chilled him. The accident had left her so frightened. Sending the girls off to the workshop might've been a bad idea. He probably should've left them with his parents or taken them to the hospital to pick up Eve. Sean contemplated turning back to get them but the school would ring if there was an issue. The last thing Eve would want was the girls bugging her.

He remembered the phone call that morning. It was very unlike Eve to call the girls. On the few occasions she'd been away without them, they hadn't heard from her. Out of sight, out of mind. She was definitely vulnerable and out of sorts. Perhaps some good would come out of the accident? Perhaps the old Eve would reappear?

She'd changed when the twins were born. Her happy and carefree nature had been replaced by a hard, distant version of herself. Eve was back at work full-time three months after their birth, employing nannies and babysitters at every opportunity.

Yes, it was hard. Yes, it was tiring, but they'd *wanted* a family. To be blessed with beautiful twin girls was incredible. Sean had cut back his hours as much as he could in the early days, but eventually his caseload grew and he was back working seventy-hour weeks.

The night of the accident Eve had asked if he'd ever considered that perhaps she'd been struggling. She'd definitely struggled, but he'd never taken the time to look at why. No one else had suggested postnatal depression or anything of the kind. Sean believed – and if he was honest, still did – she just hadn't liked the changes babies had brought to their lives.

Memories of the last seven years plagued him while he continued to the hospital, eventually turning into the multi-storey car park. They weren't all bad. They'd had some good times.

The girls' birthday was always a wonderful day. Eve went all out, ensuring everything was perfect. He liked to think that was for the girls' benefit and not purely to out-do the other mothers.

He pulled into a parking spot and sat for a moment. His life hadn't turned out how he'd thought it would. His parents had a wonderful friendship and marriage and it was what he'd assumed he'd have too. But they hadn't ever had that, not really. He'd been swept up by Eve's enthusiasm for life and for him, and had found himself moving along at her speed, never thinking to say stop or to decide whether it was really what *he* wanted.

Sean turned off the car and pushed open his door. Fifteen years and two kids later, it was a bit late to be re-evaluating.

Eve's eyes were shut when Sean entered the room, her blonde hair sticking out from under the bandages. Even with cuts, bruising, and her head wrapped in bandages, she was beautiful.

Sean's breath had caught in his throat the very first time he'd seen Leah; she was stunning. To then discover an identical twin existed had blown him away. Two women who looked like this? What would've happened if he hadn't met Eve? If he and Leah had finished that first date and had another. They would've, but Eve had sabotaged it. Not that he hadn't gone along with it.

Leah hadn't seemed to mind. In fact she couldn't get out of there quick enough when Eve had said she was interested in him. Her speedy departure led Sean to assume Leah had welcomed her sister's intervention.

Sean put the small overnight bag of clothes down beside the bed and sat in the chair next to his wife, then took her hand. Eve's eyes fluttered open and she smiled. The smile reached her eyes and lit up her face. It was as if she really was genuinely happy to see him.

'How are you?' he asked.

The smile instantly dropped. 'I rang Jackie. It was horrible. I couldn't ring anyone else.'

'I'll make the calls, if you like. Actually, I did ring Peter, in case you were supposed to work today. You've worked a lot of Sunday afternoons lately, so I thought I'd let him know. I also wasn't sure about tomorrow either, with it being a public holiday.'

Her boss had sounded rather vague when Sean had mentioned Eve working on a Sunday. The accident seemed to leave him lost for words.

'He said to give him a call first thing Tuesday and let him know how you are. There's no hurry to go back. He also said to tell you how sorry he is.'

She gave a little nod, then winced. 'Head still hurts. Thanks for calling Peter. I'll make the other calls, but I'll wait until we get home. Jackie was the hardest one.'

'Are you going to ring Grant?' Sean asked. 'He'd want to know.'

Eve's face hardened at the mention of Grant's name. He was a cheat and a liar and he could see his wife had no time for the man at all. It reminded him of how sickened Eve had been when she'd found out a colleague of Sean's was cheating on her husband. She'd made it very clear that it would be the end of their relationship if he ever strayed, and yet he'd been so sure she was seeing someone else. Obviously he'd been wrong.

Leah's thoughts flicked to her ex. How would he take the news? Probably be relieved he didn't have to deal with her again and there'd be no revenge. Although he knew her well enough to know that revenge wasn't likely.

Yes, she'd ring him all right. She'd be Eve ringing, so she'd give him a piece of her mind. His parents would want to know too.

Her heart softened and guilt replaced her anger. She'd become close with Isabelle. Grant's mother had been looking forward to welcoming Leah into the family properly. She'd often jokingly referred to her as her soon-to-be daughter. She'd be very upset.

'I'll ring him later. For now, I'd better get dressed so we can get out of here.'

Sean stood and picked up the overnight bag. 'I brought you some clothes. Comfy things, hope that's okay?'

'It's perfect. In fact, anything would be better than this hospital gown. I'll get changed and then we can go.' She tentatively moved off the bed and stood. Her body ached.

She wouldn't be able to get dressed on her own. With her arm in plaster, she couldn't undo the hospital gown or easily put on any of her clothes. Leah didn't really want Sean to do it either. He was her husband, or at least he thought he was, but he'd never actually seen her naked.

'Thanks for bringing the clothes.' She sounded awkward and cleared her throat. 'I'm going to need some help.'

'Okay,' he said. 'What do you need me to do?'

It took an excruciating five minutes to get her changed.

Sean had sucked in his breath when he saw the bruising on her body. 'You're black and blue.' He helped her pull her good arm through the sleeve of a hoodie. 'Tell me if it hurts.'

Leah grimaced. Everything hurt.

A nurse came in with her discharge papers as he finished lacing her shoe. He looked up apologetically. 'Sorry about the clothes, I wasn't really thinking. I grabbed the first things I saw. I know you'd probably want to be more stylish than this.'

'They're my clothes. I make them stylish, not the other way around.' She almost laughed when the words came out. Sometimes it was easier to sound like Eve than she'd imagined. 'Honestly, Sean, it's not important right now. What's important is getting home before the girls, and trying to establish a new normal.'

Their gazes locked. From the look in his eyes, she'd said something wrong, but Leah couldn't put her finger on what.

Sean didn't respond. He collected her belongings from around the room and helped her out past the nurses' station and through the doors to the car park.

Leah smiled as Sean helped her into the house. A huge colourful *Welcome Home Mummy!* banner was draped across the front of the stairs. The letters were coloured in all different shades and a large rainbow was drawn under it.

'They were up early,' Sean said.

'They did a great job. They can do my cast when they get home too.'

'Really?' he asked. 'I thought you were kidding when you said that yesterday.'

She stared. 'Why? They'll love decorating it.'

'I know, but it's not the sort of thing you'd normally let them do. I thought it would mess with your style.'

Leah chose to ignore the sarcasm in his statements. Whatever his problem was, it was with *Eve*, not her. She needed to tread carefully. 'It will,' she said. 'But the last twenty-four hours have put my *style* and a number of other things in perspective. Life can be short, and I've got some making up to do.'

'Making up?' Sean's eyes were full of questions. Questions she didn't understand or have answers to.

Instead she nodded. 'I'm exhausted. I might go to bed, if that's okay?'

'Of course,' he said. 'I'll go and make you a cup of tea and bring it up. Do you want something to eat?'

Leah shook her head. 'Maybe later.' She started to climb the stairs then paused. 'I understand if you need to go to work today.' She remembered Eve complaining her husband often had to work

146

weekends, which made it difficult with finding someone to look after the girls.

Eve also had often been at open homes or auctions on the weekends. It was one of the reasons they'd employed Kate. She seemed happy to work any day.

Sean shook his head. 'No, I've already rung in. I've told them I'm not sure when I'll be back. There's a lot to do, and the girls probably need more attention. Ava's very anxious. She was scared to say goodbye to me this morning. I think she was worried about me driving.'

The now familiar lump rose in her throat. The poor little thing; Ava was so sensitive. Leah gave Sean a small smile. 'We'll get through this. It'll take time but we're all tough.' She went up the stairs and turned right towards the guest room. She'd often stayed there when she babysat the girls.

'Where are you going?' he called up after her.

The guest room? What was she thinking? She backtracked to Sean and Eve's bedroom, touching her bandaged head for effect. 'I'm losing it, or lost it. My mind's really muddled, Sean. You might have to put up with some weird stuff for a while. The doctor suggested I could have some temporary memory loss.' She gave a little laugh. 'If I can't even remember where our bedroom is, he might be right.'

She tried to ignore his concerned look as she pushed open the door to the correct bedroom and looked around. She took a deep breath. Could she really get into her sister's bed?

Leah didn't even know what side Eve slept on. The bedside tables were bare, other than lamps and an alarm clock. The entire room was like Eve: orderly, neat.

She walked over to the side of the bed closest to the door and opened the bedside drawer. She found a pill packet, lube and a

147

vibrator. She quickly shut it, her face heating up. It felt like she was prying. These were her sister's very personal items.

Leah went into the walk-in wardrobe and examined Eve's clothes. She needed pyjamas, but all she could find were silky teddies and a silk robe. It was winter in Melbourne, had her sister really put sexiness above comfort? She fingered the teddies and sighed.

She needed to be warm and comfortable. She glanced over to Sean's side. There were three pairs of flannel pyjamas neatly folded and placed on one of the shelves.

Somehow she managed to undress, push the cast through the sleeve of the pyjamas, and gradually get the rest on. She slid in under the duvet and sank into the bed, exhausted. It was so comfortable, especially compared to the hospital bed.

What would happen to her own bed, her apartment? And Lewis. Oh God, she'd totally forgotten about Lewis. He'd be starving. She climbed back out of the bed, wincing when she knocked her arm.

'You okay?' Sean entered the room, tea in one hand, magazines in the other.

'I remembered Lewis. Leah's cat. He'll be starving. Someone needs to look after him.'

'I'll give your mum and dad a call, if you like. Find out if anyone's been over.'

'No, I'll ring them,' she said. 'We might have to bring him here and look after him.'

'But you hate cats,' Sean said. 'When Harry asked for one for her birthday, you said she'd have to live outside with the cat if she got one, remember?'

Leah suppressed a smile. She could imagine Eve saying that. 'She'll get a nice surprise then, won't she?'

'Really?'

'Leah loved him, Sean. We can't give him away and Mum and Dad won't be able to have him. When Oscar, their last cat, died they said they were too old, too scared of falling over another cat and breaking something.'

'Okay. Give them a ring, and if no one has gone to him, I'll go.' He put the cup of tea on the bedside table next to her. His eyes widened noticing what she was wearing.

'Hope it's okay,' she said. 'My stuff's not very comfortable with the cast and bruises.'

His eyes softened. 'Of course it's okay.' He leant down and kissed her cheek. 'Now give your mum a ring and let me know what I need to do about Lewis, then try to have a rest before the girls come home.' Sean glanced at his watch. 'Kate will be here about twelve, so I'll get her to do some jobs around the place and organise dinner. She'll be able to entertain the girls this afternoon so they don't annoy you.'

'Thank you.' In fact, it sounded anything but good. She wanted the girls around her. She didn't want to share them with Kate.

The twins loved Kate, but Leah found her very hard to warm to. She knew what was best for the girls and treated them like they were her own. Not that she could really blame her when she considered Eve's parenting style.

She picked up the phone by the bed and dialled her parents' number. It went to the answering machine. Leah started to leave a message but then heard her father's voice.

'Evie, that you?'

'Yes, Pa, it's me. How are you?'

There was a silence at the end of the phone then Leah heard her mother's voice. 'Eve, dear, are you home?'

'Yes, just got into bed. I'm a bit sore, so am going to have a bit of a rest. Is Dad okay?'

Her mother sniffed. 'He's sad, darl. We both are. We never imagined anything like this would happen. But we are so grateful that we have you with us still.'

She tried to contain her own tears. Watching her parents grieve was going to be hard. She hated that she was contributing to their pain. But she reminded herself they'd still be grieving, even if they knew the truth. It wouldn't change the fact they'd lost a daughter.

'I'm worried about Leah's cat, Mum. Has anyone gone and checked on him?'

'I didn't give him a thought,' her mother said. 'I'll send Dad over now. It will give him something to do. I guess we'll have to bring him here while we try to find a home for him.'

'No. We're going to have him. The girls will love him.'

'Really? But you hate him,' Mum said. 'You sat at my kitchen not all that long ago and referred to him as a disgusting fleabag. You said you couldn't imagine why Leah would want to be tied down by something so demanding and horrible.'

Annoyance rose. How could anyone not love Lewis? He was a beautiful Seal Point Birman. His ice-blue eyes stared out from the splash of brown on his face that contrasted to his otherwise white fluffy body. He was gorgeous.

'You even joked about his name,' her mother said. 'Said it was a stupid name for a cat. I guess you could always change that.'

Leah bit down on her rising annoyance. 'Leah loved him, Mum, and that's what matters. It'll mean we have a part of her with us. I'm sure I'll grow to love him and if I don't, the girls will have enough love to keep him happy.'

'Okay, dear – well, I'm sure Leah would be very grateful.'

'What about the rest of her stuff?'

'We haven't worked out anything yet. It's all such a shock.'

'Leave her apartment,' she said. 'I'll go through it when I'm feeling up to it. I'll get Sean to go over now and get Lewis and throw out anything perishable from the fridge. The rest can wait.'

She spoke to her mother for a few more minutes, asking them to come over the next afternoon. There were arrangements to make for Leah's funeral, and other things to discuss.

Sean popped his head into the room as Leah ended the call. 'News of the cat?'

'Would you mind going and getting him? I'm pretty sure Leah kept the cat supplies in the laundry. There should be a carry basket for him, litter tray, food, bowls and stuff like that.'

'Does he have a bed or anything?' he asked.

She was about to answer but Eve would have no idea. 'I'm not sure. Do cats sleep in beds? I thought they slept anywhere. I guess have a look around the apartment, see if there is anything cat-like and bring it back.'

Lewis did have a little blanket he liked to sleep on but if Sean didn't find it he'd find himself a comfortable spot, probably next to her on their bed if she let him. She almost smiled at that thought. It certainly would arouse suspicion for Eve the cat-hater to invite Lewis into her bed.

'Anything else?' Sean asked.

'If you could empty the fridge of any perishables and empty her bin, that would be good. It'll save going back to a smell when we go and clean it out.'

'We?'

Heat flooded into Leah's face. 'Sorry. When I clean it out. I'm not expecting you to help.'

'I didn't mean that. I thought it might be something your mum and dad wanted to do.'

'I think they'd find it too painful. Also, I'm sure Leah would like the girls to have some of her things. It'll give us a chance to look through what we might like to keep for them.'

'We'll need to wait for her will to be read first,' Sean said. 'Do you know if she had one?'

She nodded. 'She had a lawyer. There's a drop file in her home office labelled "Legal".' She noticed his raised eyebrows. 'She showed it to me once, in case anything ever happened. It has her will and his details in it.'

'Okay, I'll grab that too. I'd better go so I'm back in time to pick up the girls. Try to have some rest. I'll leave a note for Kate not to disturb you.'

Leah was woken by a heavy weight landing on her middle. She opened her eyes, the unfamiliar surrounds of Eve and Sean's bedroom bringing back everything that'd happened since the accident.

She couldn't help but smile when Lewis's face appeared over the duvet and pushed into hers.

'Hello, you,' she said. 'I hope you've had some food.'

The cat purred and continued to push against her face. She stroked him with her good hand and laughed when he moved off the bed on to the bedside table, managing to knock her phone to the floor and almost upset the lamp.

'Sorry.' Sean's voice came from the doorway. He strode across the room and grabbed the cat. 'You're coming with me, buddy. This room is definitely off limits.'

'Hold on,' she said. 'Let's let him explore. I'm going to need to get used to him so we might as well start now.'

'Really?' Sean was still holding the cat, who squirmed to get loose.

'He's a good distraction from my own thoughts, to be honest.'

He put the cat down on the floor and Lewis immediately jumped up on to the bed again and pushed his face into Leah's. She couldn't help but laugh.

Sean's eyes were wide watching them. 'I never thought I'd see you laugh at a cat doing that. Imagine if you had make-up on and he did that. You probably wouldn't find it so funny then.'

'Probably not,' she agreed. 'He might not either, if he ended up with scarlet lipstick on his white fur. But I'm not made-up, and I'm drugged up to the eyeballs so I'm probably not myself, anyway.'

He smiled.

Leah imagined him wondering how he could buy those drugs in bulk.

'I've set up his litter tray in the laundry, and he's already used it so I don't think we'll have any problems,' Sean said. 'And he had a bowl of biscuits so I imagine he'll now explore and then go to sleep. That's what they do, isn't it? Sleep?'

'No idea,' Leah said. She'd better not become a cat expert all of a sudden. 'Guess we'll find out.'

Lewis nudged the duvet cover up and crawled down inside the bedclothes. Leah felt him turn a few times before lying against her leg.

'Where'd he go?' Sean asked.

'I think his exploring is complete. It seems he's found a spot to sleep.'

Her sister's husband waggled his finger in the air. 'That's a one-off, buddy,' he said to the covers. 'No way is that becoming a regular sleeping place.' He turned to Leah. 'Kate's downstairs. Can she bring you something to eat?'

She nodded; she was starving. 'I'd love a sandwich.'

'Tuna?'

Leah stared. Eve's favourite of course, but she hated it. She shook her head and motioned towards Lewis's body. 'Better not, might have a riot on my hands if he gets a sniff. Toasted ham and cheese would be nice.'

'Really?' Sean asked.

Damn! Ever health conscious Eve would *never* ask for that.

Heat rose in Leah's cheeks. 'I guess I feel like comfort food right now.'

'I'll get her to bring it up,' he said. 'I'm going to go and get the girls. Give them the option to come home early. I'm worried about them, especially Ava. I'm thinking I should've kept them with us today.'

'Don't worry. We'll make it up to them this afternoon.'

Leah watched Sean as he left the room, a look of wonder on his face.

Was she really acting so differently from Eve?

Leah buzzed with nervous energy when a quiet knock on the door signalled Kate was outside with her lunch. How well did Kate know Eve? Not very, she hoped.

The nanny came into the room, her plump face full of concern. 'I'm so sorry about your sister, Mrs West.' She placed the tray carefully on the bed beside Leah. 'So very sorry.'

'Thank you, Kate. And call me Le— I mean Eve.'

'Are you sure?' Kate asked. 'You were very clear when I started that you preferred Mrs West.'

'I'm sure. Perhaps it's the bump to my head, but the accident seems to have put a few things into perspective. Some changes need to be made. This is a small one of course.'

The girl nodded. 'Okay, Mrs— Eve.' She said the name as if she was trying it out. Kate smiled and pointed to the lump that was now purring in the bed. 'That sounds like another change. The girls will be very excited.'

'It might help. Give them a part of Leah they can still love.' She looked down at her lunch while Kate's eyes filled with tears. 'Thanks for the sandwich. I'll eat it and try to get up before the girls come home.'

'Oh no. You must rest. I'll send them in to see you and once you've had enough, you let me know and I'll entertain them.'

She was about to object but Eve would only have put up with the girls for a few minutes.

'Also, Sean said you wanted a toasted sandwich? I made one but included a salad and some fruit for you. I thought he might've got the sandwich wrong. After all, you don't usually eat bread.'

Not eat bread? Shit, how did she not know that? Eve ate bread, didn't she? She recalled all the lunches they'd shared. Usually salads, Thai or sushi.

'The doctor said I should try to eat something more substantial than salad,' Leah lied. 'It's good for my sore head or something crazy.' She picked up the toastie. 'I'll give it a go, but thanks for the salad and fruit too.'

She took a bite of the sandwich as Kate retreated from the room. The cheese oozed into her mouth and the ham was warm, coated in butter. It was delicious.

How could Eve give up bread? She'd need to contemplate what Eve *did* eat. She'd feign memory loss and talk to Kate to work it out.

She was feeling a lot better by three o'clock when she heard the front door open and the excited chatter of the twins running up the stairs. Sean called to them, and their noise stopped.

A tentative knock on her door reminded her she was Eve. Not fun, cuddly Aunty Leah.

'Come in, if you're seven or younger.' She smiled as giggles erupted on the other side.

The door pushed open, and the girls entered the room. Ava had her soft-toy squirrel under her arm. Harriet bounded over to the bed while her sister hung back a little.

'How was your day? Was the workshop fun?' she asked.

Harriet immediately launched into a monologue of how the day had gone, who'd messed up their lines, and which part she'd enjoyed playing the most.

Ava remained quiet.

'You okay, Avie,' Leah asked. She patted the bed next to her.

'I'm sad about Aunty Leah still.'

'Me too, honey. But I've got something special that I hope might help.'

Harriet clapped her hands together. 'What? Chocolate?'

'No. Not food.' She shifted in the bed and used her good arm to pull back the covers.

Ava's eyes widened, and she gasped when Lewis's furry body was revealed.

Harriet squealed, waking the cat in the process. He stood, arched his back then stretched before sitting back down to start washing himself.

The girls moved closer and stroked him.

'Are we keeping him, Mummy?' Ava asked.

'Would you like to?' Leah said.

The little girl nodded.

'Yes, please,' Harriet said.

'Then I think we should.' Leah said. 'Your aunty would want us to love him and look after him for her. Next to you two, she loved Lewis more than anything.'

'And you.' Sean said from the doorway before he entered the room. 'How about the girls and I take Lewis downstairs for some games and give you a rest? Or not,' he added. His eyes questioned hers.

Her disappointment must've been obvious.

'We haven't decorated Mummy's cast yet,' Harriet said. 'It looks very plain.'

She held it up. 'It sure does. Definitely needs some colour on it. It's whiter than Lewis. Why don't you get your markers and get started?'

The girls dashed out of the room, Lewis close on their heels. It appeared he thought this was a game, and he was ready to play.

The twins' laughter could be heard as something crashed over, and screams of 'Oh Lewis,' filtered back to the bedroom.

Sean smiled. 'They've got a scapegoat now,' he said. 'Or *scape-cat*, I should say. Kate wanted me to check with you that you really want her to call you Eve. She's worried that the whack on the head has caused you to do strange things, and she doesn't want to get fired when you return to normal.'

Leah shook her head. 'It seems to have taken a whack to my head to make me realise I need to make some changes. Something happened last night, Sean. It was weird, but it made me see things much clearer. I don't know, it was almost like Leah came to me. Told me things. I can't explain but I do know that I need some things in my life to change. Leah dying' – the words caught in her throat as the image of Eve, her face bloody and swollen, came to her – 'is a real wake-up call. Just bear with me. I know I'm acting weird, but hopefully it's good weird?'

He nodded. 'I've got a few things to do before dinner, so I might leave the girls to colour you in. Okay?'

'Of course.'

'Send them down to Kate when you've had enough or get tired.'

'Will do.'

157

He left the room as Lewis and the girls came bounding back in, coloured markers in hand.

She held out her broken arm. 'Come on then, make me beautiful.' Leah moved so that the little girls could join her on the bed.

'Sean?' Kate poked her head into his study. 'Should I get the girls from Mrs West? I mean Eve? They're still with her, and I'm worried she might be getting tired.'

'Sick of them, more likely. I'll go up. Is dinner nearly ready? It'll be a good excuse to drag them away if she's still pretending she wants them with her.'

'Do you think she's pretending?'

Sean sighed. 'I'd like to say no, but I think that knock to her head has temporarily done something to her. That and Leah.' He coughed. 'I guess it's softened her a bit for now. She's vulnerable. In shock. It'd be nice if she stayed like this, but I wouldn't count on it.'

'We can all enjoy it while it lasts. It's nice for the girls for a change.' She reddened. 'Sorry, it's not my place to make comments like that.'

He laughed. 'You say it as you see it. No need to apologise.'

'Thank you. I'll have dinner on the table in five minutes. I'll make up a tray for Mrs— for Eve.'

'Thanks, Kate. I don't know what we'd do without you.'

Sean made his way to the stairs. He really didn't know what they would do without Kate. She kept things running. Kept a sort of balance with the girls. Provided the loving, safe environment that having two working parents didn't. The girls knew where they stood. They came home to the same person every day. It might not be a parent, but it was the next best thing.

He smiled at the sound of giggles coming from the bedroom. It wasn't a sound he heard often when it came to his wife and their daughters. To see her making such an effort was amazing. He'd assumed she would've curled up in a ball and wanted everyone and everything kept away from her while she grieved. He wouldn't be surprised if that was still to come.

Sean arrived at the room to find Ava concentrating on the picture she was drawing, and Harriet on the floor with Lewis throwing a ping pong ball. The cat was chasing and batting at it. Colour had returned to Eve's face, and she was laughing while the cat skidded all over the floor chasing the ball.

'He's crazy,' Harriet said.

'Nope,' his wife replied. 'He's a cat. That's what cats do.'

'Do you like him, Mummy?' Ava looked up from her drawing. 'It would be nice if we could keep him.'

Sean stood in the doorway and waited. Ava was smart, she knew this mood of Eve's was unlikely to last.

'We have to keep him, Aves,' Eve said. 'It's what Aunty Leah would want. And yes, I've decided I do like him. I'm not sure why I didn't like him before.'

'You said his fur got on your black pants,' Harriet said. 'You said you hated cat and dog hair getting on your work things.'

'Mmm. I'll have to make sure I don't cuddle Lewis with my work clothes on.'

Sean stared. She was actually contemplating cuddling the cat. Something *really* wasn't right with her.

Leah looked up as Sean cleared his throat from the doorway.

'Girls, dinner's ready. Why don't you bring Lewis down with you and we'll see if he wants some biscuits or a drink? I've got some special cat milk he might like.'

Ava put the final touches on her zebra picture, and clicked the lid back on her marker. 'Do you like it, Mummy? I know it doesn't really look like a zebra.'

The round body and stumpy legs could've been any animal but the black and white stripes confirmed it was a zebra. 'I love it. Best zebra I've ever seen.'

The little girl smiled. 'I'd better go and wash my hands.'

Ava got down off the bed and followed her sister, who was half carrying, half dragging Lewis with her.

Leah slowly moved herself to the side of the bed. She hoped Eve had some slippers. If her pyjamas were anything to go by, though, the slippers would probably be high-heeled.

'Do you need a hand?' Sean asked.

'No. I'll find some slippers and then come down. I'm assuming no one cares if I have dinner in your pyjamas?'

'Kate's organising you a tray so you can stay in bed.'

She shook her head. 'No, thanks. I'm getting sore lying there all the time. I need to move around a bit. Try to get rid of some of my aches and pains. And anyway, I'd rather eat with you and the girls.'

Sean's mouth dropped open.

'I don't want to be with my own thoughts, okay?' Leah added quickly. Tears welled in her eyes. While she might be pretending to be Eve, what she was saying was true. 'Every time I close my eyes, I see the kangaroo. I see the car sliding off the road and I hear the click of my sister's seatbelt. I still can't believe she did that. What was she thinking?'

'Survival. She must have thought it was the only way out.'

'For me, the only way forward is to put it out of my mind. Surrounding myself with you, the girls and even the bloody cat will help me do that.'

'*The bloody cat.* That's more like the Eve I know. I was getting worried.' He went into the walk-in wardrobe and brought back a

160

fluffy, navy robe and a pair of ankle-high UGG boots. 'I'm assuming you're not above wearing these boots tonight? Brand new, never worn. *Hideous*, if I remember your words on Mother's Day after the girls gave them to you.'

Leah grimaced. 'Did I say that?'

He nodded.

'Must be my head. It seems to be messing with my memory.'

'Really?' He ran his hand through this hair. 'Do you honestly not remember saying that?'

'It's hazy. I'm sure it is something I'd say. But I don't actually remember saying it.'

Sean's eyes narrowed. 'What else don't you remember?'

She couldn't help but laugh. 'You're asking me? How would I know if I don't remember?'

He smiled. 'Of course, sorry. I thought you were mucking about.'

'No. You'll have to tell me if it's something I've forgotten or usually do differently. I'm sure I remember most things, just not everything. But I do remember I'm starving. Let's go downstairs.'

Leah let him take her good arm and help her down the stairs.

The next morning, Leah managed to get her pyjamas and the bandage around her head off. With the waterproof bag the hospital had given her over her plaster cast, it took a while, but she was able to shower herself.

She left the gauze pad on her forehead, which covered the gash they'd stitched, but decided the bandage was overkill. With one hand she managed to wash and condition her hair and get rid of the feel of the hospital.

Her mind flashed back to the accident, to Eve, her body bloody and broken.

Her last words.

Leah's own inability to save her. Her stomach churned, and within seconds she found herself retching. The contents of her stomach quickly disappeared down the shower drain.

She gave the shower a quick clean and dressed slowly in black sweat pants and a pale pink hoodie. Eve didn't have many casual outfits but what she did have was new, branded and very comfortable.

Leah put the pyjamas on the chair next to the bed and took off a pillowcase one-handed. She needed clean sheets. She'd not showered when she'd come home from the hospital the day before and everything felt yuck. It also smelt like Eve's perfume and she needed every reminder gone.

'What're you doing?' Sean asked.

'Everything feels a bit manky. I wanted to put clean stuff on the bed.'

'Leave it for Kate,' he said. 'She'll be here in about an hour. That's one of her jobs. She won't mind doing it today.'

'She's coming this morning? I thought she didn't work on public holidays?' The fact that the nanny had the audacity to take any day off, *ever*, always had Eve complaining very loudly. 'Another thing I've forgotten?'

'No, you haven't lost your mind this time. She offered. She knew you'd be tired and thought we might want some help with the girls. They're already up, by the way. They've had breakfast and are playing outside in the cubby house.'

'That will work well. Mum and Dad are coming over after lunch. It'll be partly to talk about a funeral and to deal with Leah's affairs, so definitely good if the girls aren't around. Did you get her lawyer's file the other day by the way?'

'Yes, and I rang him. He's a colleague, so will look after us. He's going to check Leah's will and then he'll get in touch. He'll email through a copy of it to the executor and any beneficiaries. Do you know who the executor is?'

'Me.'

'Good, that'll make things simple,' Sean said. 'Did she ever talk about the type of funeral she'd want or whether she wants to be buried or cremated?'

Leah nodded. 'I know exactly what she wants. We had too many drinks one night and had a morbid discussion about death and all the things that come with it.'

'And you remember that?'

She smiled. 'Yes, even though we'd drunk far too much that night, I clearly remember her instructions. I'll go through it when Mum and Dad are here, if that's okay?'

'Okay. Now, I'll go and round up the girls and make sure they're not torturing poor Lewis. I've got no idea where he slept last night, by the way. I looked everywhere for him.'

'Oh, you know cats.' She kept her tone vague. 'They tuck themselves into the strangest of places.' She didn't let on that Lewis had slept with her all night. Sean had opted to sleep in the spare room so he didn't accidentally bump or hurt her arm and Lewis had cuddled up to Leah, like he did every night in her apartment.

The doorbell rang and her heartbeat immediately quickened. She was on edge every time the door or phone rang, expecting the police to arrive and announce that they'd identified Eve's body and knew she was Leah.

Sean ran down the stairs and Leah heard him talking. 'She's upstairs, Nicola. I'll check if she's up for visitors.'

She came out of the bedroom and stood at the top of the landing. 'I am,' she called. 'Give me a minute and I'll come down.'

Sean raced to her side to help her on the stairs.

She could smell Nicola before she saw her. Wafts of Chanel No. 5 drifted up to the landing at the top of the stairs. Leah smiled as she reached Eve's friend, who was heavily made-up, her short black skirt and boots more suitable for a night out than a Monday morning.

'You look very dressed up. Going somewhere?'

Nicola regarded her oddly, but leant in to hug Leah. 'Um, thanks. Visiting you, then I might head over to South Yarra and do some shopping.'

'Sounds nice. Feel like a coffee?'

'That'd be great. I was so worried about you, I had to drop in. Sorry it's unannounced, but your phone is going straight to voicemail.'

'Oh,' Leah said. 'I think I forgot to charge it. I'm fine though.'

'You don't look fine.' Nicola's eyes travelled the length of Leah's body.

She could imagine what Eve's friend was thinking. No make-up, sweats and a hoodie. She'd even put the UGG boots back on. They were so warm and soft. 'I know I don't look like myself, but to be honest, right now I don't feel like myself. I'm pretty sure I'm still in shock. It's a huge loss, Nic.'

'I know. I'm just used to you bouncing back from things so quickly.'

'This isn't something I'll bounce back from.' And it wasn't. Losing her sister was going to take a long time to accept. Sure, she had the distraction at the moment of taking over her life and having to learn the ropes, but she still had to come to terms with the fact that Eve was *gone*.

'Mum and Dad are coming over later to make arrangements for the funeral. I'm not sure how we're going to get through that.' Leah couldn't imagine how she'd feel standing at her own funeral, watching family and friends mourn for her while she was the only one mourning Eve.

They went through to the kitchen, where Sean was preparing a coffee for Nicola and green tea for Leah. 'I'll make these and leave you to it,' he said.

Nicola waited until Sean left the room and leant in. 'You two look rather cosy,' she said.

'What do you mean?'

'The way he helped you down the stairs. The way he's looking at you. I haven't seen either of you like that for months.'

'He's my husband, Nic. This is a huge shock for everyone. Of course it's brought us closer.'

Nicola studied her. 'What about Ben? Have you even called him?'

'Ben Styles?'

She rolled her eyes. 'Yes, Ben Styles. What other Ben would I be talking about?'

'I'm not dealing with anything work-related right now. I'll probably ask Peter to give him a call, and anyone else I was working closely with. Really, Nic, I know I was obsessed with work before the accident but it's really not a priority at the moment.'

Her sister's friend was staring. '*Work?*'

Leah nodded. 'I've got so much to do and to worry about. In addition to the funeral arrangements we also need to work out what to do about Leah's apartment and all her things. I've got the girls to think of too. To top it off I'm dealing with a dodgy memory and trying to piece together bits and pieces of my life.'

'Dodgy memory,' Nicola muttered. 'That I'll definitely agree with.'

'I hate to imagine what I've forgotten.'

'How to dress, for starters.'

Leah almost laughed but obviously the woman wasn't joking. Did she really expect Eve to care about clothes and make-up when she was sore, had a broken bone and her sister had just died?

She observed Nicola's perfectly made-up face and how over-dressed she was for a shopping trip. Her answer would most definitely be *yes*.

'It's not important right now. The girls are important, my parents are important. It's a rough time.'

'Someone needs to look after you too, Evie. And as it obviously isn't going to be you, I'll have to take charge.' She stood. 'Leave it with me. I'll make the arrangements and whisk you off to the spa. An afternoon of Tony and our regular might bring you back to earth and return you to your normal self.'

'Let's leave it for a few weeks, Nic. I'm too sore to enjoy it right now.' A whole afternoon with Nicola didn't appeal at all.

'Okay, but once those aches are gone, you're all mine. Deal?'

Leah forced a smile. Nicola wasn't someone she could imagine spending time with, but she was Eve's best friend. She was trying to do something nice. But how she wished it was Jackie sitting across from her. She'd be making her popcorn, renting movies and refusing to get out of her pyjamas. Pure comfort pampering.

They finished their drinks, but she had to force the green tea down. It was an aspect of Eve's life she doubted she'd ever embrace. To her relief, when Nicola finished her coffee, she made motions that she'd better get on with her day.

Kate arrived while Leah walked Nicola to the front door.

'Kate, would you mind doing me a favour?' Leah asked.

The nanny nodded.

'I was hoping you might change the sheets on the bed in the master bedroom. They feel a bit grotty after sleeping in them straight from the hospital.'

'Of course, Eve. I'll head straight up and do it now.'

She thanked Kate and turned back to find Nicola had walked the short distance from the front door to the drive. She stood next to her car, hand on the door handle, eyes bulging, unblinking.

'It's not a favour, Eve! It's her bloody job. Have you forgotten that too? And what's with this *Eve* stuff? She's hired help, it's *Mrs West*.'

Leah forced a smile. Nicola's voice was loud. No doubt Kate had heard every word. 'We've dropped the formalities around here. And on a public holiday, when she's not even supposed to be here, it's a favour.'

Go, you spoilt-rotten bitch. She stood and waved with her good hand as Nicola backed down the driveway.

She'd never be able to be the Eve Nicola knew. To avoid suspicion, she only had one option: to keep well away from her.

Leah was grateful Kate had taken the girls out to the park shortly after her parents arrived. The weight of their sadness was stamped clearly on their faces, and even her mum's best effort to be cheerful for the twins' sakes had failed dismally.

Harriet had rushed to show her grandparents Lewis, and chatted on like nothing had happened whereas Ava had held back. Her grandparents' sadness was mirrored on her little face.

With the girls out of the way, Sean brought the coffees Kate had made for everyone to the living room with a plate of freshly baked scones. Leah guessed the scones would most likely go untouched.

Her sister's husband handed around copies of her will. 'Leah's lawyer, Douglas Parker, said he'll be contacting each of the beneficiaries separately by mail, but seeing the will is very straightforward he's emailed it through so, we can have a look at it and ensure we follow Leah's instructions.'

Her mother's hand shook as she took the document. 'Why don't you read it to us, Sean? You're a lawyer, so it will seem official that way.'

He began reading. It only took a few minutes. He looked up at the end. 'Very straightforward. She's basically left everything to Eve, other than twenty-five thousand dollars for each of the girls to be put away in trust until they turn twenty-one. Her only other instruction is, if her parents have survived her, they're to be allowed to take any personal items they might like to keep. She's asked to be cremated, and she's pre-paid her funeral and made some basic requests with Greyson's Funeral Home. The rest she's leaving up to Eve, as her executor.' Sean addressed his in-laws. 'I'd assume from this will, Leah thought she'd outlive both of you.'

Leah turned to her parents. 'I'm happy for you to have anything at all you like, and we can sell the apartment and anything else and split the money. I'm sure Leah would've wanted you to have a share if she'd realised she'd be gone so early.'

Her father spoke for the first time since they'd arrived. 'I'd like the chess set she bought especially for me and her to play on, but other than that, we don't need her money.'

Her mother agreed. 'If you don't need it, then put it away for the girls' future. Leah would love to know she'd helped pay their school fees or contributed to their first cars or a deposit for a house once they leave home.' She wiped her eyes. 'She loved those girls so much.'

'There's probably not a lot we can do regarding her funeral until we talk to the funeral home tomorrow,' Sean said. 'Although you might want to give thought to the personal touches you'd like that Greyson's won't know about.'

'Dad, did you want anything in particular at the funeral? Bible readings or anything?' How religious would her father expect the service to be?

'No, whatever you and your mum think's best. Nothing will bring her back, so it really doesn't matter. She wasn't religious, so we'll do it how she would have wanted.'

Leah leaned back in her chair, the finality of his words sinking in. He was right. Nothing would bring her back. She watched her father rise and walk out to the backyard.

'He needs time, love,' her mother said. 'We all do. It's only been two days. We don't all have your resilience.'

That was a dig at Eve, at the way *she* was behaving. What her mother didn't realise was she was so preoccupied with ensuring she was behaving like Eve, not like herself, at times it was easy to forget her sister was dead.

Planning her own funeral was also quite surreal. She couldn't plan it as if it were for Eve, because their tastes were so different people would think it was strange. She'd never hear the end of it . . . thinking about herself and not her dead sister. So instead, she made suggestions for the personal touches she'd like at the funeral.

They still had several people to contact. While Leah and her mother discussed the funeral arrangements, Sean took on the difficult job of making the phone calls.

'He's been amazing,' she said. 'I only called Jackie, and that was hard enough. He's called everyone else.'

'He's a good man,' her mother said. 'A very good man. I sometimes worry you take him for granted.'

Leah agreed. Eve *had* taken him for granted. 'Everything's different now.'

Her mother nodded, as if understanding that the enormity of their loss would have an impact on Eve. She had tears in her eyes when she took her hand. 'It's terrible that it's taken this, but if something good comes out of it, then that will be a blessing.'

She pulled her mother to her and held her. The older woman stiffened in her arms at first; this was very unlike Eve, then eventually she relaxed and the tears flowed.

'Oh, Eve, I'm going to miss her so much,' her mother said. 'She was such a lovely girl. So generous, so loving. I'm not sure your dad and I will ever recover.'

Leah squeezed her mother; there were no words to help her.

They went back to their planning and by the time Sean finished with the phone calls, her dad returned to the living room and declared it time to leave.

He hugged her. 'Sorry, love, I can't deal with all this today. Thank you for taking charge. You always were good in a crisis.'

Sean closed the front door when they were gone and turned back to face her. 'You okay? You look done in.'

Leah nodded. 'They're a mess.'

'Particularly your dad.'

'They were so close.' She and her father had had a special bond. How she would miss that closeness.

Harriet and Ava came racing down the stairs. She hadn't even realised they'd come home. 'When did you—?'

'Lewis has gone mad, Mummy,' Harriet cried, cutting her off. 'He's at the top of the curtains; I think his claw is stuck. Kate tried to get him down, but he hissed at her.'

Ava's face crumpled when Harriet relayed the news. 'Please don't send him away, Mummy. I know he's been bad, but we'll teach him not to climb the curtains.'

Leah swallowed. Eve would've had a fit if a cat had scaled her curtains. 'Lewis isn't going anywhere. Aunty Leah would want us to look after him, and forgive him when he's naughty.' She suppressed a smile, thinking of Eve who was probably shooting daggers at her from the afterlife. 'Come on, let's go and rescue him.' Her body ached as she moved up the steps.

Sean was staring open-mouthed from the bottom of the staircase.

'I'm not going to be able to get him with my arm in a cast. We'll need your help.'

He grinned and raced up the stairs, slowing when he caught up. He took her by the good arm. 'Bet you're not so calm when you see the holes that giant fur ball's put in your designer drapes.'

Leah glared. *Giant fur ball.* That was hardly any way to talk about Lewis. No doubt Sean would interpret her display of displeasure as being angry about the curtains, which was good.

Definitely more Eve-like.

Chapter Eleven

Leah had two jobs on the Tuesday following the accident. She was grateful for Kate's early arrival to help get the girls off to school. She'd registered the surprise on the nanny's face when she'd arrived to find her in the kitchen helping the girls get their breakfast and organising their lunches.

Sean had already left for work. He'd offered to take the week off but Leah had told him to go. It would give her some time to herself, which she desperately needed. She still had to call Fitzy to tell him the news. It was the one call she'd insisted she make, not Sean. She also wanted to ring the funeral home and make an appointment to see them. Her mum wanted to go with her but her father had decided it was too hard.

'I can do the lunches, Eve,' Kate said. 'I thought you'd be in bed resting?'

She shook her head. 'No, I can go back for a rest once the girls are at school. I wanted to spend some time with them first.'

'At least let me finish the lunchboxes. It'll take you forever with one arm,' the nanny had said, taking over before Leah could object.

She'd taken her coffee to the table instead, and sat with the twins while they spread their toast with the avocado she'd managed to slice with one hand.

'You put sugar in your coffee.' Harriet giggled as she pointed at Leah's cup. 'That's poison.'

She smiled. She'd done it automatically, not even thinking about Eve's aversion to sugar. The fact she even drank coffee was surprising. Leah pointed to her head, which still had the gauze strip on it. 'I'm doing all sorts of strange stuff,' she said. 'It must be this bump on the head. You're right though, it is like adding poison.' She took a sip and moved her head closer to the girls. 'Don't tell anyone, but it actually tastes better.'

Ava stared. 'That's how Aunty Leah has her coffee. White with one sugar. You normally have it black.'

She swallowed and took Ava's hand. 'You know what, I seem to be doing a few things Aunty Leah did. I guess it makes me feel closer to her. I miss her, hon.' Tears welled in her eyes. She'd never get to talk to her sister again and it was still overwhelming.

Ava's little face crumpled. 'Don't cry, Mummy, I didn't mean to make you sad.'

'Oh darling, you didn't make me sad. Don't ever think that, okay? You and Harry are the very things that are keeping me going.'

The little girl nodded.

'Now, why don't you finish your toast and go up and brush your teeth. Kate will take you to school this morning, as I can't drive for a few weeks.'

'And you don't have a car,' Harriet said.

'That's true. I guess we could drive Aunty Leah's car once my arm's better.'

The girls looked at each other. Of course, Eve wouldn't drive her car. Eve in a Prius, even a new one? No way.

'I mean, until the insurance pays us some money and we can get a new Audi or BMW. What colour do you think we should get?'

'Blue,' Harriet said immediately.

'Purple,' Ava said. 'I've never seen a purple car. I wonder if they even have them?'

'We'll do our research and find out. Now off you two go and brush your teeth. Be back down here in ten minutes. Okay?'

The girls rushed off to get ready and Kate immediately moved over to the table and started clearing the dishes. Leah was about to tell her she'd do them, but stopped herself. Eve's practice had been to go to work, ignore her daughters and allow the nanny to do everything house-related.

She had plans to change that over time, but she didn't need to start now. Instead she stood and took her coffee to the living room. She paused at the fireplace, scanning the photos Eve had selected for the room. Tears fell looking into her sister's eyes on her wedding day and holding the twins in her arms in hospital. Photos of the girls on their second and fifth birthdays had been framed and put on the wall.

It was the photo of Eve and Leah, their arms around each other on their thirtieth birthday, that Leah paused at for the longest. Eve had organised an extravagant event, inviting both her own and Leah's friends. It was much flashier than anything she would've organised, but it'd been a wonderful night, topped off with a speech Eve had given when the giant cake had been brought out.

Her twin had made a point of saying how important her sister was to her; how they'd always been there for each other. They always knew what each other was thinking. What the other needed. She'd said how lucky she was to have a sister like Leah.

Leah had raised her glass, tears filling her eyes at her sister's uncharacteristically emotional speech. She'd mouthed 'ditto'. It was all she'd needed to say.

Looking at the photo now she thought back to those words. That they *always knew what each other needed*. Eve had been right, and it gave Leah comfort. Right now she was doing exactly what her sister needed her to do.

The call to Greyson's Funeral Home had been easy. An appointment had been arranged for the following morning, and the funeral booked for Friday at eleven a.m.

Leah had called her mother and asked her to pick her up on the way to the funeral home the next morning. Once those arrangements had been made, the next call she needed to make was to Barry Fitzpatrick.

She took a deep breath and dialled his direct number.

'Fitzpatrick, make it quick.'

'Barry, it's Eve West here. I'm Leah's—'

'Yeah, I know who you are. Real Estate agent. Better dressed version of Leah. Can you rub some of your dress sense off on her, do you think? It'd make working here more bearable. What do you want?'

God, he was so offensive. It was certainly one benefit of her new identity, not having to deal with Barry Fitzpatrick ever again.

'Leah was involved in an accident on Friday night.'

'Oh great. Let me guess, she's got you to ring in and pretend she's sick? Tell her she'll need a doctor's certificate, and if she's off at job interviews, tell her not to bother. No one will employ her.'

She was silent for a moment and then she spoke. 'Leah told me what a prick you are. A rude, crude, sexist pig and now I hear it for myself.'

Laughter erupted from the other end of the phone. 'Got a bite to you, that's what I like to see. Tell you what, Eve, if you're ever

175

looking for a job, let me know. With your straight talking you'd go a long way in my business. And another gorgeous face around here wouldn't hurt either.' His laughter boomed down the phone again. 'Now, tell your sister her hangover, or whatever's really wrong with her, had better be gone by tomorrow.'

'Not possible. She's dead.'

There was silence at the other end of the phone.

'Leah was killed in a car accident on Friday night. She won't be in tomorrow. She won't be in, ever. If you could pass the message on to the staff she worked with, it would be appreciated. Her funeral is at eleven on Friday at Greyson's on High Street in Prahran.'

'Oh, Eve.' The arrogance had been replaced by sadness in Fitzy's voice. 'I'm really—'

Leah didn't want to hear it. She ended the call. If the only time he could show any sympathy or compassion was when someone died, she didn't want to know.

Sean's hand shook as he attempted to do up his cufflinks. He took a deep breath and exhaled. He'd tried, unsuccessfully, to get rid of the feelings of guilt he had over the accident. Eve had assured him she wasn't distracted by his words. That the moment she'd picked up Leah, the two of them hadn't even talked about him. That they'd joked and laughed all the way to the party. That they were singing along to ABBA, without a care in the world. She'd tried to lighten the situation. Even told him he had tickets on himself assuming she'd have wasted so much energy on him.

He knew his wife well enough to know that could very possibly be true. She was good at blocking out things she didn't like and moving on, pretending they'd never happened. Maybe she *had* done so the night of the accident?

If she had, and *if* he believed her, why did he still feel so guilty about Leah?

The more he'd allowed himself to think about his sister-in-law, the more the truth dawned. His guilt went back a lot further than the accident. It went back to the night he and Leah had gone on their first date.

The night Eve had hijacked it – hijacked him. The night his wife had decided he was for her, *not* for Leah. His guilt went back fifteen years. To a night when he'd sat through a movie with Leah, butterflies in his stomach, itching to kiss her. To a night when he'd been swept away by Eve's energy. By her obvious attraction to him.

It was a night where he'd got a lot further than just kissing his date. Eve had done things to him that had pushed all thoughts of Leah out of his mind. She'd been able to convince him he'd made the right choice. He'd only second-guessed his decision many months later at a dinner at Eve's parents' house.

The moment his eyes connected with Leah, he'd felt it again. The butterflies. The attraction. But it had been too late.

He and Eve had been there to announce their engagement. He'd never apologised properly for that first date. For the way he'd abandoned her. With the cufflink finally secured, Sean took a last look at himself in the mirror.

His face was pale, his eyes tormented with guilt. He'd never get the chance to apologise now.

Leah had gone through Eve's wardrobe earlier in the week to find something suitable for the funeral. She'd be the best-dressed person there if she chose to be. As Eve, she had to be.

She'd settled for a black Vera Wang lace gown. It was classy, elegant and exactly the type of dress she imagined her sister would wear to a funeral. With the addition of a pair of sage green Miu Miu pumps she would definitely exude Eve's personality. She added Eve's beloved Tiffany dew drop earrings to complete the look. It always surprised her that Eve wasn't more elaborate with the jewellery she wore. She loved watches and earrings, but rarely wore any other jewellery, and had a complete aversion to rings. An aversion Leah was grateful for. The thought of having to slip Eve's wedding ring on and pretend it was hers made her shudder. Ridiculous considering she'd *slipped* Eve's entire life on, but it did.

Sean came up behind her as she tried to wrap a shawl around her shoulders. 'Here, let me help you.' He took the fabric and draped it around her. 'You look amazing,' he said.

He was dressed in a black Armani suit, silver cufflinks gleaming on his shirtsleeves and an aquamarine tie that brought out the green in his eyes. It was one Leah had given him some time ago. 'So do you,' she said.

'Leah gave me this tie.'

'I know, and I'm sure she'd want you to wear it.'

'I hope so. Now, we'd better make sure the girls are ready.' He glanced at his watch. 'The car will be here in ten minutes.'

The vehicle drew to a stop in front of Greyson's Funeral Home at ten forty-five. Leah's stomach contracted as she recognised many of her friends already milling around in the garden leading into the venue. They were here to say farewell to her. She was having an out-of-body experience.

She gripped Sean's hand as he helped her out of the car. Ava and Harriet took Kate's hands.

Leah had asked her to travel with them to look after the twins. How much she could handle today was unknown. She'd be the only person thinking of – and saying farewell to – Eve. Everyone else would be saying goodbye to *her*.

Her legs trembled when they passed through the doorway and into the reception room. She stopped. The rich, sweet fragrance of jasmine hit her first. It was exactly how she'd imagined it when she'd discussed the requirements with John Greyson earlier in the week.

The room was filled with flowers. A mixture of apricot roses and jasmine. It was pleasant, comforting. Her eyes travelled to the front of the room where her parents were standing, their backs to her, in front of the elegant mahogany coffin they'd chosen.

Leah's own instructions had been for a basic coffin, but at the funeral home she'd acted more like Eve. She'd upgraded everything to the best and insisted on paying the difference. In fact, she'd acted so much like Eve, her mother had demanded she stop.

Eve, we have to follow Leah's wishes. This isn't your funeral, it's hers.

Sean squeezed her hand.

She still hadn't moved from the doorway. She put one foot forward and walked towards her parents. Hugs were exchanged, and she smiled gratefully at Kate who was sitting with the girls, talking quietly to them and pointing out different features of the chapel.

Leah took her seat in between Sean and her mother and waited. The pews behind them started to fill. She didn't dare turn; couldn't bear to look at anyone. She was dreading the wake, and particularly seeing Jackie. Having to look her friends in the eye and make small talk as if she didn't really know them.

Music started to play and *her* friends, family and work colleagues filled the room. Leah never expected so many people would care enough to come to her farewell. She snuck a quick glance behind and spotted Fitzy towards the back. He was wiping his eyes with his handkerchief. Tears filled her own eyes and rolled down her cheeks when she glimpsed Jackie, her eyes smudged with dark circles, face pale, clinging to Richard. She knew the heartache her friend was feeling exactly.

The service began with John Greyson's welcome for everyone to the celebration of Leah's life. He read the eulogy Leah, with the help of her mother, had spent hours preparing.

It was a true reflection of her life. Leah dwelt on Eve while John's words of where she'd grown up, where she'd been to school, the places she'd travelled and more filled the room. She remembered Eve as a little girl and the things her sister had loved. The naughty things she'd convinced her to join her in doing. The protectiveness she'd shown her when Leah had been bullied in the early years of high school.

She remembered how Eve had excelled at basketball and soccer, but hardly bothered with her schoolwork. Nights out drinking and dancing with Eve and her friends. Birthdays and celebrations. Being in the birth suite when she'd delivered the twins.

Her eyes closed as memories flooded over her in waves. A squeeze of her hand brought her back to the present as John finished by saying Leah's nieces would like the opportunity to say goodbye to their aunt.

There wasn't a dry eye in the room when Harriet, hand in hand with Ava, went to the small podium and microphone. Ava's lip trembled as she clung to her sister.

Harriet smiled while the microphone was lowered to her height. 'Good morning,' she said. 'Ava and I would like you all to know our Aunty Leah was the most special aunty in the world.'

Leah felt like her heart would break watching the little girls.

'She was kind and funny and made the best cakes ever. She loved us and she loved her beautiful cat Lewis, who we are now looking after.' Harriet stepped back and pushed Ava towards the microphone. 'Your turn,' she hissed.

The look on Ava's face was of pure terror.

Leah wasn't surprised. A room full of people staring and crying; she doubted Ava would be able to speak, but the little girl proved her wrong.

'My aunty taught me and my sister many things. She taught us how to tie our shoelaces, how to play Monopoly and Twister. She even taught us how to draw animals. Especially her favourite, the zebra.'

Smiles and soft laughs could be heard throughout the room. Leah wiped her tears. The twins were doing a wonderful job. Eve would be so proud of them.

'But,' Ava said, 'the most important thing our aunty taught us, and we will always remember, is we were special to her, and she would've done anything for us.'

Harriet joined Ava now at the microphone for what was obviously a pre-planned moment.

The girls spoke at once. 'We love you, Aunty Leah. We'll think about you every day and we'll miss you forever.'

The smiles and soft laughs were immediately replaced with sniffles and more eye-wiping, as the girls returned to their seats.

'Thank you, girls, for that wonderful tribute to an aunt we can all see you loved very much,' John Greyson said. He looked over at Leah. 'And now Leah's sister, Eve, would like to say a few words.'

She took a deep breath before standing and making her way to the front of the room. She cleared her throat, acutely aware everyone was waiting for her to speak. Leah couldn't make eye contact with any of them. She'd break down.

She tried to muster a smile and shifted her focus to Ava and Harriet. Ava with her sombre little face. Harriet a beaming smile.

'Leah would've wanted to thank each of you for attending today. I think she would've been overwhelmed by how many people have come to say farewell to her. I know she would've wanted you to remember the friendships you had with her and to see you smiling, thinking of the good times.' She closed her eyes briefly. This was the only chance she'd ever get to honour Eve. There was a lot she needed to say.

She cleared her throat again. 'Last Friday, I lost a part of myself, a part that always kept me accountable and seemed to know my own mind just as well as her own. I was lucky – beyond lucky – to have a twin. We were identical in looks, but many of you will know, that's where our similarities ended. Leah was known to be gentle, loving, kind.' She smiled. 'As sisters, we had so much to learn from each other and we did. Our triumphs, our failures. We shared them together. I know that moving forward, I'll be trying to integrate the best of Leah's qualities into my own life to make sure she continues to live on for both myself and my family.' Leah wiped at the tears streaming down her face.

Many of her friends and family dabbed at their eyes.

Her voice broke as she managed a few last words. 'I will never forget you.' There was so much more she wanted to say about Eve, but she couldn't.

She walked back to her seat. Sean put an arm around her.

More tears flowed when her parents stood together and read a poem in Leah's honour. Her dad's hand shook so violently that her mum had to take the paper from him and hold it for the two of them.

They took their seats while Robbie Williams's 'Angels' filled the room.

Eve had loved that song and Leah had insisted, when planning the service, that it was the perfect song to accompany photos of her sister's life.

Following the slideshow, the congregation was invited to sprinkle rose petals on the coffin and say their goodbyes before they all stood for the Lord's Prayer. Finally, the recognisable music of

'Somewhere Over the Rainbow' filled the church, signalling it was time for people to leave.

Leah wiped her eyes and checked on how her parents were coping. They were both crying. Her father was slumped forward, his head in his hands.

She put an arm around her mother and hugged her. Her mother shuddered; her tears turning to great sobs. Leah drew her close and held her until they subsided. By the time she pulled away, the room had emptied, the music finished.

'I'm sorry, love,' her mother said dabbing at her eyes. 'This is the hardest thing I've ever had to do.'

She squeezed her hand and glanced at her father.

Sean had moved around and taken him by the arm. 'Come on, Bill,' he said. 'Let's get you out of here. Do you think you can handle the wake?'

Her father drew himself up to full height. 'For Leah, of course.'

Leah's heart swelled watching her parents. Guilt kept sweeping over her, but each time it rose she was able to push it away. She wasn't putting them through something unnecessary. The bottom line was their daughter had died.

Kate was wiping Ava's tears. Leah left her parents and went to the twins, sitting on the pew and pulling Ava into a hug.

Harriet shifted closer, but with her arm still in plaster she couldn't hug them both.

'Aunty Leah would be so proud of you. It's a very grown-up thing to speak at a funeral. This is the first time I've ever done it too. She loved you both so much.'

The twins nodded.

'Now, after a funeral we go and have a party to celebrate the person's life. There'll be food and drinks and lots of people. Some you might know, and some you won't, who might want to talk to you. Does that sound okay?'

Harriet nodded, but Ava looked uncertain.

She rubbed Ava's arm. 'If you don't like it, Ave, Kate will take you both home. Okay?'

'We'll try the drinks first,' Harriet said. 'Won't we, Avie? They might have pink lemonade.'

Leah smiled. She hoped Harriet's ability to live in the moment would rub off on Ava.

They made their way out of the funeral home to the now-crowded lawn area where a group of her work colleagues were standing together, Fitzy with them. Her extended family were gathered in a group. Her grandmother was dabbing her eyes, being comforted by one of her aunts.

There were quite a few people she didn't recognise at all. She waved at Nicola who was standing with a few of Eve's friends. She went over to them and was immediately drawn into hugs and constant murmurs of condolence. She thanked them all for coming and made a little small talk before Nicola took her aside.

'Ben's here.'

'Ben Styles?'

Eve's best friend looked at her quizzically. 'He's hoping to talk to you.'

A feeling of unease immediately settled over Leah. She didn't know Ben Styles, so why would he have attended her funeral? 'Tell him I'll see him at the wake. We're about to head off.'

Nicola squeezed her hand. 'Okay, I'll let him know.' Her sister's friend moved through the throng of people to the back.

A pair of brilliant blue eyes stared back at her from a rugged, incredibly handsome, face. It was obvious why he'd have no trouble with women. She turned as an arm touched hers. It was Sean.

'Come on, it's time to leave for the wake.'

Leah allowed him to guide her through the foyer, and out to the waiting cars.

She sank against the back seat and closed her eyes. This had been hard enough, and she hadn't even had to talk to any of her own friends yet.

Leah was pleased her parents had agreed to hold the wake at The Hove, an upmarket pub in Brighton that Eve had always called her favourite. The funeral home hadn't had a room big enough and she didn't want her parents, or herself, having the extra work of hosting it at home, so booking the pub exclusively for three hours with an open bar and finger food had seemed a perfect solution.

A murmur of conversation filled the main bar area and people were already spilling out into the beer garden. She checked that the twins were happy with Kate then disappeared to the ladies' room. She studied her reflection; she needed to do some damage control. The tears at the funeral service had left their mark. She went through the bag of Eve's she'd chosen for the service and selected her supplies.

A few minutes later she stood back, admiring her work. With scarlet lipstick, she was made up exactly as she imagined Eve would have been. She had put everything away and was zipping the bag when the door to the ladies' opened.

She froze. It was Jackie.

Her best friend took one look at her and burst into tears.

Leah immediately went to her, putting her good arm around her. 'Oh Jackie,' she said. 'I'm so sorry.'

Jackie pulled away. '*You're* sorry? God, ignore me, it's just that with you looking so much like Leah . . . it's really hard.'

'Looking *exactly* like Leah, you mean?'

She nodded. 'Although, I could always tell you apart. The way you dress, your make-up. You were both so different.' Her best

185

friend burst into tears again. 'I miss her so much, Eve. I can't even imagine how you're coping. And the girls too. Thank God you weren't badly hurt. Imagine your poor girls if—' She stopped.

Leah was glad for what she'd nearly said. Once again it reinforced she'd made the right decision.

'I was lucky,' Leah said. 'Very lucky.'

'I feel so bad for her. Everything was so messed up before she died. Grant. Then her shit of a boss. She felt like nothing was going right. She was suddenly thirty-five, single and in a job that had no future. She was really down when I last saw her.'

'Perhaps it was better that way? Imagine if she and Grant had announced their engagement, and she'd got promoted to a different department at *The Melbournian* and then *this* happened. It would seem so unfair.'

'It's unfair, regardless,' Jackie said. 'He's here you know.'

'The shit of a boss? Yes, I saw him.'

'Not him. Grant.'

Her heart raced. 'He'd better bloody *not* be. He didn't bring the pregnant girlfriend, did he?'

'He's with someone,' Jackie said.

Anger seethed through Leah. 'He does *not* get to come here and pretend he cares.' She checked herself in the mirror one more time and gave Jackie another quick hug. 'I know you were Leah's friend not mine, but I'd like to stay in touch. I think she'd want us to. Now, time to get rid of an unwanted guest. Leah would *not* want that cheating son of a bitch here.'

Jackie managed a weak grin. 'She always said you were the fiery one. You'll be doing her proud, Eve.'

With those words firmly planted in her head, she stepped out of the ladies' room. She scanned the friends and family who stood in small groups throughout the room.

Then she spotted him.

His face was pale. His suit looked new; more appropriate for a wedding than a funeral. Her anger went up a notch. Had he actually worn his *wedding suit* to her funeral?

A woman hung on to his arm. She was attractive, early thirties, long brown hair and slim. Leah assumed she was Katrina. Although she was dressed carefully, the ruffled front of her dress definitely showed a small bump.

Sean was walking towards her and she held up her hand to indicate for him to stop. She made a direct line for Grant.

He looked up as she approached him. 'Eve. I'm so—'

She grabbed him with her good arm. 'Save it. I want to speak to you outside.' Leah dragged him after her, aware that the woman was following.

The moment they were standing on the footpath outside the pub she turned on him. 'You've got a cheek showing your face here. You need to leave.'

'I needed to pay my respects.'

'Really? Respect? Do you think any of your actions in the past few months have shown Leah *respect*? You need to leave. Now.'

Grant had the good grace to look at the ground.

She glared at Grant's girlfriend. 'Make sure he treats you and your baby well. I know Leah still cared about him, but she was hurt by him – hurt badly.'

The girlfriend nodded. 'I know, and I wish I could tell her how sorry I am for what happened.'

Leah stopped. 'You knew he was in a relationship?'

She was unable to meet Leah's eyes. 'I feel awful, so awful.'

'Because she's dead, or because of what the two of you did to her?'

The look that passed between them gave her the answer. Their guilt was because she'd died, not because they'd cheated.

'You deserve each other,' she snapped. 'I only wish for Leah's sake she'd realised six years ago you weren't good enough for her.' She didn't wait for an answer, but instead turned on her heel and made her way back inside.

Jackie was waiting inside the door, a glass of champagne in each hand. She handed one to Leah. 'Good job. She'd be proud of you.'

She clinked glasses with her best friend. 'To Leah,' she said and then downed it in one gulp.

Jackie smiled. 'Leah said you didn't drink. I think she was wrong.'

'She wasn't wrong. I don't drink *much*, but today I think I'll drink her share too.'

'Your girls are super cute.'

Leah looked over to where the twins were standing together. Harriet passed Ava a cup to add to the growing pile of cups around them.

'I think Harry's decided to try all the drinks,' she said. 'The guy at the bar might have to cut them off the way they're going.' She glanced at Jackie. 'Come and meet them.'

Her friend put her glass down and followed.

The girls looked up as Leah and Jackie approached.

'This is Jackie, Aunty Leah's very best friend in the entire world.' She squeezed Jackie's arm as she saw her friend's eyes well up. 'She helped Aunty Leah through lots of hard times, and lots of good times too. She was like another sister to Aunty Leah. She probably knew her better than I did.'

'Can you tell us some stories about her, Jackie?' Harriet asked.

'Of course I can. How about we move over to those squishy chairs by the window, and I'll think of some of the things I loved best about your aunt? Now do you want to hear about when she was good or when she was naughty?'

'Good,' Ava said.

'Naughty,' cried Harriet.

Jackie laughed. 'A bit of both, perhaps?'

Leah felt a hand on her back as she watched them go.

'Just wanted to check how you are doing,' Sean said.

She took a deep breath and tried to muster a smile. 'Not very well. This is so hard.'

He pulled her to him and she sank into the comfort of his arms.

Leah closed her eyes while he stroked the back of her head.

When she opened them again her attention was captured by a set of piercing blue eyes staring at her through the window from the beer garden.

Sean felt Eve stiffen in his arms.

'You okay?'

His eyes followed her gaze. The most startling blue eyes he'd ever seen stared at them. The guy's eyes were locked with Eve's. He appeared to be in his late thirties. The cut of his designer suit leaving no question about whether he worked out or not.

The man was not someone Sean recognised. His gut churned when his wife shifted uncomfortably in his arms. He let her go. 'Who's that guy?'

'Ben Styles. He's a property developer. I've done some work for his company, and I'm supposedly working on a large development of units with him.'

'Supposedly?'

'I remember his name but that's all. Leah mentioned him to me recently. According to Nicola, I've worked with him, but I have no memory of it.'

'He looks like he wants to talk to you,' Sean said. 'Shall I come too?'

'Yes, come and meet him,' Eve said. 'I'm not really sure why he came today. I doubt he knew Leah.'

They walked outside to the beer garden. When they reached Ben Styles, Sean held out his hand and introduced himself.

Ben did the same.

'Thanks for coming today,' Sean said. 'How did you know Leah?'

'Through Eve,' he said. He leant forward and kissed Eve's cheek. 'I'm so sorry. Truly I am.'

Sean watched Eve closely. Her face was clouded in confusion. She really was having difficulty placing him.

'You might have to remind Eve how you know each other. She had a massive whack to the head in the accident and is finding it difficult to remember things.'

Ben's mouth dropped open. 'Really? You don't remember me?'

She gave an apologetic smile. 'I recognise you, and I remember a little. We've worked together before. I have a vague memory of some properties in South Melbourne. A large renovation?'

Ben glanced at him, then back to Eve. 'That's all you remember?'

Nicola joined them. She slipped her arm through Sean's. 'Could I whisk you away for a minute? I have a few questions I wanted to ask you about a legal problem I'm having.'

He glanced at his wife. 'Okay?'

Eve nodded, and he allowed himself to be dragged away by her friend.

Leah smiled at Ben as Sean was led away by Nicola. 'I have to be honest with you,' she said. 'I don't remember much about the

190

projects we've worked on together, or are supposed to be working on. I can't even get my head around why I'd be working with you on a development, other than to sell it at the end.'

He hesitated, his blue eyes piercing hers. 'You really don't remember?'

She shook her head. 'Sorry. No, I don't.'

Pain flickered across his face. 'Is your memory likely to come back?'

'I hope so. The doctors haven't been able to promise anything. You said to my husband you knew Leah through me. Had you actually met her?'

He shook his head. 'No, but you talked about her many times. I came today to show my respect and to be here for you.'

'That's very kind of you.'

'We were – are – more than work colleagues, Eve. We're very good friends too.' His eyes searched hers. 'Surely you must remember something?'

Leah shifted uncomfortably. The intensity in Ben's look suggested he did know Eve. He knew her *well*. But when she and Eve had discussed Ben Styles, her sister hadn't given any indication she knew him well, yet Nicola had implied she did.

'I'm sorry. I don't remember.'

Ben shook his head and gave a little laugh. 'I'm not sure what to say. You're looking at me like I'm a complete stranger.'

'I'm sorry, but that's how it feels. You're not the only one I'm having this trouble with if it's any consolation?'

'Not really, but I guess all we can do is wait and hope your memory comes back soon.' He leant forward and kissed her cheek again. 'Call me when you do remember me. When you remember *us*. We have something special, Eve.'

Unease filled Leah's stomach as he made his way back into the bar and out of sight. His words certainly implied something *more*

191

than friendship. She'd warned Eve about his reputation, but Eve had felt strongly about cheating.

Her reaction to the news of Grant's affair had been enough to confirm it wasn't something she'd ever condone, or do. But . . . Ben's reputation for getting women into bed was also known.

She could just imagine her sister enjoying flirting with him. It was another difference between the two of them. Eve had been a terrible flirt. She used her looks and her confidence to her advantage in all sorts of situations, but she never took it beyond the flirting stage.

Her sister had joked about finding it much easier to close a deal when she was dealing with a male client. Had Ben misread Eve's signals? Nicola certainly seemed to think something was going on between them. He might be charming, but her sister knew where to draw the line. Didn't she?

Leah walked back into the bar area. She smiled at Harriet who skipped past her into the beer garden with Ava trailing close behind.

Jackie and Richard were sitting together at the window where she'd left the girls earlier. Richard had an arm around her friend and was whispering something into her ear. Jackie gave a slight nod.

She took a deep breath, wishing with all her might she'd been able to avoid hurting Jackie, and walked over to them.

'Eve.' Richard stepped forward and kissed her on the cheek. 'How are you?'

She managed a small smile, her eyes fixed on Jackie. 'Coping, Richard. That's about all right now. How are you doing, Jackie? My girls looked like they loved hearing the stories you were telling them. Thank you for that.'

Jackie met her eyes, causing her to swallow the lump that had formed in her throat. The pain that met her gaze almost made her turn and leave. She stepped closer and took her best friend's arm.

'You know, Leah talked about you all the time. She loved you like a sister.' She managed a smile.

Tears spilt down Jackie's cheeks. 'She *was* a sister to me too. I'm not sure how I'll ever come to terms with this.'

'Me either,' Leah said. The grief at losing Jackie's friendship was as real as if *she* had died. 'It'll take time, but I hope there'll be a point when we can look back and think of all the great times rather than what's happened now.'

She nodded. 'I hope so.'

'I'm sure Leah would want you remembering that time you two snuck off to Sydney for the weekend and bumped into Kylie Minogue in George Street. Although, from what she told me, I'm surprised either of you remember anything at all. Sounds like you were completely wasted for the entire weekend.'

They were only seventeen and had decided to go and see what Kings Cross in Sydney was really like. Their adventure had included lying to their families, using most of their savings for flights and accommodation and discovering very quickly that Kings Cross was not for them. That hadn't stopped them having a fantastic time and, of course, drinking far too much.

Surprise flickered across Jackie's face. 'I didn't realise you knew about that. We swore each other to secrecy. We were taking it to our graves.' Her eyes filled with tears. 'Sorry, but you know what I mean. Not that it matters now.'

Leah could've kicked herself. She'd never told *anyone* that story. Not even Eve. She hated Jackie thinking she'd betrayed her. Even if it was years ago. 'She only told me because one of my friends saw you in Sydney at the airport. Asked me how come Leah got to go and I didn't. Don't worry, she swore me to secrecy too. I've never told anyone, until now.'

The shadow of a smile flickered across Jackie's face. 'It *was* an amazing weekend,' she said. 'I'll never forget it. Leah's face when she realised it was Kylie Minogue was priceless. You'd think she'd bumped into the queen the way she acted. She practically curtsied.' She laughed.

Jackie was right, she almost had.

'Eve,' Richard said. 'Jackie and I thought we might give our condolences to your parents, and then leave, if that's okay? The kids are with my parents but we need to get back to them. I think Jackie's probably had enough.'

Leah nodded. 'Of course. This might sound weird, but can I come out and visit you one day?'

Jackie exchanged a look with Richard.

'We don't know each other very well,' she said, 'but I feel like we should. Leah was so important to both of us. We definitely have that in common.' Butterflies flittered in her stomach as she waited for an answer.

She couldn't imagine not seeing Jackie, losing her friendship completely.

Jackie searched in her purse for a card. She handed it to Leah. 'Why don't you bring your girls with you,' she said. 'Leah was always telling me how wonderful they are. I'm sure they'd get along with our two. Poppy's six, so not far behind your twins.'

She took the card. 'I'd like that. I'll wait until my arm is better and I can drive. Then I'll give you a call.' She stepped forward and enveloped Jackie in a one-arm hug. 'She really did love you, you know.'

Her words resulted in another flood of tears from her friend, causing her own tears to spill. She was grateful for the tissue Richard held out for her.

They said a final goodbye and, with Richard's arm wrapped around Jackie's waist, moved over to where her parents stood.

Her poor parents.

Her dad had stuck close to her mother all day. His grief was so raw it was hard to look at him. She felt another stab watching him extend a hand to Richard. He was trying his hardest. He'd do anything for her.

Tears continued to flow as the family said goodbye to the last of the guests and began making their own preparations to go home. The twins were tired, yet Harriet seemed to be talking constantly.

'Is she okay?' Leah asked Sean.

He looked at his daughter and grinned. 'Harry, how many of the drinks did you try?'

A guilty flash crossed the little girl's face. She glanced from her father to Leah. 'Not many,' she said.

'It's okay. I don't mind what you drank,' Leah said.

'She tried them all,' Ava said. 'Three times each.'

Sean exploded with laughter. 'You've had fifteen sugary drinks?'

Harriet grinned. 'Guess so. I feel great. Did you know that Ava and I—'

Sean clapped a hand across his daughter's mouth. 'Time to go, Harry Barry. We'll get you home and have you run around the garden for an hour. Burn off some of that sugar.' He winked at Leah, taking Harriet's hand in one of his and Ava's in the other. 'We'll meet you out the front,' he said. He lowered his voice. 'Your dad looks like he wants to have a chat.'

Her father was waiting behind them. Her mother was talking to the pub's manager.

Leah took a step towards her father, noticing his hands were shaking. 'Dad? Are you okay?'

He shook his head and allowed her to guide him into one of the foyer's chairs.

'It's been a big day,' she said. 'A very hard day.'

Her dad's face contorted with pain. 'The hardest.'

She took his hand in hers.

'I need to ask you something, Eve,' her father said. 'Something about Leah. About the accident.'

Leah swallowed. Talking about the accident wasn't something she wanted to do at all. It was hard enough blocking out memories of the horrific crunching sounds as the car was tossed and smashed. They plagued her at different times throughout the day, particularly when she lay down to go to sleep.

The blood. Eve's final words. Her broken, dead body.

She tensed waiting for her father to speak.

He took a deep breath and brought his eyes up to meet hers. 'Did she suffer? Was she in pain?'

The truth would kill her father. Eve had been in pain. Agony, she imagined. She had known she was going to die. It'd been horrific. Her stomach churned as she relived the last few minutes of Eve's life. She brought her hand to her mouth and tried to shake the feeling. It did no good.

She excused herself and made a hurried dash to the bathroom, which luckily was situated off the foyer. She pushed open the cubicle and emptied the contents of her stomach into the bowl.

Her good hand trembled as she flushed and then came out to the sink to wash her face and mouth. She looked into the mirror. Whether she was Leah or Eve, she was a very pale version of herself.

She splashed water on her face and rinsed her mouth, her thoughts going back to her father. What on earth would he be thinking with that reaction from her? Leah could hardly tell him how traumatic she was finding even thinking about Eve.

She stood for a few moments willing some colour back into her cheeks before returning to her father.

He was sitting on the edge of his chair, her mother now next to him. He stood up when she approached. 'You okay, love?'

She nodded. 'Sorry, the day caught up with me, that's all.'

Her father shook his head. 'No. I asked you a question and thinking of the answer made you sick to your stomach.' He wiped beads of sweat from his forehead. 'That gave me my answer.'

Leah shook her head. 'No, it didn't.' Lying to her father would be the only way she could do this. 'Leah was unconscious, perhaps not even breathing, by the time the car stopped rolling. If she felt anything it would've been for a split-second only.' Tears filled her eyes. 'She never came to when I tried to revive her. She was already gone. She didn't suffer, Dad. We're the ones suffering.'

His eyes searched hers, needing confirmation she was telling the truth.

'Really. She would've been frightened, like I was, when the car left the road, but it all happened so quickly.'

Tears slid down her father's face. He pulled her to him, careful not to hurt her broken arm. 'Thank God,' he whispered in her ear. 'Thank God.'

Chapter Twelve

The stale air of the hospital corridor permeated Leah's nostrils. She shuddered as the smell brought back memories of her stay. It'd been two weeks since they'd buried her sister, three since the crash and once again, she was back staring at a crack that ran the length of the white wall.

She'd been to see her own GP the day before who'd been insistent Leah not only see a neurologist for an MRI and have further tests relating to her memory loss, but that she should also talk to someone about the accident.

When she'd originally been in the hospital, they'd given her the card of a highly recommended psychologist who dealt specifically with grief resulting from road accidents. Leah had put it aside, not wanting to go there just yet. But with her own doctor so adamant, she'd realised that perhaps it was a good idea. As the wait to see Eve's psychologist in Richmond was more than three weeks, she had called, and now, thanks to a cancellation, only twenty-four hours later, she was sitting in the waiting area.

Although the consulting rooms in the hospital were more clinical, for Leah they still held memories of a few weeks earlier.

Sean's face was buried in a magazine, his eyes scanning the page. He'd taken the morning off to bring her. She hadn't quite figured out what was going on with him. He said the right things, did the right things, but there was a huge distance between them. It wasn't because of the accident, or the fact she wasn't actually Eve. This issue existed before the accident.

The night Ava was sick, Sean had been angry with Eve. Dismissive of her working late. Her sister had commented on his moods but hadn't elaborated on the cause of them. Then there'd been the night of the accident. Eve had chosen not to talk about what Sean had said to her, but from her mood it had obviously been bad. The lack of affection between them told Leah that something was very wrong. She would have to talk to him at some stage and try to get to the bottom of it, but nerves fluttered in her stomach at the very thought.

Someone called her sister's name, jarring her. Sean looked up. 'Did you want me to come?'

She shook her head. 'No, I don't think she's expecting two of us. The appointment is for an hour, so if you want to go and get a coffee or something?'

He put the magazine back on the pile and stood. 'Okay, I'll meet you back here.'

Leah followed the receptionist past three consulting rooms before being ushered into a large office. The nameplate was embossed with the name Dr Rachael Shriver.

Dr Shriver sat at her desk, her lean fingers pounding her keyboard. She stood as Leah came into the room and rounded her desk, extending her hand. Her smile was warm and reached her green eyes. With her salt-and-pepper hair, neat black suit and thin-rimmed glasses, she exuded experience and professionalism. 'Hello, Eve, I'm Rachael.'

Leah took her hand and returned the smile.

'Come, sit down.' She indicated a small meeting area comprising two comfortable-looking armchairs and a small table on which sat a jug of water, two glasses and a small box of tissues. 'I work from the hospital two days a week but the other three I work out of my own office in Richmond. I noticed from your file that you live in Brighton, so that might be more convenient for subsequent visits.'

Leah sank into one of the chairs, grateful she hadn't been faced with a couch. She'd never seen a psychiatrist or psychologist so hadn't been sure what to expect. The clichéd scenario of lying on the doctor's couch had crossed her mind.

'How are you, Eve?'

The simple question caused tears to flood her eyes. She'd been so busy since the funeral, trying to fit in to her new role of mother and wife, she'd had little time to think of herself.

Rachael passed her the tissues.

She took one and wiped her eyes. 'Sorry, such a simple question. You'd think I could answer that.'

The woman's smile was full of sympathy. 'I think your face might've answered that for me. You've been through a terrible trauma, not only losing your sister, but the road accident itself. It'll take time.'

Leah nodded.

'I saw from the file your doctor sent across that you've been experiencing some memory loss? And you have an appointment scheduled with a neurologist next week?'

'Yes.' She would prefer not to discuss it. She lived in constant fear someone would guess she couldn't remember events because she'd never been at them.

The 'memory loss' had only been brought up with her GP because Sean had insisted on accompanying her to the appointment and was present during the consultation. He was worried about her, he'd said. Worried she was doing some strange things and wanted to hear from the doctor that it was normal, that it was a result of the concussion she'd received and hopefully temporary.

The doctor had listened to Sean's account of Leah's memory issues and referred her to a neurologist. He believed, since she was having trouble remembering incidents from before the accident, she might be suffering from retrograde amnesia. He'd warned them that there was no definite cure for amnesia, but at least if they knew what they were facing they could look at ways of helping 'Eve' moving forward. It wasn't like Leah could correct them.

'What sort of things have you been struggling to remember?' Rachael asked.

How to live a life that's not actually mine would be a good place to start. How would the psychologist react if she told her the truth? Would she call the police? Would she be allowed to?

There was probably some kind of doctor-patient confidentiality, although she doubted it would extend *that* far and she wasn't willing to find out.

'Silly things mostly,' Leah said. 'Places I've supposedly been to. Jobs I was working on. I can't remember a lot about my best friend. I know we were good friends, but I'm driving her mad as in many ways she feels like a complete stranger.'

'This is Nicola you're talking about?' She glanced up from her notes. 'The friend whose party you were travelling to on the night of the accident.'

'Yes.'

'It's quite normal to block out memories of people who you might subconsciously link to the accident.'

'It wasn't Nicola's fault,' Leah was quick to say.

'No, of course not. But she *is* closely related to that night, due to it being her birthday, her party. Our minds work in very strange ways, putting blocks in place when the trauma is so great that we feel we can't revisit it.'

Leah's lack of knowledge when it came to Nicola had nothing to do with the accident. It had to do with the fact that she hardly knew her. But she couldn't say *that*.

'Do you remember the afternoon of the accident? What you were doing before you got into the car to go to the party?'

Leah flinched as images of the accident flashed in her mind. She remembered the afternoon, Eve turning up with the costume she needed to wear, but her mind kept moving to the accident itself. She shuddered at the memory of her sister undoing her seatbelt. Nausea hit in waves and she closed her eyes.

When she opened them, Rachael was holding a glass of water out for her. She took it gratefully and sipped it, hoping to settle her stomach.

'You were remembering something painful?'

'The memories of the accident play over in my mind.' Leah glanced around the office, her eyes resting on a heavy wooden bookcase, the feature of one wall. 'They make me feel sick, to the point of vomiting.'

'That door through there' – the psychologist pointed to a small door behind her desk – 'leads to a bathroom if you need it at any time through our session.'

'Thank you, I might.'

'Let's talk about Leah,' Rachael suggested. 'You were identical twins?'

Her stomach settled as the conversation moved on to safer ground. She told Rachael about the close bond they'd had as children, the connection that remained even when they'd become more independent of each other as adults. The nausea overtook her again.

She excused herself and made it to the toilet just in time. Was it going to be like this forever? Each time she thought of the accident was she going to vomit? Was it guilt? Guilt that she had taken over Eve's life and not given their family or Eve's friends the chance to mourn her?

She shook her head. Her number one priority was the girls, and being a mother to them. It was what Eve had asked of her and she'd agreed.

Leah washed her face and rinsed her mouth before returning to the office.

Rachael was jotting down something on her notepad. 'Better?'

'Yes. Thank you.'

'Does that happen a lot? The vomiting?'

'Quite a bit. Usually when memories of the accident come up. Not so much when I'm only talking about Leah.'

'Any vomiting yesterday?'

'Yes.' Vomiting had become quite a regular thing; usually linked back to thoughts of the accident or Eve's battered body.

The previous morning, Leah had woken from a nightmare where she'd been standing on the road where the kangaroo had been and was trying to ring Eve on her mobile to tell her to stop; that she'd have an accident if she kept driving. She kept fumbling with her phone, unable to key in Eve's details and at the same time she could hear the car travelling around the winding mountain road.

Her own scream had woken her when the car had rounded the final corner, skidded to avoid her and slid through the barrier ready to travel down the hill. She'd only just made it to the toilet as her stomach heaved.

'Do you think it's anxiety related?' she asked.

Rachael stared for a moment. 'Very likely. Unless there are any other physiological reasons causing it.'

'Physiological?'

The doctor smiled gently. 'Is there any chance at all you could be pregnant?'

Pregnant?

Leah stared. Oh God, she couldn't be pregnant. Could she?

She'd had sex with Grant two or three times a week, right up to a few days before he'd ended their relationship. She closed her eyes.

How would she be able to continue the charade of being Eve if she was pregnant? What would she tell Sean?

'Eve?'

Rachael's voice jolted her, and she opened her eyes.

'You're white as a sheet. I assume pregnancy is something you hadn't considered?'

Leah shook her head and forced herself to speak. 'It's complicated.' She'd wanted a baby since she'd turned thirty. She couldn't believe she was already thirty-five, and didn't have any children.

She would've happily married Grant a year after they'd met and settled down to start a family. He hadn't been ready at the time, which was understandable. She almost laughed at the irony of it. Grant, who hadn't wanted a family, was going to be a father twice over in a very short space of time, if she *was* pregnant.

Her hand flew to her mouth, willing herself not to be sick again.

'Would you like me to organise a test for you so we can rule pregnancy out?' Rachael asked. 'It's quite likely you are experiencing a reaction based on grief and anxiety but I think we should check to make sure.'

Rachael made a phone call and ordered the test.

If she was pregnant, was there any reason she had to tell Grant? Morally, yes, but right now her behaviour was so void of any morals there was no reason she actually had to tell him. Sean and Grant had similar colouring. Would she be able to pass off the baby as Sean's? Eve often implied they had an active sex life, so there was no reason he'd question it. But could she do that to any of them?

Leah took a deep breath and waited while an assistant knocked on the door and handed Rachael a box.

The psychologist brought it over and gave it to Leah. 'You don't have to do it now. Take it home if you prefer. You can tell me the result next week when we meet.'

'Okay.' Relief settled over her. She wasn't ready to do the test now.

'We've got another ten minutes,' Rachael said. 'For now we'll assume the vomiting has been brought on by anxiety so I'll teach you a few relaxation techniques.'

Leah only half-listened.

What would she do if she was pregnant? It had the potential to ruin everything.

Leah found it hard to concentrate on Sean's questions on the ride home.

She did her best but when a stony silence fell over the car, it dawned on her that she hadn't done very well. 'Sorry. The session brought up a lot of horrible stuff about the accident. I keep seeing Leah.'

He squeezed her good hand. 'It'll take time. Do you think it was worth going?'

'I think so.' Leah's mind was already in the future, imagining a baby. *Her* baby. Assuming she let Sean think it was his, she'd be

205

having a baby with a man she'd never slept in the same bed as, let alone had sex with. Could she be *that* dishonest?

They pulled into the driveway and she excused herself, feigning exhaustion. As the girls weren't due home from school for another three hours, Sean suggested she take a nap.

She slowly climbed the stairs and made her way along the hallway to the master bedroom. She closed the door and went straight into the en suite, grateful for the lock on the door.

Leah removed the box Rachael had given her and conflicting emotions raced through her. Surely anxiety was the cause of her sickness. But if the circumstances were different – if she and Grant were about to get married – she'd be willing the test to show positive. Finally, the baby she'd always dreamed of.

She took out the plastic stick and read the instructions – she'd never done a pregnancy test before. Removing its cap she sat down on the toilet and did as instructed. Then she replaced the cap and watched the little window.

Three minutes it said it would take.

She let out a breath she'd been unaware she was holding. It didn't take three minutes. It took less than one for two pink lines to appear.

Leah stared.

She was pregnant.

Chapter Thirteen

Leah glanced around the waiting room, half expecting Sean to appear at any minute, while she waited for her credit card to be returned by the receptionist.

She'd had her cast off earlier in the week so she was allowed to drive again. She certainly hadn't wanted Sean at *this* doctor's appointment.

It had been bad enough that he'd insisted on accompanying her to the neurologist the week before. He was worried about her 'memory loss', which was understandable, but it had added a lot more stress to the appointment. The neurologist had gone through her medical history, physically examined her, run cognitive tests and booked her in for an MRI two days later.

Since she was pregnant, Leah had cancelled the appointment and told Sean it'd been rescheduled and she was waiting for a new date. It was something to avoid during pregnancy, but there was nothing wrong with her anyway.

The neurologist had looked puzzled during her examination and had explained her symptoms were representative of retro-grade amnesia, a type of amnesia where memory loss was isolated to before an injury or traumatic event. He'd suggested that the memories would most likely return over time, and assuming the MRI didn't show anything unusual, they'd continue to monitor her.

She collected her card and left the surgery. She only had space for one thought right now – her baby. Leah smiled and walked into the car park. The doctor had confirmed her pregnancy and believed she was seven or eight weeks along.

As she reached for the door handle of the Prius, she heard someone call.

'Eve?'

She turned and faced a woman who was familiar to her. Her smile slipped.

Katrina. Grant's pregnant fiancée.

The woman hesitated. 'I wanted to apologise, Eve.' Her words tumbled out in a rush. 'I know it does nothing to change the situation, but the way it was handled at Leah's funeral was really awful. I never wanted any of this.' She motioned to her slightly rounded stomach.

Leah froze, her eyes fixed on Katrina's bump. Her baby who would be a half-brother or sister to Leah's. Bile immediately rose in her throat.

'I realise this doesn't change the situation or offer any apology to Leah, but I really am sorry. I should never have been with Grant in the first place.' Katrina sighed. 'In fact, I truly wish I hadn't.'

Leah forced herself to speak. 'Things not working out between the two of you?'

She gave a disgruntled laugh. 'That's an understatement. He decided fatherhood wasn't for him. He's packed up and moved to London. He has a British passport and he told me it was a permanent move.'

Leah gasped. 'He didn't?'

'He did.'

'He'll change his mind when the baby's here.'

Katrina shook her head. 'He won't, he's made that very clear. I had a letter from his lawyer to let me know that he wants nothing to do with the child. That he'll support it financially, and is willing to pay the court expense to terminate his parental rights.'

'Can he do that?'

'Possibly. If I agree, and the judge does too. It's quite rare apparently, but if I was in another relationship and wanted my new partner to adopt the baby, then that would be a good reason.' She gave a bitter laugh. 'Not that I'll ever go near another man after this.'

'I'm really sorry, Katrina.' She couldn't wrap her head around Grant's behaviour. 'I can't see his parents letting him get way with this.'

'Isabelle, Grant's mum, is really upset,' the woman said. 'She contacted me. She and her husband said they'd help out financially and they'd like to be part of the baby's life. She said Grant had made it very clear he wasn't going to have anything to do with me, the baby, or them if they invited us into their life.'

'She'll be in shock,' Leah said. She couldn't begin to imagine how Isabelle could be coping. First the news that Leah and her son had broken up, then a baby to another woman, followed by Leah's death and Grant's sudden departure. The poor woman.

'It's a shock, I know,' Katrina said. 'Although seeing how he's behaved, I'm glad to know he's out of my life. I wouldn't want him as the father of my baby.'

'I can't believe any of it,' Leah finally managed to say. 'He and Leah seemed so happy. Well, up until the split. She thought he was going to marry her.'

The woman nodded. 'Once again, Eve, I'm so sorry about Leah. I'm sorry, firstly for my part in making her unhappy, but I'm also devastated about what happened. I didn't know her, but she's in my thoughts all the time. So are you, in fact, and your family. I can't begin to imagine how you're all coping.'

'Thank you. I appreciate that very much.' She'd hated Katrina the moment she'd learned about the affair but Grant's behaviour was his own doing. She really hadn't known the person she'd thought she was so in love with. She thought of her baby growing inside of her. Another baby for Grant to abandon, if given the chance. A chance he definitely wouldn't be given.

'I'd better get going.' Katrina rubbed her belly. 'Check-up time with the OB.'

'I hope it goes well, Katrina. And I mean that. I hope you have a beautiful pregnancy, and your family help you once your little boy or girl is born. I'm sorry that Grant turned out to be such a shit.'

'You too, Eve. I'll be thinking of you and your family.' Katrina gave one last smile and turned to cross the car park to the doctor's surgery.

Leah climbed into her own car and switched it on. She couldn't believe she'd spent so long with Grant and obviously never really knew him. She sighed. She had a few hours to fill before collecting the girls from school.

Her thoughts flickered to her father, sadness erasing everything else. He was taking things so hard. She could go see him. If nothing else, it would take her mind off Grant.

Leah took a deep breath, pushed open her car door and stepped out on to the driveway. Other than the recent coat of fresh paint, her parents' house looked exactly the same as it had when they'd purchased it nine years earlier, but the garden had been completely revamped.

The knee-high hedge that separated the driveway from the house was clipped to a perfect square and her mother's tubs of pansies and violas lined the small pathway with splashes of colour leading to the front door.

She got no response when she rang the doorbell, so she made her way around the side of the house, past the recently pruned bed of roses and into the back garden. Her father's car parked in the driveway suggested he was probably home.

Leah crossed the lush green lawn, passed the veggie patch and headed towards the garden shed. She'd spent so many hours in this garden with her father.

When her parents had first moved here she and her father had sat down and planned how they would transform the then over-grown garden. They'd spent hours clearing weeds and vines and eventually getting the soil ready to replant.

Now the overflowing flower beds, the glorious section of roses and tranquil setting of the back garden were her father's pride and joy. A vegetable garden had been added in recent years when he'd decided to try his hand at an edible garden. Whenever Leah visited she always walked away with armfuls of vegetables.

She hesitated in front of the recently painted wooden shed door. She wanted to turn back the clock, be visiting her father *before* the accident. Visiting as Leah, not Eve. Enjoy being in the warmth of her father's company.

She took another deep breath and pushed open the door.

Her father was sitting hunched over on his ride-on mower. He started at the sound of her voice. He looked up, his eyes heavy. His cheeks were sunken and drawn. He forced a smile and climbed off the mower. 'Eve, I wasn't expecting you. I'm just . . . checking all's well with the mower.'

Leah hugged him. 'How are you, Dad?'

He slipped out of her embrace and picked up a screwdriver from his tool bench. He didn't make eye contact. 'I'm doing okay,' he said. He moved towards the mower to prove he really was fixing it. 'What brings you here?'

Leah didn't answer immediately. She needed the comfort of her father. His warmth. His ability to make her feel special and loved. To not judge her; to support everything she did. *That* was what she needed. She sighed. 'I don't really know. I'm back at work next week, and I guess I wanted to see you, be near you.'

Her father raised an eyebrow. 'Really? With your busy schedule I would've thought you'd have better things to do with your time. You usually do.'

She flinched but did her best not to react to the jibe. 'Sometimes it's nice to not think, isn't it?'

'I'll agree with you on that one,' he said. 'I wish I could turn my brain off. Thinking is all I seem to do lately.'

'About Leah?'

He nodded and started unscrewing something on the mower. 'She's all I think about,' he said. 'She was special, Eve, so very special.' Her father wiped the corner of his eye with the back of his sleeve and continued tinkering with the mower.

Leah let the silence hang in the air for a few moments. 'She was, Dad, but so are *you*. She wouldn't want you being so sad. You need a distraction, something to keep your mind busy.'

'Like what?'

'How about a game of chess?' She laughed at the incredulous look he wore, as the screwdriver clattered to the floor. 'What? I know how to play chess.'

'Since when?' A smile almost appeared on his lips.

'Since forever. Leah showed me how to play, actually.' This wasn't true, but her father obviously needed some kind of explanation. 'I'm quite good.'

He continued to stare. He appeared to be weighing up his options.

'Come on,' Leah said. 'You always complain we don't spend any time together. Well, you probably don't actually complain but you should.' She grinned. 'Or are you chicken?'

A small smile found its way to his lips. 'Chicken? Not likely.' He sighed. 'Okay, then. I'm obviously not going to get any peace until I show you who's boss.' He held open the shed door and they walked across the lawn to the house.

Her father moved his knight into place and sat back in his chair. They'd been playing in a comfortable silence for over an hour. He smiled. 'Checkmate.'

She shook her head. She'd been careful not to play too well. Leah could often beat her father but certainly wasn't going to put on a great performance when she was supposed to be Eve. 'Guess you showed me who's boss. I might need a bit more practice, or a few more lessons, if I'm going to beat you.'

Her father reached across and started collecting the pieces still on the board, ready to pack away. 'You play very well. I'm surprised. Leah never mentioned you could play.'

She cleared her throat. 'I guess it was your thing, yours and Leah's. I didn't want to impose.'

'Really? You actually *wanted* to be involved?'

Leah plastered on a smile. She better act more like Eve or her father would become suspicious. 'No, of course not! Leah taught me because my boss is obsessed with chess. Playing the occasional game against him has kept me on top of his promotion list.'

Disappointment flashed across her father's face. 'Oh. I thought for a moment you might be serious. Might actually want a game from time to time.'

She took his hand. 'Dad, I'd love to play with you.'

He wore an expression of uncertainty.

'I mean it. Hopefully I'll get better and actually beat you at some stage.'

Her father smiled. 'That I doubt, but you can always try.'

Leah's eyes filled at the sight of her father's smile. The game of chess was the first time she'd seen his face light up since before the accident.

His smile was instantly replaced with concern. 'What's wrong, Evie?'

She shook her head. 'Nothing's wrong. I'm pleased to see you smile, that's all.'

'I know, love, it's not easy at the moment.' He cleared his throat. 'To be honest, I'm not sure what to do.'

'How's Mum?'

Her father cast his eyes down, suddenly unable to meet Leah's gaze.

'What is it?' she asked.

'I haven't given much thought to your mum. I've been stuck in my own misery. I imagine she's feeling as distraught as I am.'

'You need to talk to her.' She kept her words gentle. 'She needs to know you're there for her. Leah would want you to be strong, be protective of Mum. You know that.' She waited for her father's response. He needed to be jolted out of his depression, be given a reason to get up each day and keep moving; to open up and talk with her mother. They *both* needed that.

He sighed. 'You're right, love. I need to be there for her. I'll try my best.'

'Good.' Leah glanced at her watch. 'I'd better get moving. I've got a few things to do before I pick the twins up from school.' She hugged her father and made her way out of the house to her car.

The time she'd spent with him was precious. She could see how much he'd enjoyed it too.

It gave her the slightest spark of hope that a close relationship with him as Eve might be possible. Perhaps she hadn't lost him after all.

The next morning Leah stood at the kitchen bench sipping her tea, grateful Sean had gone to work for a few hours. She could have some breathing space. He'd disappeared before breakfast saying it would only be for a couple of hours, then they could spend a family Saturday afternoon together.

A growing family, including the tiny baby inside her.

She hadn't told Sean yet; she was waiting for the right moment. He was still sleeping in the spare room, and other than the occasional peck on her forehead or cheek, had not initiated any physical contact. He could no longer use her arm being in plaster as an excuse.

It was partly a relief. It would be a betrayal of both Eve and Sean, if they did sleep together, but it was something Leah also had to move through if she was going to be Sean's wife.

It was normal, expected, that they'd have sex. She only hoped she could perform like Eve would have. She'd heard enough of Eve's drunken stories to know her sister was certainly more adventurous than she was in the bedroom.

Harriet held up her drawing. 'It's of you and Aunty Leah.'

Leah sat at the kitchen table with the girls. 'It's beautiful, Harry.' She looked across to Ava's picture and was greeted with a page full of animals. 'And they look like Leah's favourites.'

The other twin smiled. 'They're my favourites too.'

'Can we do some cooking please, Mummy?' Harriet asked.

She couldn't help but notice the warning look Ava shot her sister. The little girl was still on edge most of the time, as if she expected her mother's good behaviour to come crashing down.

'Of course we can. We could make a treat for afternoon tea when Daddy's home,' she said.

Ava dropped her marker on the table and stared. 'Another treat? But we still have the cheesecake. He hasn't even tried that yet.'

'I know.' They'd stopped off at The Cheesecake Factory on their way home from school the previous day to buy a treat for dessert. Sean hadn't finished work until late, so he was yet to try it.

Leah collected her coffee cup and stood. 'But it's always nice to have a choice, and it's a lot of fun baking. How about you two come up with an idea and if we have the ingredients we'll make it?'

'Chocolate cake,' both girls said at once.

She grinned. Chocolate cake was her favourite too. She knew a recipe by heart. 'Let's have a look in the pantry. If we've got flour, sugar and cocoa, we should be in business.'

Harriet beat her to the small space, sliding open the door and rushing inside. 'We've got flour and sugar, what does cocoa look like?'

Leah came in behind her, her eyes searching the shelves. A purple box stood next to a bottle of vanilla essence on the top shelf. She reached up and took both. 'Bring the flour and sugar and we'll get some butter, eggs and milk from the fridge. Then we can start.'

Harriet flashed a brilliant smile as she carried the ingredients out to the kitchen bench. Ava had packed up the markers and drawings and washed her hands, ready to help.

Leah tried her best to ignore the constant looks that went between the twins. They were grinning in delight, acting like they were hiding a secret. She assumed it was the secret that their mother didn't usually allow them to make chocolate cakes. She wasn't going to worry. These were the sort of things the girls should be doing. She remembered spending hours in the kitchen with her own mother. Tears pricked the back of her eyes as she considered the relationship she'd had with her mother.

Being Eve meant that was now gone too.

'Are you okay, Mummy?' Ava's face clouded over, the earlier excitement now replaced with worry. 'You look so sad.'

She forced a smile and pulled Ava in for a hug. 'I'm fine baby. Just thinking of your aunty. She always loved to cook, did you know that?'

The little girl nodded. 'She let us cook sometimes when we went to her apartment. It was a lot of fun.'

Leah's smile was genuine this time. 'I'm sure it was. This is one of her recipes we're baking. I remember a few of her yummiest creations and this is one of them.'

'You tried chocolate cake?' Harriet's eyes were wide. 'Really? It has a lot of sugar in it.'

'I've tried it lots of times, but not in the last few years when I decided to cut out sugar.' She put an arm around Harriet. 'Perhaps if you and Ava can decorate this cake to look delicious, I might have the tiniest slice.'

'Really?' Ava asked.

She nodded and was rewarded with Ava flinging her arms around her waist. Leah laughed and hugged both twins to her.

'You're different, Mummy,' Harriet said. 'Since Aunty Leah died, you've changed.'

There was no point trying to hide the fact that she was a different person. She had to take care to be able to explain the reason for the change to Eve's personality. 'You're right, Harry. I feel different too.' That was certainly true. 'Aunty Leah dying made me realise I was doing a lot of things wrong. I wasn't living in the moment. Do you know what that means?'

'It means you were thinking of being other places or doing other things with other people rather than enjoying what you were doing at that exact moment,' Ava said.

Leah ruffled her hair. 'Gee, you're smart. Yes, that's exactly it. I might've been sitting here having my coffee but my mind would've been at work or thinking of going for a run, or catching up with Nicola rather than enjoying being here. When Aunty Leah died, it made me realise life can be short and I need to enjoy every moment I have with you guys and Daddy, and our life here. I don't need to be thinking of other people and other things all the time.'

'You're not going to die are you, Mummy?' Ava's face was full of concern.

'I hope not, Aves. We all will one day, but I plan to be here for many, many years to come.'

'Hopefully at least another hundred,' the little girl said.

She smiled. 'Hopefully.' She refocused them back to the cake-making. 'Now we need to add half a cup of milk and then put the mixer on for three minutes for the cake to beat.'

'I've never seen you use the mixer before,' Harriet said. 'Kate has, but have you?'

Leah shook her head. 'No, your Aunty Leah gave it to me when you girls were born. She thought I'd be doing heaps of baking and cooking.' She made a show of rolling her eyes. 'What on earth was she thinking?'

Harriet giggled. 'Have you really never used it before, Mummy?'

She assumed from their reaction to the cake-making that it was very unlikely her sister had ever used it. She shook her head. 'Nope. So let's hope for a miracle that this cake actually works.'

They waited the three minutes while the cake mixed together then poured it into a pan and put it in the oven.

'Now for the best bit,' Leah said. She handed each girl a spatula and put the mixing bowl between them. She'd almost laughed at the number of spatulas that filled the drawer. For someone who never baked, Eve certainly had an impressive kitchen of appliances and utensils. 'The most important thing with this step is how you angle the spatula. Let me show you.' She took a third spatula from the drawer and used it to clean down one section of the bowl. With the end dripping with chocolate cake mix she grinned and licked it, rolling her eyes with pleasure.

The girls followed her lead and had chocolate dripping down their chins and shirts as they licked the mixture from the spatulas.

The three of them were still giggling and making a mess when Sean walked into the kitchen.

'Daddy!' Harriet ran to Sean and threw herself against him.

Leah couldn't help but notice how good he looked in the faded jeans and white T-shirt he was wearing. The office was definitely more casual on a Saturday than through the week.

He laughed and peeled Harriet off him. 'You're a bit chocolatey to hug right now, munchkin.'

Harriet stepped back, her hand clapping over her mouth. The chocolate from her lips had smeared on his white T-shirt. She looked at Leah, fear filling her eyes. She could imagine how Eve would've reacted. The little girl was probably waiting for her to start yelling and send her upstairs.

Instead she used her finger to wipe around the mixing bowl, lifting it out with cake mixture dripping from it. She held it up and grinned at the girls. 'If you're going to smear someone with cake mix, you need to play fair,' she said.

Leah went over to Sean and wiped her finger across his lips.

Ava's gasp almost made her cry. Had her sister never had any fun with her family?

Sean raised an eyebrow, however he played along. His tongue appeared; licking the chocolate off his lips. 'Mmm. That's sensational.' He grinned and grabbed Leah's hand. 'And I think there's more.' He brought her hand up to his mouth, his eyes meeting hers as he ran his tongue along the length of her finger.

She shivered, her eyes closing while tingles of pleasure ran through her body. They were quickly replaced with guilt.

When she opened her eyes, he was staring; longing filling his features.

She smiled and turned back to the twins. 'Come on, you two, let's finish scraping down the bowl then we'd better clean up while the cake bakes. We'll ice it later, once it's cooled down.'

The girls cleaned every drip of mix from the bowl and helped Leah clean up.

Sean sat on a kitchen stool watching his family; the girls smiling and Eve laughing while they tidied the kitchen. Times like this made him grateful for the accident and the changes it'd brought about in his wife. She was so much more relaxed around the twins.

'You're home earlier than I thought you'd be,' Eve said. 'It's not even lunchtime yet.'

'I did the bare essentials. It's such a nice afternoon, I thought we should go somewhere. It feels like we've been cooped up a bit since . . . well, you know.'

'What were you thinking?'

'I don't know. Harry, Avie, what would you girls like to do?'

'Circus,' Harriet cried.

'Zoo,' Ava said.

He laughed. 'We're on the same track at least.' He glanced at Eve. 'What about you? And day spa isn't an acceptable answer.'

'I don't want to go to a day spa,' Harriet said. 'That sounds boring.'

His wife laughed. 'I think we'll go with one of your choices.' She looked at Harriet. 'Poppet, I don't think the circus is in town at the moment. They tend to come during the school holidays, but the zoo is an option. Would you like to go there?'

'Really? But you hate the zoo. Everything smells and the animals are boring.'

Sean watched Eve's face with interest. That was exactly how she'd described the zoo each time the girls had requested to go. As a result, they'd only been once – with him. There was no chance she'd choose to spend an afternoon at the zoo.

Eve grinned. 'People do change, you know. Would I have been licking sugary cake mix off the spatula a few months ago?'

The twins shook their heads.

'I did today, and I also want to go to the zoo. I'd like to see some of the zebras Aunty Leah was always going on about.' She leaned towards the girls and lowered her voice. 'Is it true the special ones have golden stripes and horns on their heads? That's what Leah always told me when we were kids.'

Sean watched the delighted expressions of his daughters. Were the changes in Eve her way of coping? Whether she was aware of it or not, she was acting more like Leah than herself. Going out of her way to do things her sister would've done. It might be her way of keeping Leah close but his real concern was whether or not it would last.

'That's settled then,' Eve said. 'We'll have some lunch then get ready for the zoo.'

'What about the cake?' Harriet asked. 'We need to ice it.'

His wife nodded. 'We can either ice it straight after lunch if it's cool enough and take it with us for afternoon tea, or leave it for tonight and have it for dessert. You girls decide.'

'Really?' Sean asked. 'Cake for dessert is an option?'

'Sure, why not? It's that or the cheesecake the girls chose for you yesterday.'

He grinned. Chocolate cake in the house was a miracle in and of itself, but allowing chocolate after dinner; that was unheard of. The twins obviously agreed with him, as they both immediately selected the dessert option.

He stood. 'Why don't you two head upstairs and get dressed in some warmer clothes for the zoo. Mummy and I will make some lunch. That way we can get going once we've eaten.'

The two little girls ran from the room, their excited laughter spilling through the house as they dashed up the stairs. Squeals and shrieks erupted when they reached their room – from the sounds of it, they'd found Lewis doing something naughty.

Sean came around the island bench and stood in front of Eve. For the first time in months he wanted her close. If the twins weren't home, he'd be taking her to bed. Instead, he took her hands in his and really looked at her. 'I'm sorry for what's happened to Leah. You'll never know how sorry, actually, but I love that we've changed as a result.'

'Me too. The girls are amazing and I want to have fun with them, be a great mum. I want this family to work. It has to.'

He pulled her to him, conscious of the tremor in her chest. Had it really been that long since he'd held his wife? Sean cupped her face in his hands and lifted it; their lips met.

Eve's eyes pierced his when he parted her lips with his tongue and explored her mouth. She relaxed, her mouth soft and inviting. Not only was she acting different, she felt different.

He stopped as her eyes filled with tears and leaned back. 'You okay?'

She tugged him back in answer, continuing their kiss. This time there was urgency. An urgency he wished he could satisfy.

The crash of footsteps on the stairs had him ending things, a soft smile playing on his lips. 'Later,' he mouthed when Harriet rushed back into the kitchen, her eyes full of mischief. She launched into a tale of what the amazing Lewis had done.

Leah snuggled the duvet over a sleeping Harriet and kissed her forehead before tiptoeing across the room and doing the same for Ava.

Both girls were exhausted.

Ava briefly opened her eyes, a soft smile forming on her lips. 'Love you, Mummy,' she said before closing her eyes again.

A lump formed in her throat thinking of Eve and all she was missing. She stood and watched the twins for a few minutes, reflecting on the excitement and laughter their day at the zoo had brought.

It was more than the animals. Sean had been attentive in a way Leah hadn't experienced. He tried on many occasions to hold her hand, often to lose out to Harry or Ava who grabbed her first.

She'd felt his hand on her lower back as they stood and stared into the cages of the animals, his fingers gently caressing her. It made her shiver to remember. There was a longing in his eyes and touch, one she imagined was going to be satisfied that night. Would she be able to go through with it? Would he be able to tell she wasn't Eve? She would feel different, act different. How would she explain that?

Leah closed the bedroom door behind her and quietly descended the stairs.

Sean was in the living room, stretched out on the couch with a glass of wine in one hand. A second glass sat on the coffee table in front of him. The lights were dim and the sounds of soft jazz floated through the room.

He patted the couch next to him, wearing a lazy smile.

She tried to push Eve out of her mind and sat down next to him – *her* husband now.

He handed her the wine glass, holding up his own ready to do a toast. She smiled. She'd need to pretend to drink this as she hadn't mustered up the nerve to tell him about the pregnancy yet. She had no idea how he'd react.

Eve hadn't wanted more children so her own reaction was going to need to be believable too. Things were going so well between them. She didn't want to ruin it, but she was going to have to tell him.

'Here's to a wonderful day.' Sean clinked her glass with his.

Leah put the glass to her lips, pretending to take a sip. She put it back on the coffee table and sank into the couch, closing her eyes. It *had* been a wonderful day.

Sean took her hand. 'You look done in,' he said.

She opened her eyes. 'I am. The girls can be pretty exhausting.'

He laughed. 'Yep, they can.'

She sat forward and looked him in the eye. 'I need you to know something.'

'What?'

Leah cleared her throat. Part of her almost blurted out that she was pregnant, but the sensible part knew it wasn't the right time. Their relationship needed to be more solid before she made that announcement. 'I'm sorry, that's all. Sorry it took the accident for me to realise what I'd been missing out on with our daughters.'

Sean squeezed her hand. 'It's okay, babe. I'm so glad you've realised. The last few weeks have been amazing. I've never seen the twins so happy, or you to be honest. Since they were born, fun Eve seemed to go into hiding. At least when you were around us.'

'I never felt ready before,' she said. 'It's hard to explain.' Eve had said various things about not being cut out for motherhood. 'But, I can do something about it now.'

He drew her to him, his lips parting hers.

Leah sank into the kiss, desire spreading through every part of her body. Years ago, when she'd first seen Sean at university, she'd imagined kissing him, undressing him, making love to him, but thanks to Eve, had never had the opportunity.

Eve. A picture of her sister filled her mind, and she pulled way.

What was she thinking? She was kissing *Eve's* husband.

He leaned back from her, his eyes searching hers. His voice was hoarse. 'You okay?'

She nodded.

'It's been too long, Eve, *way* too long.' Sean took her hand and pulled her to her feet.

They kissed again.

She tried to block out her sister. Part of her wanted Sean; wanted him badly. But she wanted him as Leah. Wanted him to want *her* as Leah too. Making love with him now felt like a betrayal of both of them.

Sean's hands moved over her body, caressing her breasts through her shirt.

Her fingers trembled when she started to unbutton it. She was going to have to get past this.

He stepped back and she reached the last button and let the shirt drop away. She undid her bra and stood partly naked before him.

His eyes drank in her body. 'You're so beautiful.'

Tears welled in her eyes. He was telling his wife, Eve, *she* was beautiful.

Sean took her hand and led her up the stairs.

Butterflies flitted in her stomach as Leah contemplated what they were about to do. An ache spread between her legs. Physically, she was ready. It was the mental part she needed to switch off.

Sean grinned and tugged her in tight the moment they reached the top of the stairs. His smile fell as a retching sound came from the girls' bedroom. He groaned. 'You've got to be kidding.'

Leah hurried out of his embrace, pulled on her shirt and pushed open the door.

Harriet was sitting up in bed, her rubbish bin in her hands, heaving violently.

'And I think this might signal the end of our night,' Sean said.

It was after three by the time Leah slipped into bed beside Sean. Poor Harriet had vomited repeatedly. She'd ended up moving the little girl to the spare room so she didn't wake Ava.

Leah had dozed beside her on the comfortable king-size bed and been ready each time Harriet had reached for the bucket.

Sean had offered to stay with them but she'd suggested he get some sleep. While she was sorry for Harriet, she was relieved their plans had been interrupted. She'd have to get over her guilt and be with Sean as his wife. It just wasn't that easy. She was terrified he'd realise she wasn't Eve. How would she explain taking things this far if he did?

She lay listening to his gentle snores. Thoughts of Eve and the girls swirled around her mind. Of Sean, and being his wife.

Eventually she drifted into a fitful sleep.

Sean intertwined his fingers in Eve's and urged her to him, stroking her hair. 'Morning, beautiful.' He leant and kissed her before she had a chance to respond. 'How's the patient?'

'She was sleeping when I crept out and back to our room around three. I think she's through the worst of it.'

He groaned. 'Her timing couldn't have been worse. It's been months, then that happens.'

He felt Eve stiffen.

'Months? Has it really been that long?'

At least. The last time they'd had sex was one night Eve had come home late from work agitated and upset about something. She hadn't told him what'd had happened, instead had dragged him to the bedroom and practically forced herself on him.

He'd been working on the Goulburn case. Sean remembered because he should've been preparing for court the next morning, not giving in to her demands. That case closed four months ago.

Eve's expression was distraught, like she couldn't believe she'd neglected him for so long. 'I can't remember the last time. But it's because of my memory, not because it wasn't memorable.'

He stroked her hair. She seemed really worried, worked up.

'How much of the last year or so do you remember?' he asked.

Eve swallowed. 'Not much, to be honest. It's not like I don't remember you or the girls, but I can't remember the detail of our day-to-day lives. There're a few days or times I do remember, most of them when Leah was over here. But I seem to have blocked out other memories. That's what Dr Shriver thinks, anyway.'

Sean stared. She really couldn't remember how awful things had been between them? How she'd worked late nearly every day, avoided spending time with the twins, and was basically detached and uninterested when she was around.

She wore so much concern now, worry that she might've let him down. He felt an overwhelming sense of love for her. The need to protect her.

He pulled her to him and kissed her gently. 'No, it hasn't been months,' he said. It wasn't true, but if she really couldn't remember, then it seemed to be what she needed to hear. 'A few weeks before the accident, from what I remember.' He grinned. 'But you know me. A week without sex feels like months.'

Eve relaxed in his arms. 'A few weeks before the accident would be like months then. So we'd better start making up for it.'

Sean grinned. He hardened immediately, his pyjama pants straining as he shifted on top of Eve. He froze when the bedroom door opened.

'Mummy, Daddy. Harry's not in her bed,' Ava said.

He let out a sigh and rolled on to his back.

'Where is she?' The little girl's forehead was creased with unease.

'She's not well, Aves,' Eve said. 'She's asleep in the spare room.'

'Oh,' Ava said. 'I hope she'll be okay to play today. We had plans to decorate the cubby house.'

Sean glanced at Eve. The dark circles under her eyes betrayed how exhausted she was. He swung his legs out of bed. 'Come on,' he said to Ava. 'We'll check on Harry. Mummy needs some sleep. She's been awake half the night.'

He was rewarded with a smile from his wife as she snuggled down under the duvet.

Leah hummed to herself as she pulled up outside the white weatherboard house. She was content, happy. A feeling she hadn't experienced for a long time.

She was glad sex with Sean had been delayed. She needed to get her head around it first. It was going to happen; it was inevitable.

He hadn't mentioned anything feeling different kissing her or touching her but surely he would notice when they had sex. She was going to have to think through how she would handle the unavoidable questions.

As guilty as she felt at times, deep down she knew she was doing the right thing. She needed to do her best to live in the moment. Do what was best for Sean and the twins, and try not to think too much.

Leah switched the car off and looked across to Jackie's recently renovated home. Richard's car was parked in the driveway and they were expecting her. She took a deep breath, collected her handbag and bag of gifts from the passenger seat, and pushed open the door of the Prius. Her visit was completely selfish, but she missed her friendship with Jackie so much.

Of everything that had happened, her parents and Jackie were her biggest regrets. Every time she had these thoughts, images of Ava and Harriet would swamp her, combined with Eve's last words.

Leah followed the curved, paved path past a colourful bed of azaleas to Jackie's blue front door. It opened before she had a chance to knock, and she was greeted by Richard's stocky frame and warm smile.

She instinctively moved to hug him but was stopped when he extended his hand towards her.

'Hello, Eve,' he said.

Of course, Richard barely knew her.

She took his hand and shook it, a lump rising in her throat.

'How are you?' he asked.

Tears immediately filled Leah's eyes. 'Sorry,' she said, blinking. 'Doesn't take much to get me going these days.'

'Come in,' Richard said. 'Jacks is in the kitchen with Poppy and Dustin. She'll be pleased to see you.'

'I hope so,' Leah said. 'I really wanted to see her. I just hope it doesn't upset her.'

He smiled. 'She's doing okay, Eve. The kids are a good distraction, although I know she thinks about Leah all the time. We've been through a few boxes of tissues since the accident.'

The lump in her throat refused to budge. She hated that she was putting her friend through this. She imagined the situation in reverse; if something had happened to Jackie, she had no idea how she'd cope.

Leah followed Richard down the long hallway to a bright, sun-filled kitchen where she could hear the quiet voices of young children talking. She hadn't seen Jackie's family for at least six months before the accident.

Three sets of hazel eyes looked up from the table strewn with different coloured home-made play dough.

'Look who I found outside,' Richard said.

Jackie rose from her chair and came over to hug her. 'Eve, it's so good to see you.'

Leah tried to smile, taking in her friend's tired, gaunt face. Lines now creased her forehead that had not been prominent before the accident. Her hazel eyes were dull, as if the light in them had flickered out. Her jeans sported a thick belt, which appeared to be the only thing holding them up. She'd lost a lot of weight.

She hugged Jackie, careful not to hold on for too long, which every fibre of her being wanted to do.

'It's good to see you too, Jackie,' Leah said. She turned to Poppy and Dustin, both mini versions of Richard with their wavy black hair and dimpled cheeks. 'And look at you guys. You've grown huge since I last saw you.' Eve had met Jackie's kids on one occasion so she was safe to say that. She put her finger to her lip, concentrating hard. 'Let me guess. Poppy, you must be fifteen and Dustin, twelve. Am I right?'

Giggles erupted from the children.

Poppy was quick to speak. 'I'm six,' she proudly announced, 'and Dusty is four.'

She dropped her mouth open in mock surprise. 'No way. But you're so tall and grown up. I was sure you were older.' She grinned. 'But I'm also relieved, because I brought a little something for you and it probably isn't suitable for teenagers.' She rummaged through the gift bag, pretending not to notice the look that passed between Richard and Jackie. 'Aha!' Leah presented two beautifully wrapped parcels. 'I knew I had something in here for you both.'

Huge smiles appeared on the children's faces. 'Thank you,' Poppy said at once.

She nudged Dustin, whose eyes were wide, and he looked like he was holding his breath.

Poppy turned to Jackie. 'Can we open them, Mummy?'

'Of course,' Jackie said. She turned to Leah. 'That was so kind of you, Eve. You really didn't need to.'

'I wanted to. I'm sure Leah would have brought a gift.'

Tears filled her friend's eyes.

She regretted bringing up her own name. 'Sorry, I didn't come here to make you sad.'

Jackie shook her head, seeming to force a smile. 'It's good sad, don't worry. You're right, Leah would've brought them gifts.' She laughed. 'Way over-the-top gifts.'

'She told me she loved to spoil them.'

Poppy gasped when the paper came off her gift. She stared up. 'How did you know I wanted this Lego? I was going to write to Santa for Elsa's castle.'

'I guessed. My nie—' She cleared her throat. She'd nearly messed up. 'I mean, my Ava, has asked for it non-stop too. She's only a bit older than you, so I thought you might like it.'

'Wow, I love it.' The little girl hugged the box to her chest.

'I think your presents are a hit.' Richard pointed to Dustin. 'How on earth did you know he's obsessed with garbage trucks? We won't hear from him for hours – days even.'

She laughed when the little boy placed one of the small bins on the opposite side of the kitchen and pushed the truck she'd given him over to empty it.

'Thank you, Eve,' Jackie said. 'They're really amazing presents.'

'Come on,' Richard said to the kids. 'Let's leave Mummy and Eve to chat. Poppy, bring the Lego into the playroom and you can use the table to start building it. Dusty, you can bring your truck and bin too.'

Jackie smiled gratefully as they left the room.

'They're great kids, Jackie. You guys should be proud.'

'Thanks. Now, a cuppa?'

'I'd love one.' Leah sat on a stool at the long island bench while her friend started fiddling with the coffee machine.

'How do you have it?'

'White with one.'

'Coming up. You and Leah have the same taste in coffee.'

'Makes it easy to remember.'

Confusion crossed her friend's expression. 'I remember Leah telling me you were the pillar of health. No junk food, no sugar, no alcohol.'

'I've fallen off the health wagon a bit since the accident,' Leah said. 'Realised I might as well enjoy life. You never know what's around the corner.'

Jackie's eyes met hers. 'How are you?'

She stared at her friend. *She* was the cause of so much pain for Jackie, yet the woman was genuinely concerned about Leah's sister.

'I'm doing okay. The girls and Sean have helped make things easier. They're a good distraction.'

'And work too, I guess. Leah always said you worked long hours.'

Leah shook her head. 'No, I haven't gone back yet. In fact, I start tomorrow. I was supposed to go back once I got the cast off my arm, but decided to leave it a bit longer. I plan to cut back my hours. Losing Leah has woken me up to so many things. The twins were practically being raised by the nanny. I hardly saw Sean, or spent any time with the family. That's all changed. They're my life, and I want to make sure they realise that.'

Jackie placed a cup of coffee in front of her and went back to making a cup for herself. 'That's wonderful to hear,' she said. 'Leah would be very proud of you. I know she had some reservations about the nanny.'

She burst out laughing. 'Some? That's an understatement. I think you and I both know what Leah thought of my parenting. Don't worry, she made it very clear I'd been given a gift and wasn't appreciating it.'

'I'm sure she was just concerned for the girls and you.'

Leah nodded. 'Oh yes, I wasn't suggesting she was mean about it. She was, in fact, very diplomatic but I knew what she was thinking. I didn't need my twin radar to work that one out. Now, let's talk about you. As Leah has probably told you, I'm very direct.'

'And?' Jackie asked.

'And so I need to know what's going on and why you look like a walking skeleton. Leah would kill you if she could see you. You know that, don't you?' She took Jackie's hand the moment the words left her mouth. Her friend would take the words to heart, and she meant her to.

They'd upset her. Tears spilled down Jackie's face. 'I don't have any desire to eat or do anything. Getting up in the morning is a big enough job. Poor Richard has been left to do nearly everything for the kids. Most days he comes home from work to find me still in my pyjamas, and the kids in front of the TV.'

'Oh, Jackie.' Tears filled her own eyes. 'That's not healthy for any of you.'

'I know. Richard wants me to go and see someone. Talk to a psychologist, but even that feels like too big an effort.'

'I can imagine. You should, you know that, don't you? What would Leah say to you if she could see you now?'

Jackie sniffled. 'She'd tell me I was a selfish cow, and to get my shit together and be happy I'm alive.'

She laughed. 'I'm not sure she'd say that exactly. I can't imagine her calling you a selfish cow, but you're right about getting your shit together. Do it for her. Do it for Richard and the kids. I know a great psychologist. Would you be okay if I made an appointment for you?'

'You don't have to do that. I'm sure I can get a referral from my doctor.'

'Let me,' Leah said. 'That way, I'll know that you've gone and if you don't I'll be back on your doorstep and will drive you there myself.'

'Thank you,' Jackie said. 'Really, Eve. Thank you.'

Leah leant forward and hugged her friend. It was so good to see her, even in this weird situation.

Jackie stared when they drew apart. 'You know you're much more like Leah than I ever realised. I had a completely different impression of you before now. Don't take this the wrong way, but you were always a little scary when we were growing up and rarely wanted to spend time with Leah and me, even when we were little kids. I guess I made assumptions about you but never really got to know you.'

Heat rose in her cheeks. She needed to inject a bit more Eve into her personality around Jackie. If anyone could see through her act it would be her friend.

'Don't worry, I'm on my best behaviour,' she joked. 'The real me, the scary one, appears after a few hours.' Leah didn't let Jackie respond. 'Tell me more about your kids. I met them that one time at the party in the park Leah had, but I don't know much about them. What do they like to do?'

They sat chatting comfortably while they drank their coffee. Jackie made them each a second cup and when she got to the end of it, Leah decided it was time to leave. Visiting as Eve she might be overstaying her welcome. As Leah, she would've stayed all day and possibly the night, but Jackie didn't know Eve all that well and a few hours was probably more than enough.

Richard and the children reappeared to say their goodbyes.

The smile on Jackie's face was genuine when she hugged her. 'Thank you so much for visiting,' she said. 'It's exactly what I needed.'

'Me, too,' Leah said, which was the absolute truth. 'Can I come back again?'

'Yes!' both children and Jackie said at the same time.

Richard laughed. 'That's a big definite *yes* from all of us.' He put an arm around Jackie. 'This is the first time in weeks I've seen a glimpse of my wife.'

'Ring me,' Leah said, 'if she disappears again. We've had a chat, which I'm sure she'll fill you in on.' Her gaze met her friend's. 'I'll organise that appointment tomorrow and send you the details. No backing out. Promise?'

She nodded. 'Promise.'

'And I'll be back for a visit in a few weeks.'

Leah hugged Jackie one last time before high-fiving the kids and walking back down the path to her car. She fixed a smile on her face and waved as she drew away from the kerb.

That smile remained plastered until she turned the corner and burst into tears.

Chapter Fourteen

Leah poured herself a cup of peppermint tea. It was still early, and the house was quiet. Monday had rolled around far too quickly.

She'd arrived back from Jackie's only to find Sean and the girls entrenched in a game of Monopoly. She'd joined in and before they knew it, it was dinner time and they'd all enjoyed a delicious meal of takeaway Thai and the remains of the chocolate cake and scrumptious strawberry cheesecake. Sean had work to do after dinner, which left Leah to put the twins to bed and read them a story.

She'd fallen asleep sometime after ten; her late night with Harriet had caught up with her. She'd woken again at two to find Sean asleep next to her but had no idea what time he'd come to bed.

Leah couldn't avoid the issue of sex for much longer, nor could she avoid news of the pregnancy. She was going to have to tell him soon. She had no idea how he'd react. Eve was the one who hadn't wanted more children. She remembered there'd been talk at one time about Sean wanting another baby, hoping for a boy.

She sipped her tea. It was after six. She'd left him snoring and was getting a start on the day. She was supposed to be going into the office today for a few hours.

The office. She'd need to get used to the fact that that meant the real estate office. Not *The Melbournian*. She was familiar with property from the reporting angle, but had limited ideas of how one went about selling it. How was she going to cope? She'd have to rely on 'memory loss' to get her through the day.

The front door opened and Leah's heart sank a little. Sharing the girls with the nanny was difficult. It was astonishing how in such a short space of time she had become jealous of Kate, rather than grateful for her help. Eventually the nanny would have to go, but for now it wasn't practical. She needed to get on top of the work situation first and determine whether cutting her hours back to school hours was even an option.

She forced a smile when Kate came into the kitchen in her usual faded blue jeans and long tomboy-style white shirt. 'How was your weekend?'

The nanny hesitated. 'Um, good, thanks, Mrs West.'

'Leah – call me Leah. Mrs West makes me feel really old.'

Kate stared, her amber eyes widening. 'Are you okay, Mrs— I mean, Eve?'

She nodded. 'Of course, why?'

'You asked me to call you Leah.'

Leah's hand flew to her mouth. Had she really done that?

She took a deep breath hoping to calm her heart rate. For Kate's benefit, she gave a little laugh. 'Really? I'm sorry, Kate. Leah's been on my mind all morning. Obviously more than I realised.'

Sympathy flooded the young woman's face.

God, she needed to be more careful. Leah was doing enough weird things in the eyes of Sean and the twins as it was. She smiled. 'I'd better get ready for work. I need to go in to the office today. Would you mind getting the girls organised?'

Surprise flickered across Kate's eyes. 'Mind?' She laughed. 'It's why I'm here. I'll give them another ten minutes to sleep while I make their lunches and then wake them. Don't worry, you won't even hear them, I'll make sure they don't interrupt you.'

Leah wanted to say 'Let them interrupt', wanted them to run in and throw their little arms around her, but her 'Call me Leah' mess-up was probably enough for this morning.

Leah dressed carefully in one of Eve's more conservative pantsuits. She felt more like herself in the tailored black pants and jacket, even though she'd never had Gucci in her own wardrobe.

Her eyes travelled the length of her sister's extensive shoe collection. While the selection of Manolo Blahnik, Jimmy Choo and Louis Vuitton was impressive, they were hardly practical. How much had Eve spent on shoes? She was staring at thousands and thousands of dollars. Eve wore them to work considering them regular shoes . . . that blew her away. She might dare to wear a pair if she was going to a wedding or black-tie event, but to work? Leah breathed a sigh of relief when she found a pair of ankle length boots. They'd be perfect.

Sean came into the walk-in wardrobe, his hands slipping around her waist as he drew her to him. 'Morning, Mrs West.'

'Mr West.' She laughed and leant up to kiss him.

He kissed her then held her at arm's length, eyeing her from top to toe. 'You're looking super sexy today. They might not recognise you at the office.'

Leah smiled, surprised he'd find the more conservative look sexy. 'They might need to get used to it. I'm thinking I need a new look. More understated. As gorgeous as some of my other outfits are, they don't feel quite right.'

Sean laughed. 'Shame it took you a million dollars in clothes to make that decision.'

'Would you mind if I dressed a bit more casually?' she asked. 'I feel like something's shifted in me, and I can't explain it, but it doesn't feel right.'

He nodded, a twinkle in his eye. 'Of course, but keep in mind what you're wearing right now doesn't look casual. You look incredible. In fact, I might need to get you to take that suit off right now and show me exactly how you put it on.' He reached for her and started to slip the jacket off her shoulders when giggles and screams erupted from outside the bedroom.

Sean sighed. 'Nothing kills the mood better than that.'

She swatted his arm and moved back into the bedroom. Harriet and Ava stopped when they saw her.

Harriet's eyes lit up. 'You look lovely, Mummy,' she said. 'Are you going back to work?'

Leah noticed Ava's expression fall. 'Just for a few hours today. I need to catch up on what's been going on.' *And learn how to be a real estate agent.* She ruffled Ava's blonde hair. 'What's wrong, sweetheart?'

'I like it better when you're home,' the little girl said. 'We never see you when you're at work.'

She squeezed her tight. 'That's going to change. I'm going to talk to Peter about reducing my hours and definitely not working late at night.' She caught Sean's surprise above Ava's head. 'Is that all right with you?'

'Of course it is.'

'Money will be okay if I reduce my hours?'

He laughed. 'Eve, I know you've forgotten some things but surely my hourly rate isn't one of them. I know you love your work too much to give it up, but we could more than survive if you did. Cut back to whatever hours you want, if they'll let you. You've always said how they expect long hours. Do you think it will be an option?'

Leah shrugged. 'One way to find out.' She turned to the girls. 'Now, let's get your teeth brushed, then we'd better all get going. Kate's going to drop you at school this morning, so I want lots of cuddles before you go.'

The twins squealed and rushed to the bathroom.

Sean moved back to her and took her in his arms again. 'You're full of surprises at the moment.'

She pushed her body against his, feeling him harden against her. 'Surprises I hope you like?'

He nodded and ended the conversation by bringing his mouth to hers.

Leah switched her car off as she parked at North to South Realty. She took a deep breath and pushed open the door of the Prius. It hadn't been hard to convince Sean that she should drive Leah's car until they had time to replace her Audi. She saw no need at all to replace the Audi, but hadn't told him yet.

She entered the reception area of the real estate agency, relieved to find Linda, the long-time receptionist, sitting at the front desk. She'd known Linda briefly from coordinating visits for properties she'd reported on for *The Melbournian*, and also from the few times she'd come to the office to meet Eve for lunch.

'Eve!' The receptionist jumped up from her seat and rushed around to give Leah a hug. 'We're so glad you're back. Everyone's been worried sick about you, and so upset about Leah.' Tears filled Linda's eyes.

She gave her a squeeze, surprised Linda would feel so emotional. She hardly knew her – as Leah. 'Thank you. It's good to be back.'

'Peter will want to see you when he gets in,' Linda said. 'Shall I send him down to your office?'

'Yes, please.' She'd never actually ventured past the reception desk, so finding her office could get interesting.

'I'll bring you a green tea once you're settled,' the receptionist added. 'I'm sure Penny will be here any minute too.' She glanced at the clock. 'She's been a little later than usual since you've been away.'

Ugh, green tea. 'I guess I'll need to have a word with her about that.' There was no way Eve would let her assistant get away with anything. 'And actually, a coffee would be great. White with one.'

Linda stared. 'Really? I thought you only ever drank it black?'

She shrugged. 'Life's too short to not enjoy things.'

The receptionist's eyes filled with tears again.

She squeezed Linda's arm. 'Thank you for caring so much. Leah would be touched.'

The woman gave a small smile. 'I'll get you that coffee.'

Leah moved away from the reception desk.

'Oh, and Eve,' the receptionist called, 'a delivery came for you this morning. It's on your desk.'

She took another deep breath and continued down the corridor in the direction Eve always appeared from when they'd met here. From the first office she passed, a man waved to her, his face breaking into a delighted grin while he spoke on the phone. Eve had spoken of the boss, Peter, and had mentioned Zelda and Curt. As Linda had suggested Peter wasn't in yet, this must be Curt. Leah had met Zelda before briefly at a function so would at least recognise her. From what Eve had said they were not friends; rivals if anything.

She smiled, seeing the name Eve West in large letters on the outside of one of the office doors. It was the only door to have a name on it. Typical of Eve, but she was grateful on this occasion for her sister's ego. It'd saved the embarrassment of asking.

Leah pushed open the door and went inside, scanning the room. A stunning bunch of light pink and white lilies had been positioned in a crystal vase to one side of the desk. Clean lines, expensive furniture, tastefully decorated. The office was definitely Eve.

She sat in her sister's chair and took the card from the flowers.

> *Welcome back, Eve. I hope you'll remember us soon. B.*

Us? A shiver ran down Leah's spine. She assumed the flowers were from Ben. She moved them off the desk to the window ledge. The very thought of Ben Styles made her uneasy. He and Eve obviously had some kind of friendship or connection. Ben wouldn't be pursuing her if they hadn't.

She returned to the desk and glanced at the paperwork. There wasn't much. She assumed Eve's workload had been handed off to one of the other agents. Leah opened the top drawer of her sister's desk to find it neat and orderly. Stationery supplies, a pile of business cards and a loyalty card for the local coffee place.

She was about to close the drawer when she noticed something else at the back. Her fingers latched on to a phone. It was a basic mobile, certainly not one she'd ever seen, or imagined Eve using. She tried to switch it on but nothing happened. She found the charger in the drawer too. She'd charge it up and see if there was anything on it later.

Her own phone rang as she plugged in the charger. It was Nicola. She answered and couldn't help but smile at the enthusiastic voice at the other end of the line.

'No arguments,' her sister's best friend said. 'Meet me at Café Zee at one. It's been far too long since I saw you, to the point that I think you've been avoiding me.'

Leah forced a laugh. Yes, she *had* been avoiding her. She had nothing in common with her sister's best friend, and Nicola was smart. Smart enough to see through her story and realise she wasn't Eve.

'I can't, Nic, not today. I'm only just back to work and everything's a bit overwhelming. I'm trying to get away early to pick the girls up too. I won't have time.'

There was a moment's silence at the end of the phone. 'You're leaving early to pick up the girls?' Nicola's voice was incredulous. 'Please tell me there's a good reason. Has the nanny run off or something?'

'No, I want to today. How about we have lunch later in the week?'

'Done,' she said. 'Café Zee, tomorrow at one. See you there.'

Before Leah had a chance to point out that tomorrow wasn't really much later in the week, Nicola had hung up, leaving her staring at the phone.

Chapter Fifteen

Sean pushed open the front door, inhaling the sweet aroma of fresh baking. He smiled. He could imagine the mess the twins had made with Kate.

He put his computer bag in his office before making his way to the kitchen. Sean stopped in the doorway, the scene in front of him making him catch his breath.

Eve was standing at the kitchen table, her face and hair smeared with flour, laughing as she watched their daughters add food colouring to icing. A ton of cupcakes sat in the middle of the table, ready to be iced.

She looked up at him, her smile reaching her blue eyes. 'You're home early.'

'So are you,' he said. He kissed her on the forehead before ruffling the girls' hair. 'Where's Kate?'

'I gave her the afternoon off.'

Sean raised an eyebrow.

'I left work early. I wanted to pick up the girls and spend some time with them. Kate made us dinner. We'll finish decorating these, then I'll reheat it. Cottage pie, if that's okay?'

Sean nodded. 'And cupcakes for dessert?'

'No, Daddy,' Ava said. 'These are for school. We're having a tea party tomorrow and Mummy said she'd make the cakes. There's one for everyone.'

'We had to look up a recipe,' Harriet said. 'Mummy's never made cupcakes before but she said if you can read a recipe, then you can bake.' Her eyes widened with delight as she pointed at the cupcakes. 'And she was right.'

'I think they'll look fantastic,' Sean said.

'Why don't you grab yourself a beer and relax?' Eve suggested. 'I think there's a game on tonight, isn't there?'

He grinned. A beer on a Monday night? Eve really had relaxed since the accident. 'There'll be a game somewhere.' Sean opened the fridge. 'Do you want a beer?' If she said yes, then it would tell him something *was* really wrong. Eve hated beer.

She shook her head.

Sean flipped the top off his Corona with the bottle opener, kissed Eve's floury forehead again, and headed for the media room. This was what he called living.

Eve seemed serious and slightly nervous when she exited the en suite and joined him in bed.

'Everything okay?' Sean asked. He gave a small laugh to lighten the mood. 'Don't worry, the twins are definitely asleep. No one's going to interrupt us tonight.'

His wife smiled as she drew the covers over her. 'Good, but first there's something I need to tell you.'

He braced himself. She looked scared. 'You're worrying me.'

It was unusual for Eve to be so nervous. 'Sorry, I'm a bit on edge. I'm not sure how you're going to react.'

Sean returned her smile. 'One way to find out.'

246

She took his hand, her eyes focused on their fingers. She seemed to be trying to gather the courage to share her news. Then she raised her head and stared into his eyes.

'I know that before the accident I said I didn't want any more children.'

Sean breathed a sigh of relief. He'd been worried. Now he laughed. 'That's an understatement. I think your exact words were you'd kill yourself, or the baby, if it ever happened.'

Shock flashed in Eve's eyes. She hesitated before she spoke. 'Things have changed since the accident. What I want has changed. The girls are amazing. I can see that, and I know I've missed out.'

'What're you saying? You want more kids?'

Eve nodded.

Sean was silent. He'd tried to initiate many conversations about having another baby after the twins were born. He'd given up. Her flat-out refusal, plus her lack of interest in the two children they already had confirmed it was the right decision.

She broke the silence. 'How would you feel about that?'

'If I thought you really meant it, I'd be ecstatic.'

'I do really mean it.' She took a deep breath. 'The thing is—' Eve stopped, as if she was unsure whether or not to continue.

It was so unlike her to be so hesitant. 'Tell me, babe, what's going on? I'm happy to talk about having another baby, definitely. You don't need to be so nervous.'

'I do actually. I'm really not sure what you'll think.' She closed her eyes briefly. 'The thing is, I'm pregnant.'

He stared before retracting his hand. *Damn her.* For the first time in what felt like years, he'd actually had hope for their marriage. Bile rose in his throat.

Why was she staring at him so adoringly? Surely she must realise what this would mean for them? Sean had managed to convince himself there'd never been an affair. Eve's time away from

247

home before the accident had been work-related. God, he was a fool.

He slipped from the bed.

Eve sat up, her face flushed. 'Stop! What's wrong? I hoped you'd be happy.'

'Happy? What the *fuck* are you thinking?'

He didn't wait for her reaction. Instead he grabbed the clothes he'd discarded only minutes before and headed out of the door.

Leah was grateful to be able to rely on Kate the next morning to get the twins ready for school. She moved through her own routine of dressing for work, gulping her tea, and trying to smile and interact with the girls, in a daze.

She'd lain awake most of the night trying to work out why Sean had reacted the way he had. She'd heard him drive off shortly after he'd left their bedroom and he hadn't returned.

She knew he and Eve had decided not to have any more children. Her sister had had an awful pregnancy and coping with two babies at once had taken her down a route of depression. She'd rushed back to work as soon as possible, employing a nanny. Eve had told her how relieved she'd been not to be in charge the whole time, and that if she'd known what it would be like she would've never had them. How Eve felt about having more children hadn't been a mystery, but Sean hadn't felt the same way. He'd even said he'd be ecstatic to discuss having more. His reaction the previous night, however, suggested otherwise.

He had no reason to suspect the baby wasn't his, did he? Leah thought back to her discussions with Eve before the accident. She'd been fed up with Sean and his moods and on the night of the accident had said he'd behaved like an arsehole. A flicker of doubt settled in her stomach. Sean and Eve had obviously been having problems, but they were still close enough to have been sleeping together. He'd told her that even though it had felt like months, it had only been a few weeks before the accident. What reason did he have to lie about that? It didn't make any sense.

Leah stacked her cup in the dishwasher and turned to Ava, whose face was scrunched up in frustration.

'You're not listening, Mummy. I need to know where the cupcakes are.'

She took the little girl's hand. 'Sorry, darling, I was miles away.' She led her over to the fridge. 'I put them all in here. There are two containers full. I'll help you carry them down to the classroom this morning.'

Ava smiled. 'You're taking us to school?'

Kate was staring. 'I can take them,' the nanny volunteered.

Leah shook her head. 'No, I promised I would and anyway, I want to.' She looked back at Ava. 'Now go and brush your teeth and hair and tell Harry to hurry up. I'll be a few minutes, then we'd better jump in the car.'

Ava grinned and dashed out of the kitchen, her footsteps falling heavily on the stairs.

Leah took the cupcakes from the fridge and put them next to the girls' school bags.

Kate was pushing lunchboxes and drink bottles into them. 'Feel free to leave me a note if you want me to do any baking with the girls for school,' she said.

Leah stared at the nanny. Her sister had let Kate do pretty much everything when it came to the twins, yet Leah was getting involved and taking over a lot of the jobs.

Kate was looking at her strangely. 'You're very different since the accident.'

Her heart quickened. Had she acted too differently? 'In what way?'

Kate shrugged. 'You're doing things you've always said you hate doing. Picking the girls up, making cakes, letting them eat sugar and treats.'

Was the nanny merely observing or complaining? 'Things I should always have been doing. The accident has given me a different perspective. Showed me what's important and that life can be short. That it needs to be celebrated and enjoyed.' A lump formed in her throat.

Kate nodded. 'I understand. The changes have come as a bit of a surprise, that's all.' She gave a little laugh. 'Are you sure you need a nanny?'

She didn't answer immediately. At this stage, she still needed Kate's help. She probably could manage work and the twins on her own but it wasn't the right time to do that. Perhaps when the baby came, and she was home full-time, she could do without the extra help.

'We do for now, Kate. The girls love you and you've been so wonderful for our family. But, and this is between you and me, I'm pregnant. When the baby comes, I plan to stop work, and will be around for the twins and the new baby. I'm not sure how much extra help we'll need then.'

Kate's eyes went wide. 'Pregnant?'

Leah nodded.

The nanny gave a soft whistle. 'Wow.'

The whistle and *wow* were not congratulatory; more said in disbelief.

'Is it that big a shock?' Leah asked.

Kate snapped out of her shocked expression and managed a smile. 'I'm sorry. It wasn't what I was expecting. How's Sean taking the news?'

She swallowed, managing to make her voice sound jokey. 'You make it sound like it's bad news. I'm very happy about this.'

The woman's smile appeared forced. 'Congratulations, then. I hope Sean feels the same way.' She continued packing the girls' school bags.

Leah made her way out of the kitchen. She still needed to brush her own teeth and finish her make-up.

Ava and Harriet rushed past her on the stairs, their giggles and laughter hardly registering.

Kate's reaction to the pregnancy news wasn't much better than Sean's.

Leah worked with Penny for most of the morning, going over the client files she was supposed to be working with. She'd apologised on numerous occasions, explaining the memory loss she'd suffered was affecting her recollection.

Stepping into Eve's role with no formal real estate training was going to be hard, if not impossible, to pull off.

She breathed a sigh of relief when Penny declared at twelve-thirty it was lunchtime and headed out of the office. It gave Leah a few minutes to google where Café Zee was. She didn't know the food eatery scene around Eve's office well. She discovered it was less than a five-minute walk and collected her bag and coat, smiling at Linda when she passed reception and walked out to the bustle of Chapel Street.

Only moments later she found herself sitting across from Nicola, feeling as uncomfortable as she had in the office. Playing the role of Eve in both situations left her feeling even more vulnerable to discovery and was definitely the most stressful.

'You're what?'

'Pregnant,' Leah said through a mouthful of sticky rice.

'Pregnant? Jesus, Eve, what're you going to do? Does he know?'

She swallowed her rice and nodded. How she wished it was Jackie sitting across from her. She'd know exactly what to say, and certainly wouldn't have turned ghostly pale.

'I told him. He acted really strangely, to be honest. I stupidly thought he'd be happy.'

Her sister's best friend dropped her sandwich on the plate, her eyes wide. 'Happy? What? Do you think he's going to leave his wife? What about Sean? What about the girls? I know you love him, Eve, but you said it'd never lead to anything more than what the two of you had. I don't know that a baby is going to be as welcome as you think.'

Leah's stomach churned. 'Nicola.' She formed the words slowly, almost too scared to ask. 'Who are you talking about? Who's not going to leave his wife?'

'Ben. Who else?'

They stared at each other until recognition dawned in Nicola's eyes, and she broke the silence. 'Eve, do you remember anything about your relationship with Ben?'

She shook her head. The uneasy feeling she'd had looking at the flowers the previous day returned.

'So, you have no idea you've been sleeping with him for at least twelve months? You've been talking about him non-stop. You told me you wished it was an option to be with him permanently.'

Leah closed her eyes. *Oh God.* 'No. I'd never cheat on Sean. Maybe we were just friends or something?'

Nicola shook her head. 'You were much more than that. Much more. You spoke to him at Leah's funeral, didn't you?'

'He said we were friends, that's all.'

'He hasn't contacted you since the funeral?'

She swallowed, thinking of the flowers on her desk. 'Penny mentioned he'd rung a few times, but she passed him through to Curt. Curt's dealing with the South Melbourne development now, not me. He sent me an email yesterday, but it was professional.'

'You were completely in love with the man, and him you. I don't know what's going on with your memory, but when it comes back, you'll remember everything.'

Leah shook her head. She didn't want to believe Eve was capable of this.

'Your phone,' her sister's friend said. 'Surely that's enough evidence for you. All the texts and phone messages he sent you?'

'He wasn't even a contact in my phone, Nic. There are no texts or messages.'

'You had a separate phone. You never used your own phone, in case Sean saw a message.'

Heat flooded her cheeks. The mobile phone in the office. She'd put it on to charge the previous day and forgotten about it.

'From everything you told me before the accident, this baby is his,' Nicola said. 'It can't be Sean's.'

'Yes, it can,' Leah said. 'It definitely can.'

'Oh.' Nicola frowned. She lowered her voice. 'I didn't realise you and Sean were, you know, still sleeping together.'

Her mouth went dry. 'He's my husband, of course we are.' She hoped she sounded more confident than she felt. Again she thought back to the conversation she and Sean had had about it being months since they'd made love and then him correcting himself and saying it was only weeks. It didn't make sense for him to have lied.

Confusion clouded Nicola's face. 'The way you spoke before the accident, I thought it'd been months. You said you were worried he'd get suspicious at some stage, and were surprised that he wasn't pushing for it.'

Leah's throat constricted. She couldn't believe Eve had had an affair. She wanted to doubt Nicola, but the woman seemed certain – of everything.

Sean storming out would make complete sense if he knew about the affair. But why would he have tried to make love to her if he thought she'd cheated on him?

Oh God, what a mess. Here she was trying to convince her *best* friend the baby she was carrying was her husband's, not her lover's, when in fact it was her ex-boyfriend's.

She needed to play it carefully with Nicola. 'We weren't doing it much, but enough to be able to get pregnant. It could definitely be Sean's. Couldn't it?'

'If the dates work and you can pass it off for Sean's, then great,' Nicola said. 'But what about Ben? What're you going to tell him?'

'Nothing,' she said. 'It's not his, and as I have no recollection of ever being with him, it would seem weird.' That was an understatement.

Nicola signalled to the waitress. She ordered a vodka martini and looked expectantly at Leah, who pointed at her stomach and shook her head.

'And anyway,' she said after the waitress retreated. 'I have to go back to work after this.'

'So do I,' her sister's best friend said, 'but I'm in shock. Pregnant and the affair's over? The hours I've listened to you talk about Ben and how important he is to you. I find it hard to believe you can forget it – him – so easily.'

Leah hesitated. It wasn't a case of forgetting it. It was a case of trying to get her head around the fact Eve had cheated. 'Firstly, I can't even remember it, but even if I could, the accident changed everything. It's put so many things into perspective. I need to make my family work. I've been distant with the girls, and cheating hardly makes me a good wife. It's time to fix that.'

254

Nicola managed a wry smile. 'That whack on the head has a lot to answer for. I'm worried that when you get your memory back, you'll have a change of heart. Are you involved at all with the development project of Ben's?'

Peter had come into her office the previous day, his delight in her return quite overwhelming. It'd brought tears to Leah's eyes, knowing how much Eve was respected. She'd spoken to him about the accident and how it'd changed her outlook on her life.

Luckily for her, Eve's boss was a man who put family before everything. He'd agreed to a trial of a reduced working week, even gave her the flexibility of deciding her own hours. He'd mentioned the development in South Melbourne that she'd been asked to consult on with Ben. Curt had been looking after the project in her absence and from all reports was doing a fantastic job. Leah had convinced him to leave the project with her co-worker. She'd said she would be happy to visit the site if required, but as she was reducing her hours, it made sense to hand over a big project like that.

Peter had then spoken with Ben, who'd been fine with the change, although he'd sent her an email that afternoon saying if her memory returned and she'd like to work on the *development*, to be in touch.

To Nicola, however, she shook her head. 'I've completely handed it over to Curt. I'm reducing my hours, and it makes sense to step aside from large projects. I don't think Ben minded. The email he sent yesterday said to get back in touch if my memory returns.'

Her sister's best friend stared as if she was looking at a stranger. 'I bet it did.' She downed the rest of her drink in one gulp.

Chapter Sixteen

Leah sat in her car outside her parents' house. She opened her handbag and retrieved the small black phone. Her lunch with Nicola had left her rattled. After she'd left Café Zee, she'd rung Kate and arranged for her to collect the girls from school before stopping at the office.

She made up an excuse as to why she needed to leave early, and collected the phone. She wanted to believe Eve wouldn't have strayed, but Nicola had been so adamant and Sean's reaction certainly confirmed it. She took a deep breath and switched it on. It had a password lock. She keyed in 1184, half hoping Eve's standard password wouldn't work this time.

But it did.

The screen opened showing fifteen missed calls.

Leah opened the recent call history. Fifteen missed calls from one number. One name. *Ben.*

She closed the phone and slipped it back into her bag. She'd seen enough. Even though she didn't want to believe Eve was capable of an affair, there was enough evidence to suggest she was.

Her own phone chimed. A text from Kate.

Have picked up girls. Stopping at the park for a play.

She quickly sent a message back telling them to have fun and stepped out of the car. She wanted the comfort of her mum. Leah wanted to tell her about the pregnancy and have at least one person be excited for her.

The curtain flapped in the living room as she made her way towards the front door and she smiled. Her mother had always spied on visitors. The minute she heard a car in the driveway, she was at the curtain, thinking no one noticed.

The front door opened.

'Eve!' Her mother's arms were around her before she even had time to say hello.

She sank into the comfort of the embrace.

'What a lovely surprise,' her mother said, leading her inside. 'Shouldn't you be at work?'

'I left a bit early. Kate's picking up the twins from school so I thought I'd pop in and see you.'

They made their way through to the kitchen.

'Cuppa?'

Leah nodded and sat down at the kitchen table while her mother switched on the kettle and organised some cups.

'Where's Dad?'

Her mum gestured towards the back. 'He'll either be in the veggie garden or sitting on the ride-on mower in the shed.'

'Still sitting on the mower? Does he ever come inside?'

She sighed. 'Rarely. The garden seems to be the only place he's at peace. I guess he and Leah had a connection there, and he feels close to her. He hasn't been coping very well.'

Tears pricked Leah's eyes. Her poor dad. He hadn't shared a close bond with Eve. She'd always been very dismissive of their parents. They were too old and out-dated to be of use, she'd often said. Although she'd been quite happy to leave her daughters with them on weekends when it suited her.

A steaming cup was put in front of her. 'Decaffeinated green tea with a squeeze of lemon. Exactly how you like it.'

Leah smiled through her tears. This was probably not the time to ask for a cup of tea with sugar.

Her mother sat across from her. 'So, what brings you here this afternoon?'

'Do I have to have a reason?'

Her mother's eyes widened. She reached across the table and patted her hand. 'Hon, don't take this the wrong way, but I don't think you've ever dropped in without calling first. Did you need me to look after the girls for you? You know we're always happy to do that. We love having them.'

Leah shook her head. 'No, it's not that. I've got some news and I'm hoping you'll be more excited for me than Sean or Nicola have been.'

'Go on.'

She took a deep breath. 'I'm pregnant.'

Her mum's mouth dropped open. 'Really? Are you sure?'

'One hundred per cent sure.'

Her mother pushed her chair back from the table, stood and went to shut the window that opened out on to the backyard.

'Why're you shutting that?' Leah asked.

'In case your father isn't in the shed. I'd prefer he didn't hear the rest of our conversation.'

'I thought he'd be happy. In fact, I hoped you would be too.'

She whirled back to face her. 'Of course I'm happy. I'm delighted. Another grandchild. With Leah gone, I'd assumed Ava and Harry were going to be it. It's not that, and you know it.'

She swallowed at her mother's piercing stare. Her eyes were full of questions.

'You know exactly why I'm concerned. Don't you?'

Surely her mother couldn't know about the affair?

'How did Sean take the news?'

Her hand trembled reaching for her tea. 'He stormed out last night and didn't come home.'

Her mother's smile was mixed with compassion and concern. 'He knows.'

'That I'm pregnant?'

'Oh, come on, Eve. I warned you months ago you were playing with fire. That he'd find out and it would ruin your marriage. To walk out on you like that suggests to me, he's aware of what's been going on.'

Heat rushed to her face. Her mother *did* know. She couldn't believe Eve had told her mother, but not her.

'I'm trying not to be judgmental. But you've created this mess, and now you'll have to deal with the fallout.'

'The baby could be Sean's.'

'Really?' Her mother was silent for a moment, digesting this news. 'That's excellent. You'll need to prove it to him. They can do those DNA tests these days. You might even be able to find out while you're pregnant.'

A DNA test was hardly going to smooth things over with Sean. It would open a completely different can of worms. His reaction certainly made sense if he knew of the affair, but what Leah couldn't work out was why he hadn't mentioned it, and why he'd wanted to take her to bed.

'Are you going to tell the other man?'

She shook her head. 'I'm not sure what I'm going to do. Assuming Sean knows about the affair, it's probably the end of our marriage.'

The marriage that had only just begun for Leah. Over the last few weeks, Sean had started off distant but it hadn't taken long for him to relax around her. He'd kissed her, attempted to be intimate – which would've happened if not for the twins interrupting.

Why would he do all that if he knew about the affair?

Leah shook her head. 'I'm really hoping he doesn't know and his reaction was due to something else.' Even as the words left Leah's lips she knew the likelihood of them being true was very slim.

Her mother gave her a wry smile. 'I hope so, love, I really do hope so.'

Sean shivered as the cold breeze from the ocean ripped through him. He pulled his knees up to his chest, shifting to find a more comfortable position on the rock he'd chosen.

He hadn't been down to the beach since he'd brought his daughters last summer. He rubbed his chin, the roughness of yesterday's stubble confirming his decision to ring in sick today had been the right one. He looked like shit.

He shook his head. He still didn't understand how she'd been able to deliver the pregnancy news so calmly, as if she'd actually expected he might be *happy*. All the pregnancy did was confirm his suspicions that Eve had been having an affair.

She'd cheated on him.

Sean's mind drifted to the place it'd been many times in the months leading up to the accident: considering the guys his wife worked with, the mutual acquaintances they had – men Eve could have been having an affair with. Who else knew? Was he a laughing stock amongst their friends?

No doubt Nicola thought the whole thing was hilarious. In fact, he wouldn't be surprised if she'd introduced Eve to the guy in the first place. Anger surged through him, thinking back to the lies she'd told. She'd been able to look him in the eye and deny having an affair. He should've done more when he first suspected. Had her followed. He wouldn't be going through this pain now if he had. He would've left her ages ago.

Sean rested his head on his knees, a huge weight on top of him. He thought of the girls and what this meant for them. Two homes. Divorced parents.

He'd never wanted this. He'd tried to make allowances for Eve. Tried to understand that she needed her space, but this? From the woman who'd only a few years back said if she fell pregnant again she'd terminate it in a flash. Declared she'd never go through what she did with the twins again. If he wanted a son, he was going to have to adopt and raise it himself.

The same woman who'd gazed at him adoringly last night and told him she was pregnant. Pregnant with a child they both knew couldn't be his.

He shook his head. Nothing made sense.

The afternoon passed slowly for Leah. Not even the girls or their constant babble were enough to distract her from her swirling thoughts.

Dread settled in the pit of her stomach while she went through the motions of helping the twins with their homework. She couldn't begin to plan what she'd say to Sean.

How did she admit to, or deny an affair she had no knowledge of? She had enough evidence now to know it certainly had taken place. She had no idea what Eve would've done in this situation. Then again, her sister wasn't pregnant and probably never intended to be.

Leah's mind was a jumble when her phone chimed with a text message. It was from Sean.

At mum and dad's. Had a few drinks. Will be home tomorrow night.

'Who was that, Mummy?' Ava asked.

She looked up at the twins, who were both waiting for her to speak. She smiled. 'Daddy. He won't be back until tomorrow night. He was letting us know, and' – she put an arm around each of them and drew them close – 'he wanted me to give you both this.'

They hugged her back.

Harriet was the first to pull away, declaring it time to get on with their work. They wrote their spelling words in sentences.

Leah was relieved. She couldn't handle talking to Sean tonight. It was all too overwhelming. She needed to get it straight in her head before she even considered talking to him. She'd been given twenty-four hours' reprieve.

The next evening, Sean pushed the front door open a little before six. He'd contemplated staying out until his daughters were in bed but had changed his mind. He wanted to see them.

A small smile crept on to his lips as he heard Harriet's scream from the floor above followed by the twins collapsing with shrieks of laughter. The crash that followed silenced them momentarily before Harriet bellowed, 'Lewis!'

That cat was a source of constant entertainment and the centre of many disasters. It still amazed him that Eve had decided to adopt Lewis, and that she hadn't threatened to get rid of him yet.

Breaking into his thoughts, she appeared from the kitchen.

She stopped, her face colouring when she saw him. 'Are you okay?'

Sean stared. She was genuinely concerned. Worried about him even. He shook his head. More likely, Eve was worried about the consequences. She'd cheated on him. And he was now certain he knew who it was with.

'Mummy.' The shriek caused them both to look upstairs. 'Mummy!'

Eve dropped her gaze and hurried up the steps.

Sean remained rooted to the spot.

Harriet's high-pitched voice was telling Eve how naughty Lewis was; that he'd broken the lamp, and she was asking if they could still keep him.

His wife's laughter and reassurance left him shaking his head again. He needed a drink. He moved into the kitchen and was hit by the smell of freshly baked bread as he made his way to the fridge.

Sean's stomach growled, reminding him he'd survived all day on coffee. Kate's bread was always amazing. He grabbed a Corona, wrenched off the cap with a bottle opener and took a long swig. He was going to need a few of these tonight. He sat on the kitchen bench and waited.

Leah told the twins to clean up for dinner while she collected the broken pieces from the lamp Lewis had pushed over. Luckily, it'd broken into five large pieces rather than shattering everywhere.

She smiled, remembering the girls' faces transforming from anxiety to delight when she'd confirmed Lewis, whilst certainly in trouble, would be allowed to stay. She still saw signs of anxiety, particularly from Ava, but was relieved it seemed to be less and less often. They'd settled into a comfortable routine but now and then, at times like this, the child's insecurities and concerns rose to the surface.

Leah put the last bits of the lamp into the empty box she'd used to clean up and called for the girls. 'Come on, dinner's ready, and

I think Daddy might even be downstairs somewhere.' She swallowed. Sean.

He'd looked terrible. He was dressed in the old jumper and track pants he'd been wearing the night he'd stormed out, so presumably he hadn't been to work. Had he been with his parents all day? Had he told them? The more she thought about the situation and his reaction the more it was obvious he must know about the affair.

Damn Eve. Why had she gone and messed with a marriage that was so good? What was Leah supposed to say? Did she apologise? Admit to the affair? Did she deny it completely? If he and Eve hadn't been sleeping together then denying it certainly wouldn't help the situation.

'Are you okay, Mummy?' Ava was staring up at her.

She reached out and ruffled her hair. 'Of course, I was thinking, that's all.'

'You seem sad,' the little girl said. Her eyes filled with tears. 'You're not having second thoughts about Lewis, are you? It was an accident. He didn't mean to break your lamp. I can buy a new one with the money I saved. I have at least thirty dollars. Would that be enough?'

'Aves, I love Lewis. Of course, he's not going to be sent away. I'll never send him away, no matter what he does. Okay? I promise.'

'Good, but why are you so sad? Were you thinking of Aunty Leah?'

'For a moment I was.' She could hardly tell Ava the truth.

'Do you think she would've been mad with Lewis?'

Leah shook her head and placed an arm around the small girl. 'No, she loved everything about him. Even his craziness and habit of breaking things. She would've said "Oh, Lewis", then probably given him a cat treat.'

'Oh yes,' Ava said. 'You're right. We should probably get him one too.'

She laughed and called for Harriet. She kept an arm around Ava and walked her to the top of the stairs. 'I'm not sure I want to reward him, but we can certainly fuss over him a bit later. Now come on, it's time to eat.'

The twins proved an easy distraction at dinner. Both gabbed on about their days, filling Sean in on what they hadn't already told him. The bread disappeared quickly, each of them dipping it into the rich minestrone soup Leah had made earlier.

'You've eaten five pieces already, Daddy,' Harriet said as he reached for another slice.

He grinned. 'I know, I can't stop. Kate's bread is the best bread in the universe.'

Harriet giggled. 'You mean, *our bread*. Kate didn't come this afternoon.'

Sean's eyes locked with Leah's. 'Didn't come?'

She shook her head. 'No, I'm finishing early now on Mondays, Thursdays and Fridays. So I picked the girls up, and we came home and made the bread.'

'Have you reduced Kate's hours?'

Leah hesitated. The look on Sean's face shouted she should've spoken to him first. 'Not officially. I told her things had changed a little since the accident, and you and I needed to discuss how we move forward.'

'You can say that again,' he muttered.

She ignored him. 'I don't think we need her on the days I'm only working school hours.'

'I doubt she'll agree to only working two days a week.' Sean's eyes flashed with anger.

Leah took a deep breath. 'Why don't we chat about it later, once the girls are in bed. I know they have lots of news about their day to share with us.'

He picked up his beer and took a swig while Harriet launched into a full replay of what'd happened that day.

Leah pulled the door to the twins' bedroom shut and leaned against the outside. Harriet was already asleep and Ava not far off. They'd giggled their way through a bubble bath followed by three stories.

She took a deep breath.

Sean was waiting in the living room. Disappointment, anger and hurt radiated from him.

Her stomach clenched. She'd unintentionally caused this. Slowly Leah peeled herself from the door and forced herself to walk down the stairs. If she hadn't been pregnant, she would've gone via the kitchen and poured herself a large glass of Dutch courage.

Sean snapped the television off as she went into the living room. She forced a smile and sat opposite him. Then waited.

He stared. 'Well?'

'Well, what?' Did he want to talk about Kate first or the baby?

'Don't you have something to say to me?'

She swallowed. The lump in her throat threatened to constrict her breathing at any moment. 'Do you want to talk about Kate?'

Sean leaped to his feet. 'No, I don't want to talk about Kate. You know *exactly* what I want to talk about.'

'Our baby?'

He shook his head. 'You've got to be kidding me! Even now you're still going to try to pass it off as mine?'

Her gut contracted. 'What do you mean, pass it off?'

'We both know damn well it can't be my baby. How could you, Eve? Why didn't you tell me you wanted to end our marriage, rather than do this? You stood in the kitchen the night of the accident and blatantly denied having an affair. It was that guy, wasn't it? The one at the funeral? The one who hardly knew Leah but turned up to be supportive.'

A tear escaped the corner of her eye. The hurt in Sean's voice was heartbreaking. *Oh, Eve, how could you have done this to him?*

Now *she* was the one that was going to have to live with the consequences. Unless she admitted the truth to him. She dismissed this thought. She'd made a promise to Eve. One she intended to keep.

'I assume so,' she finally said.

Sean stopped his pacing and stared. 'You *assume* so? What the hell is that supposed to mean? You cheated with more than one?'

She shook her head. 'No, I have no recollection of being with him.' This part was at least true. 'I'm assuming it is to do with the whack to the head I got in the accident, but at the funeral, I can honestly say I'd never seen him before. He looked familiar, but that's about it.'

'But you think it was him? That the baby is his?'

'Possibly. Hopefully it's yours, but if it's not, then I assume it is.'

'If you have no recollection of him, *why* do you think the baby is his? Couldn't it be anyone's? You could have been sleeping with ten people for all you remember.' His voice was bitter.

Leah met his eyes. 'Both Nicola and Mum have confirmed that I had conversations with them about Ben.'

'Your mum?' Sean's eyes were wide. 'Peggy knew? Nicola doesn't surprise me, she probably encouraged it, but your mum?' His ashen face and strain to his voice conveyed exactly how hurt he was.

She said nothing. She agreed with Sean. She found it hard to believe her mother would condone Eve's behaviour. Maybe not condone the behaviour but she'd kept her secret.

'What do you want me to do?'

Shock washed over her. She'd been expecting Sean to declare the marriage over and storm out. 'Forgive me?' Leah's voice was barely a whisper. 'Pray that the baby is yours.'

Sean sat beside her, sighing. 'Part of me wants to kill you, but part of me feels like I'm dealing with a totally different person. You really don't remember, do you?'

She stared. 'Remember what?'

'There's no way the baby can be mine. We hadn't had sex for months before the accident.'

Leah shut her eyes, her worst fear confirmed. There was no way he'd accept the baby as his. 'But you said it'd only been a few weeks.'

He nodded. 'You didn't remember, and you seemed surprised at how awful our relationship had turned. I said it because I felt bad. You were making such an effort, and for the first time in ages things seemed good. I figured it wouldn't make any difference. I didn't want to upset you. What an idiot I am.' He crumpled and put his head between his hands.

She had to stop herself from rubbing his back. *Damn Eve.* Guilt flooded her the moment the words hit her brain. Her sister was *dead*. Leah taking over her life was hardly Eve's fault.

It was hard to believe Eve and Sean's marriage had been on the rocks. Leah knew there were problems but nothing this serious. She swallowed. She hated that Sean thought so little of her now. She could fix that by admitting she was Leah, but she couldn't do that to him or to the twins.

Leah had to keep her promise to Eve.

She took a risk and reached for his hand. He allowed her to take it. 'Sean, I need you to know one thing.'

268

His eyes met hers. 'What?'

'I'm truly sorry. I can't even imagine what I must've been thinking. I love you and the girls so much. I don't want to lose you.' As the words came out it hit her just how true they were.

He closed his eyes before tugging his hand from hers and standing. 'I don't think I can do it, Eve.'

Panic rose within Leah. 'Do what?'

'The baby. Our marriage. Any of it. I'm not sure I can do it.' Sean hesitated. 'Even if you got rid of the baby, I don't know if I could forgive you. It's not like you even want more children. You've made that very clear over the years.'

Her heart raced. *Get rid of the baby?* He wanted her to terminate the pregnancy? There was no way she'd snuff out the life of a baby, not even at this early stage. Sean was right, though. Eve definitely hadn't wanted more kids and had actively supported abortion and the right to terminate.

'I know I said that before. But now I'm actually pregnant and it's not so easy. I don't think I could.'

He sighed again. 'Jesus, what a mess. I never thought I'd want that either, but raising someone else's baby and pretending it's mine? I couldn't.'

Without looking at her again, he left the living room. Moments later she heard the front door click shut.

Tears ran down Leah's cheeks while she processed the enormity of what'd happened. She didn't blame him for walking out. He was such a good guy. She still couldn't work out why her sister would've felt the need to stray.

One thing was certain, her short marriage to Sean was over.

She closed her eyes. She'd thought she was doing the right thing stepping in as Eve, but now it appeared she'd given up her own life unnecessarily. She needed to undo the damage she'd done. But how?

Chapter Seventeen

Friday passed in a blur for Sean. He'd left the house early, worked a long day and arrived home well after midnight. He'd slept in the guest room and left again the moment the sun rose.

Now he was walking aimlessly along the beach, hands stuffed in his pockets as the cool morning breeze whipped across his cheeks. How he wished he could escape his own thoughts, but he couldn't.

His phone pinged at eight with a text from Eve. She asked if he could come home by eleven. She wanted to visit her parents without the girls, and hoped he could stay with them. Her message said she would take them if it didn't suit him, but would prefer not to on this occasion.

Sean had left the house before anyone had woken that morning. He couldn't bear to look at his wife right now. Was he more upset about her having an affair, or trying to pass the baby off as his? Things had been going so well between them. The accident had changed her. A change that'd been needed. One that could've saved their marriage – until this.

He sent back a text agreeing to be home at eleven. The old Eve wouldn't have *asked* him to be home by eleven, she would've told him in no uncertain terms to be there.

Not that he would've dreamed to go out on a Saturday on his own without checking with her first. His wife had always made it very clear because he was out so much during the week, it was her turn on the weekend to have a break, and basically do whatever she wanted – which rarely included him or their daughters. Now it wasn't a mystery exactly what those *other things* were.

He kicked at a piece of cuttlefish and turned back in the direction of the car and the car park. He had time to grab a coffee and a bite to eat before going home. He wouldn't get there a minute earlier than eleven.

Sean waited for the roller door to open, and a mixture of emotions flooded through him. While he wanted to see his daughters, dread at having to look at Eve overcame him. As he drove into the garage, she appeared through the internal access door. She gave him an uncertain smile and opened the door to Leah's Prius.

Sean was surprised she hadn't been at him to replace the practical car for something more to her taste. She'd said she liked it and that the small vehicle kept her close to her sister but, for a woman who up until six weeks ago was obsessed with brands, it seemed rather strange.

His wife stood next to the open door, waiting to talk to him. Her words streamed out too quickly; her voice wavered, showing exactly how nervous she was. 'I thought I'd go straight away, I know you don't want to see me right now.' She waited, as if hoping he might correct her.

He didn't respond.

'The girls are upstairs, making cards and I should only be a few hours.'

'Don't hurry back,' Sean said. 'I'm going to take them out somewhere this afternoon. We'll probably end up seeing a movie and having some dinner. I'll bring them back in time for bed.'

Eve hesitated, a flash of concern crossing her face.

'And don't say it.'

'Say what?'

'Remind me about not giving them soft drinks or lollies or junk for dinner.'

Hurt flashed in her eyes. 'I hadn't planned on saying anything. I was going to mention, your mum rang. She's invited us all over tomorrow for lunch. I wasn't sure how you'd feel about that so said you'd call her back.'

'Okay. I will. Now I'd better get upstairs to the girls.' He turned his back on her and walked into the house.

Leah sat across the table from her mother, steam rising from the freshly made cup of tea in front of her.

'So, he knows,' her mother said.

Tears welled in her eyes. 'He looked at me like he hates me. I was wrong, it definitely isn't his.'

Her mother patted her arm. 'I'm sorry, Eve.'

'But?'

'But like I said to you months ago, playing with fire usually ends in disaster.'

'The worst thing is I don't remember Ben properly. I have no real recollection of ever being with him. Ever feeling anything for him.'

'I can guarantee, you had very strong feelings for him,' her mother said. 'If it's any consolation, it wasn't just a fling. I'm sure you said more to Nicola than to me. You might want to talk to her about it.'

Leah nodded. She had no intention of talking to anyone. What she needed from her mother were some words of wisdom. 'How do I fix things?' she asked.

Her mother went over to the pantry, took out a large box of chocolate biscuits and placed them in front of her. 'You might not eat this junk, but I need something. It's too early for a drink, so this is the next best thing.'

She agreed and, ignoring her mother's raised eyebrows, helped herself to a biscuit.

'I'm not sure if you can fix things,' her mother said.

'Sean asked if I would have an abortion.'

Her mother sucked in a breath. 'Would you?'

She shook her head. 'Of course not. It's my baby.'

'What about Ben? You'd have to tell him. A baby's father has the right to know.'

Leah's stomach clenched. *Grant.* From what Katrina said, she didn't see any reason to tell him. He certainly wasn't going to welcome the news. 'Where's Dad?' she asked, changing the subject.

'Playing golf. He should be home any minute.'

She managed a smile. 'That's good news. He's finally out of the house.'

'He's started to whistle again too. They're small steps, but I think he's beginning to come back to us.'

'That's great news, Mum.' She meant it. It'd been awful seeing her father caught in such a deep depression.

'I don't suggest you tell him anything about this, not until you know what's happening with you and Sean and the baby. Leah's death . . .' Her mother stumbled on the word. She cleared her throat. 'Leah's death has been particularly hard on your father. I'm not sure what has brought him back out of his despair, but whatever it is I'm very grateful.' She wiped at her eyes. 'I was beginning to think I'd lost him too.'

Leah squeezed her hand, for the second time wishing she could turn back time to before the accident. She was no longer sure her choice had been the right one.

In fact, she was convinced it wasn't.

'I won't say anything,' she said.

They sipped their drinks until the opening of the garage door broke the silence.

'Here he is now,' her mother said. 'Fingers crossed he's in a good mood.' Worry crossed her face.

Her poor mother. She was dealing with a lot more than her own grief.

Her dad came in through the kitchen door, his face expressionless.

'Hello, love,' her mother said.

Her father's face broke into a smile as he saw Leah. 'Eve, I wasn't expecting to see your car out the front. I wouldn't have played golf if I'd realised you'd be stopping by. How are you, love?'

Leah smiled. He was genuinely pleased to see her. She couldn't help but notice the look of surprise that flashed across her mother's face. 'I'm good, Dad. Only just got here, and if it's okay with you both, I might hang around for a few hours. Sean's taking the girls to the movies this afternoon, so I'm at a bit of a loose end.'

Her dad laughed. 'You, a loose end? What about all those friends you like to lunch with, drink with? You always complained that with the restrictions of the girls, you never got to see them enough.'

'I feel like a quieter day. Perhaps another chess challenge?'

'Chess?' her mother asked. 'That's Leah's thing, not yours.'

Her father laughed again.

The surprise on her mother's face suggested her mother probably hadn't heard her husband laugh for some time.

'She's a dark horse, our Eve. Was around here the other week. Almost beat me. Turns out she's had some expert Leah training.'

'Well, that's very unexpected,' her mother said. 'And you were here, visiting?'

'Only once. You were out. It gave me and Dad a chance to hang out.'

'Give me a minute to wash up and I'll get the board set up,' her dad said. 'I'll tell you about my golf game while we play.' His laughter boomed down the hall on his way to the bathroom. 'That'll bore you into defeat for sure.'

Her mother's jaw dropped.

'What's wrong, Mum?'

'Nothing's wrong. It's only that I've hardly seen your father crack a smile since the accident. Sounds like your chess game might've snapped him out of it.' She smiled. 'Sorry, I shouldn't be acting so surprised. Whatever brings him back to life I'm grateful for.'

'Definitely,' Leah said.

'Ready?' The holler came from her father's study.

She finished her tea, grinned as she stole another biscuit from the tin, and went in search of her father.

Sean stopped in the kitchen and took a deep breath. Moving forward was going to be tough on all of them. He was being realistic at least when he thought about that. It would be hard enough breaking the news to the girls, but having to look at Eve every time they dropped the children with each other, having to talk to her; it made him feel ill.

Her betrayal hurt. It was that simple.

Laughter floated down the stairs. He forced a smile. He needed to be fun dad today, not this miserable, depressed version of himself.

Sean pushed Eve far from his mind, and took the steps two at a time.

'Daddy,' Harriet cried, when he reached their playroom. She dropped her pencil and leapt up to throw her arms around him. 'Why did you have to go to work so early? It's Saturday.'

He laughed and squeezed his daughter close. 'Work? Who said anything about work? I was out planning our day.'

'Mummy said you'd gone to work early because of some case you were working on,' Ava said. 'Why would she say that if it wasn't true?'

Because Mummy's very good at lying. 'I'm working on the case of "let's have fun on Saturday". It's a very special case, and needs good detectives to ensure it's solved. Think you can help me?'

Harriet cheered. 'I can, Daddy. I'm a great detective.'

'How about you, Ave?' he asked, noticing his daughter seemed concerned, rather than excited.

'Is Mummy coming, too?'

He ruffled the serious little girl's hair. 'No, hon, she's gone to visit Gram and Gramps.'

'Without us? Why?' Ava asked. 'I want to see them too.'

Sean sighed. *So much for getting on and having fun.* 'They're still very sad, Aves. Mummy wanted to spend some time with them on her own. She was worried it would be a bit depressing, and maybe even boring for you guys. So you and I are going to have some fun instead.' He clapped his hands and glanced at Harriet. At least he'd be able to get her excited about the day. 'I'm thinking we head out this afternoon to the movies. We might take your bikes and go to the duck-pond park afterwards for a ride and then go out for dinner on the way home. How does that sound?'

Harriet cheered again. 'Can we take bread for the ducks?'

'Yep. We can do anything you want.'

A sly smile crossed Harriet's lips. 'Can we buy lollies to eat at the movie?'

'Yep. Maybe an ice cream too.'

Ava's face lit up. 'Really, one of those choc-tops? I've never had one of those.'

Sean picked her up and swung her around. 'What? Seven years old and never had a choc-top? That's definitely not right, and we need to fix it immediately.'

Ava giggled.

'We need to finish our cards first,' Harriet said. 'Will we have time?'

Sean placed Ava back on the floor. 'Heaps of time. We'll have lunch here and head off around one.' He pulled up one of the small chairs next to the craft table the twins were working at. 'Let's see what you are doing.'

A lump rose in his throat while his daughters proudly showed him the cards they'd been making.

'They're for Gran,' Ava explained.

'It's her birthday on Monday,' Harriet said. 'Mummy thought it would be nice if we made some cards for her.

'Mummy remembered Gran's birthday?' That was a first.

'She said it was in her diary, and as she's turning sixty we should do something special.'

God, they were right, his mum *was* turning sixty. He'd been so caught up with everything he hadn't given her a second thought. Thank goodness Eve had remembered. He still had time to get her a present and make a fuss of her.

'Mummy's much better at remembering these days,' Harriet said. 'She laughed when she told us about Gran's birthday. Said Gran would probably get a shock that we'd all remembered.'

'She doesn't remember everything,' Ava said. 'She still says and does some weird stuff.'

'Like what?' Sean asked.

'Silly stuff,' the serious twin said. 'Like, she can't always find things in the house or doesn't remember the names of people. Mrs

Jensen from across the road came over to see how we're doing. She even brought a big lasagne for dinner and Mum had no idea who she was.'

'Really?' Eve hadn't mentioned anything. 'When did this happen?'

Ava stopped drawing and sat up, her pen resting against her little lip. 'It must've been on Tuesday,' she said. 'It was after swimming lessons.'

'What other things does Mummy forget?'

'She hardly recognises any of the mums or kids at school,' Harriet said. 'She always has to ask us who they are.'

'Did she know any of them before the accident?' he asked. 'Kate used to take you to and from school every day.'

'She knew who Jemima and Shilo and Lisa were,' Harriet said. 'They've been here to play with us before.'

He nodded. 'And she didn't recognise any of them?'

Harriet shook her head and got back to her card.

'Do you think she's sick?' Ava asked. 'Is her brain sick?'

Sean took one look at his daughter's panic-stricken face and pulled her to him. 'Of course not, sweetie. When she bumped her head in the accident, it affected her memory.' For God's sake, she didn't even remember having an affair. 'Hopefully it'll come back to her soon, but if it doesn't we have to keep helping her and reminding her of things.'

'I hope it doesn't come back,' Harriet said. 'She might remember she prefers going to work than being with us. Or that sugar is evil and we can't bake cakes with her anymore. I like her better when she can't remember things.'

'I like her better, too,' Ava said. 'Our family is nicer since she had the accident. You and Mummy don't argue and you kiss and hold hands. You're like proper parents.'

'Proper parents? We weren't before?' Sean asked.

Ava shook her head and began colouring in the flower she'd drawn on the card. 'Mummy was always mad at you, and never wanted to do things as a family. Since she hurt her head, we've done everything together. We've had lots of fun. More fun than I can ever remember.'

'Yeah,' Harriet agreed. 'It's really different. I wish Aunty Leah hadn't been in the car when Mummy had her accident, but I'm not sorry she had the accident. It's changed her, and I love it.'

'I don't have to worry anymore either,' Ava whispered.

'Worry?'

She wouldn't meet his eyes and continued to colour. 'That you're getting a divorce. Oliver in my class, his parents are splitting up and he hates it. He has to live in two different houses, and if he forgets his favourite toy, he has to wait a full week to see it again. His mum and dad fight the whole time too. He cries a lot at school. He's really sad, and it's all their fault.'

Sean swallowed the lump that seemed to have grown to gigantic proportions in his throat. *Damn Eve. Damn her.*

She'd ruined everything and now, in the eyes of his daughters, when they split up he was going to be as bad as *she* was.

'You'd better ring Gran,' Ava said. 'Did Mummy tell you she rang?'

'She wants us all to go for a barbecue tomorrow,' Harriet said. 'I can't wait.'

Ava looked up at him. 'Mummy is coming, isn't she, Daddy? It's our chance to celebrate Gran's birthday.'

He hesitated. It would be a bit hard to explain why Eve couldn't be there to his daughters *and* his parents. 'Of course she's coming. Now I'd better go and give Gran a quick ring and confirm everything.' He did his best to smile. 'Finish your cards and when we're out this afternoon, we'll buy her a lovely present.'

He left the twins to put the finishing touches on their art and went down to the kitchen.

So much for putting Eve out of his mind. Sean needed to put his lawyer hat on, detach emotionally. It was his job; what he did best. It shouldn't be *that* hard. Right?

'Come on, Dad,' Leah said, removing one of his bishops from the board. 'That's not like you to be losing pieces so early.'

Bill smiled. 'I think my mind's still back on the sixteenth green. Perfect putt it was. At least eight feet, straight into the hole.'

'It's nice to hear you sounding enthusiastic again.'

Darkness clouded her father's face.

She touched his arm. 'She'd want you to be happy. She'd want you to keep living.'

Her father studied the board. 'I feel guilty.' He didn't look up.

'The accident wasn't your fault. You didn't even know we were going to a party.'

'I feel guilty that I'm alive,' he said. 'I've had a long life; Leah was only thirty-five. She had so much still to do. Marriage, kids, happiness. It was all just waiting for her. I wish it had been me.'

Her heart contracted. His words rang true. He would've changed places with her if it was an option.

'I'd give anything to have her back, you know,' her father said. 'Anything at all.'

She was silent, her eyes on the board. She was beginning to believe she'd made the biggest mistake of her life.

Being Eve, lying to everyone.

She shouldn't have messed with the universe. If she hadn't, she'd be pregnant, single and supporting her family and Sean as best she could. Instead she was living a ridiculously complicated life of lies.

Leah jolted when her father squeezed her hand.

'There's one good thing that's come from this, Evie. And that's you and me. I've seen a different side to you since the accident. Caring, compassionate. The real you. The you I always knew was there deep inside.' Dad gave a small laugh. 'You kept it well hidden behind that brittle façade of yours. The expensive clothes, the make-up, the fancy haircuts. It never felt real to me. It felt like you were hiding something.'

'Hiding something?'

Her father nodded. 'Hiding the real you. The vulnerable you. You put up this strong front, like nothing could touch you, but deep down we both know that doesn't work. You're more like me than I ever realised.'

She stared. He was comparing himself to Eve? She'd known Eve better than anyone, and she disagreed with his belief that it was a façade. It was just Eve. Who she'd been.

'You know, it's *you* who's helped me face the world again, don't you?' he said.

'What do you mean?'

'You coming and sitting with me. Playing chess, being here. You've got the same calm nature Leah had. Makes me proud to be your dad. The way you've changed your approach with the girls. Softened, moved in different directions, better directions. It's made me realise I can keep going. I've lost something very precious to me, but at the same time I've gained.'

'Gained what?'

'Gained *you*. Gained belief. Watching you makes me realise there's a bigger picture to all this. I'd say if you'd kept going the way you were then your marriage would've ended and the girls would probably, if given the choice, have chosen to be with Sean. A lot of miserable lives as a result. Instead, Leah's death has inspired you to be a great mum. To love those twins with all your might.'

'Like I should have from the start?'

'That's the ideal, but it doesn't happen for everyone. It's not easy having twins.' He winked. 'Believe me, I know.'

'Do you think people should always be honest, Dad?' Leah asked. 'Is it always for the best?'

He seemed to think about it for a moment, then shook his head. 'Definitely not.'

She couldn't help but laugh. 'I was sure you'd say they should.'

Her father shook his head. 'I like to say I live an honest life, but there're times when the truth isn't always the kindest thing to share with people. I don't condone telling lies for self-advancement or anything of that sort, but I do condone lying if it is done to protect people and basically for the right reasons.'

'Protecting people often means others are hurt. One lie can have so many knock-on effects.'

He studied her for a moment. 'Is everything okay, love? Got yourself into a situation, have you?'

Leah's bottom lip trembled. 'You could say that.'

'I'm here if you want some advice.'

Tears filled her eyes. Oh, how she'd love some advice. The problem was her father was one of the many people *her* lies had hurt. 'No, I'll be fine. A few things to work out that's all.'

Her dad patted her hand. 'I won't pry, love, but I'm always here. I won't judge you.'

She forced a smile. How could he not judge her if he knew the truth? His relationship with her would never be the same again. That much was certain.

Chapter Eighteen

'You definitely want me to come?' Leah glanced at Sean as she finished unloading the dishwasher. 'I'll understand if you don't.'

For the first time since she'd announced her pregnancy, Sean had stayed in the same room for more than five minutes. They'd had breakfast with the girls, trying to act normal for their sake.

Ava hadn't been fooled.

'What's wrong with you?' the little girl had asked Sean when he'd snapped *no* to Leah's question of whether he'd like another coffee.

He'd run his hands through his hair and forced a smile. 'Nothing, honey, I'm a bit tired.'

'You should apologise to Mummy,' Ava said. 'She made us a yummy breakfast, and offered you another coffee and you were horrible to her.'

'You're right. I'm a bit of a grump this morning.' He'd turned to Leah with a big smile that didn't reach his eyes. 'I'd love one, thank you.'

That had placated Ava, and she'd dug into her Bircher muesli.

Now the twins were upstairs putting the finishing touches on the birthday sign they'd made in addition to the cards for their grandmother.

The moment they'd left the room he'd stopped pretending, and an icy chill had filled the kitchen.

'No, I don't want you to come. But right now, it's going to look pretty strange if you don't. I'm not ready to tell anyone what's going on, and my mum is worried about you. Worried how you're coping since the accident. Other than you suddenly becoming ill, which would worry her even more, I can't think of any good reason for you not to come. The twins will be suspicious too.'

She didn't know June or Abe very well, but from what Eve had said about her in-laws, she hadn't had a close relationship with them. Other than at the funeral, Leah had met them at a few celebrations: Eve and Sean's wedding, the girls' birthday parties. They'd always been friendly. Chatted about the twins and asked Leah about her work.

Her sister hadn't had much time for her own parents so it wasn't a surprise she'd viewed the get-togethers with Sean's as inconvenient obligations.

'Okay. I'll go and get dressed then. You said you bought a present yesterday, didn't you?'

Sean nodded. 'Presents. The girls are giving her perfume and chocolates and we're giving her a five-night getaway from all of us for her and dad.'

She smiled. 'Sounds lovely. Where to?'

He hesitated.

'Come on, Sean. I know I've put us in an awful situation' – understatement of the century – 'but for the sake of the girls, and everyone around us, we need to at least be able to talk to each other.'

'The Hunter Valley. And yes, you have put us in an awful situation. And no, I don't agree that we need to be able to talk to each other. For now, let's keep it to an absolute need-to-know basis. Okay?' He didn't wait for her response, but instead picked his car

284

keys up off the bench. 'I'm going to get Mum some flowers. I'll be back in about an hour. We need to leave at eleven.'

The familiar nauseous feeling rose within Leah, reminding her exactly *why* they were in this situation.

The front door of Sean's parents' much-loved Federation bungalow opened and June's plump arms flew open to embrace the twins as they launched themselves at her.

'Settle down,' Leah said, laughing when she caught up with them, holding a large bunch of lilies in her arms. 'You'll knock Gran over.'

'They're fine,' Sean's mum said. 'Excited to see me, aren't you, girls?'

'Happy birthday, Gran,' Harriet said.

'For tomorrow,' Ava added.

'Thank you.' She looked at the flowers Leah had with her. 'Although today wasn't supposed to be about me. It was a chance to have you over. See your mum too, as we haven't seen much of her since . . . well, since, you know.' June flushed, stumbling over her words.

Leah squeezed her arm. 'No, we haven't seen much of you. So today will be an extra special celebration.'

'And today *is* about you, Gran,' Harriet said. 'We have banners and cards and presents and everything to prove it. Ava and I'll go and help Daddy. There's tons of stuff to bring in.'

'Tons? Is that right?' June winked, her chestnut eyes dancing playfully. 'Come on in, Eve, it's lovely to see you. Abe's out the back somewhere getting the barbecue ready and organising skittles and other games.'

Leah smiled and followed her into the living room. The mantelpiece was filled with family photos. 'Happy birthday,' she said.

'My favourite.' The older woman beamed, accepting the flowers.

'Sean takes the credit for them,' she said. 'He went out early to make sure he could find exactly the right ones.'

'He's a good boy. Take a seat while I pop into the kitchen and find a vase.'

Leah sat on the faded leather couch, her eyes fixing on the portrait of Sean, aged around ten, with younger versions of his smiling parents that took up most of one wall. Yes, he *was* a good boy. Too good for her now that she'd complicated things so spectacularly. How she wished she could talk to Jackie, tell her everything.

There was *no one* she could turn to. No one she could tell the full truth to. She was so alone.

Sean's mother returned with the flowers arranged in a beautiful crystal vase as Sean, the twins, and Abe appeared. It was easy to see where Sean's height and lean frame came from. He was very much his father's son in build and temperament. Other than eye colour, his mother hardly got a look in.

The living room quickly turned to chaos as greetings and hugs were exchanged and the girls hopped from foot to foot, desperate to give their gran her banner and cards.

'This is spectacular.' June held up the birthday banner. 'It must've taken you days to make. Look at the detail on these pictures. I love the zebras, and this wonderful fluffy cat.'

'That's Lewis,' Ava said. 'He was Aunty Leah's cat, but he lives with us now.'

June locked eyes with Leah for a split second, her eyes full of sympathy. 'That must be lovely, to have something your aunt loved so much to look after. You'll have to be extra nice to him. He probably misses Leah.'

Harriet shook her head. 'No, he's right at home. He climbs the curtains all the time. Gets into the pantry to look for treats. Sleeps on my bed and even Mummy's sometimes. In fact, he really loves Mummy the best. He always follows her around.'

She shrugged. 'Animals usually pick the people that like them least and stick to them like glue.'

Ava gasped. 'But you love him, Mummy. You said so.'

Leah ruffled Ava's hair. 'I do now, sweetie, but when Leah was alive, I wasn't so keen on cats. It wasn't personal towards Lewis. I just didn't really like them.'

'But you do now?'

'Of course.' That was true at least. Lewis was the only part of her old life that she'd been able to keep.

Abe took the bottle of Veuve Clicquot from Sean and the salad and cheesecake Leah had made, then disappeared into the kitchen.

'Open your presents, Gran.' Harriet took the gift bag from Sean and handed it to her grandmother. 'The best ones are from me and Ava. The one that's a boring card and voucher is from Mummy and Daddy.' She rolled her eyes.

June's genuine delight when she opened each of the presents had the twins smiling from ear to ear. She was equally delighted when she opened the voucher for the Hunter Valley holiday. 'Airfares too,' she scolded. 'You shouldn't have.'

'Of course we should,' Sean answered. 'You don't turn sixty every day, and it'll be a nice break for you and Dad. There are some lovely wineries up there.'

His mother clapped her hands. 'I can see it now, sitting in front of an open fire, glass of red, nice music. Heaven!'

Leah smiled at Sean. He'd certainly done a good job with the presents.

'Now,' June said to the girls. 'How about you two go out the back and see what Pops has set up for you to play. Take a pen and paper from the kitchen and use it to make a score sheet. You can have a proper battle.'

The twins giggled and made their way through to the kitchen and out of the French doors to the backyard.

'What can we do to help, June?' Leah asked.

June's eyes widened at her offer but she was quick to compose herself. 'How about you head out and help your father, Sean, and Eve, you come with me?' She winked. 'I think I'll need help opening that bottle of champagne.'

Leah followed her into the recently renovated kitchen, glad to be separated from Sean. She found it hard to even look at him at the moment.

'So how are you, love?' Eve's mother-in-law asked.

She tried to smile, but it wouldn't come. She was suddenly so overwhelmed she burst into tears.

The older woman moved towards her immediately and embraced her. 'Oh, you poor girl. What an awful time you've had. I can only imagine what you've been going through.'

Leah took the tissue June offered her and wiped her tears. It was all too much. Losing Eve, trying to fit into her life. The trust the two little girls now had in her. The new baby. Sean. Her parents' pain. Jackie's.

How she'd kept it together until now she had no idea.

It took a few minutes, but she managed to compose herself. 'Sorry. I'm not sure where that came from. I think it's been so busy since the accident I haven't had enough time to grieve.'

'You need a break,' June said. She looked out of the window to where Sean was opening a beer and passing it to his father. The older man was turning sausages on the barbecue. 'Perhaps Abe and I could have the twins for a few days? Let you and Sean have some time to yourselves. Get away somewhere.'

Leah's face must've given away her thoughts on that kind suggestion.

'Or perhaps you need a few days to yourself?' Sean's mother added.

'Perhaps,' she said. She leant forward and hugged June again. 'I appreciate the offer and will definitely let you know if I want to take you up on it.' She stood. 'I might use the bathroom and freshen up before we have lunch.'

'Of course, dear. You take your time. I'll finish preparing the salads and we'll join the others.'

Only a few sausages and some salad remained on the table when they'd all finished eating. Sean leaned back in his chair, his hands wrapped around his empty beer bottle as he watched the twins return to their skittles duel and Leah stand, ready to help June clear the table.

'You sit down,' the older woman insisted. 'Chat with Sean and Abe. I can do this.'

'Absolutely not. You should be the one sitting down. It's your birthday.'

'Not until tomorrow, and this lunch wasn't supposed to be for my birthday.'

'No arguments,' Leah said. 'I'm helping, at least.'

'Fine, but let's just put it all inside and go and join the girls. They look like they're having so much fun. We'll clean up properly later. The boys can stay here and chat. Get Sean another beer, Abe. He looks like he could use one.'

'She's right, you know,' Sean's dad said, while Eve and June took the plates and made their way inside. 'You do look like you could use one. Everything okay?'

Sean sighed. 'Yes. No. Sort of.' He ran his hand through his hair. 'Don't know really, Dad. Not sure if I want to talk about it.'

They sat in silence, both nursing their beers, their eyes on the twins.

June and Eve reappeared and joined in with the game of skittles. The shrieks from the twins grew louder when his mum managed to knock down all ten pins at once. Harriet frowned in concentration as she stood the pins back up, took the ball in hand and lined up ready for her turn.

'Looks like it's getting serious,' his father said.

Sean smiled. 'After Mum's strike, Harry will be dying to do the same.'

The little girl released the ball, fists clenched while she waited. Nine of the pins fell down immediately. The tenth teetered to and fro before finally crashing to the ground.

The screams this time were twice as loud as they had been for June, with both Eve and his mum joining in. Eve swept Harriet up in a huge hug and spun her around. The two of them laughed and cheered.

'Eve seems different,' his dad commented. 'Much more relaxed around the kids than usual.'

Sean nodded. 'The accident shook her up, a lot. In some ways she's been very different since then.'

'Really? What's she been doing?'

'Choosing to spend time with the girls and me. Cutting back her work. Baking with them, letting them have treats. Not yelling at them like she used to. She's been doing half of the jobs Kate was doing before. Kate's only coming two days a week, not five. Realistically, we probably don't even need her anymore.'

'You don't look very happy about it. Did you prefer the other version of Eve?' His father asked.

He didn't respond immediately.

'Or is it Kate? Are you disappointed she might not be around so much?'

Sean looked up at his father, reading the real question in his eyes very quickly. He almost laughed out loud. 'What, me and Kate? No, Dad, that's definitely not what the problem is. Kate's been a great nanny, and that's all.'

'Good to hear, son.' He took another swig of his beer. 'So, what is it then? You have a new and improved wife, and you look like you can't stand her.'

'It's complicated.'

'It's usually not all that complicated. It's what we make of a problem that complicates things.'

He gave a half smile. 'Let me assure you, Dad, this *is* complicated and nothing I've done has contributed to it.'

His father leant back in his chair, his eyes fixed on the lively game of skittles on the other side of the garden. 'So, Eve's messed up.'

'Understatement. She's pregnant.' Why had he added that information? He hadn't planned to talk to his father about what was really going on.

'That's great news, surely? Or is it twins and you can't bear the thought of two screaming babies at once again?'

'It's too early to tell. She hasn't had an ultrasound yet.'

'How's she messed up then? Hate to tell you, but it takes two to make a baby. I'd say you might've contributed.'

Sean sighed again. 'I'm more than aware of that, Dad. I wasn't one of the two.'

'Oh.'

They sat in renewed silence.

Sean stole a look at his father. *Oh.* That was all he had to say?

His dad appeared to be deep in thought. Eventually he spoke. 'You sure it isn't yours?'

'Definitely. Things hadn't been good between us before the accident. To make things worse, she tried to pass it off as mine.'

'Even though she knew it couldn't be?'

'Her memory from before the accident is a bit hazy. She doesn't seem to remember how bad things were between us. That I'd been sleeping in the other room. She doesn't even remember having an affair.'

'But she definitely did?'

'Her own mum and best friend seem to know a lot more about it than she does. She's also pregnant. She definitely had an affair.'

'But it's stopped now?'

Sean nodded.

'That's one thing, at least. What does it mean for the two of you?'

'It's over. I haven't worked out how we move forward from here. We have the girls to think of.'

'Of course . . .'

'What?' Sean could see his father had more to say but was choosing to keep silent.

The older man met his eye. 'Life is difficult, son. It's how we handle what's thrown at us that makes us men.'

'What? You think I should forgive her and raise some other guy's kid?'

'I didn't say that. But things aren't always black and white.'

'This *is*. She had an affair and got pregnant. The affair itself was enough to end the marriage. Let alone the pregnancy.'

'You've never thought about being with someone else before?'

Heat rushed to Sean's cheeks. 'Put it this way, I've never acted on it.'

'And there's no way you'd be willing to take things slowly. In light of the accident and how much she's changed? See if it's worth giving her a second chance?'

Sean watched as Eve drew Ava to her in an embrace and then started tickling her. Ava giggled and tried to escape his wife's clutches.

'Let me tell you a story,' his dad said before he could reply. 'A story I don't want you repeating. Okay?'

'Okay.'

His father stared at his beer bottle. 'Your mother is the most amazing woman I've ever met.'

He smiled. 'I know, Dad. You two have a great marriage, you're lucky.'

His father met Sean's eyes. 'No thanks to me. When you were about two, I was travelling a lot for work and if I'm honest, I was glad to be. Babies and toddlers weren't really my thing. Your mum was terrific with you but I found the crying and nap times and constant attention you seemed to need really wearing. I also got a bit jealous that your mum's time was now so devoted to you. You were her priority, not me. So, I found comfort elsewhere.'

'What?' He couldn't believe what he was hearing. His parent's marriage was like an institution. Something he'd respected and looked up to all through his life. It was the thing that had made him want to get married. To have the same bond with someone. To enjoy a family, to grow old together. Of course, Eve hadn't exactly fulfilled the role of wife and mother that he'd imagined.

'It went on for about a year. I was travelling to Sydney most weeks, and she'd come and stay with me.'

'Did Mum find out?'

His father nodded. 'Eventually. The other woman, Denise, tracked me down in Melbourne. I came home to find her having a cup of tea with your mum at the kitchen table. I'd been lying to both of them. Denise didn't know I was married.'

'Oh shit,' Sean said.

'You can say that again. I'll tell you, your mother was remarkable. While Denise was in the house, she stayed calm. Practically apologised on my behalf. Offered her a meal, which, thankfully, she didn't stay for. It was the most excruciating experience, mainly because of the way your mum behaved. She even gave me time to speak to Denise on my own before she left.'

'What did you tell Denise?'

'What *could* I tell her? I apologised. Told her how much I'd enjoyed our time together and I was sorry I'd led her on. She slapped me across the face and left.'

'And Mum?'

'Your mum got out the whisky, placed the bottle and two glasses on the table and made me sit down and talk to her. She made me tell her exactly why I'd felt the need to stray. It took quite a few drinks, but we ended up having the discussion we should've had before I went looking elsewhere. She had no idea how I'd felt about you and how the changes in our life because of having a baby had affected me. Turns out she was finding it hard too, particularly when I was gone half the time and not helping out much when I was around.'

'What did you do? You obviously stayed together.'

'Your mother offered me six months. She said she wasn't going to stay in the marriage if I was unfaithful again. She suggested we take on board everything the whisky had given us the guts to say and see if we could make the situation happy for all three of us.'

'And you did?'

'We did. We also had whisky night every Friday night. We never drank so much as we did that first night, but a couple of drinks each helped us to be honest. Really share our feelings. After a while we didn't need the whisky anymore. We seemed to be able to communicate a lot better.'

'And you didn't stray again?'

'No. Never had the need. If anything, our marriage was stronger because of what'd happened. Mind you, only because of the way your mother made us handle it. Like I said, she's an incredible woman.'

Sean looked across to his mother, who caught his gaze and smiled back. 'Okay, reverse the situation then. Let's say Mum was the one who'd had the affair and came back pregnant. Would you have stayed?'

'Probably not.' His father didn't hesitate.

He laughed. 'So why tell me this whole story then?'

'I wouldn't have stayed, because there's no way I would've sat down and had a conversation with your mother. My pride wouldn't have allowed me to find out why she'd had an affair. I would've walked out and that would've been it. I'm telling you the story so hopefully you don't act like me, but consider acting like your mother. I'm not saying it'll be easy. I'm not guaranteeing it'll fix anything. Raising someone else's kid is a whole other thing. But you and Eve have been together for a long time. You have a history. You have two beautiful girls. It's a lot to throw away.'

It *was* a lot to throw away.

'It would've been an easier decision before the accident,' Sean said. 'We'd grown so far apart. I'm not sure if that was because Eve was having an affair or if there were other reasons too.'

'But now?'

'She's so different. It's like I have the wife I've always wanted. Look at her with the girls. She's so natural with them. So loving and kind. As awful as this sounds, I think I have Leah dying to thank for this dramatic change. Some of the qualities I'm seeing in Eve now are more like her sister. I didn't know Leah all that well, but there was an underlying kindness in her. It's like part of Leah's soul merged with Eve.'

'Tragedy changes people. Eve went through a terrible trauma seeing her sister die. A *twin* sister too. The connection between twins, as you know, is so strong. Eve survived the accident and has come out the other side a better person. Sure, the pregnancy creates an issue you'd prefer not to deal with, but it's not the end of the world. You need to take the pregnancy out of the equation if you can. Could you forgive Eve for the affair based on the fact that *she* ended it, doesn't seem to remember it, and has changed so much?'

Sean closed his eyes. If only he couldn't remember before the accident. That would make things a lot easier. 'I don't know, Dad. I really don't know.'

'Whatever you decide, son, your mother and I will be here to support you. But don't rush into any decisions. Push your pride aside if you can and try to live in the present. Don't look back. Look at what you have right now with Eve and the girls, and go from there.'

Sean placed his empty bottle on the table and stood. 'I'll get us another beer. And, Dad, thanks.'

Sean crossed the lawn and headed towards the kitchen to get some more drinks.

Eve lined the ball up and rolled it with all her might at the skittles. Much to the girls' delight, all ten skittles went flying.

He smiled when the twins rushed to hug his wife. She caught his eye, her smile hesitant as their gazes connected.

A flood of emotions swept through him. She was so beautiful, not only in looks but since Leah's death, in her nature too.

Did he have it in him to forgive her? To move on? Sean closed his eyes when no answer presented itself. He opened them again. 'Great shot,' he called before continuing on.

Leah had never been so pleased for Monday, and work, to roll around. Sean had been a little nicer after they'd left June and Abe's. She'd put it down to the excessive number of beers he'd drunk.

He'd certainly felt it that morning, crashing around the kitchen like a bear with a sore head. He'd grunted at her and disappeared out the door before the girls had surfaced. She'd been relieved when his car backed out of the driveway and sped off down the street. A hangover on top of his already foul mood wasn't going to be good for any of them.

Leah had left the girls with Kate to take to school to ensure she'd be in the office well before the nine o'clock staff meeting. She had a lot of preparations to do for the week. One of the accounts she was managing was going to auction on Thursday and she needed to confirm two more open houses with the owners.

There was a knock on her door as she picked up the phone to make some calls. It was Peter.

'Got a minute?'

'Of course. Everything okay?'

Peter smiled and sat in a chair opposite her. 'It is with me. It's you I'm worried about. Although you're certainly looking a little more like yourself today, which is a good sign.'

She gripped her hands together under the desk. Leah was only looking like *herself*, or the old Eve, because she'd agreed to have lunch with Nicola. She'd taken extra care that morning to look more the part of her sister. However, that wasn't going to help her now. She'd known her poor work performance would catch up with her.

'The thing is, I'm worried you've come back to work too soon. Your memory issues are really affecting the quality of your work.' Peter's smile, kind and gentle, reached his eyes. 'Don't take this the wrong way, Eve. You're brilliant at what you do – we both know that. But I think right now you need to recover. Get your memory back. Come back when you know you're back up at your best, or near it, at least.'

She swallowed. 'Are you firing me?'

Concern flooded his face. 'Of course not. You're the best sales person we've ever had. I just think for the moment it'd be best for everyone if you took some time off. I'm happy to match whatever holiday time you have owing with paid leave. Take a month. Take two if you need it.'

Leah stared. He was willing to pay for Eve to take more time off? She blinked back the tears that were threatening to fill her eyes once again.

'I'm sorry,' Peter said. 'I didn't want to upset you.'

She shook her head. 'I'm not upset. I'm totally overwhelmed you'd offer to do that for me.'

'We want to look after you,' he said gently. 'And we want you to look after yourself. That's the priority right now. We'll be fine for the short-term covering your accounts.'

Leah nodded. Her lies were affecting his business, his bottom line. Again, not something she'd considered when making the decision to become Eve.

'Curt's out until eleven. When he gets back, brief him on any new developments since you took back your portfolio. He's up to speed with most of your accounts so it shouldn't take long. Keep in touch with me and your office is here waiting when you feel you're up to it. And I mean *really* up to it, Eve.'

Until Leah had some clue of what a real estate agent actually did was the underlying message.

She spent the morning organising her files and cleaning her office of all personal items while she waited for Curt. It didn't take long to hand the files back over to him, and by a little after twelve they were finished.

Leah took a last look around her office and collected her bag and coat. She stuck her head in to Peter's office to say she was leaving.

He got up and gave her a hug. 'I want you better, Eve. You've been through a lot, and you need to process it. Grieve. Get your head together. It won't happen overnight.'

She hugged him back. What an amazing boss Eve had. She couldn't imagine Fitzy saying anything like this.

Leah said her goodbyes to the other staff and made her way out of the office to meet Nicola.

Nicola raised an eyebrow when Leah put her hand across the top of the wine glass and shook her head.

'Really? No wine?'

'I'm pregnant, Nic, or did you forget? I'll stick with mineral water.'

Her sister's friend poured herself a glass and shook her head. 'Didn't stop you the first time around.'

'Really? I drank when I was pregnant with the twins?'

'You don't remember?'

She shook her head. 'Considering I hardly drink, that seems weird.'

'*You* seem weird.'

Leah laughed at the direct comment. 'Really? How?'

'Just different.' Her eyes grazed over Leah's face and down to her clothes. 'Since the accident, I hardly recognise you, physically and personality wise.'

She'd purposefully applied more make-up than she'd been wearing and dressed in one of Eve's designer suits. She'd even worn high, uncomfortable heels, all because she was meeting Nicola. Yet her sister's friend was saying she looked physically different? 'Physically?'

'You look more like yourself today,' Nicola said. 'Although you'd never have been caught dead wearing such a pale shade of lipstick. Whatever happened to bold reds being your *power lips? Lips no one could resist?*'

Leah spluttered on her mineral water. 'I actually said that?'

'Far out, Evie! Have you been back to see the doctor? How can you not remember that sort of stuff? It's one thing to not remember saying it, but to have stopped wearing it too? Where did you get that natural shade you're wearing today? You must've gone out to buy it. There's no way the Eve I know would own that. Or what? Did you inherit Leah's make-up?'

Heat flushed her cheeks. *Busted.* Yes, she'd taken all her make-up from her flat and added it to her drawers in Eve's bathroom. She needed to feel comfortable in her own skin, even if she was pretending to be someone else.

Nicola took her hand. 'Sorry, didn't mean to bring up Leah. But do you honestly think she'd want to see you change so much? You've become a different person. It's like you're trying to be Leah, or something weird.'

'Why, because I'm spending more time with my family and less time worrying about superficial things like make-up and clothes?'

'Exactly.' She smiled, relieved that *Eve* finally understood. 'It's not like you. You've always hated so many of the things you say you're doing now. Picking up the girls. Doing homework with them. Cooking meals. All the things you hired the nanny for. You're becoming the nanny.'

Leah shook her head. That was how Nicola saw her now? As the nanny? 'Not the nanny, Nic. I think I'm finally learning how to be a good mother.'

Her sister's friend snorted. 'Boring. What about your work? Ben? Your life?'

'Things have changed.'

'Have they ever.' The woman sipped her wine.

'I can't explain exactly how or why, but they've changed. You're right, I am a different person. I feel different. What's important is different. The girls are my life, and that's not going to change. Yes, it took a tragedy and a huge whack on the head to see that, but I do now.' Leah squeezed her hand. 'I'm sorry that's not what you want to hear.'

Nicola pulled back. 'It's your life, Eve. I know you lost a lot in the accident, and I'm glad if you feel that your life's better now, but I feel like I lost a lot in the accident too. I feel like I lost my best friend.'

Tears flooded Leah's eyes. Nicola couldn't realise how true her words were. She *had* lost her best friend.

They both had.

Leah hardly saw Sean during the week that followed. He had a heavy caseload and was working late every night. He made sure he was up with the girls each morning so he saw them, but he usually left during their breakfast-time.

She hadn't expected much from him. If anything, she'd been surprised to receive the occasional smile. She'd told him that she'd been asked to take some time off from work because she'd been doing a pretty horrible job of it.

He'd been sympathetic when she'd explained what Peter had said. Sean had also been concerned to learn that her memory loss had had such an impact on her job. He'd stated it wasn't normal to forget how to do your job, and suggested she make another doctor's appointment as soon as possible.

She was thinking of Sean while she waited for the girls on Friday after school. His nicer behaviour didn't mean much, long-term. She rubbed her stomach, still amazed that a little person was growing inside her.

The twelve-week scan was only two weeks away. She hadn't imagined seeing her baby for the first time by herself, but it was out of the question to ask Sean to come with her. She could ask her mother but was unsure how her mum really felt about it.

It was all such a mess.

Jackie was who she really needed around her right now. That wasn't realistic either. Her phone pinged with a text message and she smiled reading it.

Eve, was so lovely to see you. Thank you again for the presents you brought for Poppy and Dustin. I'd love to see you again. I'll be up your way tomorrow morning. Any chance you'd be free for a coffee? Jackie xx

Before the accident there were many times Leah would be thinking about Jackie and within minutes, she'd receive a text message or phone call from her friend. They'd always laugh about it. Say it was ESP. It appeared that hadn't changed.

She sent her a quick text back saying she'd love to and suggested they meet at Roast in Brighton at ten.

Leah sent the message before realising that suggesting their usual catch up spot might not have been the most sensitive suggestion.

She relaxed when a smiley face came back and, *CU then.*

The classroom door burst open and twenty-five seven-year-olds came tumbling out. Harriet, her blue shoe laces giving away her identity, came out before Ava. She was smiling and chatting with a friend. She waved to Leah and ran to get her bag.

Ava appeared at the back of the group. She looked worried as she still did most afternoons. Her eyes searched the waiting parents and her face broke into a huge smile the moment she saw Leah.

Her heart contracted. The little girl was still so anxious. Leah shuddered. Her whole reason for becoming Eve had been to protect the girls. Provide security. It certainly wasn't to put them through the trauma of divorce.

Leah, much to the delight of Ava and Harriet, tossed the last of the pancakes up into the air and all three of them watched as it came back down half landing on the plate and half on the bench.

They all cheered.

'Well done, Mummy,' Harriet said. 'You're getting much better at flipping. Almost equal to Aunty Leah.'

Leah was an expert at pancake flipping, but for the twins' benefit, she'd been working her way up to looking like she knew what she was doing.

It'd all started a few weeks back when Harriet had watched her make pancakes and told her that the real secret to them tasting yummy was to flip them. She'd pretended to be doubtful and then tossed the first pancake up and feigned horror when it had stuck to the ceiling.

The twins had watched open-mouthed, their glances alternating between the ceiling and their mother's reaction. Sean had walked in to find them in fits of laughter watching the final piece of pancake gradually fall to the floor.

Since then, Leah's flipping abilities had slowly improved. The first pancake she'd managed to land on a plate earned her a huge round of applause. She still ensured at least one pancake hit the roof, partly for the hilarity, but also to ensure she didn't look too skilled.

Part of this morning's effort was still hanging waiting to fall.

The girls took their plates with the pancakes that'd survived and sat down at the table, while Leah popped some bread into the toaster for her own breakfast and set about making a pot of tea.

'Don't you drink coffee anymore?' Ava asked.

She'd cut down to one coffee a day since discovering she was pregnant. 'I'm meeting Jackie for a coffee this morning. I don't want to overdo it with too many.'

'You're meeting Jackie? Why?'

Her stomach clenched when Sean walked into the kitchen and sat at the island bench.

'Because she asked,' Leah said. 'It helps her feel connected to Leah and it's good for me too.'

He smiled. 'I hope it goes okay. That she's not too sad.'

She hesitated. Two smiles in less than twenty-four hours. 'We had a really nice catch-up when I visited at her house. She said then she wanted to stay in touch, so I assume that's all this is. Tea?'

'Yes, please.' A third smile.

Leah took another cup from the shelf as Sean moved and sat at the table with the girls. Their conversation turned to laughter very quickly, further fuelled by Lewis who jumped up on to the table.

'Lewis!' The cry came from the twins simultaneously.

Leah scooped him off the table with one arm. 'Come on, you naughty pussycat. I'll get you some breakfast.'

Ava's smile vanished and worry appeared in her eyes. She'd called Lewis naughty in a jokey way, yet the little girl still seemed to be on edge, worried that the old Eve would return. Leah made a point of lifting Lewis high into the air and spinning him around before putting him on the floor and rubbing him under the chin.

'I can hear him purring from here,' Harriet said. 'He loves you so much, Mummy.'

'And me him.' Her eyes connected with Ava's while she spoke. 'He's completely changed my view on cats. I can't imagine life without him.'

Ava visibly relaxed and tucked back into her pancakes as Leah poured some biscuits into Lewis's bowl.

'What time are you meeting Jackie?' Sean asked.

'Ten, if that's okay? I won't be out for too long. I can drop the girls at Mum and Dad's on the way if you have work to do. I already checked with them.'

'No, I'm not working this weekend. I was thinking after lunch we could drive up to Belgrave. Puffing Billy leaves at two thirty and I managed to get some tickets this morning. What do you all think?'

The twins squealed in delight.

Leah smiled at their excitement, but inside was disappointed. Another Saturday spent on her own. For Sean, it was a lot easier to get out of the house with the kids than be around her. She spooned the tea leaves into the pot while the girls asked Sean questions about Puffing Billy. They'd never been on the iconic steam train before.

'Sound good, Eve?' he asked. 'Do you think you'd be back by one, so we can head off? We could have a wander through Belgrave first if we're early.'

Leah stared. 'You bought tickets for all four of us?'

He nodded, his eyes searching hers. 'Yes. I thought it would be a nice thing to do as a family.'

'You will come, won't you, Mummy?' Ava asked.

She stared at Sean. *Doing things as a family?*

'Mummy,' Ava said again. 'You will come?'

Leah ruffled her hair. 'Of course. I haven't been on Puffing Billy since I was about your age. I wouldn't miss it. I'll definitely be home before one. In fact, I should be home in time to make us all lunch before we go.'

'No,' Sean said. 'We'll have lunch ready. If you're not back in time, we'll pack yours up and you can eat it in the car. Okay?'

He was going out of his way to be nice. What was the catch?

'Sounds lovely.' She grabbed her toast and picked up the teapot to head to the table.

Sean immediately reached across her plate and stole a piece of toast.

The twins giggled.

Leah pointed in the direction of the toaster. 'For that, you will be sentenced to making more toast. Extra slices too for the girls, and of course Lewis.'

He leapt up and bowed continuously on the way to the toaster. 'Yes, Your Majesty. Of course, Your Majesty. And what would Sir Lewis like on his toast? Smoked salmon, perhaps?'

Leah and the girls laughed at Sean's ridiculous act and the mood continued to be cheerful while they ate their breakfast.

Harriet filled her father in on everything important that'd happened to her that week, and he was also given a full run-down of everything funny Lewis had done. He laughed with his daughters, occasionally winking at Leah.

It would've been lovely if it wasn't so unnerving.

She drank the last of her tea and put her cup down. 'I'd better get ready. I need to leave soon.'

'We'll clean up, Mummy,' Ava said.

'Yes,' agreed Sean. 'Our turn.'

A wicked glint appeared in Harriet's eye. 'You'll have to get the ladder, Daddy. There's a pancake on the roof.'

His eyes went up to the ceiling where the last piece of pancake still clung on. He darted a look at Leah, who shrugged. He shook his head and burst out laughing.

Leah searched the tables at Roast but saw no sign of Jackie. The coffee shop was busy, with most tables in use and other customers standing by the counter waiting for takeaways. Music played in the background but could hardly be heard over the buzz of chatter and brewing coffee. The delicious aroma of freshly ground beans filled Leah's senses and she wished drinking coffee wasn't discouraged during pregnancy. She placed an order and made her way to an empty table tucked away at the back of the store.

A few minutes later, her best friend appeared at the front door. Her eyes scanned the shop and she smiled when she saw Leah waving.

She jumped up when Jackie reached the table and hugged her.

'You look so much better than you did the other week,' Leah said.

Jackie did. Her face had filled out a little, a shine had returned to her hair, and her smile reached her eyes.

'I'm feeling better. Your visit really helped give me the kick up the bum I needed. It made me realise I'll get through this. I will cope.' She smiled. 'Now, should we order?'

'Already did,' Leah said, and immediately regretted it. Eve would hardly remember how Jackie took her coffee. 'Latte macchiato. Right?'

Surprise lit Jackie's face. 'How on earth did you know that?'

'We had coffee a few times with Leah.'

'But that was years ago. You have an amazing memory.'

She forced a laugh. 'Only because I'd never heard of it before you ordered it. So, tell me, how's Richard? How are the kids?'

Jackie gave a quick summary of how her family were, and politely asked the same about Sean and the twins.

'I hope you didn't think it was strange me asking you to have coffee,' she said, after a waiter delivered their steaming cups. 'It's just, your visit was so lovely. I felt like I had part of Leah with me.'

'You do. She'll always be with you. She'll be a big piece in all our hearts.'

'I know, but it was more than that. I had this strange feeling when you were there. It brought me a kind of peace. I feel it now too. Your connection to Leah is so strong. It's like I can feel her.'

Tears filled Leah's eyes. Of course she could feel it. Only she didn't know she was being deceived.

Jackie put her hand on Leah's. 'Oh, Eve. I'm sorry, I didn't mean to upset you.'

Tears poured down her cheeks as she tried to smile. She shook her head and wiped her eyes on the back of her sleeve. 'Sorry, I'm a bit emotional at the moment.'

Jackie nodded. 'I'm like that too. It only takes a few words, and the grief hits me all over again. I wonder if it'll ever go away?'

A lump formed in Leah's throat and the tears kept coming. She couldn't stop. *She'd* caused Jackie's pain. One of the people she loved best was hurting so much and it was for *nothing*. She'd completely failed Eve's wishes to look after her family. Instead she'd hurt them, and her friends, in the process.

Jackie passed a serviette across the table. Her face was full of concern. 'I'm so sorry,' she kept saying.

Leah closed her eyes. She blew her nose and wiped her eyes before releasing a huge breath. 'You don't need to be sorry, Jacks, it's nothing that you've done.'

Jackie paused and gave Leah a long look.

Oh God, she'd called her *Jacks*. Eve hadn't known her well enough to be so familiar. She continued, hoping it would be overlooked. 'I've got a lot going on right now. More than just missing my sister to worry about.'

'Oh no, that's all you need. Can I help at all?'

She hesitated, glad Jackie hadn't commented on her use of the nickname but also realising that talking to Jackie was exactly what she needed. The problem was she couldn't tell her the full story. She could tell her part of it, though.

'I'm pregnant. And it's not Sean's.' The words were out before she could stop them.

Shock registered on Jackie's face. 'Oh, Eve,' she said. 'You poor thing.'

More tears flowed. This was why Jackie had been her best friend for so long. No judgement. Pure compassion.

Leah put her head in her hands. 'I've made such a mess of things. Such a mess.'

'Does Sean know?'

'He does, and he's being very strange. He was angry and hurt when I told him, and acted like we were splitting up. Then the last few days, he's been really nice. I'm not sure what he's thinking.'

'Have you asked him?'

She shook her head. 'I'm too scared. I can't imagine telling the girls we're getting a divorce. Not after what they've been through in the past few months. Poor Ava's anxious enough as it is.'

'What about the guy whose baby it is? Does he know?'

What a shock Grant would get if she announced she was pregnant. He'd have two children only a few months apart. 'No, I haven't told him. I haven't seen him since Leah's funeral.'

'He was at the funeral?'

309

Leah nodded. That was true at least. Grant *had* been at the funeral. 'He's about to have a baby with someone else. I don't think he'll be very pleased to hear about this one.'

'Do you want him to be involved?'

'The bastard cheated on me. I don't want anything to do with Grant ever again.'

Jackie visibly drew back at these words. Disbelief clouded her face and she stared, seemingly unable to speak.

Leah closed her eyes. She'd said *Grant*. She hadn't meant to name him.

God, what would Jackie think now?

'You're pregnant by Grant?' Her best friend's voice was practically a whisper. '*Leah's* Grant? The Grant that cheated on her and was having a baby with someone else? That someone else is you?'

'He doesn't know I'm pregnant.'

Anger replaced Jackie's previously calm voice. 'Let me get this straight. Leah's boyfriend of six years was cheating with you *and* someone else, and managed to get you *both* pregnant? How were you planning on explaining this to Leah, Eve? Or was the accident a nice convenient way to get out of having to?'

She sucked in a breath.

Jackie was shaking, she was so angry. She got to her feet. 'I can't sit here and listen to anymore. Leah loved you. For all your faults, she loved you. And this is how you thank her. You're an absolute disgrace.'

Leah sat open-mouthed while her best friend collected her bag and stormed towards the door.

Chapter Nineteen

Leah sat stunned for a moment. How had their conversation turned to this?

She should never have mentioned the pregnancy. She could've kicked herself for saying Grant instead of Ben. Her stomach contracted. The look on Jackie's face. The shock. The hurt. The fury.

She couldn't leave it like this. She grabbed her bag and rushed to the door, hoping to catch Jackie before she drove off.

Her car was parked across the street in front of the hedged entrance to Brimble Park. Jackie wasn't in the car; she was walking very briskly into the park. Leah crossed the road and hurried after her. She called her, but Jackie didn't turn or slow.

'Jackie,' she yelled again as they neared a small lake.

This time her best friend turned, her face contorted with anger; cheeks stained with tears. 'Get away from me, Eve, I mean it. Pregnant or not, I'm likely to push you in the lake. Or worse.'

She had to suppress a smile. Jackie would never do that, it wasn't in her make-up. 'Can we talk for a minute? There's a lot you don't know.'

'I can't imagine one thing you could say that would make this better. Your sister was miserable when she died, and a large part of that was due to Grant ending their relationship. She thought he was going to propose. Did you know that? That anniversary dinner was supposed to be a proposal. Not the end. And there you are, laughing behind her back. Having sex with the man she loved. You should've died in that accident, Eve, not Leah.' Jackie's face froze as the words left her lips.

Leah tried to hold back the tears but she couldn't. They streamed down her cheeks again. She'd never heard her friend, so angry, so passionate and so protective of her.

Jackie approached her. 'I'm sorry, that was an awful thing to say. I didn't mean it. The bit about you dying.'

She shook her head. 'No, based on everything I've told you, you're right. The thing is—' Tears overcame her.

Jackie led her to a bench overlooking the lake.

'Oh God,' Leah breathed. 'I've made such a mess of things. You'll never forgive me, Jacks.'

'It's not *me* that needs to forgive you, Eve. Your husband. Your family. That's who you need to ask forgiveness from. You can't ask Leah, it's too late.'

She took a deep breath. 'I have to tell you something. But I need you to listen to *all* of it, and I need you to know I'm so sorry for what I've put you through. My decision to do what I did wasn't made lightly, and I agonised over how it would impact you. I'm so sorry.'

Worry flooded Jackie's face. Leah's friend would – naturally – be struggling to think of anything Eve could've done to hurt her.

She took another deep breath, her stomach churning. She might vomit at any moment. 'When the accident happened, there was some confusion at both the accident site, and then in the hospital. Before she died, my sister asked me to do one thing for her, and I made her a promise that I would.'

Jackie was waiting expectantly. 'And?'

Leah looked her friend in the eye. 'Jacks, Eve asked me to look after the girls for her. To become their mum. And I did.'

Sean and the girls set up a production line in the kitchen. Bread, sandwich fillings, cookie cutters and plates filled the counter.

'I'll cut the sandwiches into shapes,' Harriet said. 'Ava, you put the fillings in and Daddy, you . . .' She hesitated, looking around for a job for Sean. 'You go out to the garden and pick some flowers so we can decorate the plates with petals. Mummy will love that.'

He ruffled her hair. 'Yes, Chef!'

The twins giggled while he left them to make the sandwiches and went out to the back garden. He wondered how Eve's catch-up with Jackie was going? Would she tell Jackie about the baby, or would they only talk about Leah?

How awful it was that Leah's life had been cut so short. She'd never have the things she wanted. Marriage, children. She would've been a good mother too. She'd been so good with the twins.

The way Eve was behaving reminded him of Leah. The spark in her eye, her endless patience for their daughters. He'd often found himself comparing the two sisters. Even with everything that'd happened, he was still lucky.

Not only had Eve survived the accident, but it'd been a massive wake-up call for her. She really *had* changed. The occasional glimpse of the old Eve appeared from time-to-time. In a look or a sharp word spoken, but they were usually immediately softened or apologised for. The girls were happier than he'd ever seen them.

He kicked at a rock and leaned to pick a flower. *Damn her.* Why had she gone and wrecked it? Pregnant by someone else. An affair was bad enough. It was a deal breaker; something he'd always said he wouldn't tolerate, but *this* was so much worse.

Sean sighed and pulled his jacket tight as the cool morning air cut through him. If she wasn't pregnant, would he forgive the affair? She couldn't even remember it, and certainly appeared remorseful.

He believed that. It might be stupid of him, especially when she'd been lying non-stop before the accident, but there was something vulnerable about Eve right now that told him she was telling him the truth.

His mother had given his father a second chance. Their marriage had gone from strength to strength.

He picked another flower. He probably *could* move past the affair. The circumstances had changed. Life had changed since the accident and put many things into perspective. But looking at someone else's baby every day would be a constant reminder of what she'd done.

Ironically, Sean was the one who'd wanted another baby. Another girl would be lovely, but deep down he'd always wanted a son. It was Eve who'd said absolutely no way. Now it was possible. The baby might be a boy. Even if it wasn't, Eve seemed open to the idea of more kids.

Why did everything have to be so bloody difficult? There was part of him that almost wished he and Eve had been having sex before the accident, so that it could've been his.

Ignorance, in this case, would certainly be bliss.

Jackie stared at Leah. Her face paled as her mouth dropped open. Leah waited, allowing her friend time to comprehend what she'd just heard. Finally Jackie spoke.

'Leah?' Her voice was barely a whisper. 'It's you?'

She nodded.

A range of emotions passed over Jackie's face. Shock, doubt, confusion.

She took her hand. 'I'm sorry, Jackie. I really am. I know what I've put your through and I'm so, so sorry.'

Her friend withdrew her hand. 'Why? *Why* would you do that to your family? To Sean? To me and your other friends?'

'Because Eve asked me. It was horrific, Jacks, absolutely horrific.' Leah wiped a tear before she could continue. 'She was so badly injured, so broken. She had blood pouring from her and the only thing she was worried about were her girls. She asked me to promise I'd look after them for her, to become like a mum to them.'

Tears ran down Jackie's face. 'But she wouldn't have meant for you to literally become their mum.'

'I think she did. And then there was confusion at the accident scene because we were dressed identically and they thought I was Eve. The same happened in the hospital, and I think shock got the better of me and I never corrected them. At first I figured Sean or my parents would clear everything up when they arrived. I wasn't thinking properly. Then Sean was so relieved Eve was alive that I didn't know what to do. The reality was things weren't going well in my life and I had the chance to save a lot of people from unnecessary grief. I was doing it for them; for Eve, for the twins.'

Jackie was shaking her head. 'But what about all the people that love *you*? What about *us*?'

'My parents were so relieved the girls hadn't lost their mother. When they visited, I convinced myself I was doing the right thing. They didn't need to lose their mum at seven. How would Sean have coped? How would any of them have coped?'

'They would've coped. It might've been hard, but they would have. They had no choice. But what about your parents? Eve's friends? They don't even know she's gone. They haven't been given a chance to say their goodbyes. To mourn their daughter, their friend.'

'I know. I've made such a mess of things.' Leah started to cry again. 'It was for Eve. Those final moments were awful. I had to do it for her.'

Jackie stared for a moment then put an arm around her and pulled her close. 'Oh Lee-Lee, you poor thing. You always put Eve first, always. But this is too extreme.'

They sat in silence for a few minutes, both deep in their own thoughts.

Eventually Leah drew back from the comfort of her best friend's embrace. 'Everything's such a mess. I didn't know that Eve and Sean's marriage was on the rocks, that she'd been having an affair. That there was no way a baby could be his.'

'No way?'

She shook her head. 'No, he'd been sleeping in the spare room for months. I only found all this out when I announced I was pregnant. Stupid me thought he'd be happy. Instead, it confirmed Eve, or as far as he's concerned, *I*, had had an affair. He was devastated.'

'Was or is?'

'I'm not sure. He's acting very strangely. His nice behaviour the last few days feels like it's the calm before the storm.'

'You have to tell him, Leah. You can't let him believe you're Eve. It's not fair on Eve either. Did she actually have an affair?'

'She did, but it's highly unlikely she was pregnant.'

'Geez.' Jackie ran her hand through her hair. 'This really is a mess.'

'I can't bear the thought of the girls finding out. Of them having to live without a mother. We've become so close too.'

'Lee, you're living a *lie*. A lie so ginormous I can't even get my head around it. Your intentions may have been good, but I don't think it's going to be the happy ending you'd envisaged. You need to tell the truth to Sean and your parents at least. Go from there.'

She sat in silence. She had made a big mistake. *Ginormous*, Jackie had said. She couldn't begin to imagine the fallout if she told the truth.

Leah hugged Jackie tight as they said their goodbyes.

Her best friend confessed she was still in shock. 'But, Lee,' she said, tears welling in her eyes again. 'I'm also so happy. I know you didn't want to hurt me. You were trying to do your best for Eve and her girls.' She shook her head. 'I can't believe you're alive. I really can't.'

Leah waved goodbye and climbed into her car. Her heart was heavy. Telling the truth to Sean and the girls still may not be the best thing. Could she even do it? She drove home slowly, making an effort to pull herself out of the overwhelming sadness. She needed to put on a happy act for the twins and their afternoon plans.

She arrived back at the house close to twelve thirty, and made her way through the garage. She was met with Harriet's cheers as she entered the kitchen.

'Perfect timing, Mummy. Lunch is ready and we're about to eat.'

She couldn't imagine being able to eat a thing. Leah allowed Harriet to bustle her into her seat and smiled when a plate of sandwiches, all cut into shapes with the cookie cutters, was placed in front of her. The plate was decorated with flower petals. 'This looks wonderful. You've both been very busy.'

'The sandwiches are healthy, too,' Ava added.

'Except for the dessert one,' Harriet said. 'That's not healthy.'

'A dessert sandwich? I've never had one of those,' Leah said. 'What's in it?'

'Peanut butter and strawberry jam,' Ava said. 'I thought peanut butter and jelly meant wobbly jelly. Daddy explained jelly is

317

what Americans call jam, so we wanted to try it. That's okay, isn't it, Mummy?'

'Of course. Peanut butter and jelly is one of my favourites.'

'Really?' Sean asked. 'I wouldn't have thought you'd ever have tried it.'

Perhaps she was feeling over-sensitive, but she wasn't in the mood for a dig. She glared. 'Do you really need to question everything I say?'

Silence fell around the table and Ava's face immediately crumbled.

Sean looked contrite. 'Sorry, babe, I didn't mean it in a nasty way. You've been so into clean eating. White bread, sugar and peanut butter aren't really high on your list of foods. Or at least didn't use to be.'

Guilt rushed over Leah.

The girls waited for her response; Ava hardly daring to breathe.

She squeezed Ava's arm. 'Oh, well, that makes sense. I probably should've said it was my favourite when I was little. I remember trying it for the first time on a family holiday when we went to Fraser Island in Queensland. Your Aunty Leah was experimenting with all types of sandwich fillings, and that was one of them. We also decided banana and peanut butter was nice, Vegemite and Cheetos a real hit, but we weren't so keen on tuna and marmalade.'

'Oh yuck!' Harriet said. 'That would be disgusting.'

Leah nodded. 'Sure was.'

'Will you try our dessert sandwich, Mummy?' Ava asked.

'Of course.' She smiled. 'It'll bring back lots of memories.' She didn't exhale until they started eating their lunch.

It was the first time she'd really snapped at Sean since the accident. The first time the girls had seen her be the old Eve. She would almost have laughed at that irony, except laughter was far from her thoughts.

Jackie's words kept playing in her head. *You need to tell the truth to Sean and your parents.*

Sean packed the last of the lunch dishes into the dishwasher and checked the clock on the microwave. It was nearly one. 'Time to go,' he called.

The girls had been instructed to wash the jam and peanut butter off their faces and get anything they wanted to bring with them in the car.

He hadn't meant to upset Eve by questioning her favourite sandwich. She was definitely on edge. He sighed. He couldn't blame her. He'd been pretty awful to her. His father's advice continued to play over and over in his mind. His mother was such a strong person to be able to put the situation behind them and move forward in a loving and generous way.

He shook himself. He wanted an afternoon free of thinking about the situation. Hopefully they could all have some fun.

Ava and Harriet hurried into the kitchen; Ava with her much-loved toy squirrel under her arm and Harriet lugging the large struggling white mass of Lewis.

'Ready, Daddy,' she giggled.

He couldn't help but laugh. 'You can't bring Lewis, Harry.'

'But you said bring anything you want for the car.' The little girl grinned from ear to ear. 'I chose Lewis.'

Eve came in behind her and scooped the cat from her arms. 'I think that's a great idea, Harry. Perhaps Lewis could drive us there? Now, everyone say your prayers, wrap yourself in bubble wrap and we should be good to go.'

They all laughed.

'Okay, fine I won't bring him then,' Harriet said. 'He'll be lonely without us.'

His wife put Lewis on the floor and he dashed from the kitchen. They heard him plodding on the stairs as he raced up to the girls' bedroom.

'I think he'll be fine,' Sean said. 'Now, let's go.'

Sean smiled, watching Eve and the twins take great delight in sitting on the windowsills, dangling their legs outside of the train. He remembered the wind whistling through his hair and soot filling his eyes as he'd hung on to the black safety bars across the open windows when he was a boy. He hadn't been sure if safety laws would still allow it. He was glad they did, even though it also meant they were dealing with the soot and smoke of the steam engine.

Luckily Eve had thought to bring the girls' sunglasses, so at least it was only their clothes that were getting specks of black and they weren't having to contend with tears from stinging eyes.

The train tooted as it chugged along the line between Belgrave and Lakeside. They'd already had a short stop at Menzies Creek and expected one more at Emerald before continuing on to the lake where they could get out and explore for forty-five minutes before returning on the four fifteen train.

'You should hang out the window too, Daddy,' Ava said. 'It's so much fun.'

'Yeah, Daddy, you're missing the best bit,' Harriet added.

Sean had been standing behind the girls, his arms around each of their shoulders. 'Okay,' he said. 'I'll give it a go.'

Eve shuffled across, giving him room to slip in between her and Ava. He hauled himself up and laughed as he struggled to get his legs through the bars. 'There was a lot more room to do this when I was a kid.'

320

'That's better,' Ava said once he was settled. 'Now we can all really enjoy it.'

Sean felt Eve stiffen when he slipped in next to her. She was probably waiting for his announcement that he wanted a divorce. What she didn't realise was how hard that would be for him to do. They had their daughters. They had a history, and since the accident he'd had so much hope for their future.

The fact that she'd thought she could pass the baby off as his was another thing. Although, what did he really believe? If she didn't remember the affair, or the state of their relationship before the accident, then perhaps she really *had* thought it was his. To believe she hadn't deliberately tried to deceive him was a comforting thought.

He shut his eyes. The cool air of the Dandenongs whipped against his face while the train chugged along.

Sean wanted to get past this. It was up to him, of course. *He* had to be the one to end the marriage, or to accept the situation and try to make it work. He opened his eyes and turned to Eve.

She appeared to be deep in thought. Her face was pale, filled with regret, as she stared out at the passing trees and bushes. The level of remorse she felt had been clear since her announcement. He was grateful for that at least.

Sean swallowed. She was his wife. The mother of his children. He took her hand and squeezed it.

Eve looked at him and offered a small smile when she squeezed his hand back.

He dropped her fingers and put an arm around her shoulders, tugging her close and kissing her head gently. He felt her relax against him.

On his other side, the twins were nudging each other and giggling.

'Mummy and Daddy sitting in a tree . . .' Harriet began.

He laughed. 'Okay, that's enough. Look, we're coming into Emerald station. See if you can count how many people are waiting to get on the train.'

His daughters' focus instantly moved from watching their parents to counting passengers.

Sean's heart swelled. Right at this moment, with Eve snuggled against him and the girls having a wonderful time, he was content.

Leah was quiet while they drove back from Belgrave. They'd had a wonderful day out; the girls had wanted Puffing Billy to last a lot longer than it had, and were disappointed when it was time to disembark from their return journey.

They'd been lucky that it hadn't been too busy on the train so they'd been able to sit with legs hanging out of the window in both directions. Unfortunately, she was certainly feeling it now. The window ledges weren't the most comfortable of places to sit for more than an hour at a time.

They'd only had a short time at Lakeside to wander around, enjoy an ice cream and have a quick look at a model railway. They'd all agreed to come back again on an earlier train so they could spend the day there.

Harriet begged to go on a paddleboat on the lake but there wasn't time.

'Another day,' Sean had promised.

Something had changed in him. He was making such an effort. He'd taken Leah's hand as they'd walked around and pulled her close to him a few times, stroking her arm.

She found herself fighting tears most of the day. While Leah had originally told herself her only reason for stepping into Eve's shoes was for the twins, that wasn't completely true.

She loved Sean.

He was kind, caring, a wonderful father. She was attracted to him, always had been. But their relationship was based on a lie. A well-meaning, but poorly thought-through lie. Leah hated to imagine how he'd react if she told him. How much extra pain she'd inflict on him. It hurt because she'd let Eve down too.

'You okay?' Sean squeezed her knee.

'I'm fine.' She took a deep breath. Her decision was made that moment. 'But we need to talk. Tonight, when the girls go to bed.'

He smiled. 'I was going to suggest the same. It's been a difficult few weeks, but yes, we need to talk. Need to work out how we move forward.'

She nodded.

'There's something I want to say to the twins first, a bit of a surprise.' Sean smiled again. 'It'll be a surprise for you too. I'll do it at dinner. Then you and I can talk properly once they're in bed.'

Leah closed her eyes for the remainder of the trip home. Her stomach churned considering the girls. Particularly Ava.

Sean waited until dessert to make his announcement. It was time to step up; to take a leaf out of his mother's way of operating.

He waited until each had fruit salad in front of them then picked up his water glass and tapped against it with a spoon. 'Attention please!'

His daughters' chatter stopped as they waited.

Eve watched him, her face guarded. She obviously had no idea what he was about to say, and by the looks of her, she was terrified at the prospect.

He took his wife's hand. 'Your mother and I have some news.'

'What is it?' Harriet asked.

'Shh,' Ava hissed. 'Let him speak.'

'Your mother and I are very pleased to share some news with you. Sometime in March next year, we will be welcoming your new baby brother or sister.'

Eve's sharp intake of breath was audible. She snatched her hand from his.

Sean turned to her, worry rushing over him. 'Sorry, should I have not said anything?'

Eve shook her head, tears filling her eyes while she smiled. 'No, of course not. I wasn't expecting you to tell them, that's all.'

'Why not, Mummy?' Ava asked. 'Did you think we wouldn't be pleased?'

She shook her head again, tears streaming down her face. 'Mummies get very emotional when they're pregnant, that's all.'

'They're good tears?' Harriet asked.

'Definitely,' she said, squeezing her niece's hand.

'I hope it's a girl,' Ava said. 'Imagine having a baby sister.'

'I already do,' Harriet smirked. 'I'm two minutes older than you, don't forget that.'

Ava stuck out her tongue. 'That doesn't count, and anyway you act about two years younger.'

Sean laughed. 'She's got you there, Harry. So, now that you know the exciting news, there's lots you're both going to have to do.'

'Like what?' Ava asked.

'Like help Mummy out a bit more, particularly when her tummy starts to get big when the baby grows. Closer to the time he or she is born we'll need your help to set up a nursery for the baby and buy some toys.'

'We'll need to train Lewis, too,' Harriet said. 'He might get jealous that he's not the newest member of the house. We'll sit him down and talk to him before the baby's born.'

'I'm going to make a card for the baby,' Ava said. 'To welcome her. And maybe a banner.' She clapped her hands. 'This is so exciting. I wish you could have the baby right now, Mummy.'

Sean grinned at his daughters. 'I knew you'd both be excited.' He squeezed Eve's hand. 'Imagine us, a family of five.'

'Six,' Ava corrected. 'Don't forget Lewis.'

'Maybe seven,' Harriet said. 'Mummy might be having twins or more!'

He laughed. 'God help us, if that's the case.'

Leah finished reading story number four to the twins and tucked them into bed.

'I'm so happy, Mummy,' Ava said. 'A baby brother or sister. It's so exciting.'

'It sure is.' She leaned down and kissed the little girl's forehead. 'Now you sleep well, won't you?'

She moved across the room to tuck Harriet in and kissed her too. 'Sweet dreams, Harry.'

'You too, Mummy.' The child's voice was soft. The excitement of Puffing Billy had taken it out of her; she was almost asleep.

Leah switched off the light. 'I love you, girls.'

'Love you, Mummy,' they replied.

She closed the door quietly and leaned against it. She certainly hadn't counted on Sean making the *happy* announcement at dinner. There was no way he would've done that if he was planning to tell her he wanted a divorce.

Leah descended the stairs to the kitchen. It was empty. She could hear voices from the television, so she followed the sound into the living room.

Sean smiled at her, flicked the television off and patted the seat on the couch next to him. 'I'm sorry I put you on the spot with the girls. I thought it was a nice way of telling them, and telling you I'm okay with it. I'll consider this baby mine, treat him . . .' He grinned. 'Hopefully *him*, exactly as if he was mine. I want us to move past this, Eve. Get on with living our lives and enjoying each other.'

The lump in Leah's throat shot pain down into her chest. It hurt so much she couldn't talk.

'Things have changed since the accident. You've changed, we've changed, and it is all for the better. I never imagined we'd have another baby, never thought you'd *want* one. But maybe, unless this one is twins, too, that's something we might want to consider again down the track.'

Leah still hadn't been able to speak.

'Are you okay?'

She shook her head and opened her mouth but the words wouldn't come. Instead, she found herself suddenly overcome with tears. Her body convulsed with sobs.

Sean pulled her to him, stroking her back. 'Hey, it's okay. That's what I'm telling you. Everything will be okay. I checked the calendar and have cleared my morning on the fifteenth so I can come with you for the twelve-week scan. I want to be part of this; I want you, and I want this baby.'

She continued to sob. How on earth was she going to tell him? He'd forgiven her, even agreed to father this child.

He held her tight, continuing to stroke her back. 'Come on, Eve,' he said. 'You're beginning to worry me. Happy tears are fine but I'm not convinced this is what these are.'

Leah moved out of his embrace and excused herself. She went to the downstairs bathroom, blew her nose and dried her tears.

She perched her hands on the edge of the bathroom vanity and took a number of deep breaths in the hope of calming her churning stomach.

After a few minutes passed, there was a gentle knock on the door.

'Babe, are you okay?' Sean's voice was full of concern.

'Be out in a sec.' She took another deep breath and opened the bathroom door. 'Sorry,' was all she offered.

He took her hand and led her back to the living room to the couch. 'I thought you'd be happy?' he said, sitting next to her. 'This is what you wanted, isn't it?'

Leah nodded. 'It is – well, was. Oh, Jesus.' She stood and paced the length of the room.

'Eve—'

She couldn't meet his eyes. 'I can't do this right now. I'm going for a run.'

'But it's late. You can't—'

She ignored Sean and was out of the house within seconds. She closed the front door behind her and ran down the path to the front gate. She didn't stop until she was far enough down the street to be out of view. By then she was gasping for air.

She slowed to a walk and continued in the direction of the park. She needed to think. To work out what she should do. She'd been so clear in her own mind that she should tell Sean.

But now? How could she?

Leah tried to imagine what Eve would want her to do. Would she want her to continue living this enormous lie? Had she really meant for Leah to take over her life?

Jackie's words haunted her. *But she wouldn't have meant for you to literally become their mum.*

She took a deep breath. Jackie was right. Eve wouldn't have meant it literally. She would've meant for Leah to spend time with the girls. Be close to them. Help fill the gap her death had left behind.

As she reached the wide, open playing fields of Johnstone Park, she was overcome with sadness. She wished Eve was still here. That none of this had ever happened.

Somehow Leah had managed to turn a tragic event into something even worse. Tears spilled while she continued along the walking track. She'd been so preoccupied most of the time, trying to be Eve, that she'd barely had time to grieve for her sister, to miss her.

She stopped at a bench and sat. She was crying so hard she could no longer see where she was going. How would she ever come to terms with losing her twin?

Leah hadn't even been able to talk about her to anyone. Her parents and Sean of course were grieving for *her*, Leah, and were able to talk about her, share stories. There was no one she'd been able to share stories of *Eve* with, to grieve with.

The tears continued to flow. Leah closed her eyes trying to get a hold of herself. She was grateful it was getting late and there was no one else around.

She took deep breaths, trying to bring herself under control. Eventually, she wiped her eyes and stood.

Sean would be worried sick.

She owed him an explanation.

Leah pushed open the front door.

Sean immediately appeared in the hallway, his face full of concern. 'Eve—'

She put her hand up to silence him. 'Can you let me talk please, Sean? Let me say everything I need to before you ask questions or get angry or react in any way. Please.'

He nodded. His eyes filled with fear.

They moved into the living room and Leah sat opposite Sean. 'Before I tell you anything, I need you to know how sorry I am. I never imagined things would spiral so quickly out of control.' She swallowed, the lump in her throat pushing painfully against her. She held her hand up again when it looked like he was going to speak. 'Let me finish, please.

'On the night of the accident, things were crazy. Shock, confusion, terror, you name it.' Leah took a deep breath. 'I lied about my sister's death. I didn't want anyone to know what she went through. She wasn't unconscious when the car finally stopped, she was with it for a few more minutes; long enough to ask me to do something for her. To beg me, in fact. When she died, I was beside myself. My head was throbbing. All I could think about was you and the girls and my parents and everyone close to us. I couldn't bear the thought of the pain any of us were going to have to go through. Then the paramedics came, and next thing I knew I was in the hospital. A mistake had been made, and I hadn't corrected it. I assumed when you arrived, it would all be fixed, but then you came and I realised I couldn't do it. Sean, I was in shock. I was so confused, but it was the one thing that made sense at the time. It was *the* one thing I could do to make things better, and it was the one thing she asked me to do.'

'What did she ask?'

'She asked me to be her, Sean. She asked me to be Eve.'

Chapter Twenty

Sean stared at the woman sitting in front of him. 'What?'

Tears ran down her face. 'Eve asked me to be her. She asked me to be a mum to the girls. She couldn't bear the thought of the pain that any of you would go through.'

'Eve's . . . Eve's dead?'

Leah nodded, her eyes brimming with tears.

Air whooshed from his gut, as if he'd been punched.

His wife, the mother of his girls was dead?

He was looking at Leah, not Eve.

Sean took his head in his hands. How could he have been so stupid? How could Leah have done this to them?

Anger rose within him staring at his sister-in-law. 'And you said yes?' His voice shook. 'You thought you could just slip in and *be* Eve? That you could steal her life?'

Tears spilled down Leah's cheeks. She quickly wiped them with her sleeve. 'I wasn't thinking straight. The doctors were calling me Eve because of a mistake at the accident site. We were dressed identically. There was no way they knew which of us was which. I had Eve's final words ringing in my head, then you turned up. You were so happy Eve was alive. So grateful she'd been spared. Then when the girls came to visit it also felt like the right decision. I wasn't stealing her life. I was fulfilling a promise. Trying to reduce the pain and suffering you and the girls would go through.'

'But what about Eve? She's gone and no one has mourned her. There's been no celebration of her life. Nothing.'

She didn't respond. Her face was pale. Her hands trembled.

Sean couldn't wrap his head around the enormity of what she'd done. 'You gave up your entire life, your parents, your friends, your work, to *become* Eve?' He paced around the living room. Then stopped by the liquor cabinet and – hand shaking as much as hers – poured himself a large Scotch.

He threw it back in one gulp, and left his empty glass next to the bottle, sitting back on the couch taking his head in his hands.

Eve was dead.

Sean looked up at Leah, tears filling his eyes. 'How am I supposed to tell them? *How* do I tell them that their mother died and about what you've done? How are two little girls going to deal with losing you both at once?'

'I wasn't trying to deceive anyone, Sean. I thought I was doing the best for everyone.'

'Why tell me now then? After putting me through thinking my wife is pregnant by another man, you decide, on the night I tell you I'm willing to accept this baby as my own, it would be a good idea to come clean? Why not keep the charade up? Let me go on believing you're my wife? Ironically our relationship has been better than it has been in years. Before the accident, Eve and I were heading towards divorce. Now, for the first time in years, I could see a future for us.'

'I realised that the vomiting isn't just morning sickness, Sean. I look at you and the girls every day and realise how much I want to be here, how much I love you all and then I feel guilt. We're living a colossal lie.'

'That's an understatement,' he said. 'So, what do we do now? Legally you're dead. Your entire family thinks you're dead. So do your friends and work colleagues. Are you expecting them to accept you back into their lives like you'd never died? They've grieved for you, missed you.'

'I have *no* idea what to do. Jackie knows. I told her this morning. I don't know if our friendship will ever be the same.'

'I doubt *anything* will ever be the same. There will be legal consequences too. Do you realise that? You can't pretend to be dead and take over someone else's identity.'

She shook her head. 'It wasn't high on my list of concerns. I was more worried about you and the girls, and Mum and Dad.'

He stared for a long moment. Had she really done this for them? He stood. 'I'm going out. I need to clear my head.'

She watched as he turned and left the room.

Sean pushed himself harder and harder through the dark streets of Brighton towards the beach, his chest burning.

He'd been running for over fifteen minutes, counting the rhythmic thud of his footsteps as he pounded along the path. The counting was helping to push all other thoughts from his head. He slowed when he reached the running track overlooking the beach.

It was dark but the streetlights lit up enough to be able to see the dark ripple of the sea. The salty smell of seaweed and ocean filled his nostrils. He breathed deeply, trying to catch his breath. He slowed to a gradual walk, eventually stopping at a picnic table.

Sean sat on the table, his feet resting on the bench seat as he gazed out to sea. The sky was filled with stars. He shivered; a jumper would've been a good idea.

Tears filled his eyes. Eve was dead.

She'd hardly been the perfect wife, and it was true, prior to the accident he'd been seriously thinking of asking her for a divorce, but he wouldn't ever wish her dead.

He shook his head. How could Leah have done it? Didn't she realise how many people she'd hurt? How would they move forward? Another funeral? This time, for Eve? How would Peggy and Bill react?

The grieving would start again. Eve's friends, Nicola and . . . Sean stopped there. Other than Nicola, she hadn't had any close friends. A lot of colleagues and acquaintances, but not that many friends. Still, they'd all be very upset to learn of her death.

To think that Leah had not only been passing herself off as Eve West, wife and mother, but she'd been going to work too. It certainly made sense as to why Peter had asked her to take some time off.

She'd been visiting her parents, catching up with Nicola. Everyone commented about how different she'd become since the accident; so much warmer, a better wife, a better mother. Not one of them, including him, had ever suspected she *wasn't* Eve.

She was being treated for memory loss, for goodness' sake. Of course she didn't have Eve's memories. They weren't *hers* to have.

All the soul-searching he'd done since talking to his father – weighing up whether or not he could take on another man's baby – paled in comparison to the conversation he was going to have to have with Ava and Harriet. He was a single dad, a widower. How on earth was he going to make *that* work?

His thoughts shifted to Leah. He'd grown close to her. Thought he'd fallen back in love with his wife.

It made so much sense now. All the things he'd fallen in love with – her kindness, her gentle nature and adoration of the girls – were not traits Eve had ever possessed. She'd happily accepted Lewis into their home, started drinking coffee and eating bread and sugar. Baking cakes and other treats.

These should have been sure-fire signals that all was *not* okay, but he hadn't focused on any of it. He'd put everything unusual down to the accident and, if anything, had been immensely grateful for the changes. Even her protectiveness of the baby growing inside her.

Two years after the twins were born, Eve had thought she might be pregnant. It'd turned out to be a false alarm, but Sean had been shocked at the time when she'd announced she'd be making an appointment immediately to terminate the pregnancy. There was no way she was going through labour and the nightmare of another newborn. It definitely wasn't for her. That time, it would've been *his* baby.

For Eve to have been so adamant she was keeping the baby should've been another big red flag. The post-accident changes in 'Eve' had been enough to accept this too.

He climbed off the table and started walking in the direction of home, his mind shifting to the girls. They'd lost more than their mother. The happiness, the love they'd received from the woman they thought was Eve was about to be ripped away from them.

Guilt settled like a rock in the pit of his stomach. He'd been happier in the past weeks than he had been in *years*, and from their behaviour, the girls had too. Part of him wished Eve *had* been more like Leah when she was alive. It was unfair, but true.

Leah had shown them how happy a family could be. How loved they could feel. She wasn't faking her feelings towards him or the girls. They were genuine. She'd said that she loved all of them. His feelings had been real too. Or at least he thought they were; now he didn't know what to believe.

He sighed. His anger gave way to a small level of understanding. It was her nature. She always was the one to try to put things right.

Sean had no idea what the next steps were. Did they have a funeral for Eve? What repercussions would Leah face legally? How were the girls going to take this?

He shook his head. He still couldn't believe she'd done it. Given up her own life to become Eve? It made no sense at all.

Leah wasn't in the living room when Sean got back. He went upstairs. The light was on in their bedroom.

The morning he'd brought her home from the hospital, he remembered, she'd made her way towards the guest room before realising she wasn't a guest. That she was supposed to be sleeping in the main room.

Sean knocked and poked his head in to the room. 'Can I come in?'

Leah was sitting up in bed, tissues in one hand and stroking Lewis, who was stretched out beside her, with the other. She nodded.

He came around and sat on the edge of the bed. 'I don't really know what to say or do right now. I need time to process everything. What I do know is what you did was for Eve, me and the girls. It was a huge sacrifice.'

'You don't hate me?' she asked.

'No, I don't hate you. I'm freaked out, though. I'm sad for Eve, sad for the girls. I'm sad for all of us. But I also recognise we lost Eve that night, and we already knew that. The *Eve* that returned from the hospital wasn't the same person, and for that I was grateful. Eve wasn't cut out for motherhood and that has always worried me. Something changed in her when she had the girls. Or at least it appeared that way.'

He sighed. 'I think having two people dependent on her was overwhelming and she rejected the idea of motherhood. She chose not to breastfeed. Went back to work when they were three months old. She wasn't maternal, and fought against the idea of bonding with them. It made me very sad. I'd hoped when they got older she'd change. But she didn't. She found them more tolerable, but that was about it. Ava was scared of her.'

Tears flowed down Leah's cheeks again. 'I know Eve was trying her best. We talked about it before the accident. She was going to make more of an effort. She never got the chance.'

He stared. 'I'm glad she was at least aware she needed to change. But *you* changed Eve for us. For starters, Ava's not scared of her mother anymore. I don't know how she's going to cope when she finds out the truth. Eve constantly let her down, and she didn't trust her. After this, I can't imagine she's going to trust anyone.'

'I'm sorry, Sean. I know they're only words, and they don't fix anything, but I need you to know I *am* truly sorry.'

'I know that. Like I said, I know you thought you were doing this for all the right reasons.'

'Do you want me to move out?' Leah asked. 'I can go tomorrow if you like.'

'Where would you go?'

'To Mum and Dad's, I guess. If they'll have me. There's no guarantee of that, of course. I could probably stay at Jackie's until I get myself sorted out.'

Sean shook his head. 'No, for now I'd like you to stay. I'm not sure I want to tell the girls, yet. I need some time to think about things. I want to look into what it means for you too. Whether there'll be legal ramifications. Do you mind being Eve for a few more days?'

'That's fine. I won't talk to Mum and Dad until we've told the twins and worked out how to move forward.' She hesitated. 'Sean, I love the girls. I wish I was their mother. There was no pretending when it came to that. All of my feelings were true. Not only for the girls, but for you too.'

He stood. 'I'm going to have a shower and sleep in the spare room. Let's do our best to act like nothing has changed in the morning.'

'Okay.'

'And, Leah,' He turned when he reached the bedroom door, 'as big a mess as this all is, I do know your heart was in the right place.'

Leah was glad for the companionship of Lewis that night. She hardly slept, but was comforted by his constant purrs and occasional snores.

She lay awake obsessing about Eve. About their childhood and how she'd constantly got into trouble for being involved in her sister's mostly hare-brained schemes. They'd never been thought through. Her twin had acted on impulse and her enthusiasm for whatever mad plan she'd thought up was usually contagious. *This* situation was no different.

She dozed off around four and was woken by giggles a little after seven.

'Mummy, you've slept in,' Ava said. 'You need to get up. We have to go to school.'

Leah glanced at the clock and groaned. 'Oh gosh, sorry girls. We're going to have to be quick.' She focused on the twins, who stood in front of her in their school uniforms. 'You're dressed already?'

'Yep, and we had breakfast too,' Harriet said. 'Daddy was snoring in the spare room.'

'Why did he sleep there?' Ava asked. 'Did you have a fight?'

She shook her head. 'No, he worked late and said he didn't want to wake me when he came to bed. Lewis was here with me.' She looked around the room. 'I wonder where he's gone.'

'He's downstairs having breakfast,' Ava said. She whispered to Harriet. 'Did you put his bowl back on the floor?'

Harriet's eyes widened and her little mouth hung open, then she dashed out of the room.

Leah laughed. 'I take it Lewis was set a place at the table while you ate your breakfast.'

Ava nodded. 'Are you mad, Mummy? We thought it was easier because he kept jumping up trying to eat our cereal. We knew you wouldn't want us sharing that with him.'

Leah clambered out of bed and ruffled Ava's hair. 'It's fine, honey. But let's not make a habit of it. Now, let me quickly get ready and I'll be down in a minute to make your lunches. Tell Harriet to brush her teeth and we'll be on time. You two have done a great job this morning, I'm really proud of you.'

Ava beamed.

'We'd better wake Daddy too,' Leah said. 'He'll be late for work otherwise.'

Sean pulled out of the driveway, a piece of toast in one hand, the other on the steering wheel.

Leah had made him coffee, which was sitting in the drink holder of the Mercedes. He almost laughed at the absurdity of it. Eve wouldn't have allowed anything to be eaten or drunk in either of their cars, let alone handed him a piece of toast to take.

The morning had been a mad rush, thanks to both of them sleeping in. Leah's decision to cut back Kate's hours to only two days a week certainly hadn't been appreciated by either of them today.

From the dark circles under Leah's eyes he assumed she'd managed about the same amount of sleep he had.

He'd been wracked with guilt all night. Sean could never take back his final words to Eve. Guilt also nagged because he hadn't shed a tear since learning Eve really was gone. He was just . . . numb. Yet at the hospital when he'd been told Leah had died, he'd felt like he'd been stabbed. He'd been so shocked and so upset.

Sean joined the throngs of traffic on Nepean Highway heading towards the CBD. His mind was a jumble.

He took a deep breath. The first thing he planned to do when he arrived at the office was look into the legal ramifications for Leah. They couldn't be good.

The day dragged for Leah. After dropping the twins at school, she'd returned home and spent most of the morning on the couch with the comfort of Lewis beside her.

She'd stroked her beautiful cat, trying not to think about the fact that she'd be saying goodbye to him when she moved out. There was no way she could take him from the girls now that they were so attached. It was all such a mess, although Sean's reaction was above and beyond anything she would've imagined. He seemed to understand *why* she'd done what she had and wasn't furious with her. It was a relief. Was it too much to hope that her parents would feel the same way?

Eventually Leah dragged herself up off the couch, cleaned up the breakfast dishes and put on a load of washing. Her thoughts continually flicked back to the accident, to Eve. To her last moments.

She wiped the dampness from her cheeks. How she wished she could turn back time. That she could do something to prevent the accident from happening in the first place.

It wouldn't have stopped the twins from going through the pain of their parent's divorcing, assuming Sean and Eve's relationship had come to that, but she wouldn't be responsible for any of it. And she'd have been there to pick up the pieces, support Eve and Sean and help with their daughters, without feeling any guilt.

Leah opened the cupboard in the laundry and took out the cleaning supplies. She needed to distract herself, keep busy. Nothing like cleaning bathrooms to do that.

Even with the twins home to keep her occupied, the afternoon had continued to drag.

Sean arrived in time for dinner, and they both did their best to have fun with the girls and not give them any reason to worry. They put them to bed and sat down together in the living room.

'I need to know something,' he said. 'The night of the accident, Eve and I had a huge fight. I said things I can never take back.' He ran a hand through his sandy blonde hair. 'Things I'll always regret. I was worried it might've affected her driving. That perhaps the accident was avoidable if she hadn't had that glass of wine and wasn't so riled up.'

'Eve wasn't driving. When she picked me up, she said she'd had a drink and could feel it. She asked me to drive. I've gone over it a million times. The kangaroo appeared out of nowhere. I didn't have time to do anything but swerve. If the barrier hadn't been broken at that point on the road we probably would've hit it and stopped.'

Sean stared. 'She wasn't driving?'

'No.'

'That's one thing at least. But I said terrible things to her that night.'

'And she said terrible things to you many times, too,' Leah said. 'She called you a prick when she got in the car and spent most of the drive to the party laughing and talking about other things. Whatever you said didn't seem to concern her too much.'

'Really?'

She nodded. She'd never be certain how Eve had been feeling about Sean, although her sister mentioning something did suggest it'd affected her. Confirming that now wasn't going to achieve anything.

He sat in silence for a few minutes, digesting this information.

Leah's stomach churned. She dreaded telling the girls and her parents. What were they all going to think of her? Would they be able to see she was trying to do the right thing, or would they think she was trying to have a life that was better than her own? She couldn't imagine how any of them would react.

'I have a proposition for you.'

Sean broke into her thoughts.

'I did some research at work, and think there's a way you can come clean without it looking like it was something you orchestrated for personal gain.'

'Really? How?' Leah hadn't given any consideration to the legal consequences behind her actions. Her concerns had been for her family.

'You received considerable head trauma during the accident, which everyone around you has been led to believe is the reason for you forgetting things. The doctors have gone as far as suggesting retrograde amnesia. I think we can take that a step further and convince everyone that you believed you *were* Eve. That things have felt very strange since the accident, but you put that down to grief and your memory loss.'

'Will anyone buy that?'

'If I'm by your side agreeing *I* believe, they will. Legally, your appointments with the doctor and psychologist where there's a record of memory loss and disorientation will help to corroborate the story. It means we don't have to tell your parents that you did this by choice. The girls too. I'm worried how they'll feel towards you if they know you deliberately deceived them.'

Leah nodded. Was it possible there might be a way out of this? 'Where do we start?'

'I think we should tell your parents first, before we tell the twins. We'll then tell the authorities and get the legal side of things sorted out. After we tell the girls, we'll let Eve's friends and colleagues know. You'll probably want to tell Nicola yourself.'

'And then what? What do *you* want me to do?'

'Be here for me and the girls,' Sean said. 'We're going to need you. There's a funeral to arrange. Eve's things to be gone through. You gave so much of your own furniture and belongings away. The money from the sale of your apartment is still in the bank account. I'll sign that over to you. The life insurance money is there too. You'll need to pay that back to the insurance company. I'll add in some more money for you so you can buy new furniture and belongings for when you want to move into your own place.'

Leah took a deep breath, allowing all that Sean had suggested to sink in.

'You'll always be welcome to visit, Leah. We'll always want and need you as part of our family.'

She was doing her best not to cry. The last few months had been both the worst and – at times – the happiest of her life. Those two little girls made life worth living. She'd never realised how encompassing love for another person could be.

However, she *did* have own baby to think of now. She'd feel that same love for him or her, of that she was sure.

'You okay?' Sean asked.

'It sounds like the best way out of this. When do we tell my mum and dad?'

'I've asked my parents to have the girls for a sleepover on Saturday night. I thought we'd invite your parents to dinner. Tell them then.'

'There's probably no point making a meal if we're dropping this news on them.'

Sadness filled Sean's eyes. He shook his head. 'No, probably not.'

Saturday night came around too quickly. Leah dreaded the visit from her parents. It was the start of inflicting pain and hurt on so many people.

The colour drained from her mother's face when Sean finished explaining what had happened; that Leah's memory had come back in full and what it meant for them.

'Leah?' her dad had whispered. 'It's really you?'

She'd burst into tears while her father hugged her tight.

Her mum was next to hug her. 'My darling, what an awful, awful time you've had. You poor, poor thing. You attended your own funeral. Thought you'd had an affair. Oh goodness me.'

'Affair?' her father asked. 'Who had an affair?'

'No one, Dad,' Leah assured him when Sean's face tightened at the mention.

'Our beautiful Evie has gone.' He sat on the chair in the living room and looked at Sean. 'Whisky?'

He nodded and stood. 'Can I get you something, Peggy?'

'I'll have the same, thank you, Sean.' She sat next to Bill and took his hand. 'I can't believe this.'

'I can't believe that none of us realised we had Leah with us, and not Evie,' her dad said. 'And it was obvious. What about the chess game? You said Leah had taught you how to play.'

'I did teach Eve how to play. She wasn't all that good at it.'

343

'When you played against me, did you really think you were Eve and Leah had taught you the game?'

Heat rose up her neck. She hoped her cheeks weren't glowing. 'I guess so, Dad. It's hard to explain. Some things seemed really strange to me, or I didn't remember or know the answer to them. It makes sense now why.'

He nodded.

Sean returned to the room with the drinks, and passed a box of tissues to her mother.

She wiped at her eyes. 'Thank you, Sean. This is all a huge shock, as you can imagine. Have you told the girls?'

Leah glanced at Sean and shook her head. 'Not yet, we wanted you to know first.'

'The doctors only finished with Leah yesterday,' he lied. 'They wanted to check that she was completely okay so ran a bunch of tests. Luckily she is, and it seems her memory has fully returned.'

'What does it mean for Eve, then?' her mum asked. 'We need to say goodbye to her. Honour her life.'

'Of course,' Sean said. 'We thought that once the girls knew, perhaps, if you're in agreement, we could organise a memorial service to celebrate her life. A proper funeral will be a bit difficult. Her body was cremated at what we thought was Leah's funeral.'

'God, what a mess,' her father said. The whisky was helping bring some colour back into his cheeks.

'The poor girls,' her mother said. 'We'll be here for you, Sean, with whatever you need. Please know that. I'm sure your parents will be too. Do they know?'

He shook his head. 'I'm going to stay behind tomorrow morning when we go to pick up the twins. I'll tell them then.'

'How will you manage? There's so much to do.'

'Leah has offered to stay and help me for the next little while. Which is very generous of her.'

Leah felt the familiar prickling sensation of tears, listening to him talk.

'Once we feel that the twins are settled into a new routine, she'll work out where she's going to go. Whether she buys a new apartment, or whatever is next for her.'

'But the baby,' her mother said. 'Whose is it then?'

'Grant's,' Leah answered. 'And no, he won't be having anything to do with it. That's a story for another day though, Mum.' She forced a smile. 'Don't worry. I'll be fine.'

More tears filled her mother's eyes. 'Poor Evie. My poor Evie.'

She swallowed the lump in her throat as her father drew her mother towards him.

They sat together, her father's eyes were squeezed shut, tears formed at the edges and began to tumble down. He opened his eyes and rubbed them roughly with his sleeve. 'We might go now,' he said. 'Come on, Peg, let me get you home.'

'I'll drive you,' Sean said. 'I'll drive you in your car and get a taxi back. The shock and the whisky and all that.'

Her father handed him his keys without needing to be convinced. He moved to Leah and drew her into another tight hug. 'It's a gift that we have you here, Leah. A true gift.'

Her mother hugged her and she managed to hold herself together until she heard the sound of the car reversing down the driveway. Then she collapsed on the couch in a flood of tears.

The next morning Leah and Sean arrived in separate cars at his parents' to pick up the girls.

She and the twins said their goodbyes and left him to spend some time with June and Abe. Leah could only imagine how they'd react to the news.

Sean arrived home before lunch and asked everyone to come into the living room for a family meeting. He told Harriet no when she's asked whether she should go and wake Lewis from his morning nap.

'Why can't Lewis be part of the family meeting,' the little girl asked. 'He's a very important part of the family.'

He smiled at his daughter, who sat with her arms crossed, a scowl fixed firmly on her face. 'He's asleep, Harry. I don't think he'd be very happy if you woke him. You can fill him in later. Okay?'

She nodded.

'Are you okay, Mummy,' Ava asked. 'You look strange – kind of green.'

'I'm okay, sweetie, thanks for asking.' Leah was anything *but* okay. She'd spent a good part of the morning vomiting. She dreaded this discussion. When she'd been in the hospital, she'd thought she'd avoided them ever having to go through this.

Sean cleared his throat. 'We have something very important to discuss with you both. You need to know we love you both very much and *that* will never change.'

Ava stared to cry. 'You're getting a divorce, aren't you?'

'No,' he said. 'It's a bit more complicated than that. Please let me tell you everything, Ava, and then you'll understand what's happened.'

The little girl continued to cry and her sister's scowl was replaced with fear. Her eyes widened.

'This week Le—' He hesitated. 'This week, Mummy's memory has returned. All the things she'd forgotten, she can now remember. The doctors have been able to say she's now a hundred per cent better from the accident.'

'But that's a good thing, isn't it?' Ava asked through her tears.

'Except we'll never bake or eat chocolate cakes again,' Harriet said, her scowl returning. 'Mummy will return to what she was like

346

before the accident now. Won't you?' The accusation hung in the silence of the room.

Leah took a deep breath. 'No, honey, that's not going to happen. There's a lot more to it than we realised.' She took one hand of each twin. 'When the accident happened, there was a lot of confusion. I was scared and couldn't remember a lot about what'd happened, or even who I was. The paramedics at the accident site and the doctors at the hospital all called me *Eve* and told me that my sister had died. I remembered some things about myself but not everything. I knew that I loved you guys, and I loved cats and chocolate and things, but the rest, I just let you all fill in for me.'

'But you didn't love all those things,' Harriet said. 'Except us, maybe.'

'I do, actually.' Leah took a deep breath. 'The thing is I've been so confused I didn't realise who I was. I'm not Eve, I'm actually Leah.'

Shock registered on the girls' faces.

'You're not our mummy?' Ava said.

She shook her head. 'I'm sorry, honey, but no. It was Mummy who died in the accident.'

'Our mummy died?' Harriet said as if she couldn't begin to believe it.

Sean moved to the twins and took them both into his arms. Tears ran down his face when the little girls began to cry.

Leah had to leave the room. She couldn't take any more tears. Couldn't bear to watch the pain her actions had inflicted on the girls. She'd tried to convince herself it wasn't her fault, that the girls would've grieved when the accident happened, but it wasn't true.

Being the mother they'd always wanted and now taking her away was definitely *her* doing.

Leah poked her head into the twins' room that evening after they'd had their bath and were in bed. They were so tired from the emotion of the day. She'd made them their favourite pizzas for dinner but they'd hardly eaten a thing.

'Can I come in?' she asked.

'Yes,' Harriet answered.

Ava turned and faced the wall.

She sat on Harriet's bed. 'I love you guys as much as if you were my daughters. I want you to know that. I also know that your mummy would want me to spend time with you both and look after you. She'd want me to be a big part of your lives right up until you're old enough to tell me you don't want me around anymore.'

Ava turned back over and faced her.

'It was a real shock for me this week when everything suddenly came back. When I realised I was Leah. It made me very sad too. The last few months living with you guys, being your mum, has been the best time of my whole life. I want you to both know that. I love you both and your daddy very much.'

'Then why can't you stay?' Harriet asked. 'We could still be a family.'

'She's not our mummy,' Ava said. 'She never could be, even if she pretends.'

'That's true.' Ava's words stabbed into her heart. 'Your mummy's in heaven and will be looking down on you every day. She wouldn't want someone else to replace her. She loved you both very much. It was the two of you she was talking about before she died.'

'What did she say?' Ava asked.

'She said you were the most important thing in her life and she asked me to be part of your life, to look after you.'

That was true at least.

'She actually said that?' A small smile appeared on Ava's face. 'That we were important?'

Leah shifted to Ava's bed and pulled the little girl into a hug. 'Of course she did, Aves. People have different ways of showing how they love people, but I can guarantee your mummy loved you very much.'

'I'm glad,' Ava said. 'I was never really sure. We used to annoy her all the time, and she'd always get Kate to do everything for us. I thought she hated us.'

'She wasn't much fun,' Harriet said. 'Although, sometimes she did funny things.'

'Like what?' Leah asked. She sat back and listened to the girls speak of the funny things they could remember about their mother.

Giggles erupted when they spoke of Eve's attempts at roller-skating, and how she'd been unable to stand up without holding on to the side barriers.

Leah smiled, glad Eve had at least done some normal things with the girls.

The twins' laughter quickly turned to tears when the reality – that their mother was gone – sank in.

She held them close and wiped their tears and went on to tell them a number of funny stories about her sister from when they were children. The trouble they used to get into and what a wonderful sister she'd been.

Lewis joined them part way through the discussion, jumping from bed to bed, enjoying plenty of strokes and cuddles.

'Time for sleep, girls.' Sean came into the room. 'It's a special night, I know, but it's also getting late.'

She hugged the girls tight.

'Can Lewis stay with us tonight?' Ava asked.

'Of course.'

'Will you live with us?' Harriet's question was urgent. 'Or will you and Lewis move out?'

The lump reappeared in Leah's throat.

'Nothing's been decided yet,' Sean said. 'Let's get through the next few days. Plan a nice celebration for Mummy's life and go from there. There's no hurry for anything else.'

The girls seemed content with this response, and Leah and Sean left the room.

There were some muffled whispers as the twins argued over whose bed Lewis would prefer to sleep on.

Leah heard quiet sobs when she passed the girls' bedroom the next morning. She pushed the door open to find Ava lying on her bed, head buried in her pillow.

Harriet was nowhere to be seen.

She sat on the bed. 'You okay, Aves?'

The little girl rubbed her face on the pillow before looking up. 'I'm sad about Mummy.'

She reached for her and took her into her arms. 'Me too, Avie. We are all going to miss her very much.'

'What if something happens to Daddy?' Ava asked. 'Then Harry and I would have no one.'

Leah squeezed her. 'Do you really believe that?'

She nodded. 'We'd be orphans, like Annie.'

Leah had to suppress a smile. *Little Orphan Annie* had always been a favourite with Ava. 'You'd have me, and two sets of grandparents. And Lewis of course,' she added as a white ball of fluff appeared at the door. 'But I don't think anything is going to happen to Daddy.'

'We didn't think anything would happen to Mummy.'

'That's true, we didn't. But what happened to Mummy was very unlucky. The likelihood of it happening to anyone else in our family is very, very slim. But, if it did, then I'd ask you and Harry to come and live with me, and Lewis of course.'

Ava snuggled against her. 'I'm glad you're alive still, Aunty Leah. I just wish everyone was.'

Leah stroked the little girl's hair. 'Me too, Aves, me too.'

Chapter Twenty-One

It took several weeks for the legalities surrounding Leah and Eve's switch of identity to be worked out. Luckily the doctors and psychologist reports contained enough information for Sean to be able to convince the authorities Leah was as much a victim of all that'd happened as Eve. She'd gone through further medical testing to ensure that her brain function was clear of trauma and it appeared that it was.

She'd been filled with guilt listening to him discuss what she'd been through. He was a very good lawyer. She could see that in the way he presented the facts, even if those facts had been manipulated.

He'd said absolutely no to her when she'd suggested telling the authorities the truth. Sean had said it might clear her conscience but would also most likely land her in jail. That was hardly any use to the girls, or anyone around them, and certainly not what Eve would've envisaged when she asked Leah to look after her family.

In the end, he'd pointed out her parents would also need to know the full truth if she did confess, and she'd been forced to agree with him.

Peggy and Bill seemed to have aged another ten years since the revelation that Leah was alive and their other daughter had died in the accident. They'd mourned in different ways for Eve, assuring

Leah how much they had loved Eve but also how blessed they felt that they still had her with them.

The task of telling Eve's friends and colleagues the truth was a difficult one, but one she tackled one person at a time. She'd started with Nicola who'd been upset, but strangely not all that surprised.

She'd said something hadn't made sense to her. The enormous changes in 'Eve's' personality since the accident hadn't felt right. For starters, there was no way Eve would be caught dead in half of the outfits she'd seen Leah in since the funeral, and her make-up attempts were pitiful. When her tears had subsided, Nicola almost seemed relieved. She'd promised to pass the information of the memorial, or celebration of life, on to friends who Leah didn't have contact details for.

She had planned to speak to Ben over the phone, but because of how close Eve and Ben had been, she decided to pay him a visit. When she'd first arrived at his office, his eyes had lit up and he'd immediately taken her arm and led her to a private room.

Leah had started out by telling him she'd regained her memory and had had to pull out of his embrace when he'd assumed this meant her feelings for him had returned. She'd very gently told him what'd happened, that Eve had been the one to die in the accident, not her.

His shock and tears had brought tears to her eyes. If Eve hadn't been happy in her marriage, she was at least glad she had found comfort in a man who obviously adored her. Leah invited him to attend the celebration for Eve, but suggested he do his best to stay right away from Sean.

Her sister's work colleagues had shown great compassion towards her. Peter had managed a small smile and said it did help explain 'Eve's' lack of performance since the accident. He suggested Leah either get qualified, or go back to journalism instead of real estate. He also promised to let their clients know about the celebration.

Now, four months since her death, plans were put in motion to give Eve the send-off she deserved.

The sun sank low over the beautiful gardens as the last of the guests gave their condolences and said their goodbyes.

Leah's idea to have the service and wake at The Gables, the same venue Sean and Eve had been married at, had been met with approval from both Sean and her parents.

Her sister had spent hours planning every detail of her wedding and The Gables had been her first choice of venue. She'd insisted they marry in September to ensure the jasmine would be in flower, and the garden smelt sweet through the pre-dinner drinks and canapés. The weather had been perfect for the wedding and her twin had been equally stunning.

'I think she would've liked this.' Her father's voice was low when they spoke after the service when drinks were being served in the garden. 'It's classy. Like Eve was. I think she would've preferred this to the funeral home.'

Leah shuddered at the memory.

She'd spent time chatting with Eve's friends and watching the twins, ensuring Harriet didn't take to climbing any of the trees. The wake in the garden definitely felt like a celebration. They'd paid for drinks and finger food for a three-hour period and Eve's friends were making the most of it.

It appeared she had many more friends, mainly through Nicola, who Sean hadn't been aware of. She'd heard a number of anecdotal stories about her sister she'd never heard before. The story of Eve without a stitch on trying to find her hotel room in Las Vegas was one that had them all laughing.

Sean took her arm. 'Got a minute?'

Leah nodded.

'That guy over by the fountain. It's *him*. Isn't it?'

Leah's stomach clenched at the sight of Ben. He was standing with a beer in hand looking into the fountain.

For Sean's sake, she shouldn't have invited him.

'Yes.' She was beyond lying to him at this stage. 'That's Ben Styles.'

Sean's eyes were fixed on the dark-haired man. 'I'm going to go and have a word.'

Before Leah could stop him, Sean went to Ben.

Her sister's lover immediately took a step backward, surprise registering on his face when Sean put his hand out. She couldn't hear the actual exchange between them, but it was short and when Sean looked at her, he smiled.

Ben turned back to the fountain, his shoulders hunched as he stared into the water.

Leah waited until Sean had moved away and walked over to Ben. 'Everything okay?' she asked.

'Yes, I'll finish my beer and head off. I know it sounds silly, especially when she was cremated months ago and isn't here, but I wanted to be close to her.'

'What did Sean say to you?'

Ben met her gaze. 'He asked if I'd been sleeping with his wife.'

Leah gasped. 'He actually asked you that?'

He nodded. 'I said no. I said I'd wanted to, but she'd said she wouldn't cheat on her husband. It wasn't true, but I thought he'd probably been through enough. I also didn't want to end up head first in the fountain.'

'Thank you. I know Eve would appreciate you doing that.'

'I loved her, Leah.' Ben's eyes glistened with tears. 'We were good together. We never would've left our marriages, but what we had was special, very special. I don't expect you or anyone else to understand, but it was real.'

A small part of her felt sorry for him, she could see how much he was suffering, but another part didn't. Infidelity was inexcusable. It didn't matter which way you tried to spin it.

Ben drank the last of his beer and placed the empty glass on a tray as one of the many waiters came past. 'Time for me to leave. Thank you, Leah. It was generous of you to include me today.'

He leaned forward and kissed her on the cheek before striding through the gardens of The Gables on his way to the car park.

Sean gave both his daughters one last cuddle each as he and Leah tucked them into bed. 'Sweet dreams,' he said while they moved to the doorway to switch off the light.

'Sweet dreams to you, too,' the girls chorused.

The twins had returned from the service and wake in different moods. Harriet had given them a running commentary about the differences between the two funerals all the way home to Brighton while Ava sat quietly, her face turned towards the window.

'You okay, Aves?' Leah asked.

'I'm thinking about Mummy,' she said. 'Did you know on the night of the accident, when she couldn't come out to dinner with us, she'd told us to have caramel sundaes? And she told us she loved us.'

Sean smiled, pleased by Ava's final memories of Eve.

The conversation, driven by Harriet, quickly returned to the celebration for Eve and most importantly the drinks and food. The twins both agreed The Gables had better pink lemonade and the best sausage rolls they'd ever had.

'I had seven,' Harriet boasted. 'One for each year I am.'

Leah laughed. 'Lucky you're not eighty-eight then.'

The atmosphere in the car had become joyous, a complete contrast to the first funeral.

Sean assumed it was because they'd dealt with a lot of their shock and grief back then. Yes, they were saying goodbye to Eve, not Leah, but the girls were handling it a lot better. So was he.

He reflected on his brief conversation with Ben Styles. The guy had lied straight to his face. Sean was a lawyer; he could read people well and could see the dishonesty in Ben's eyes. All of Eve's actions before the accident had indicated an affair, and both Nicola and Peggy had confirmed it when they thought it was Eve who was alive and pregnant by another man.

While part of him would happily have punched Ben in the face, he'd not pursued it. Sean had the tiniest – tiniest – amount of respect for the man. He'd openly admitted he wanted Sean's wife but said she was the one to put a stop to it. He'd been protecting Eve. He could see that. The person Eve had gone to instead of him actually cared about her, but it was up in the air whether or not that was a good thing.

Sean was going to do his best to put it out of his mind. There was nothing he could do now to change anything that'd happened. All he could influence was what happened from now on.

He pulled the door to the girls' room shut and, with a hand on the small of her back, guided Leah down the stairs to the living room. 'You must be exhausted. Today was a big day. A lot of emotion. The speech you gave for Eve was beautiful.'

'The twins did an amazing job too. Ava, in particular. And Mum and Dad. I didn't think they'd get through that reading.'

'They have incredible strength. They'd have to with what they've been put through the past few months.'

'No thanks to me,' Leah said as they both sat on the couch.

'You'll need to stop thinking like that,' Sean said. 'I think we both need to do our best to move on. Live in the moment, or at least *not* in the past. You did what you did with the very best of intentions, and that's all that really matters.' He smiled. 'My guess is Eve would be having a good laugh right about now, about how spectacularly messed up everything got. I think she'd also be pretty happy with the send-off she got today too. Her glamour squad was there. You'd have believed they were going to a fashion show, not a memorial service.'

She laughed. 'Yes, I can see now why Nicola was so suspicious of me. Eve actually dressed quite understated compared to most of them.'

He moved closer and took her hand. 'As messed up as this has all been, I have realised one thing. You mean a lot to me, Leah. You always have. I don't want you to move out. I'd like you to stay, see what happens when it's *you* and me. Not you pretending to be my wife. The girls love you and I . . .' He hesitated. 'I'd like the chance to spend time with you as *Leah*.' Sean placed his hand gently on her stomach. 'You're going to need some help here, too, when the baby's born, and I'd like to be here for you through that.'

'But this is someone else's baby.'

'I know. But it's very unlikely Grant's going to want anything to do with the baby. On top of that, it's a lot easier to accept you and your baby than a baby that's the result of my wife having an affair. I come with baggage too, don't forget. Twins to be exact.'

'They're family. That's a bit different.'

'Not to me,' Sean said. 'What do you say? Shall we at least give it a go? No pressure, no expectations, just see where it might lead? Eve got in the way of that opportunity fifteen years ago, and I think we deserve the chance to see how it might've played out.'

Leah squeezed his hand. 'I think we do too.'

ACKNOWLEDGMENTS

My warmest thanks to the many people who helped me take *A Life Worth Living* from draft form to publication.

To my early readers, Judy, Maggie, Ray, Robyn and Tracy, your input helped transform the story – thank you!

Dr Peter Garrett, thank you for sharing your knowledge and advice on the medical elements of the plot.

Thank you to Chrissy Szarek and Laila Miller for your invaluable input.

To the exceptional Lake Union Publishing team – a huge thank you!

And lastly, and most importantly, my love and thanks to my husband Ray and my mother Judy for everything they do to help me write each novel.

ABOUT THE AUTHOR

Louise Guy has enjoyed working in marketing, recruitment and film production, all of which have helped steer her towards her current and most loved role—writer.

Originally from Melbourne, a trip around Australia led Louise and her husband to Queensland's stunning Sunshine Coast, where they now live with their two sons, gorgeous fluffball of a cat and an abundance of visiting wildlife—the kangaroos and wallabies the most welcome, the snakes the least!

Awed by her beautiful surrounds, Louise loves to take advantage of the opportunities the coast provides for swimming, hiking, mountain biking and kayaking. When she's not writing or out adventuring, Louise loves any available opportunity to curl up with a glass of red wine, switch on her Kindle and indulge in a new release from a favourite author.

To get in touch with Louise, or to join her mailing list, visit: www.LouiseGuy.com.

Made in the USA
Middletown, DE
31 October 2020